ABT

HITLER'S PEACE

HITLER'S PEACE

A NOVEL OF THE
SECOND WORLD WAR

PHILIP KERR

A MARIAN WOOD BOOK

PUBLISHED BY G. P. PUTNAM'S SONS

A MEMBER OF THE PENGUIN GROUP (USA) INC.

NEW YORK

A MARIAN WOOD BOOK
Published by G. P. Putnam's Sons
Publishers Since 1838
A member of the Penguin Group
Penguin Group (USA) Inc., 375 Hudson Street, New York, New York
10014, USA · Penguin Group (Canada), 10 Alcorn Avenue, Toronto,
Ontario M4V 3B2, Canada (a division of Pearson Penguin Canada Inc.) ·
Penguin Books Ltd, 80 Strand, London WC2R 0RL, England ·
Penguin Ireland, 25 St Stephen's Green, Dublin 2, Ireland (a division of
Penguin Books Ltd) · Penguin Group (Australia), 250 Camberwell Road,
Camberwell, Victoria 3124, Australia (a division of Pearson Australia Group
Pty Ltd) · Penguin Books India Pvt Ltd, 11 Community Centre, Panchsheel
Park, New Delhi–110 017, India · Penguin Group (NZ), Cnr Airborne and
Rosedale Roads, Albany, Auckland 1310, New Zealand (a division of
Pearson New Zealand Ltd) · Penguin Books (South Africa) (Pty) Ltd,
24 Sturdee Avenue, Rosebank, Johannesburg 2196, South Africa

Penguin Books Ltd, Registered Offices:
80 Strand, London WC2R 0RL, England

Library of Congress Cataloging-in-Publication Data

Kerr, Philip.
Hitler's peace: a novel of the Second World War / Philip Kerr.
p. cm.
"A Marian Wood book."
ISBN 0-399-15269-5
1. World War, 1939–1945—Peace—Fiction.   2. Teheran
Conference (1943)—Fiction.   I. Title.
PR6061.E784H58   2005   2004043170
823'.914—dc22

Printed in the United States of America
1   3   5   7   9   10   8   6   4   2

This book is printed on acid-free paper. ∞

In Memoriam,
A. H. R. Brodie (1931–2004)

To be empirical is to be guided by experience, not by sophists, charlatans, priests, and demagogues.

WILLARD MAYER, *On Being Empirical*

HITLER'S PEACE

I

Friday, October 1, 1943, Washington, D.C.

History was all around me. I could smell it in everything from the French Empire clock ticking on the elegant mantelpiece to the bright red wallpaper that gave the Red Room its name. I had experienced it the moment I entered the White House and was ushered into this antechamber to await the president's secretary. The idea that Abraham Lincoln might have stood on the same Savonnerie carpet where I was standing now, staring up at an enormous chandelier, or that Teddy Roosevelt might have sat on one of the room's red-and-gold upholstered chairs took hold of me like the eyes of the beautiful woman whose portrait hung above the white marble fireplace. I wondered why she reminded me of my own Diana, and formed the conclusion that it had something to do with the smile on her alabaster white face. She seemed to say, "You should have cleaned your shoes, Willard. Better still, you should have worn a different pair. Those look like you walked here from Monticello."

Hardly daring to use the ornate-looking sofa for fear of sitting on Dolley Madison's ghost, I sat on a dining chair by the doorway. Being at the White House contrasted sharply with the way I had been intending to spend the evening. I had arranged to take Diana to the Loew's movie theater on Third and F streets, to see Gary Cooper and Ingrid Bergman in *For Whom the Bell Tolls*. War, or indeed a movie about a war, could not have seemed more remote among the richly carved and finished woods of that elegant red mausoleum.

Another minute passed, then one of the room's handsome

doors opened to admit a tall, well-groomed woman of a certain age, who flashed me the kind of look that said she thought I might have left a mark on one of the chairs, and then invited me, tonelessly, to follow her.

She was more headmistress than woman, and wore a pencil skirt that made a rustling, sibilant sound, as if it might have bitten the hand that dared to approach its zipper.

Turning left out of the Red Room, we walked over the red carpet of the Cross Hall and then stepped into an elevator where a Negro usher wearing white gloves conducted us up to the second floor. Leaving the elevator, the woman with the noisy skirt led me through the West Sitting Hall and along the Center Hall, before halting in front of the president's study door, where she knocked and then entered without waiting for an answer.

In contrast to the elegance I had just left, the president's study was informal and, with its ziggurats of books, piles of yellowing papers tied with string, and cluttered desk, I thought it resembled the shabby little office I had once occupied at Princeton.

"Mr. President, this is Professor Mayer," she said. And then left, closing the doors behind her.

The president was sitting in a wheelchair, cocktail shaker in hand, facing a small table on which stood several liquor bottles. He was listening to the *Symphony Hour* on WINX.

"I'm just mixing a jug of martinis," he said. "I hope you'll join me. I'm told that my martinis are too cold, but that's the way I like them. I can't abide warm alcohol. It seems to defeat the whole point of drinking in the first place."

"A martini would be very welcome, Mr. President."

"Good, good. Come on in and sit down." Franklin D. Roosevelt nodded toward the sofa opposite the desk. He turned off the radio and poured the martinis. "Here." He held one up and I came around the table to collect it. "Take the jug as well, in case we need a refill."

"Yes, sir." I took the jug and returned to the sofa.

Roosevelt turned the wheelchair away from the liquor table and pushed himself toward me. The chair was a makeshift affair, not the kind you would see in a hospital or an old people's home, but more like a wooden kitchen chair with the legs cut off, as if whoever built it had meant to conceal its true purpose from the American electorate, who might have balked at voting for a cripple.

"If you don't mind me saying so, you seem young to be a professor."

"I'm thirty-five. Besides, I was only an associate professor when I left Princeton. That's a little like saying you're a company vice-president."

"Thirty-five, I guess that's not so young. Not these days. In the army they'd think you were an old man. They're only boys, most of them. Sometimes it just breaks my heart to think how young our soldiers are." He raised his glass in a silent toast.

I returned it, then sipped the martini. It had way too much gin for my taste, and it was not too cold if you like drinking liquid hydrogen. Still, it wasn't every day the president of the United States mixed you a cocktail, and so I drank it with a proper show of pleasure.

While we drank, I took note of the small things about Roosevelt's appearance that only this kind of proximity could have revealed: the pince-nez that I had always mistaken for spectacles; the man's smallish ears—or maybe his head was just too big; the missing tooth on the lower jaw; the way the metal braces on his legs had been painted black to blend in with his trousers; the black shoes that looked poignantly unworn on their leather soles; the bow tie and the worn smoking jacket with leather patches on the elbows; and the gas mask that hung off the side of the wheelchair. I noticed a little black Scotch terrier lying in front of the fire and looking more like a small rug. The president watched me slowly sip the liquid hydrogen, and I saw a faint smile pull at the corners of his mouth.

"So you're a philosopher," he said. "I can't say I know very much about philosophy."

"The traditional disputes of philosophers are, for the most part, as unwarranted as they are unfruitful." It sounded pompous, but then, that goes with the territory.

"Philosophers sound a lot like politicians."

"Except that philosophers are accountable to no one. Just logic. If philosophers were obliged to appeal to an electorate, we'd all be out of a job, sir. We're more interesting to ourselves than we are to other people."

"But not on this particular occasion," observed the president. "Else you wouldn't be here now."

"There's not much to tell, sir."

"But you're a famous American philosopher, aren't you?"

"Being an American philosopher is a little like saying you play baseball for Canada."

"What about your family? Isn't your mother one of the Cleveland von Dorffs?"

"Yes, sir. My father, Hans Mayer, is a German Jew who was brought up and educated in the United States and joined the diplomatic corps after college. He met and married my mother in 1905. A year or two later she inherited a family fortune based on rubber tires, which explains why I've always had such a smooth ride in life. I went to Groton. Then to Harvard where I studied philosophy, which was a great disappointment to my father, who's inclined to believe that all philosophers are mad German syphilitics who think that God is dead. As a matter of fact, my whole family is inclined to the view that I've wasted my life.

"After college I stayed on at Harvard. Got myself a Ph.D. and won the Sheldon Traveling Fellowship. So I went to Vienna, by way of Cambridge, and published a very dull book. I stayed on in Vienna and after a while took up a lectureship at the University of Berlin. After Munich I returned to Harvard and published another very dull book."

"I read your book, Professor. One of them, anyway. *On Being Empirical.* I don't pretend to understand all of it, but it seems to me that you put an awful lot of faith in science."

"I don't know that I'd call it faith, but I believe that if a philosopher wants to make a contribution toward the growth of human knowledge, he must be more scientific in how that knowledge is grasped. My book argues that we should take less for granted on the basis of guesswork and supposition."

Roosevelt turned toward his desk and collected a book that was lying next to a bronze ship's steering clock. It was one of my own. "It's when you use that method to suggest that morality is pretty much a dead cat that I begin to have a problem." He opened the book, found the sentences he had underlined, and read aloud:

" 'Aesthetics and morality are coterminous in that neither can be said to possess an objective validity, and it makes no more sense to assert that telling the truth is verifiably a good thing than it does to say that a painting by Rembrandt is verifiably a good painting. Neither statement has any factual meaning.' "

Roosevelt shook his head. "Quite apart from the dangers that are inherent in arguing such a position at a time when the Nazis are hell-bent on the destruction of all previously held notions of morality, it seems to me that you're missing a trick. An ethical judgment is very often merely the factual classification of an action that verifiably tends to arouse people in a certain kind of way. In other words, the common objects of moral disapproval are actions or classes of actions that can be tested empirically as a matter of fact."

I smiled back at the president, liking him for taking the trouble to read some of my book and for taking me on. I was about to answer him when he tossed my book aside and said:

"But I didn't ask you here to have a discussion about philosophy."

"No, sir."

"Tell me, how did you get involved with Donovan's outfit?"

"Soon after I returned from Europe I was offered a post at Princeton, where I became an associate professor of philosophy. After Pearl Harbor, I applied for a commission in the Naval Reserve, but before my application could be processed I had lunch with a friend of my dad's, a lawyer named Allen Dulles. He persuaded me to join the Central Office of Information. When our part of the COI became the OSS, I came to Washington. I'm now a German intelligence analyst."

Roosevelt turned in his wheelchair as rain hit the window, his big shoulders and thick neck straining against the collar of his shirt; by contrast, his legs were hardly there at all, as if his maker had attached them to the wrong body. The combination of the chair, the pince-nez, and the six-inch ivory cigarette holder clenched between his teeth gave Roosevelt the look of a Hollywood movie director.

"I didn't know it was raining so hard," he said, removing the cigarette from his holder and fitting another from the packet of Camels that lay on the desk. Roosevelt offered one to me. I took it at the same time as I found the silver Dunhill in my vest pocket and then lit us both.

The president accepted the light, thanked me in German, and then continued the conversation in that language, mentioning the latest American war casualty toll—115,000—and some pretty savage fighting that was currently taking place at Salerno, in southern Italy. His German wasn't so bad. Then he suddenly switched subjects and reverted to English.

"I've a job for you, Professor Mayer. A sensitive job, as it happens. Too sensitive to give to the State Department. This has to be between you and me, and only you and me. The trouble with those bastards at State is that they can't keep their fucking mouths shut. Worse than that, the whole department is riven with factionalism. I think you might know what I'm talking about."

It was generally well known around Washington that Roosevelt had never really respected his secretary of state. Cordell Hull's grasp of foreign affairs was held to be poor, and, at the age of seventy-two, he tired easily. For a long time after Pearl, FDR had come to rely on the assistant secretary of state, Sumner Welles, to do most of the administration's real foreign-policy work. Then, just the previous week, Sumner Welles had suddenly tendered his resignation, and the scuttlebutt around the better-informed sections of government and the intelligence services was that Welles had been obliged to resign following the commission of an act of grave moral turpitude with a Negro railway porter while aboard the presidential train on its way to Virginia.

"I don't mind telling you that these goddamned snobs at State are in for one hell of a shake-up. Half of them are pro-British and the other half anti-Semitic. Mince them all up and you wouldn't have enough guts to make one decent American." Roosevelt sipped his martini and sighed. "What do you know about a place called Katyn Forest?"

"A few months ago Berlin radio reported the discovery of a mass grave in the Katyn Forest, near Smolensk. The Germans allege it contained the remains of five thousand or so Polish officers who had surrendered to the Red Army in 1940, following the non-aggression pact between the Germans and the Soviets, only to be murdered on Stalin's orders. Goebbels has been making a lot of political capital out of it. Katyn's been the wind breaking from the tailpipe of the German propaganda machine since the summer."

"For that reason alone, in the beginning I was half-inclined to believe the story was just Nazi propaganda," Roosevelt said. "But there are Polish-American radio stations in Detroit and Buffalo that insist the atrocity occurred. It's even been alleged that this administration has been covering up the facts so as not to endanger our alliance with the Russians. Since the story first broke, I've received a report from our liaison officer to the Polish army in exile, another from our own naval attaché in Istanbul, and one from Prime Minister Churchill. I've even received a report from Germany's own War Crimes Bureau. In August, Churchill wrote to me asking for my thoughts, and I passed all the files over to State and asked them to look into it."

Roosevelt shook his head wearily.

"You can guess what happened. Not a goddamned thing! Hull is blaming everything on Welles, of course, claiming Welles must have been sitting on these files for weeks.

"It's true, I had given the files to Welles and asked him to get

7

someone on the German desk at State to make a report. Then Welles had his heart attack, and cleared his desk, offering me his resignation. Which I refused.

"Meanwhile, Hull told the fellow on the German desk, Thornton Cole, to give the files to Bill Bullitt, to see what our former ambassador to Soviet Russia might make of them. Bullitt fancies himself a Russia expert.

"I don't actually know if Bullitt looked at the files. He'd been after Welles's job for a while and I suspect he was too busy lobbying for it to pay them much attention. When I asked Hull about Katyn Forest, he and Bullshitt realized that they'd fucked up and decided to quietly return the files to Welles's office and blame him for not having done anything. Of course Hull made sure to have Cole back up his story." Roosevelt shrugged. "That's Welles's best guess about what must have happened. And I think I agree with him."

It was about then that I remembered I had once introduced Welles to Cole, at Washington's Metropolitan Club.

"When Hull returned the files and told me that we weren't in a position to have any kind of view on Katyn Forest," Roosevelt continued, "I used every short word known to a sailor. And the upshot of all this is that nothing has been done." The president pointed at some dusty-looking files stacked on a bookshelf. "Would you mind fetching them down for me? They're up there."

I retrieved the files, laid them on the sofa beside the president, and then inspected my hands. The job did not augur well, given the amount of grime on my fingers.

"It's no great secret that sometime before Christmas I'm going to have a conference with Churchill and Stalin. Not that I've any clue where that will be. Stalin has rejected coming to London, so we could wind up almost anywhere. But wherever we end up meeting I want to have a clear idea on this Katyn Forest situation, because it seems certain to affect the future of Poland. The Russians have already broken off diplomatic relations with the Polish government in London. The British, of course, feel a special loyalty to the Poles. After all, they went to war for Poland. So, as you can see, it's a delicate situation."

The president lit another cigarette and then rested a hand on the bundle of files.

"Which brings me to you, Professor Mayer. I want you to conduct your own investigation into these Katyn Forest claims. Start by making an objective assessment of what the files contain, but don't feel you have to limit yourself to them. Speak to anyone you think would be of use. Make up your own mind and then write a report for my eyes only. Nothing too long. Just a summary of your findings with some suggested courses of action. I've cleared it with Donovan, so this takes priority over anything else you're doing."

Taking out his own handkerchief, he wiped his hand clean of dust, and didn't touch the files again.

"How long do I have, Mr. President?"

"Two or three weeks. It's not long, I know, for a matter of such gravity, but as you can appreciate, that can't be helped. Not now."

"When you say 'speak to anyone who might be of use,' does that include people in London? Members of the Polish government in exile? People in the British Foreign Office? And how much of a nuisance am I allowed to make of myself?"

"Speak to whomever you like," insisted Roosevelt. "If you do decide to go to London, it will help if you say that you're my special representative. That will open every door to you. My secretary, Grace Tully, will organize the necessary paperwork for you. Only, try not to express any opinions. And avoid saying anything that will make people think you're speaking in my name. As I said, this is a very delicate situation, but whatever happens, I'd very much like to avoid this coming between myself and Stalin. Is that clearly understood?"

Clear enough. I was to be a mutt with no balls and just my master's collar to let people know I had the right to piss on his flowers. But I fixed a smile to my face and, brushing some stars and stripes onto my words, piped, "Yes, sir, I understand you perfectly."

9

WHEN I GOT BACK HOME, Diana was waiting for me, full of excited questions.

"Well?" she said. "What happened?"

"He makes a terrible martini," I said. "That's what happened."

"You had drinks with him?"

"Just the two of us. As if he was Nick and I was Nora Charles."

"What was it like?"

"Too much gin. And way too cold. Like a country house party in England."

"I meant, what did you talk about?"

"Among other things, philosophy."

"Philosophy?" Diana pulled a face, and sat down. Already she was looking less excited. "That's easier on the stomach than sleeping pills, I guess."

Diana Vandervelden was rich, loud, glamorous, and drily funny in a way that always put me in mind of one of Hollywood's tougher leading ladies, say Bette Davis or Katharine Hepburn. Formidably intelligent, she was easily bored and had given up a place at Bryn Mawr to play women's golf, almost winning the U.S. Women's Amateur title in 1936. The year after that she had quit competition golf to marry a senator. "When I met my husband it was love at first sight," she was fond of saying. "But that's because I was too cheap to buy glasses." Diana was herself not very political, preferring writers and artists to senators, and, despite her many accomplishments in the salon—she was an excellent cook and was famous for giving some of the best dinner parties in Washington—she had quickly tired of being married to her lawyer husband: "I was always cooking for his Republican friends," she later complained to me. "Pearls before swine. And you needed the whole damn oyster farm." When she left her husband in 1940, Diana had set up her own decorating business, which was how she and I had first met. Soon after I moved to Washington, a mutual friend had suggested I hire her to fix up my home in Kalorama Heights. "A philosopher's house, huh? Let's see, now. How would that look? How about a lot of mirrors, all at navel height?" Our friends expected us to get married, but Diana took a dim view of marriage. So did I.

Right from the beginning my relationship with Diana had been intensely sexual, which suited us both just fine. We were very fond of each other, but neither of us ever talked much about love. "We love each other," I had told Diana the previous Christmas, "in the way people do when they love themselves just a little more."

And I loved it that Diana hated philosophy. The last thing I was looking for was someone who wanted to talk about my subject. I liked women. Especially when they were as intelligent and witty as Diana. I just didn't like it when they wanted to talk about logic. Philosophy can be a stimulating companion in the salon, but it's a dreadful bore in the bedroom.

"What else did Roosevelt talk about?"

"War work. He wants me to write a report on something."

"How very heroic," she said, lighting a cigarette. "What do you get for *that*? A medal on a typewriter ribbon?"

I grinned, enjoying her show of scorn. Both Diana's brothers had enlisted in the Canadian Air Force in 1939 and, as she never failed to remind me, both of them had been decorated.

"Anyone might think you don't believe that intelligence work is important, darling." I went over to the liquor tray and poured myself a scotch. "Drink?"

"No, thanks. You know, I think I worked out why it's called intelligence. It's because intelligent people like you always manage to stay well out of harm's way."

"Someone has to keep an eye on what the Germans are up to." I swallowed some of the scotch, which tasted good and warmed my insides pleasingly after Roosevelt's embalming fluid. "But if it gives you a kick trying to make me feel yellow, then go ahead. I can take it."

"Maybe that's what bothers me most."

"I'm not bothered that you're bothered."

"So that's how it works. Philosophy." Diana leaned forward in her armchair and stubbed out her cigarette. "What's this report about, anyway? That the president of the United States wants you to write."

"I can't tell you."

"I don't see what there is to be cagey about."

"I'm not being cagey. I'm being secretive. There's a big difference. If I were being cagey, I might let you stroke my fur, fold my ears, and tickle it out of me. Secretive means that I'll swallow my poison pill before I let that happen."

For a moment her nostrils looked pinched. "Never put off what you can do today," she said.

"Thank you, dear. But I can tell you this. I'm going to have to go to London for a week or two."

Her face relaxed a little and a smile played a quiet little duet on her lips.

"London? Haven't you heard, Willy dear? The Germans are bombing the place. It might be dangerous for you." Her voice was gently mocking.

"I did kind of hear that, yes," I said. "Which is why I'm glad to be going. So I can look myself in the eye when I'm shaving in the morning. After fifteen months sitting behind a desk on Twenty-third Street, it strikes me that maybe I should have joined the navy after all."

"Goodness. Such heroism. I think I will have that drink."

I poured her one, the way she preferred it, neat, like the Bryn Mawr way Diana occupied a chair, knees pressed chastely together. As I handed it to her, she took it out of my fingers and then held my hand, pressing it close to her marble-cool cheek. "You know I don't mean a word of anything I say, don't you?"

"Of course. It's one of the reasons I'm so fond of you."

"Some people fight bulls, ride to hounds, shoot birds. Me, I like to talk. It's one of the two things I do really well."

"Darling, you're the Ladies Grand Champion of talk."

She swallowed her scotch and bit her thumbnail as if to let me know it was just an appetizer and there were parts of me she would like to try her little bite on. Then she stood up and kissed me, her eyelids flickering as she kept on opening and closing them to see if I was ready to climb aboard the pleasure boat she had chartered for us.

"Why don't we go upstairs and I'll show you the other thing I do really well?"

I kissed her again, putting my whole self into it, like some ham who'd understudied John Barrymore.

"You go ahead," I said when, after a while, we came up for air. "I'll be there shortly. I have a little reading to do first. Some papers the president gave me."

Her body stiffened in my arms and she seemed about to make another cutting remark. Then she checked herself.

"Don't get the idea that you can use that excuse more than once," she said. "I'm as patriotic as the next person. But I'm a woman, too."

I nodded and kissed her again. "That's the bit about you I like most of all."

Diana pushed me away gently and grinned. "All right. Just don't be too long. And if I'm asleep, see if you can use that giant brain of yours to figure out a way to wake me up."

"I'll try to think of something, Princess Aurora."

I watched her go upstairs. She was worth watching. Her legs seemed designed to sell tickets at the Corcoran. I watched them to the tops of her stockings and then well beyond. For purely philosophical reasons, of course. All philosophers, Nietzsche said, have little understanding of women. But, then, he never watched Diana walk up a flight of stairs. I didn't know a way of understanding ultimate reality that came close to observing the lacy, veined phenomenon that was Diana's underwear.

Trying to shake this particular natural knowledge from my mind, I made myself a pot of coffee, found a new packet of cigarettes on the desk in my study, and sat down to look through the files given to me by Roosevelt.

The report compiled by the German War Crimes Bureau contained the most detail. But it was the British report, written by Sir

Owen O'Malley, ambassador to the Polish government in exile, and prepared with the help of the Polish army, that detained me the longest. O'Malley's exhaustive report was vividly written and included gruesome descriptions of how officers and men of the Soviet NKVD had shot the 4,500 men—in the back of the head, some with their hands tied, some with sawdust stuffed into their mouths to prevent them from crying out—before burying them in a mass grave.

Finishing the report a little after midnight, I found it impossible not to agree with O'Malley's conclusion that, beyond any shadow of a doubt, the Soviets were guilty. O'Malley's warning to Winston Churchill that the murders in the Katyn Forest would have long-lasting "moral repercussions" seemed understated. But following my talk with the president, I reckoned that any conclusions I formed from my own investigations would have to take second place to a perception I had already formed of the president's desire for more cordial relations between himself and the murderous, Pole-hating Joseph Stalin.

Any report on the massacre that I myself compiled could be nothing more than a formality, a way for Roosevelt to cover his ass. I might even have viewed my presidential commission as something of a bore had it not been for the fact that I had managed to talk myself into a trip to London. London would be fun, and after months of inaction in one of the four redbrick buildings that comprised the "Campus"—the local nickname for the OSS and its predominantly academic staff—I was desperate for some excitement. A week in London might be just what the doctor ordered, especially now that Diana had started to make digs about my staying out of the line of fire.

I got up and went to the window. Looking out at the street, I tried to imagine all those murdered Polish officers lying in a mass grave somewhere near Smolensk. I drained the last of the whiskey from my glass. In the moonlight the lawn in front of my house was the color of blood and the restless silver sky had a spectral look, as if death itself had its great white whale of an eye upon me. Not that it mattered much who killed you. The Germans or the Russians, the British or the Americans, your own side or the enemy. Once you were dead you were dead, and nothing, not even a presidential inquiry, could change that fact. But I was one of the lucky ones, and upstairs, life's affirmative act beckoned my attendance.

I switched off the lights and went to find Diana.

II

SUNDAY, OCTOBER 3, 1943,
BERLIN

STANDING UP, Joachim von Ribbentrop, the German foreign minister, came around his huge marble-topped desk and crossed the thickly carpeted room to face the two men seated on an ornate Biedermeier salon set upholstered in striped green-and-white silk. On the table in front of them lay a pile of curling photographs, each the size of a magazine, each the facsimile of a document that had been removed, covertly, from the safe of the British ambassador in Ankara, Sir Hughe Knatchbull-Hugessen. Von Ribbentrop sat down, and, trying to ignore the stalactite of rainwater dripping off the Maria Theresa crystal chandelier and collecting, noisily, in a metal bucket, he studied each picture, and then the swarthy-looking thug who had brought them to Berlin, with a show of weary disdain.

"It all looks too good to be true," he said.

"That is, of course, possible, Herr Reichsminister."

"People don't suddenly become spies, for no good reason, Herr Moyzisch," said von Ribbentrop. "Especially the valets of English gentlemen."

"Bazna wanted money."

"And it sounds as if he has had it. How much did you say that Schellenberg has given him?"

"Twenty thousand pounds, so far."

Von Ribbentrop tossed the photographs back onto the table and one of them slipped to the floor. It was retrieved by Rudolf Linkus, his closest associate in the Foreign Ministry.

"And who trained him to use a camera with such apparent expertise?" said von Ribbentrop. "The British? Has it occurred to you that this might be disinformation?"

Ludwig Moyzisch endured the Reichsminister's cold stare, wishing he were back in Ankara, and wondering why, of all the people who had examined these documents provided by his agent Bazna (code-named Cicero), von Ribbentrop was the only one to doubt their authenticity. Even Kaltenbrunner, the chief of the Reich Security Service and Walter Schellenberg's boss, had been convinced the information was accurate. Thinking to make the case for Cicero's material, Moyzisch said that Kaltenbrunner himself now held the opinion that the documents were probably genuine.

"Kaltenbrunner is ill, is he not?" Von Ribbentrop's contempt for the SD chief was well known inside the Foreign Ministry. "Phlebitis, I heard. Doubtless his mind, what there is of it, has been much affected by his condition. Besides, I yield to no man, least of all a drunken, sadistic moron, in my knowledge of the British. When I was German ambassador to the Court of St. James, I got to know some of them quite well, and I tell you that this is a trick dreamt up by the English spymasters. Disinformation calculated to divert our so-called intelligence service from their proper tasks." With one of his watery blue eyes half-closed, he faced his subordinate.

Ludwig Moyzisch nodded with what he hoped looked like proper deference. As the SD's man in Ankara, he reported to General Schellenberg; but his position was complicated by the fact that his cover as the German commercial attaché to Turkey meant that he also answered to von Ribbentrop. Which was how he found himself justifying Cicero's work to both the SD *and* the Reich Foreign Ministry. It was a situation that was enough to make any man nervous, since von Ribbentrop was no less vindictive than Ernst Kaltenbrunner. Von Ribbentrop may have looked weak and artificial, but Moyzisch knew it would be a mistake to underestimate him. The days of von Ribbentrop's diplomatic triumphs might be behind him, but he was still a general in the SS and a friend of Himmler's.

"Yes, sir," said Moyzisch. "I am sure you're right to question this, Herr Minister."

"I think we are finished here." Von Ribbentrop stood up abruptly.

Moyzisch rose quickly to his feet but, in his anxiety to be out of the Reichsminister's presence, knocked over his chair. "I'm sorry, Herr Reichsminister," he said, picking it up again.

"Don't bother." Von Ribbentrop waved his hand at the dripping ceiling. "As you can see, we are not yet recovered from the last visit of the RAF. The top floor of the ministry is gone, as are many of the windows on this floor. There is no heat, of course, but we prefer to stay on in Berlin rather than hide ourselves away at Rastenburg or the Berchtesgaden."

Von Ribbentrop escorted Linkus and Moyzisch to the door of his office. To Moyzisch's surprise, the Reichsminister seemed quite courteous now, almost as if there might be something he wanted from him. There was even the faintest hint of a smile playing on his face.

"Might I ask what you will be telling General Schellenberg about this meeting?" With one hand tucked into the pocket of his Savile Row suit, he was clinking a bunch of keys nervously.

"I will tell him what the Reichsminister himself has told me," said Moyzisch. "That this is disinformation. A crude trick perpetrated by British intelligence."

"Exactly," von Ribbentrop said, as if agreeing with an opinion Moyzisch had first voiced himself. "Tell Schellenberg he's wasting his money. To act on this information would be folly. Don't you agree?"

"Unquestionably, Herr Reichsminister."

"Have a safe trip back to Turkey, Herr Moyzisch." And, turning to Linkus, he said, "Show Herr Moyzisch out and then tell Fritz to bring the car around to the front door. We leave for the railway station in five minutes."

Von Ribbentrop closed the door and returned to the Biedermeier table, where he gathered up Cicero's photographs and placed them carefully in his saddle-leather briefcase. He thought Moyzsich was almost certainly right, that the documents were perfectly genuine, but he had no wish to lend any support to them in Schellenberg's eyes, lest the SD general be prompted to try to take advantage of this new and important information with some stupid, theatrical military stunt. The last thing he wanted was the SD pulling off another "special mission" like the one a month before, when Otto Skorzeny and a team of 108 SS men had parachuted onto a mountaintop in Abruzzi and rescued Mussolini from the traitorous Badoglio faction that had tried to surrender Italy to the Allies. Rescuing Mussolini was one thing; but knowing what to do with him afterward was quite another. It fell to him to deal with the problem. Installing Il Duce in the city-state Republic of Salo, on Lake Garda, had been one of the more pointless diplomatic endeavors of his career. If anyone had bothered to ask him, he would have left Mussolini in Abruzzi to face an Allied court-martial.

These Cicero documents were another thing entirely. They were a real chance to put his career back on track, to prove he was indeed, as Hitler had once called him—after the successful negotiation of the nonaggression pact with the Soviet Union—"a second Bismarck." War was inimical to diplomacy, but now that it was clear the war could not be won, the time for diplomacy—von Ribbentrop's diplomacy—had returned, and he had no intention of allowing the SD with their stupid heroics to ruin Germany's chances of a negotiated peace.

He would speak to Himmler. Only Himmler had the foresight and vision to understand the tremendous opportunity that was provided by Cicero's very timely information. Von Ribbentrop closed his briefcase and headed for the street.

By the tall lamppost that flanked the building's entrance, von Ribbentrop found the two aides who were to accompany him on his train journey: Rudolf Linkus and Paul Schmidt. Linkus relieved him of his briefcase and placed it in the trunk of the enormous black Mercedes that was waiting to drive him to the Anhalter Bahnhof— the railway station. Sniffing the damp night air charged with the smell of cordite from the antiaircraft batteries on nearby Pariser Platz and Leipziger Platz, he climbed into the backseat.

They drove south down Wilhelmstrasse, past Gestapo headquarters and onto Königgratzerstrasse, turning right into the station, which was full of aged pensioners and women and children taking advantage of Gauleiter Goebbels's decree permitting them to escape the Allied bombing campaign. The Mercedes drew up at a platform well away from Berlin's less distinguished travelers, alongside a streamlined, dark green train that was building up a head of steam. Standing on the platform, at five-meter intervals, a troop of SS men stood guard over its twelve coaches and two flak wagons armed with 200-millimeter quadruple antiaircraft guns. This was the special train *Heinrich* used by the Reichsführer-SS, Heinrich Himmler, and, after the *Führerzug*, the most important train in Germany.

Von Ribbentrop climbed aboard one of the two coaches reserved for the use of the Reich Foreign Minister and his staff. Already the noise of clattering typewriters and waiters laying out china and cutlery in the dining car that separated von Ribbentrop's personal coach from that of the Reichsführer-SS made the train seem as noisy as any government office. At exactly eight o'clock the *Heinrich* headed east, toward what had once been Poland.

At eight-thirty, von Ribbentrop went into his sleeping compartment to change for dinner. His SS general's uniform was already laid out on the bed, complete with black tunic and cap, crossbelts, black riding breeches, and polished black riding boots. Von Ribbentrop, who had held the honorary rank of SS-Gruppenführer since 1936, enjoyed wearing the uniform, and his friend Himmler seemed to appreciate him wearing it. On this particular occasion, however, the SS uniform was mandatory, and when the minister came out of his compartment, the rest of his Foreign Ministry staff aboard the train were also dressed in their coal black uniforms. Von Ribbentrop found himself smiling, for he liked to see his staff looking smart and performing at a level of efficiency that only the proximity of the Reichsführer-SS seemed able to command, and instinctively he saluted them. They saluted back, and Paul Schmidt, who was an SS colonel, presented his master with a sheet of ministry notepaper on which was typed a summary of the points von Ribbentrop had wanted to make to Himmler during their dinner meeting. These included his suggestion that any Allied air crew captured after a bombing raid be handed over to the local population and lynched; and the issue raised by SD agent Cicero's photographed documents. To the minister's irritation, the issue of the deportation of Jews from Norway, Italy, and Hungary was also on the agenda. Von Ribbentrop read this last item once more and then tossed the summary onto the table, his face coloring with irritation. "Who typed this?" he asked.

"Fräulein Mundt," said Schmidt. "Is there a problem, Herr Reichsminister?"

Von Ribbentrop turned on the heel of his boot and walked into the next carriage, where several stenographers, seeing the minister, left off typing and stood up respectfully. He approached Fräulein Mundt, searched her out tray, and silently removed the carbon copy she had made of Schmidt's summary before returning to his private carriage. There, he placed the carbon copy on the table and, thrusting his hands into the pockets of his SS tunic, he faced Schmidt with sullen displeasure.

"Because you were too damned lazy to do what I asked, you risk all our lives," he told Schmidt. "By committing the specific details of this Moellhausen matter to paper—to an official document, I might add—you are repeating the very same offense for which he is to be severely reprimanded."

Eiten Moellhausen was the Foreign Ministry's consul in Rome, and the previous week he had sent a cable to Berlin alerting the ministry to the SD's intention to deport 8,000 Italian Jews to the Mauthausen concentration camp in Austria, "for liquidation." This had caused consternation, for von Ribbentrop had given strict orders that words such as "liquidation" should never appear in Foreign Ministry papers, in case they fell into Allied hands.

"Suppose this train were captured by British commandos," he

shouted. "Your stupid summary would condemn us just as surely as Moellhausen's cable. I've said it before, but it seems I have to say it again. 'Removal.' 'Resettlement.' 'Displacement.' Those are the proper words to use in all Foreign Ministry documents relating to the solution of Europe's Jewish problem. The next man who forgets this will go the same way as Luther." Von Ribbentrop picked up the offending summary and carbon copy, thrust them at Schmidt. "Destroy these. And have Fräulein Mundt retype this summary immediately."

"At once, Herr Reichsminister."

Von Ribbentrop poured himself a glass of Fachinger water and waited, impatiently, for Schmidt to return with the retyped document. While he was waiting, there was a knock at the other door of the carriage and an aide opened it to admit a small, plain-looking SS-Standartenführer, a man not dissimilar in appearance to that of his master, for this was Dr. Rudolf Brandt, Himmler's personal assistant and the most industrious of the Reichsführer's entourage. Brandt clicked his heels and bowed stiffly to von Ribbentrop, who smiled back at him ingratiatingly.

"The Reichsführer's compliments, Herr General," said Brandt. "He wonders if you are free to join him in his car."

Schmidt returned with the new summary sheet, and von Ribbentrop received it without a word, then followed Brandt through the concertina gangway that joined the two coaches.

Himmler's car was paneled with polished wood. A brass lamp stood on a little desk beside the window. The chairs were upholstered in green leather, which matched the color of the car's thick velour. There was a gramophone and a radio, too, though Himmler had little time for such distractions. Even so, the Reichsführer was hardly the monkish ascetic he projected to the public. To von Ribbentrop, who knew Himmler well, his reputation for ruthlessness seemed ill deserved; he was capable of being very generous to those who served him well. Indeed, Heinrich Himmler was not a man without charm, and his conversation was lively and more often than not laced with humor. It was true that, like the Führer, he disliked people smoking cigarettes around him, but on occasion he himself enjoyed a good cigar; no more was he a teetotaler, and often drank a glass or two of red wine in the evening. Von Ribbentrop found Himmler with a bottle of Herrenberg-Honigsächel already open on the desk, and a large Cuban cigar burning in a crystal ashtray that lay on top of a Brockhaus atlas and a Morocco-bound copy of the Bhagavad Gita, a book that Himmler was seldom, if ever, without.

Seeing von Ribbentrop, Himmler put down his notorious green pencil and jumped to his feet.

"My dear von Ribbentrop," he said in his quiet voice, with its light Bavarian twang that sometimes reminded von Ribbentrop of Hitler's Austrian accent. There were even some who said that Himmler's accent was consciously modeled on Hitler's own voice in an attempt to ingratiate himself still further with the Führer. "How nice to see you. I was just working on tomorrow's speech."

This was the purpose of their rail journey to Poland: the following day in Posen, the old Polish capital that was now the site of an intelligence school run by Colonel Gehlen for German military forces in Russia, Himmler would address all of the generals, or "troop leaders," in the SS. Forty-eight hours later, he would give the same speech to all of Europe's Reichsleiters and Gauleiters.

"And how is that coming along?"

Himmler showed the foreign minister the typewritten text on which he had been working all afternoon, covered as it was with his spidery green handwriting.

"A little long, perhaps," admitted Himmler, "at three and a half hours."

Von Ribbentrop groaned silently. Given by anyone else, Goebbels or Göring or even Hitler, he would have risked taking a nap, but Himmler was the kind of man who later asked you questions about his speech, and what in particular you thought had been its strongest points.

"That can't be helped, of course," Himmler said airily. "There's a lot of ground to be covered."

"I can imagine. Of course, I've been looking forward to this, since your new appointment."

It was just two months since Himmler had taken over from Frank as minister of the interior, and the speech at Posen was meant to demonstrate that the change was not merely cosmetic: whereas previously the Führer had counted on the support of the German people, Himmler intended to show that now he relied exclusively on the power of the SS.

"Thank you, my dear fellow. Some wine?"

"Yes, thanks."

As Himmler poured the wine, he asked, "How is Annelies? And your son?"

"Well, thank you. And Haschen?"

Haschen was what Himmler called his bigamous wife, Hedwig. The Reichsführer was not yet divorced from his wife, Marga. Twelve years younger than the forty-three-year-old Himmler, Haschen was his former secretary and the proud mother of his two-year-old son, Helge—try as he might, von Ribbentrop couldn't get used to calling children by these new Aryan names.

"She is well, too."

"Will she be joining us in Posen? It's your birthday this week, isn't it?"

"Yes, it is. But, no, we're going to meet at Hochwald. The Führer has invited us to the Wolfschanze."

The Wolfschanze was Hitler's field headquarters in East Prussia, and Hochwald was the house Himmler had built, twenty-five kilometers to the east of the Führer's sprawling compound in the forest.

"We don't see you there very much anymore, von Ribbentrop."

"There's very little a diplomat can do at a military headquarters, Heinrich. So I prefer to stay in Berlin, where I can be of more use to the Führer."

"You're quite right to avoid it, my dear fellow. It's a terrible place. Stifling in summer and freezing in winter. Thank God I don't have to stay there. My own house is in a considerably healthier part of the countryside. Sometimes I think the only reason the

Führer endures the place is so he can feel at one with the privations endured by the ordinary German soldier."

"There's that. And another reason, of course. So long as he stays there he doesn't have to see the bomb damage in Berlin."

"Perhaps. Either way, it's Munich's turn tonight."

"Is it?"

"Some three hundred RAF bombers."

"Christ!"

"I dread what is to come, Joachim. I don't mind telling you. That is why we must do all we can to succeed with our diplomatic efforts. It is imperative that we make a peace with the Allies before they open a second front next year." Himmler relit his cigar and puffed it carefully. "Let us hope that the Americans can yet be persuaded to put aside this insane business of unconditional surrender."

"I still think you should have allowed the Foreign Ministry to speak to this man Hewitt. After all, I've lived in America."

"Come now, Joachim. It was Canada, was it not?"

"No. New York, too. For a month or two, anyway."

Himmler remained silent for a moment, studying the end of his cigar with diplomatic interest.

Von Ribbentrop smoothed his graying blond hair and tried to control the muscle twitching in his right cheek that seemed only too obviously a manifestation of his irritation with the Reichsführer-SS. That Himmler should have sent Dr. Felix Kersten to Stockholm to conduct secret negotiations with Roosevelt's special representative instead of him was a matter of no small exasperation to the foreign minister.

"Surely, you can see how ridiculous it is," von Ribbentrop persisted, "that I, an experienced diplomat, should have to take a backseat to—to your chiropractor."

"Not just mine. I seem to remember he treated you, too, Joachim. Successfully, I might add. But there were two reasons why I asked Felix to go to Stockholm. For one thing, he's Scandinavian himself and able to conduct himself in the open. Unlike you. And, well, you've met Felix and you know how gifted he is and how persuasive he can be. I don't think magnetic is too strong a word for the effect he can have on people. He even managed to persuade this American, Abram Hewitt, to let him treat him for back pain, which provided a very useful cover for their talks." Himmler shook his head. "I confess I did think it was possible that under the circumstances Felix might actually achieve some influence on Hewitt. But so far, this has not proved to be the case."

"Abram. Is he a Jew?"

"I'm not sure. But, yes, probably." Himmler shrugged. "But that can't be allowed to matter."

"You've spoken to Kersten?"

"This evening on the telephone, before I left Berlin. Hewitt told Felix that he thought negotiations could only begin after we have made a move to get rid of Hitler."

At this mention of the unmentionable, both men grew silent.

Then von Ribbentrop said, "The Russians aren't nearly so narrow in their thinking. As you know, I've met Madame de Kollontay, their ambassador in Sweden, on a number of occasions. She says Marshal Stalin was shocked that Roosevelt made this demand for unconditional surrender without even consulting him. All the Soviet Union really cares about is the restoration of its pre-1940 borders and a proper level of financial compensation for her losses."

"Money, of course," snorted Himmler. "It goes without saying that's the only thing these Communists are interested in. All Stalin really wants is Russia's factories rebuilt at Germany's expense. And Eastern Europe handed to him on a plate, of course. Yes, by God, the Allies are going to find out damn soon that we're all that stands between them and the Popovs.

"You know, I've made a special study of the Popovs," continued Himmler, "and it's my conservative calculation that so far the war has cost the Red Army more than two million dead, prisoners, and disabled. It's one of the things I'm going to speak about in Posen. I expect them to sacrifice at least another two million during their winter offensive. Already the SS Division 'Das Reich' reports that, in some cases, the divisions opposing us have contained whole companies of fourteen-year-old boys. Mark my words, by next spring they'll be using twelve-year-old girls to fight us. What happens to Russian youth is a matter of total indifference to me, of course, but it tells me that human life means absolutely nothing to them. And it never ceases to amaze me that the British and the Americans can accept as their allies a people capable of sacrificing ten thousand women and children to build a tank ditch. If that is what the British and the Americans are willing to base their continued existence on, then I don't see how they're in any position to lecture us on the proper conduct of the war."

Von Ribbentrop sipped some of Himmler's wine, although he much preferred the champagne he had been drinking in his own carriage, and shook his head. "I don't believe that Roosevelt knows the nature of the beast to which he has chained himself," he said. "Churchill is much better informed about the Bolshevik and, as he has said, he would make an ally of the devil in order to defeat Germany. But I really don't think Roosevelt can have any real conception of the gross brutality of his ally."

"And yet we know for a fact he was informed of the Katyn Forest massacre's true authors," said Himmler.

"Yes, but did he believe it?"

"How could he not believe it? The evidence was incontrovertible. The dossier that was compiled by the German War Crimes Bureau would have established Russian guilt in the eyes of even the most impartial observer."

"But surely that's the point," said von Ribbentrop. "Roosevelt is hardly impartial. With the Russians continuing to deny their culpability, Roosevelt can choose not to believe the authority of his own eyes. If he had believed it, we would have heard something. It's the only possible explanation."

"I fear you may be right. They prefer to believe the Russians to us. And there's little chance of proving otherwise. Not now that Smolensk is back under Russian control. So we must find another way to enlighten the Americans." Himmler collected a thick file off his desk and handed it to von Ribbentrop, who, noticing that

Himmler was wearing not one but two gold rings, wondered for a moment if they were both wedding bands from each of his two wives. "Yes, I think that I might send him that," said Himmler.

Von Ribbentrop put on reading glasses and moved to open the file. "What is it?" he asked, suspiciously.

"I call it the Beketovka File. Beketovka is a Soviet labor camp near Stalingrad, run by the NKVD. After the defeat of the Sixth Army in February, some quarter of a million German soldiers were taken prisoner by the Russians and held in camps like Beketovka, which was the largest."

"Was?"

"The file was put together by one of Colonel Gehlen's agents in the NKVD and has only just come into my hands. It's a remarkable piece of work. Very thorough. Gehlen does recruit some very capable people. There are photographs, statistics, eyewitness accounts. According to the camp register, approximately fifty thousand German soldiers arrived at Beketovka last February. Today less than five thousand of them are still alive."

Von Ribbentrop heard himself gasp. "You're joking."

"About such a thing as this? I think not. Go ahead, Joachim. Open it. You'll find it quite edifying."

As a rule, the minister tried to avoid the reports arriving at the Foreign Ministry's Department Deutschland. These were filed by the SS and the SD and detailed the deaths of countless Jews in the extermination camps in the East. But he could hardly be indifferent to the fate of German soldiers, especially when his own son was a soldier, a lieutenant with the Leibstandarte-SS and, mercifully, still alive. What if it had been his son who had been taken prisoner at Stalingrad? He opened the file.

Von Ribbentrop found himself looking at a photograph of what at first glance resembled an illustration he had once seen by Gustave Doré, in Milton's *Paradise Lost*. It was a second or two before he realized that these were the naked bodies not of angels, or even devils, but human beings, apparently frozen hard and stacked six or seven deep, one on top of the other, like beef carcasses in some hellish deep freeze. "My God," he said, realizing that the line of carcasses was eighty or ninety meters long. "My God. These are German soldiers?"

Himmler nodded.

"How did they die? Were they shot?"

"Perhaps a lucky few were shot," said Himmler. "Mostly they died of starvation, cold, sickness, exhaustion, and neglect. You really should read the account of one of the prisoners, a young lieutenant from the Seventy-sixth Infantry Division. It was smuggled out of the camp in the vain hope that the Luftwaffe might be able to mount some sort of bombing raid and put them out of their misery. It gives a pretty good picture of life at Beketovka. Yes, it's a quite remarkable piece of reportage."

Von Ribbentrop's weak blue eyes passed quickly over the next photograph, a close-up shot of a pile of frozen corpses. "Perhaps later," he said, removing his glasses.

"No, von Ribbentrop, read it now," insisted Himmler. "Please. The man who wrote this account is, or was, just twenty-two, the same age as your own son. We owe it to all those who won't ever come back to the Fatherland to understand their suffering and their sacrifice. To read such things, that is what will make us hard enough to do what must be done. There's no room here for human weakness. Don't you agree?"

Von Ribbentrop's face stiffened as he replaced his reading glasses. He disliked being cornered, but could see no alternative to reading the document, as Himmler had bidden.

"Better still," the Reichsführer said, "read aloud to me what young Zahler has written."

"Aloud?"

"Yes, aloud. The truth is, I have only read it once myself, as I could not bear to read it again. Read it to me now, Joachim, and then we will talk about what we must do."

The foreign minister cleared his throat nervously, recalling the last occasion on which he had read a document aloud. He remembered the day exactly: June 22, 1941—the day when he had an nounced to the press that Germany had invaded the Soviet Union; and as von Ribbentrop proceeded to read, the sense of irony was not lost on him.

When he had finished reading, he removed his glasses, swallowing uncomfortably. Heinrich Zahler's account of life and death at Beketovka seemed to have conspired with the motion of the train and the smell of Himmler's cigar to leave him feeling a little off-color. He stood up unsteadily and, excusing himself for a moment, walked into the concertina gangway between the coaches to draw a breath of fresh air into his lungs.

When the minister returned to the Reichsführer's private car, Himmler seemed to read his thoughts.

"You were thinking of your own son, perhaps. A very brave young man. How many times has he been wounded?"

"Three times."

"He does you great credit, Joachim. Let us pray that Rudolf is never captured by the Russians. Particularly as he is SS. Elsewhere the Beketovka File makes reference to the especially murderous treatment that the Russians have inflicted on SS POWs. They are taken to Wrangel Island. Shall I show you where that is?"

Himmler picked up his Brockhaus atlas and found the relevant map. "Look there," he said, pointing with a well-manicured fingernail at a speck in a patch of pale-looking blue. "In the East Siberian Sea. There. Do you see? Three and a half thousand kilometers east of Moscow." Himmler shook his head. "It's the *size* of Russia that overwhelms, is it not?" He snapped the atlas shut. "No, I'm afraid we will not see those comrades again."

"Has the Führer seen this file?" asked von Ribbentrop.

"Good God, no," said Himmler. "And he never will. If he knew about this file and the conditions in which German soldiers are kept in Russian POW camps, do you think he would ever contemplate making a peace with the Soviets?"

Von Ribbentrop shook his head. "No," he said. "I suppose not."

"But I was thinking that if the Americans saw it," said Himmler. "Then . . ."

"Then it might help to drive a wedge between them and the Russians."

"Precisely. Perhaps it might also help to authenticate evidence we have already provided of the Russians being to blame for the Katyn Forest massacre."

"I assume," said von Ribbentrop, "that Kaltenbrunner has already informed you of this man Cicero's intelligence coup?"

"About the Big Three and their forthcoming conference in Teheran? Yes."

"I'm thinking, Heinrich—before Churchill and Roosevelt see Stalin, they're going to Cairo, to meet Chiang Kai-shek. That would be a good place for this Beketovka File to fall into their hands."

"Yes, possibly."

"It would give them something to think about. Perhaps it might even affect their subsequent relations with Stalin. Frankly, I don't expect any of this material would surprise Churchill very much. He's always hated the Bolsheviks. But Roosevelt is a very different saucer of milk. If the American newspapers are to be believed, he seems intent on charming Marshal Stalin."

"Is such a thing possible?" grinned Himmler. "You've met the man. Could he ever be charmed?"

"Charmed? I sincerely doubt that Jesus Christ himself could charm Stalin. But that's not to say Roosevelt doesn't think he can succeed where Christ might fail. But then again, he might lose his will to charm if he were made aware of just what sort of monster he's dealing with."

"It's worth a try."

"But the file would have to come into their hands from the right quarter. And I fear that neither the SS nor the Reich Foreign Ministry could bring the appropriate degree of impartiality to such a sensitive matter."

"I think I have just the man," said Himmler. "There's a Major Max Reichleitner. Of the Abwehr. He was part of the war crimes team that investigated the Katyn massacre. Of late he's been doing some useful work for me in Turkey."

"In Turkey?" Von Ribbentrop was tempted to ask what kind of work Major Reichleitner was doing for Himmler and the Abwehr in Turkey. He hadn't forgotten that Ankara was where the SD's agent Cicero was also operating. Was this just a coincidence, or was there perhaps something he wasn't being told?

"Yes. In Turkey."

Himmler did not elaborate. Major Reichleitner had been carrying the diplomatic correspondence on another secret peace initiative, this one conducted with the Americans by Franz von Papen, the former German chancellor, on behalf of a group of senior officers in the Wehrmacht. Von Papen was the German ambassador in Turkey and, as such, von Ribbentrop's subordinate. Himmler considered von Ribbentrop useful in a number of ways; but the Reichsminister was acutely sensitive about his position and, as such, was sometimes something of a nuisance. The plain fact of the matter was that Himmler enjoyed reminding the foreign minister of how little he really knew and how much he now relied on the Reichsführer, rather than Hitler, to remain close to the center of power.

"I believe there may be something else we might do to take advantage of this forthcoming conference," the foreign minister said. "I was thinking that we might attempt to seek further clarification of exactly what Roosevelt meant when he told reporters at Casablanca of his demand for Germany's unconditional surrender."

Himmler nodded thoughtfully and puffed at his cigar. The president's remark had caused as much disquiet in Britain and Russia as it had in Germany, and, according to intelligence reports from the Abwehr, it had generated the fear among certain American generals that unconditional surrender would make the Germans fight all the harder, thereby prolonging the war.

"We might use Teheran," continued Ribbentrop, "to discover if Roosevelt's remark was a rhetorical flourish, a negotiating ploy intended to force us to talk, or if he meant us to take it literally."

"Exactly how might we obtain such a clarification?"

"I was thinking that the Führer might be persuaded to write

three letters. Addressed to Roosevelt, Stalin, and Churchill. Stalin is a great admirer of the Führer. A letter from him might prompt Stalin to question why Roosevelt and Churchill don't want a negotiated peace. Could it be that they would like to see the Red Army annihilated in Europe before committing themselves to an invasion next year? The Russians have never trusted the British. Not since the Hess mission.

"Equally, letters to Roosevelt and Churchill might make something of the brutal treatment of German POWS by the Russians, not to mention those Polish officers murdered at Katyn. The Führer could also mention a number of pragmatic considerations which Roosevelt and Churchill might think could weigh against a European landing."

"Such as?" asked Himmler.

Von Ribbentrop shook his head, unwilling to show the Reichsführer all his best cards and telling himself that Himmler wasn't the only one who could withhold information. "I wouldn't want to go into the details right now," he said smoothly, now quite convinced that Cicero's discovery of the Big Three at Teheran might be the beginning of a very real diplomatic initiative, perhaps the most important since he had negotiated the nonaggression pact with the Soviet Union. Von Ribbentrop smiled to himself at the idea of pulling off another diplomatic coup like that one. These letters to the Big Three from the Führer would be written by himself, of course. He would show those bastards Göring and Goebbels that he was still a force to be reckoned with.

"Yes," said Himmler, "I might mention the idea to Hitler when I go to the Wolfschanze on Wednesday."

Von Ribbentrop's face fell. "I was thinking that I might mention the idea to Hitler myself," he said. "After all, this is a diplomatic initiative rather than a matter for the Ministry of the Interior."

The Reichsführer-SS thought for a moment, considered the possibility that Hitler might not like the idea. There was a strong chance that any negotiated peace might require Germany to have a new leader, and while Himmler believed there was no one better than himself to replace the Führer, he did not want Hitler to think that he was planning some sort of coup d'état.

"Yes," he said, "I think perhaps you're right. It should be you who mentions this to the Führer, Joachim. A diplomatic initiative like this one should originate in the Foreign Ministry."

"Thank you, Heinrich."

"Don't mention it, my dear fellow. We will have your diplomatic effort and my Beketovka File. Either way, we must not fail. Unless we can make some sort of a peace, or successfully detach the Soviet Union from her Western allies, I fear Germany is finished."

Since the purpose of the speech Himmler was to make at Posen the next day was the subject of defeatism, Ribbentrop proceeded cautiously.

"You are being frank," he said carefully. "So let me also be frank with you, Heinrich."

"Of course."

Von Ribbentrop could hardly forget he was speaking to the most powerful man in Germany. Himmler could easily order the train stopped and Ribbentrop shot summarily by the side of the railway track. The foreign minister had no doubt that the Reichsführer could justify such an action to the Führer at a later date, and, aware of the secrecy of the subject he was about to broach, Ribbentrop found himself struggling for the words that might still leave him at arm's length from being complicit in Germany's crusade against the Jews.

In late 1941, he had become aware of mass executions of Jews by Einsatzgruppen—SS special action groups in Eastern Europe— and since then had tried his best to avoid reading all SS and SD reports that were filed, as a matter of routine, with Department III of the Foreign Ministry. These Special Action Groups were no longer shooting thousands of Jews but organizing their deportation to special camps in Poland and the Ukraine. Von Ribbentrop knew the purpose of these camps—he could hardly fail to know it, having visited Belzec in secret—but it bothered him a great deal that the Allies might also know their purpose.

"Is it possible," he asked Himmler, "that the Allies are aware of the purpose behind the evacuation of Jews to Eastern Europe? That this is the true reason they have ignored evidence of Russian atrocities?"

"We agreed that we are speaking frankly, Joachim," said Himmler, "so let us do just that. You are referring to the systematic extirpation of the Jews, are you not?"

Von Ribbentrop nodded uncomfortably.

"Look," continued Himmler. "We have the moral right to protect ourselves. A duty to our own people to destroy all saboteurs, agitators, and slander-mongers who want to destroy us. But to answer your question specifically, I will say this. I think it's possible that they do know of the existence of our grand solution to the Jewish problem, yes. But I would suggest that currently they imagine that accounts of what goes on in Eastern Europe have been dramatically exaggerated.

"If I might be allowed to pat myself on the back, it is incredible just what has been achieved. You have no idea. Nevertheless, none of us forgets that this is a chapter in German history that can never be written. But rest assured, Joachim, as soon as a peace has been negotiated, all the camps will be destroyed and all evidence that they ever existed erased. People will say Jews were murdered. Thousands of Jews, hundreds of thousands of Jews—yes, they will say that, too. But this is war. 'Total war,' Goebbels calls it, and for once I agree with him. People get killed in wartime. That is an unfortunate fact of life. Who knows how many the RAF will kill tonight in Munich? Old men, women and children?" Himmler shook his head. "So, Joachim, I give you my word that people will not believe it was possible so many Jews died. Faced with the menace of European Bolshevism, they will not *want* to believe it. No, they could never believe it. No one could."

III

MONDAY, OCTOBER 4, 1943,
POSEN, POLAND

NAMED AFTER THE LEADING POET of Polish romanticism, the Adam Mickiewicz Square in Posen was one of the old city's most attractive sights. On the eastern side of the square was a castle built for Kaiser Wilhelm II in 1910, when Posen had been part of the Prussian empire. In truth, it hardly looked like a castle, more like a town hall or a city museum, with a facade that was fronted not by a moat but by a large wrought-iron railing protecting a neatly kept lawn and an open graveled area that resembled a parade ground. On this particular day, that spot had been given up to at least a dozen SS staff cars. Parked in front of the railing were several Hannomag troop carriers, each containing fifteen Waffen-SS Panzergrenadiers, and there were almost as many patrolling the castle's perimeter. The Polish passengers riding on a tram along the eastern side of Adam Mickiewicz Square glanced in at the castle and shuddered, for this was the headquarters of the SS in Poland, and even as they looked, still more SS staff cars could be seen going through the heavily guarded gates and dropping SS officers at the tree-lined entrance.

The inhabitants of Posen, formerly known as Poznań, had endured the SS in their city since September 1939, but no one on the tram could remember ever seeing so many SS at the Königliches Residenzschloss; it was almost as if the SS were holding some sort of rally at the castle. If the people on the tram had dared to look more closely, they would have noticed that every one of the SS officers arriving at the castle that morning was a general.

One such general was a handsome, dapper-looking man of

medium height in his early thirties. Unlike most of his brother senior officers, this particular SS general stopped for a moment to smoke a cigarette and look with a critical eye at the exterior of the castle, with its ignoble, suburban clock tower and high mansard roof from which were hung a number of long swastika banners. Then, looking one last time across Adam Mickiewicz Square, he ground the cigarette under the heel of his well-polished boot and went inside.

The general was Walter Schellenberg, and he was no stranger to Posen. His second wife, Irene, had come from Posen, something he had discovered not from her but from his then boss and the former chief of the SD, Reinhard Heydrich. Six months after marrying Irene, in May 1940, Schellenberg had been given a file by Heydrich. It revealed that Irene's aunt was married to a Jew. Heydrich's meaning had been clear enough: Schellenberg now belonged to Heydrich, at least as long as he cared anything about his wife's relations. But two years later Heydrich was dead, murdered by Czech partisans, and Department 6 (Amt VI) of the foreign intelligence section of the Reich Security Office, one of the key administrations formerly commanded by Heydrich, was given to Schellenberg.

In the castle's Golden Hall there were perhaps only two notable absentees: Heydrich's replacement as chief of the Reich Security Office (which included the SD and the Gestapo), Ernst Kaltenbrunner; and Himmler's former adjutant, Karl Wolff, now the supreme SS representative in Italy. It had been given out that both men were too ill to attend Himmler's conference in Posen, that Kaltenbrunner was suffering from phlebitis and Wolff was recovering from an operation to remove a kidney stone. But Schellenberg, a man as well informed as he was resourceful, knew the truth. On Himmler's orders Kaltenbrunner, an alcoholic, was drying out in a Swiss sanatorium, while Wolff and his former boss were no longer on speaking terms after the Reichsführer-SS had refused Wolff permission to divorce his wife, Frieda, in order to marry a tasty blonde named Grafin—a permission subsequently granted by

Hitler himself when (quite unforgivably, in Himmler's eyes) Wolff went over Himmler's head.

There was, Schellenberg thought to himself as he sauntered into the hall, never a dull moment in the SS. Well, almost never. A speech by Himmler was not something he could view with anything other than dread, for the Reichsführer had a tendency to long-windedness, and given the number of SS generals who were gathered in architect Franz Schwechten's Golden Hall, Schellenberg expected a speech of Mahabharatan length and dullness. The Mahabharata was a book the young general had made himself read so that he might better understand Heinrich Himmler, who was its most passionate advocate; and having read it, Schellenberg had certainly found it easier to see where Himmler got some of his crazier ideas concerning duty, discipline, and, a favorite Himmler word, sacrifice. And Schellenberg did not think it too fanciful to view Himmler as someone who regarded himself as an avatar of the supreme god, Vishnu—or, at the very least, his high priest, descended to earth in human form to rescue Law, Good Deeds, Right, and Virtue. Schellenberg had also formed the impression that Himmler thought of Jews in the same way that the Mahabharata spoke of the one hundred *Dhartarashtras*—the grotesque human incarnations of demons who were the perpetual enemies of the gods. For all Schellenberg knew, Hitler held the same opinion, although he thought it much more likely that the Führer simply hated Jews, which wasn't exactly unusual in Germany and Austria. Schellenberg himself had nothing at all against the Jews; his own father had been a piano manufacturer in Saarbrücken and then in Luxembourg, and many of his best customers had been Jews. So it was fortunate that Schellenberg's own department was obliged to pay little more than lip service to all the usual Aryanist claptrap about Jewish subhumans and vermin. Those anti-Semites who did work in Amt VI—and there were quite a few—knew better than to give vent to their hatred in the presence of Walter Schellenberg. The young Foreign Intelligence head was interested only in what a British secret agent, Captain Arthur Connolly, had once called "the

Great Game"—the game in question being espionage, intrigue, and clandestine military adventure.

Schellenberg helped himself to coffee from an enormous refectory table, and, his eyes hardly noticing the enormous portrait of the Führer hanging underneath one of three enormous arched windows, he fixed a smile on his clever schoolboy's face and meandered toward a pair of officers he recognized.

Arthur Nebe, head of the Criminal Police, was a man much admired by Schellenberg. He hoped he might get a chance to warn Nebe of a whispered rumor making the rounds in Berlin. In 1941, according to the gossips, Nebe, in command of a Special Action Group in occupied Russia, had not only falsified his report of the slaughter of thousands of Jews, but also had allowed many to escape.

No such rumors attended the record of the second officer, Otto Ohlendorf, now chief of the SD's Domestic Intelligence Department and responsible for, among other things, compiling reports regarding German public opinion. The Einsatzgruppe commanded by Ohlendorf in the Crimea had been regarded as one of the most successful, slaughtering more than a hundred thousand Jews.

"So here he is," said Nebe, "our youngest brother, Benjamin." Nebe was repeating a remark made by Himmler about Schellenberg being the youngest general in the SS.

"I expect to grow older and wiser this morning," said Schellenberg.

"I can guarantee you'll grow older," said Ohlendorf. "Last time I went to one of these affairs it was in Wewelsburg. I think Himmler got all of it straight out of a Richard Wagner libretto. 'Never forget we are a knightly order from which one cannot withdraw and to which one is recruited by blood.' Or words to that effect." Ohlendorf shook his head, wearily. "Anyway, it was all very inspiring. And long. Very, very long. Like a rather slow performance of *Parsifal*."

"It wasn't blood that got me into this knightly order," said Nebe. "But that's certainly been the end result."

"All that 'knightly' order stuff makes me sick," said Ohlendorf. "Dreamed up by that lunatic Hildebrandt." He nodded at another

SS-Gruppenführer who was engaged in earnest-looking conversation with Oswald Pohl. Hildebrandt's own department, the Race and Resettlement Office, was subordinate to the Administration Office of the SS, of which Pohl was the head. "My God, I detest that bastard."

"Me, too," murmured Nebe.

"Doesn't everyone?" remarked Schellenberg, who had an extra reason to hate and fear Hildebrandt: one of Hildebrandt's principal functions was to investigate the racial purity of SS men's families. Schellenberg lived with the fear that just such an investigation might discover that there was more than one Jew in his family.

"There's Müller," said Ohlendorf. "I had better go and make my peace with him and the Gestapo." And putting down his coffee cup, he went to speak to the diminutive Gestapo chief, leaving Nebe and Schellenberg to their own conversation.

Nebe was a small, tough-looking man with gray, almost silver hair, a thin slit of a mouth, and a policeman's inquiring nose. He spoke in a thick Berlin accent.

"Listen carefully," said Nebe. "Don't ask questions, just listen. I know what I know because I used to be in the Gestapo, when Diels was still in charge. And I still have a few friends there who tell me things. Such as the fact that the Gestapo have you under surveillance. No, don't ask me why because I don't know. Here—" Nebe took out a cigarette case shaped like a coffin and opened it to reveal the little flat cigarettes he smoked. "Have a nail."

"And here I was thinking that I might have to warn *you* about something."

"Like what, for instance?"

"There's a rumor going around the SD that you falsified the figures for your Einsatzgruppe in Byelorussia."

"Everyone did," said Nebe. "What of it?"

"But for different reasons. It's said that you actually tried to put a brake on the slaughter."

"What can you do about such slanders? Himmler himself inspected my theater of operations, in Minsk. So, as you can see, accusing me of going easy on some Russian Jews is the same thing as saying that Himmler wasn't clever enough to spot anything wrong. And we can't have that, can we?" Nebe smiled coolly and lit their cigarettes. "No, I'm in the clear about that one, old boy, whatever the rumors say. But thanks. I appreciate it." He sucked hard at his cigarette and nodded warmly at Schellenberg.

Schellenberg's mind was already racing out of the castle and back to his hometown of Saarbrücken. Not long before he died, Heydrich had given Schellenberg the file about his wife's Jewish uncle. But had Heydrich kept a copy that was now in the possession of the Gestapo? And was it possible that the Gestapo might now suspect that he himself was Jewish? Berg was a German surname, but it could hardly be denied that there were more than a few Jews who had used the name as a prefix or suffix in an attempt to Germanize their own Hebraic names. Could that be what they were out to prove? To destroy him with the insinuation that he himself was Jewish? After all, the Gestapo had tried to destroy Heydrich with the suggestion that the "blond Moses" was also a Jew. Except that, in Heydrich's case, this was a suggestion that turned out to be partly true.

After Heydrich's murder, Himmler had shown Schellenberg a file that proved Heydrich's father, Bruno, a piano teacher from Halle, had been Jewish. (His nickname in Halle had been Isidor Suess.) Schellenberg had thought it was a strange thing for Himmler to have done so soon after Heydrich's death until he realized that this was the Reichsführer's way of persuading Schellenberg that he should forget about his former boss, that his loyalty now lay with the Reichsführer himself. But with Schellenberg's own father, a piano maker, Schellenberg did not think it so very far-fetched that someone in the Gestapo, jealous of his precocious success—at thirty-three he was the youngest general in the SS—should have considered it worth the Gestapo's time to investigate the possibility of his being Jewish, too.

He was about to ask Nebe a question, but the Berliner was already shaking his head and looking over Schellenberg's shoulder.

And as soon as Schellenberg turned, he saw a heavyset man with a bull neck and a shaven head who greeted him like an old friend.

"My dear friend," he said. "How nice to see you. I wanted to ask if there was any news about Kaltenbrunner."

"He's ill," said Schellenberg.

"Yes, yes, but what is it that ails him? What is this illness he has?"

"The doctors say it's phlebitis."

"Phlebitis? And what's that when it's not in a medical dictionary?"

"Inflammation of the veins," said Schellenberg, who was anxious to get away from the man, hating the familiarity with which Richard Gluecks had spoken to him. Schellenberg had only ever met him once before, but it was not a day he was likely to forget.

Richard Gluecks was in charge of the concentration camps. Not long after his appointment as chief of the SD, Kaltenbrunner had insisted on taking Schellenberg to see a special camp. Schellenberg looked into Gluecks's florid face as the man began to speculate on what might have caused Kaltenbrunner's illness and remembered that dreadful day in Mauthausen in all too vivid detail: the ferocious dogs, the smell of burning corpses, the unhinged cruelty of the officers, the absolute freedom of the swaggering guards to maim or kill, the distant gunshots, and the stench of the prisoners' barracks. The whole camp had been an insane laboratory of malice and violence. But the thing that Schellenberg remembered most vividly of all had been the drunkenness. Everyone on that tour of the special camp, himself included, had been drunk. Being drunk made things easier, of course. Easier not to care. Easier to torture someone or kill them. Easier to conduct hideous medical experiments on prisoners. Easier to force a thin smile onto your face and compliment your brother SS officers on a job well done. Small wonder that Kaltenbrunner was an alcoholic. Schellenberg told himself that if he had had to visit a special camp more than once, by now he would have killed himself with drink. The only wonder was that not every SS man serving in the special camps was addicted in the same way as Ernst Kaltenbrunner.

"I'm not in Berlin very much," said Gluecks. "My work keeps me in the East, of course. So if you see him, please tell Ernst I was asking for him."

"Yes, I will." With relief Schellenberg turned away from Gluecks, only to find himself face-to-face with a man he regarded with no less loathing: Joachim von Ribbentrop. Since he knew that the foreign minister was well aware of Schellenberg's pivotal role in the attempt of his former aide, Martin Luther, to discredit him with the Reichsführer-SS, Schellenberg expected to be cold-shouldered. Instead, much to the intelligence chief's surprise, the foreign minister actually spoke to him.

"Ah, yes, Schellenberg, there you are. I hoped to have a chance to talk to you."

"Yes, Herr Reichsminister?"

"I've been speaking to that fellow of yours, Ludwig Moyzisch. About Agent Cicero and the supposed contents of the British ambassador's safe in Ankara. I'm surprised to hear that you think Cicero's material is genuine. You see, I know the British very well. Better than you, I think. I've even met their ambassador to Turkey, Sir Hughe, and I know the kind of man he is. Not a complete fool, you know. I mean he only had to run a background check on this fellow—Bazna, isn't it? Cicero's real name? All he had to do was ask one or two questions to have discovered that one of Bazna's former employers in Ankara was my own brother-in-law, Alfred. Shall I tell you what I think, Schellenberg?"

"Please, Herr Reichsminister. I should be pleased to hear your opinion."

"I think Sir Hughe did ask; and having discovered that he had been Alfred's employee, they decided to put some information his way. False information. For our benefit. Take my word for it. This is the Big Three we're talking about. You don't just stumble across top-secret information about when and where they are meeting. If you ask me, this Cicero is a complete charlatan. But speak to my brother-in-law yourself, if you like. He'll confirm what I say."

Schellenberg nodded. "I don't think that will be necessary," he said. "But I did speak to our own former ambassador to Persia. At length. He tells me that Sir Hughe was British ambassador there from '34 to '36, and that Sir Hughe has never been particularly careful about security. Even then, he was, apparently, often in the habit of taking sensitive documents home with him. You see, the Abwehr tried to steal them as long ago as 1935. As a matter of fact, they have quite a large file on Sir Hughe relating to his time in Teheran. 'Snatch,' as he is better known to those who were at Balliol with Sir Hughe, is privately considered by no less a figure than your opposite number in England, Sir Anthony Eden, to be leakier than a sieve. And none too intelligent, either. The Ankara posting was seen as a means of keeping him safely out of harm's way. At least, it was until the outbreak of war, when the small matter of Turkish neutrality came up. In short, everything I have learned in assessing the intelligence from Cicero has led me to suppose that Sir Hughe was too lazy and trusting to make thorough enquiries about Bazna. Indeed it seems that he was much more concerned with hiring a good servant than with vetting a potential security risk. And with all due respect, Herr Reichsminister, I think you are mistaken in judging him by your own highly efficient standards."

"What an imagination you have, Schellenberg. But then I suppose that is your job. Well, good luck to you. Only don't say I didn't warn you." With that von Ribbentrop turned on his heel and walked off in the opposite direction, finally coming to a halt next to Generals Frank, Lörner, and Kammler.

Schellenberg lit a cigarette and continued to watch von Ribbentrop. It was interesting, he thought, that the foreign minister should have been prepared to overcome his loathing of him long enough to try to discredit Bazna and suggest his material was of no value. Which seemed to indicate that von Ribbentrop held quite the opposite opinion and was trying to prevent Amt VI from acting on Cicero's intelligence. Schellenberg had formed no particular plans in this matter, but given von Ribbentrop's interest in the affair, he began to wonder if he should try to think of one, if only to irritate the most pompous minister in the Reich.

"Can't you do without a cigarette in your mouth for just five minutes?"

It was Himmler, pointing at the Golden Hall's magnificent Neo-Romanesque ceiling, where a thin cloud of smoke was already gathering above the heads of the SS troop leaders. "Look at the air in here," he said irritably. "I don't mind the odd cigar in the evening, but first thing in the morning?"

Schellenberg was relieved to see that Himmler's antismoking remarks were addressed not just to him but also to several other officers who were smoking. He looked around for an ashtray.

"I don't mind you killing yourself with nicotine, but I do object to your poisoning me with it. If my throat doesn't hold up through the next three and a half hours, I shall hold all of you responsible."

Himmler marched off to the podium, his boots knocking loudly on the polished wooden floor, leaving Schellenberg to finish his cigarette in peace and to reflect upon the imminent prospect of a three-and-a-half-hour speech from the Reichsführer-SS. Three and a half hours was 210 minutes, and for that you needed something a lot stronger than a cup of coffee and a cigarette.

Schellenberg unbuttoned the breast pocket of his tunic and took out a pillbox from which he removed a Benzedrine tablet. In the beginning he had taken Benzedrine for his hay fever, but it wasn't very long before the drug's effect in the prevention of sleep made itself well known. Mostly, he preferred to take Benzedrine in situations involving pleasure rather than work. In Paris, he had used it liberally. But a 210-minute speech by Himmler was something of an emergency, and, swallowing the tablet quickly with the dregs of his coffee, he went to take his seat.

At midday, a strong smell of hot food came up the stairs from the castle's basement kitchens, arriving in the Golden Hall to torture the nostrils and stomachs of ninety-two SS troop leaders waiting for Himmler to finish. Schellenberg glanced at his wristwatch. The Reichsführer had been speaking for 150 minutes, which meant that there was still a whole hour to go. He was speaking about bravery as one of the virtues of the SS man.

"Part of bravery is composed of faith. And in this I don't think we can be outdone by anyone in the world. It's faith that wins battles, faith that achieves victories. We don't want pessimists in our ranks, people who have lost their faith. It doesn't make any difference what a man's job is—a man who has lost the will to believe shall not live among us in our ranks. . . ."

Schellenberg glanced around, wondering how many of his fellow SS troop leaders were still possessed of the faith that could win victories. Since Stalingrad, there had been precious little reason for optimism; and with an Allied landing in Europe expected sometime in the next year, it seemed more likely that many of the generals in the Golden Hall were less concerned with victory than with avoiding the retribution of Allied military tribunals after the war was over. And yet Schellenberg couldn't help thinking that there was still a way that victory might yet be won. If Germany could strike decisively at the Allies with the same surprise and effect that had been achieved by the Japanese at Pearl Harbor, they might still turn the tide of the war. Hadn't he been presented with just such an opportunity in agent Cicero's information? Didn't he already know that as of Sunday, November 21, Roosevelt and Churchill would be in Cairo for almost a week? And then in Teheran with Stalin until Saturday, December 4?

Schellenberg shook his head, puzzled. What on earth could have possessed them to pick Teheran for a conference in the first place? It seemed likely that Stalin must have insisted on the two other leaders coming to him. Doubtless he would have given them some excuse about the necessity of his being near his soldiers at the front; but all the same, Schellenberg wondered if either Churchill or Roosevelt was aware of the real reason behind Stalin's insistence that they meet in Teheran. According to Schellenberg's sources in the NKVD, Stalin had a morbid fear of flying and could no more have countenanced a long-distance flight to Newfoundland (which was the location favored by Churchill and Roosevelt) or even Cairo, than he could have bought himself a seat on the New York Stock Exchange. The chances were that Stalin had chosen Teheran because he could spend a large part of the journey on his armored train, making only a short flight at the end of it.

He imagined that the Big Three would never have picked Teheran if Operation Franz had ever gone into action. A joint operation of the Luftwaffe's elite 200 Squadron and the Friedenthal Section of Amt VI, the plan had been to fly a Junkers 290 carrying one hundred men from an airfield in the Crimea and drop them by parachute near a large salt lake southeast of Teheran. With the help of local tribesmen, F Section—many of whom spoke Persian—would then have interrupted American supplies for Russia that were being carried on the Iran–Iraq railway. The plan had been delayed following damage to the Junkers and the arrest of several of those pro-German Iranian tribesmen. By the time they were ready to go again, the best of the men in F Section, commanded by Otto Skorzeny, had been ordered to try to rescue Mussolini from his Italian mountaintop prison, and Operation Franz had been scrubbed. But the more Schellenberg thought about the situation now, the more it looked like a plan. F Section, with its Persian-speaking officers and special equipment, was, as far as he was aware, still intact; and there were the Big Three, heading for the very country in which F Section had been trained to operate. And there was no reason why such a plan should be restricted to a ground attack force. Schellenberg thought a commando team in Teheran might operate in tandem with a very specialized form of attack from the air. And he resolved to speak to a man he knew was coming to Posen that evening for the Reichsführer's speech the following day: Air Inspector General Erhard Milch.

Himmler's speech finally ended, but Schellenberg was too excited to have lunch. Using a borrowed office in the castle, he telephoned his deputy in Berlin, Martin Sandberger. "It's me—Schellenberg."

"Hello, boss. How's Posen?"

"Never mind that now, just listen. I want you to drive over to Friedenthal and find out what state F Section is in. Specifically, whether they're up for another shot at Operation Franz. And, Martin, if he's there, I want you to bring that baron fellow back to Berlin."

"Von Holten-Pflug?"

"That's him. Then I want you to set up a department meeting for first thing on Wednesday morning. Reichert, Buchman, Janssen, Weisinger, and whoever's running the Turkish and Iranian desk these days."

"That would be Major Schubach. He reports to Colonel Tschierschky. Shall I ask him, too?"

"Yes."

After the call Schellenberg went to his room and tried to sleep, but his mind was still fizzing with the mechanics of a plan he was already calling Operation Long Jump. He could see no obvious reason why the plan couldn't work. It was daring and audacious, yes, but that was what was called for. And while he disliked Skorzeny, the man had at least proved that the apparently impossible could be pulled off. At the same time, the last person he wanted in command of such an operation was Skorzeny—that went without saying. Skorzeny was much too hard to control. And, besides, the Luftwaffe would never have agreed to Skorzeny, not after Abruzzi. Of the dozen glider pilots who had landed near Il Duce's makeshift prison on the loftiest peak in the Italian Apennines, all had been killed or captured—not to mention the 108 SS parachutists who had accompanied Skorzeny. Just three men had flown off that mountain: Mussolini, Skorzeny, and the pilot of their light aircraft. Abruzzi might have been worth the heavy sacrifice of men and materials if something useful had been achieved. But Schellenberg thought Il Duce was finished and that rescuing him seemed pointless. The Führer might have been delighted enough to award Skorzeny the Knight's Cross, but Schellenberg and quite a few others had regarded the whole operation as something of a disaster; and he had told Skorzeny as much on the train to Paris. Predictably, Skorzeny, a large and violent man, had been furious and would probably have attacked and possibly even tried to kill Schellenberg but for the silenced Mauser pistol the young general had produced from underneath his folded leather coat. You didn't criticize a man like Skorzeny to his face without having something in reserve.

Schellenberg finally fell asleep, only to be awoken at eight o'clock that evening by an SS-Oberscharführer who told him Field Marshal Milch had arrived and was waiting for him in the officers' bar.

Like everyone who worked for Hermann Göring, Erhard Milch looked rich. Thick-set, smallish, dark-haired, and balding, he offset his unremarkable appearance with a gold marshal's baton that was a smaller version of the one Göring carried, and when he offered Schellenberg a cigarette from a gold case and a glass of champagne from the bottle of Taittinger on the table, the SD man's keen eyes quickly took in the gold Glashütte wristwatch and the gold signet ring on Milch's stubby little finger.

As with Heydrich, it was strongly rumored that Milch was of Jewish blood. But Schellenberg knew this for a fact, just as he also knew how, thanks to Göring, this was not a problem for the former director of the German national airline, Lufthansa. Göring had fixed everything for his ex-deputy in the Reich Air Ministry when he had persuaded Milch's gentile mother to sign a legal affidavit stating that her Jewish husband was not Erhard's true father. It was a common enough practice in the Third Reich, and in this way the authorities were able to certify Milch as an honorary Aryan. These days, however, Göring and Milch were no longer close, the latter having criticized the Luftwaffe for its poor performance on the Russian front, a criticism that Göring was not likely to forget. As a result it was also believed that Milch had transferred his allegiance to Albert Speer, the minister of armaments—a rumor that had only been fueled by their arrival together in Posen.

Over champagne, Schellenberg told Milch about Agent Cicero's intelligence, and then came quickly to the point: "I was thinking of resurrecting Operation Franz. Only instead of disrupting supplies on the Iran–Iraq railway, F team would try to assassinate the Big Three. We could coordinate their attack with a bombing raid."

"A bombing raid?" Milch laughed. "Even our longest-range bomber would barely make it there and back. And even if a few bombers did get there, enemy fighters would shoot them down before they could do any damage. No, I'm afraid you'd better think again on that one, Walter."

"There *is* a plane that could do the job. The Focke Wulf FW 200 Condor."

"That's not a bomber, it's a reconnaissance plane."

"A long-range reconnaissance plane. I was thinking of four of them, each armed with two thousand-kilogram bombs. My team on the ground would knock out the enemy radar to give them a chance. Come on, Erhard, what do you say?"

Milch was shaking his head. "I don't know."

"They wouldn't have to fly from Germany, but from German-held territory in the Ukraine. Vinnica. I've worked it out. From Vinnica it's eighteen hundred kilometers to Teheran. There and back is just within the 200's standard fuel range."

"Actually it's just outside, by forty-four kilometers," said Milch. "The published figures on the 200's range were inflated. Wrongly."

"So they throw something out to save a bit of fuel."

"One of the pilots, perhaps."

"If necessary, yes. Or one of the pilots could take the place of the navigator."

"Actually, I suppose that with overload fuel it might be possible to extend the range," admitted Milch. "With a light bomb load, such as you describe, maybe. Perhaps."

"Erhard, if we manage to kill the Big Three, we could force the Allies to the negotiating table. Think of it. Like Pearl Harbor. A decisive strike that completely changes the course of the war. Isn't that what you said? And you're right, of course. If we kill the Big Three there won't be an Allied landing in Europe in '44. Perhaps not at all. It's *that* simple."

"You know, things are not so good between myself and Göring right now, Walter."

"I'd heard something."

"He won't be so easy to persuade."

"What would you suggest?"

"That perhaps we should work around him. I'll speak to Schmid at the Kurfürst." Milch was referring to the intelligence arm of the Luftwaffe. "And to General Student in airborne."

Schellenberg nodded: it was Student who had helped Skorzeny plan the air assault on the Hotel Campo Imperatore on the Gran Sasso in the Apennines.

"Then let's drink to our plan," said Milch and ordered another bottle of champagne.

"With your agreement, Erhard, I propose to call this plan of ours Operation Long Jump."

"I like that. It has an appropriately athletic ring. Only this will have to be a world record, Walter. As if it were that black fellow from the last Olympiad in Berlin doing the long jumping."

"Jesse Owens."

"That's the one. Marvelous athlete. When were you thinking of carrying out this operation of ours?"

Schellenberg unbuttoned his tunic pocket and took out his SS pocket diary. "This is the best part of the plan," he grinned. "The part I haven't yet told you about. Look here. I want to do this exactly eight weeks from tomorrow. On Tuesday, November thirtieth. At precisely nine P.M."

"You're very precise. I like that. But why that day in particular? And at that time?"

"Because on that day not only do I know that Winston Churchill will be in Teheran, I also happen to know that he'll be hosting his own birthday party that night, at the British embassy in Teheran."

"Was that also in agent Cicero's information?"

"No. You see it's obvious just from the location of this confer-ence that the Americans are out to accommodate the Russians in whatever way they can. Why else would a president who is also a cripple be prepared to fly all that way? Now, that will discomfort the British, who, as the weakest of the three powers, will be looking for ways to try to control the situation. What better way to do it than to host a birthday party? To remind everyone that Churchill is the oldest of the three. And the longest-serving war leader. So the

British will give a party. And everyone will drink to Churchill's health and tell him what a great war leader he has been. And then a bomb from one of your airplanes will land on the embassy. Hopefully more than one bomb. And, if there is anyone left alive after that, my Waffen-SS team will finish them off."

A waiter arrived with a second bottle of champagne, and as soon as it was open, Milch poured two glasses and raised his to Schellenberg. "Happy birthday, Mr. Churchill."

IV

WEDNESDAY, OCTOBER 6, 1943,
BERLIN

AMT VI (DEPARTMENT 6) of the SD had its offices in the southwest part of the city, in a curvilinear, four-story modern building. Constructed in 1930, it had been a Jewish old people's home until October 1941, when all the residents were transferred directly to the ghetto at Lodz. Surrounded by vegetable gardens and blocks of apartments, only the flagpole on top of the roof and one or two official cars parked outside the front door gave any clue that 22 Berkaerstrasse was the headquarters of the Foreign Intelligence Section of the Reich Security Office.

Schellenberg liked being well away from his masters in the Wilhelmstrasse and on Unter den Linden. Berkaerstrasse, in Wilmersdorf, on the edge of the Grunewald Forest, was a good twenty-minute drive from Kaltenbrunner's office, and this meant that he was usually left alone to do much as he pleased. But being alone in this way was not without its own peculiar disadvantage, insofar as Schellenberg was obliged to live and work among a group of men several of whom he considered, privately at least, to be dangerous psychopaths, and he was always wary of how he enforced discipline among his subordinate officers. Indeed, he had come to regard his colleagues much as a zookeeper in the reptile house at the Berlin Zoo might have regarded a pit full of alligators and vipers. Men who had killed with such alacrity and in such numbers were not to be trifled with.

Men like Martin Sandberger, Schellenberg's second in command, who had recently arrived back in Berlin after leading a special action commando battalion in Estonia, where, it was bruited, his unit had murdered more than 65,000 Jews. Or Karl Tschierschky, who headed up Amt VI's Group C, dealing with Turkey, Iran, and Afghanistan, and who had been seconded to Schellenberg's department with a similarly murderous background in Riga. Then there was Captain Horst Janssen, who had led a Sonderkommando in Kiev, executing 33,000 Jews. The plain fact of the matter was that Schellenberg's department, much like any department in the SD, was thick with killers, some of whom were just as willing to kill a German as they had been to murder Jews. Albert Rapp, for example, another veteran of the special action groups and Tschierschky's predecessor at the Turkish desk, had been killed in a hit-and-run accident. It was generally assumed Captain Reichert, another officer in Amt VI, was the driver. Reichert had become aware of a relationship between his wife and the late Albert Rapp: the baby-faced Captain Reichert did not look like a murderer, but then again, so few of them did.

Schellenberg himself had only escaped doing service in one of Heydrich's murderous battalions by virtue of his precocious appointment as head of the SD's Counterespionage/Inland Department in September 1939. Could he ever have murdered so many innocent people so very blithely? It was a question Schellenberg seldom asked himself, for the simple reason that he did not have an answer. Schellenberg subscribed to the view that a man did not really know what infamy he was capable of until he was actually required to do it.

Unlike most of his colleagues, Schellenberg had rarely fired a gun in anger; but concern for his own safety among so many proven murderers meant that he carried a Mauser in a shoulder holster, a C96 in his briefcase, a Schmeisser MP40 under the driver's seat of his car, and two MP40s in his mahogany partner's desk—one in each drawer. His precautions did not end there, however; underneath the blue stone on his gold signet ring was a cyanide capsule, while the windows of his top-floor office were sheathed in an electrically charged wire net that would sound an alarm if breached from the outside.

Waiting behind his desk for his subordinates to arrive for the meeting, Schellenberg turned to a nearby trolley table and pressed the button that activated the room's secret microphones. Then he pressed the button that switched on the green light outside his door, signaling that it was permitted to come in. When everyone was assembled and the door light was changed to red, he outlined the bare bones of Operation Long Jump and then invited comments.

Colonel Martin Sandberger went first. He had a lawyer's way of speaking—measured and slightly pedantic—which was not surprising, given his background as an assistant judge in the Inner Administration of Württemberg. It was always a source of surprise to Schellenberg how many lawyers were involved at the sharp end of genocide; that a man could be teaching the philosophy of law one week and executing Jews in Estonia the next was, Schellenberg had decided, a real clue as to the shallowness of human civilization. Even so, the thirty-three-year-old Sandberger, with his wide jaw, thick lips, broad nose, and heavy brow, looked more a thug than a lawyer.

"Yesterday," said Sandberger, "as instructed, I drove out to the Special Section at Friedenthal, where I met SS Sturmbannführer von Holten-Pflug." Here, Sandberger nodded at a young, aristocratic-looking Waffen-SS major who was sitting opposite him.

Schellenberg regarded the major with something close to amusement—even without their names he could always tell the aristocrats. It was the tailoring that gave them away. Most officers had their uniforms made up by the SS-Bekleidungswerke, a clothing factory in a special camp where Jewish tailors were put to work; but von Holten-Pflug's uniform looked made to measure, and Schellenberg guessed it had come from Wilhelm Holters, in Tauentzienstrasse. The quality was quite unmistakable. Schellenberg himself bought his uniforms from Holters, as did the Führer.

"Sturmbannführer von Holten-Pflug and I conducted a materials check," continued Sandberger, "with a view to the present readiness for Operation Long Jump. We found that some weapons and ammunition had been requisitioned by Hauptsturmführer Skorzeny for the Mussolini rescue. Apart from that, however, everything is pretty much there. SS winter uniforms, SS fall- and spring-pattern uniforms, all the usual gear. Most important of all, the special stores we put together as gifts for the local Kashgai tribesmen are still there, too. The silver-inlay K98 rifles, and the gold-plated Walther pistols."

"It's not stores we lack," said von Holten-Pflug. "It's men. Skorzeny left us very shorthanded. Fortunately, those men who remain in the section are Farsi-speakers. I myself also speak a little Gilaki, which is the language of the northern Persian tribesmen. Of course, most of their leaders have some German. But given that we'll very likely be up against Russian troops, I'd like to make a recommendation that we use a team of Ukrainians, and base the operation at Vinnica."

"How many men do you think you would need?" asked Schellenberg.

"About eighty to a hundred Ukrainians, and another ten or fifteen German officers and NCOs, commanded by myself."

"And then?"

Von Holten-Pflug unfolded a map of Iran and spread it out on the table in front of him.

"I recommend that we stick to the plan from Operation Franz and fly from Vinnica. Six groups of ten men wearing Russian uniforms to parachute into the country near the holy city of Qom, and another four groups near Qazvin. Once there, we'll rendezvous with our agents in Iran and head for the safe houses in Teheran. We can then reconnoiter the embassy areas and radio precise coordinates back to Berlin for the air strikes. After the bombing, the ground force will move in and deal with any survivors. Then we'll make our way to Turkey, assuming that it remains a neutral country."

Schellenberg smiled. Von Holten-Pflug made the whole operation sound as straightforward as a stroll around the Tiergarten. "Tell me more about these Ukrainians," he said.

"They're Zeppelin volunteers. Naturally I'll need to go to Vinnica to sort things out. There's a local intelligence officer I'd like to use. Fellow named Oster."

"No relation, I hope," said Schellenberg.

Von Holten-Pflug adjusted the monocle in his eye and regarded Schellenberg blankly.

"There was an Oster in the Abwehr," explained Sandberger. "Until a month or two ago. A lieutenant colonel. He was dismissed and transferred to the Wehrmacht on the Russian front."

"This Oster is a captain in the Waffen-SS."

"I'm very glad to hear it."

Von Holten-Pflug smiled uncertainly, and to Schellenberg it was plain to see that the major had no idea of the intense rivalry that existed between Amt VI of the SD and the Abwehr. Indeed, Schellenberg thought "rivalry" hardly strong enough to describe his relations with German military intelligence and the man who was its chief, Admiral Wilhelm Canaris. For it was Schellenberg's greatest ambition that Amt VI should absorb the largely ineffective Abwehr; and yet, for some reason Schellenberg was unable to fathom, Himmler—and perhaps also Hitler—hesitated to give Schellenberg what he wanted. In Schellenberg's view, there were obvious economies of scale a merger of the two agencies would bring. As things now stood, resources ended up being duplicated, and sometimes operational initiatives as well. Schellenberg understood Canaris wanting to hang on to power. He would have felt the same way. But it was quite futile for Canaris to resist a change that everyone—even Himmler—saw as inevitable. It was just a question of time.

"Captain Oster speaks Ukrainian and some Russian," said von Holten-Pflug. "He used to work for the Wannsee Institute. And he seems to know how to handle the Popovs."

"I think we have to be careful here," said Schellenberg. "After the Vlasov affair, the Führer is not at all keen on using so-called subhuman military resources."

Captured by the Germans in the spring of 1942, Andrei Vlasov was a Soviet general who had been "persuaded" to create an army of Russian POWs to fight for Hitler. Schellenberg had worked hard to achieve the independence of Vlasov's "Russian Liberation Movement"; but Hitler, infuriated by the very idea of a Slav army fighting for Germany, had ordered Vlasov returned to a POW camp and forbade any mention of the plan again.

"I haven't given up on Vlasov and his army," continued Schellenberg, "but at Posen, Himmler made a special mention of his being ostracized, and it would be unwise not to be mindful of that."

The Zeppelin volunteers were not much different from Vlasov's RLM; these were also Russian prisoners fighting for the German army, except that they had been organized into guerrilla partisan units and then parachuted deep into Soviet territory.

"I don't think a team of Zeppelin volunteers is likely to meet with the Reichsführer's approval any more than a unit from Vlasov's army." Schellenberg turned to Captain Janssen. "No, we'd best try to make this an SS operation from top to bottom. Horst, you were in the Ukraine. What's the name of the Ukrainian Waffen-SS division that's fighting there?"

"The Galicia Division. Waffen-SS Fourteenth Grenadiers."

"Who's the commanding officer?"

"General Walther Schimana. I believe the enlistment of Ukrainian cadres is going on even as we speak."

"I thought as much. Speak to this General Schimana and see if we can have our Zeps operate from within the Galicia Division. As long as I can refer to our men as Waffen-SS instead of Ukrainians, or Zeps, then I think we can make Himmler happy.

"Go back to Friedenthal," he told von Holten-Pflug, "and take everything—men, stores, money, the lot—to the Ukraine. You and the other officers can stay at Himmler's place in Zhitomir. It's an old officers' training college, about eighty kilometers north of Hitler's Wehrwolf HQ, at Vinnica, so you'll be quite comfortable there. I'll clear it with Himmler myself. I doubt he'll be needing it again. And be careful. Tell your men to stay out of the Russian villages, and to leave the women alone. Last time I was there, Himmler's pilot got himself murdered in the most horrible circumstances by local partisans after he went chasing some local skirt. If your boys want to relax, tell them to play tennis. There's quite a good court there, as I recall. As soon as your team is operational I want you to come back here and make your report. Use the Wehrmacht's courier plane to Warsaw, and then by train to Berlin. Got that?"

Schellenberg concluded the meeting and left his office. He had parked his car on Hohenzollerndamm instead of his usual place outside the front door, reasoning that the walk might afford him an opportunity to see if he was being followed. He recognized most of the cars parked outside the offices of Amt VI; but further up the street, toward the taxi file on the corner of Teplitzer Strasse, he saw a black Opel Type 6 limousine with two occupants. It was parked facing north, the same direction as Schellenberg's gray Audi. But for Arthur Nebe's warning he would have paid it little or no attention. As soon as he got into his car, Schellenberg picked up the shortwave transmitter and called his office, asking his secretary, Christiane, to check on the license plate he read off in his rearview mirror. Then he turned the car around and drove south toward the Grunewald Forest.

He drove slowly, with one eye on his mirror. He saw the black Opel make a U-turn on Hohenzollerndamm and then come after him at the same leisurely speed. After a few minutes, Christiane came on the radio again.

"I have that Kfz-Schein," she said. "The car is registered to Department Four, at the Reich Main Security Office, on Prinz Albrechtstrasse."

So it was the Gestapo who were following him.

Schellenberg thanked her and switched off the radio. He could hardly let them follow him to where he was going—Himmler would never have approved of what he had arranged. But equally, he didn't want to make it too obvious that he was trying to lose them; so long as the Gestapo were unaware that he had been tipped off about them, he had a small advantage.

He stopped at a tobacconist and bought some cigarettes, which gave him the opportunity to turn around without it looking like he'd spotted the tail. Then he drove north until he reached the Kurfürstendamm, turning east toward the city center.

Near the Kaiser Wilhelm Memorial Church, he turned south onto Tauenzienstrasse and pulled up outside the Ka-De-We department store on Wittenberg Platz. Berlin's biggest department store was full of people, and it was a comparatively simple matter for Schellenberg to give the Gestapo the slip. Entering the store by one door, he left by another, picking up a taxi at the stand on Kurfürstenstrasse. The driver took him north, up Potsdamer Strasse toward the Tiergarten, and then dropped him close to the Brandenburg Gate. Schellenberg thought Berlin's famous monument was looking a little scarred from the bombings. On top of the quadriga roof, the four horses drawing Eirene in her chariot seemed rather more apocalyptic than triumphal these days. Schellenberg crossed the street, glanced over this shoulder one last time to check that he was no longer being followed, and hurried through the door of the Adlon, Berlin's best hotel. Before the war the Adlon had been known as "little Switzerland" because of all the diplomatic activity that took place there, which was probably one reason why Hitler had always avoided it; more important, however, the SS avoided the Adlon, too, preferring the Kaiserhof in Wilhelmstrasse, which was why Schellenberg always conducted his liaisons with Lina at the Adlon.

His suite was on the third floor of the hotel, with a view of Unter den Linden. Before the National Socialist Party had cut down the trees to facilitate military displays, it had been just about the nicest view in Berlin, with the possible exception of Lina Heydrich's bare behind.

As soon as he was inside the room he picked up the telephone and ordered some champagne and a cold lunch. Despite the war, the kitchens at the Adlon still managed to turn out food that was as good as anywhere in Europe. He moved the telephone away from the bed and buried it under a heap of cushions. Schellenberg knew that the Forschungsamt, the intelligence agency established by Göring and charged with signal surveillance and wiretapping, had planted listening devices in all of the Adlon's four hundred bedroom phones.

Schellenberg took off his jacket and settled down in an armchair with the *Illustrierte Beobachter* and read a highly romanticized account of life on the Russian front that seemed to suggest not only that German soldiers were holding back the enemy masses, but also that in the end German heroism would prevail.

There was a knock at the door. It was a waiter with a trolley. He started to open the champagne but Schellenberg, tipping him generously, told him to go. It was one of the bottles of Dom Perignon 1937 he had brought from Paris—a whole case he had left with the Adlon's sommelier—and he had no intention of letting anyone but himself open what was perhaps one of the last good bottles of champagne in Berlin.

Ten minutes later the door opened a second time and a tall, blue-eyed, corn-haired woman wearing a neatly tailored brown tweed suit and a checked flannel blouse entered the suite. Lina Heydrich kissed him, a little sadly, which was always the way she kissed Schellenberg when she saw him again, before sitting down in an armchair and lighting a cigarette. He opened the champagne expertly and poured a glass, then brought it to her, sitting down on the arm of her chair and stroking her hair gently.

"How have you been?" he asked.

"Good, thank you. And you? How was Paris?"

"I brought you a present."

"Walter," she said, smiling, although no less sadly than before. "You shouldn't have."

He handed her a gift-wrapped package and watched as she unwrapped it.

"Perfume," she said. "How clever of you to know it's in short supply here."

Schellenberg smiled. "I'm an intelligence officer."

"Mais Oui, by Bourjois." She removed the seal and the scallop-shaped stopper and dabbed some on her wrists. "It's nice. I like it." Her smile grew a little warmer. "You're very good at presents, aren't you, Walter? Very thoughtful. Reinhard was never good at presents. Not even on birthdays or anniversaries."

"He was a busy man."

"No, that wasn't it. He was a womanizer, that's what he was, Walter. Him and that awful friend of his."

"Eichmann."

She nodded. "Oh, I heard all the stories. What they were up to in the nightclubs. Especially the ones in Paris."

"Paris is very different now," said Schellenberg. "But I can't say I ever heard anything."

"For an intelligence chief you're a terrible liar. I hope you're better at lying to Hitler than you are to me. You must have heard the story of the Moulin Rouge firing squad?"

Everyone in the SD had heard the story of Heydrich and Eichmann lining up ten naked girls in the famous Paris nightclub, then bending them over so that they could fire champagne corks at their bare behinds. He shrugged. "Those stories have a habit of being exaggerated. Especially after someone has died."

Lina gave Schellenberg a penetrating sideways look. "Sometimes I wonder what you get up to when you go to Paris."

"Nothing so vulgar, I can assure you."

She took his hand and kissed it affectionately.

Lina von Osten was thirty-one years old. She had married Heydrich in 1931 when she was just eighteen and already an enthusiastic National Socialist. It was rumored that it was she who had persuaded her new husband to join the SS. Schellenberg himself thought the rumor was probably true, for Lina was a strong woman as well as a handsome one. Not a great beauty but well made, and wholesome looking, like one of those paragons of Aryan womanhood from the Nazi Women's League you'd see exercising in a propaganda film.

She took off her jacket to reveal a peasant-style bodice that seemed to enhance the size of her breasts; then she unpinned her golden hair so that it fell about her shoulders. Standing up, she started to undress and they began their usual game: for each question he answered truthfully about what Amt VI was doing, she would remove an article of clothing. By the time he had told her all about Agent Cicero and the documents in Sir Hughe's safe and his plan to assassinate the Big Three at Teheran, she was naked and seated on his lap.

"What does Himmler have to say about this?" she asked.

"I don't know. I haven't told him yet. I'm still putting the plan together."

"This could save us from disaster, Walter."

"It's a possibility."

"A strong possibility." Lina kissed him happily. "How clever you are, Walter."

"We'll see."

"No, really, you are. It hardly matters if you kill Roosevelt, I think. After all, he's a sick man and the vice president would replace him. But Churchill personifies the British war effort, and killing him would be a real body blow for the English. Then again, the British hardly matter, do they? Not next to the Americans and the Russians. No, it's the Russians that would be affected the most. If Churchill personifies the British war effort, then Stalin personifies the whole Soviet system. To kill all three would be splendid. It would put the Allies in total chaos. But just to kill Stalin would end the war in Europe. There would be another revolution in Russia. You might even get that Russian general of yours to lead it."

"Vlasov?"

"Yes, Vlasov. The Russians are more terrified of Stalin than they are of Hitler, I think. That's what makes them fight. That's what makes them tolerate such enormous losses and still fight on. There are only so many planes and tanks that they can make, but men seem to be in limitless supply. That's Russian arithmetic. They think they can win because at the end, when every German is dead, they'll still have lots of Russians left alive. But you kill Stalin and everything changes. He's shot everyone capable of replacing him, hasn't he? Who's left?"

"You," smiled Schellenberg. "I think you'd make a fine dictator. Especially the way you are now. Magnificent."

Lina punched him playfully on the shoulder, although it still hurt. She was stronger than she thought. "I'm serious, Walter. You have to make this plan happen. For all our sakes." She shook her head. "Otherwise, I don't know what's going to become of us, really I don't. I saw Goebbels the other day and he told me that if the Russians ever get to Germany we are facing nothing less than the Bolshevization of the Reich."

"He always says that. It's his job to scare us with the idea of what it might be like to live as Communists."

"That just shows you haven't been listening, Walter. They won't be handing out copies of Marx and Engels when they get here. We're facing nothing less than the liquidation of our entire intelligentsia and the descent of our people into Bolshevist-Jewish slavery. And behind the terror, mass starvation and total anarchy."

To Schellenberg's well-informed ears this sounded like a pamphlet from the Propaganda Ministry that had come through his letterbox the previous week, but he didn't interrupt Lina.

"What do you suppose happened to all those German soldiers who were captured at Stalingrad? They're in forced labor battalions, of course. Working in the Siberian tundra. And all those Polish officers executed at Katyn. That's the fate that awaits us all, Walter. My sons are in the Hitler Youth. What do you think will become of them? Or for that matter their two sisters, Silke and Marte?" Lina closed her eyes and pressed her face against Schellenberg's chest. "I'm so afraid of what might happen."

He folded her in his arms.

"I've been thinking of speaking to Himmler," she said quietly. "Of asking his permission to get my boys out of the Hitler Youth. I've already given a husband to Germany. I wouldn't want to lose a child as well."

"Would you like me to speak to him, Lina?"

Lina smiled at him. "You're so good to me, Walter. But, no, I'll do it myself. Himmler always feels guilty when he talks to me. He'll be more likely to give in to me than to you." She kissed him, and this time she gave herself up to it and they were soon in bed, each striving to please the other and then themselves.

In the early part of the afternoon, Schellenberg left Lina in the Adlon and walked to the Air Ministry. It was housed in a squared-off, functional-looking building, and to prevent it from becoming a target for enemy bombers it displayed no flags.

Schellenberg was shown to a large conference room on the fourth floor, where he was quickly joined by a number of senior officers: General Schmid, General Korten, General Koller, General Student, General Galland, and a lieutenant named Welter who took notes. It was General Schmid, better known to the Luftwaffe as "Beppo," who spoke first.

"On the basis of what Milch told us, we've examined the feasibility of using a squadron of four Focke Wulf 200s. It is, as you have already worked out for yourself, the best aeroplane for the job. It has a service ceiling of almost six thousand meters and, carrying extra fuel, a range of forty-four hundred kilometers. However, to facilitate targeting, we would recommend not carrying a bomb load, but rather two Henschel HS293 radio-controlled missiles. The Henschel acts like a small aircraft, with a motor to boost it to its maximum-level speed, after which a radio controller on the plane guides it to its target."

"Radio-controlled?" Schellenberg was impressed. "How does that work?"

"The weapon is top secret, so you'll understand if we don't say too much about it. But the operation of the missile is quite simple. However, the bombardier must keep the missile in sight, and environmental conditions such as cloud, haze, or smoke could interfere with the targeting. Tracers from light AA fire could also make it difficult to pick out the missile." Schmid paused to light a cigarette. "Of course, all that is somewhat academic. Everything really depends on your ground team's being able to knock out the enemy radar. If they manage to have fighters up in the air waiting for us, our Condors would be easy booty for them."

Schellenberg nodded. "I don't think I can overstate the risks involved in this mission, gentlemen," he said. "I believe as soon as we've knocked out their radar they'll put fighters up anyway, just to be on the safe side. There's a strong possibility that none of your air crews will get back to Germany in one piece. But I can improve their chances."

"Before you do," General Student interrupted, "I should like to know what happened to the signals commando that was parachuted into Iran back in March. As the first stage of Operation Franz."

Six men, all of them veterans of Ukrainian murder squads from F Section, had been met on the ground in Iran by Frank Mayr, an SS man who had been living with Kashgai tribesmen since 1940. One of the six had died immediately from typhoid; but the others had been successful, at least insofar as establishing communications with the Havelinstitut—the SS radio center at Wannsee.

"When Operation Franz was downgraded because of Skorzeny's Mussolini rescue," explained Schellenberg, "they encountered a number of difficulties. They entered Teheran and survived there for almost five months, living with a group of pistachio-nut farmers and Iranian wrestlers before they were picked up by the Americans. They're currently being held in a POW camp near Sultanabad."

"I only asked about them," said General Student, "because you seem very confident of knocking out the enemy radar in Teheran. Will your men be doing that by themselves, or will you have more wrestlers to help you?"

Schellenberg saw the smiles on the faces of some of the other officers and shifted uncomfortably on his chair.

"In Iran, wrestlers are regarded as men of high social status," he said. "Rather like matadors in Spain. Being physically fit, they are frequently called upon to become policemen, bodyguards, sometimes even assassins."

"They sound like the SS," observed Student.

Schellenberg turned back to General Schmid and asked him if the Luftwaffe was willing to proceed with the plan to kill the Big Three, assuming Hitler himself approved it. Schmid glanced around the table and, finding no opposition to Operation Long Jump, nodded slowly.

"The Führer knows that the Luftwaffe will do anything that helps to win the war," he said.

After the meeting, Schellenberg took a taxi back to Wittenberg Platz and returned to where he had left his car near the Ka-De-We. Before the war, the store had served forty different kinds of bread and 180 kinds of cheese and fish, but choice was rather more limited in the autumn of 1943. Approaching his car, he glanced around, hoping the black Opel had gone; but it was still there, which seemed to heighten the gravity of his situation. The Gestapo were not about to let the small matter of his having given them the slip for several hours deter them from whatever it was they wanted to find out. As soon as he drove off, the Opel came after him, and he resolved to find out before the afternoon was over exactly what it was they were investigating—his supposed Jewishness, his affair with Lina Heydrich, or something else.

He drove quickly now, back the way he had come, until he reached the edge of the Grunewald Forest—the city's green window—where, on an empty, wide, firebreak road that ran between two armies of facing trees, he pulled over. Leaving the car's engine still running and the driver's door open, he grabbed the Schmeisser MP40, hid it under his coat, and ran into the woods. He ran at a right angle to the road for almost thirty meters before turning and running parallel to the road for almost a hundred more in the direction from which he had just driven. Returning cautiously to the edge of the tree line near the road, he saw that he was no more than twenty meters behind the Opel, which had halted at what the driver must have considered to be a discreet distance. Crouching behind a large red oak, Schellenberg unfolded the MP40's stock and worked the slide action slowly and quietly, to ready the weapon's thirty-two-round magazine. Surely they wouldn't want to lose him twice in one day. The driver's door of his own car was wide open. At first the two Gestapo men inside the Opel would assume that he had gotten out to take a leak, but when he didn't return, curiosity would surely overcome them. They would have to get out of the car.

Ten minutes passed with no sign of movement in the Opel. And then the driver's door opened and a man wearing a black leather coat and a dark-green Austrian-style hat got out and fetched a pair of binoculars from the trunk, which was Schellenberg's cue to step out of the trees and walk quickly up to the Opel.

"Tell your friend to get out of the car with his hands empty."

"Jürgen," said the man with the binoculars. "Come here, please. He's here and he has a machine pistol. So please be careful."

The second Gestapo man stepped slowly out of the car with his hands raised. Taller than his colleague, with a broken nose and a boxer's ear, he was wearing a dark pinstripe suit and sensible Birkenstock shoes. Neither was more than thirty and both wore the cynical smiles of men who were used to being feared and who knew that nothing could ever happen to them. Schellenberg jerked the gun toward the trees.

"Move," he said.

The two men walked through the line of trees with Schellenberg following at a distance of three or four meters until, at a small clearing about forty meters from the road, he ordered them to stop.

"You're making a serious mistake," said the smaller one, who was still holding the binoculars. "We're Gestapo."

"I know that," said Schellenberg. "On your knees, gentlemen. With your hands on your heads, please."

When they were kneeling, he told them to throw their guns as far as they could and then show him some kind of identification. Reluctantly the two men obeyed, each tossing away a Mauser automatic and showing him the small steel warrant disc that all Gestapo men were obliged to carry.

"Why were you following me?"

"We weren't following you," said the man with the boxer's ear, still holding out the warrant disc in the palm of his hand like a beggar who had just received alms. "There's been a mistake. We thought you were someone else, that's all."

"You've been following me all day," said Schellenberg. "You were outside my office on Berkaerstrasse this morning, and you were outside the Ka-De-We this afternoon."

Neither man replied.

"Which section of the Gestapo are you in?"

"Section A," said the one with the binoculars, which were now lying on the ground in front of him.

"Come on," snapped Schellenberg. "Don't waste my time. Section A *what?*"

"Section A3."

Schellenberg frowned. "But that's the section that deals with matters of malicious opposition to the government. What on earth are you following *me* for?"

"As I said, there must have been a mistake. We've been tailing the wrong man, that's all. Happens sometimes."

"Don't move until I tell you to move," said Schellenberg. "So I'm not who you thought I was, eh?"

"We were tailing a suspected saboteur."

"Does he have a name, this saboteur?"

"I'm not at liberty to disclose that."

"How do you know that I'm not an associate of this saboteur of yours? If I was, I might shoot you. Perhaps I'll shoot you anyway."

"You won't shoot us."

"Don't be so sure. I don't like people following me."

"This is Germany. We're at war. People get followed all the time. It's normal."

"Then maybe I'll shoot you both to get you off my ass."

"I don't think so. You don't look like the type."

"If I don't look like the type, then why were you following me?"

"We weren't following you, we were following your car," said the other man.

"My car?" Schellenberg smiled. "Why, then you must know who I am. You've had plenty of time to get a Kfz-Schein on my car. That would easily have told you who and what I am." He shook his head. "I think I'll shoot you after all, just for being such bad liars."

"You won't shoot us."

"Why not? Do you think anyone's going to miss an ugly bastard like you?"

"We're on the same side, that's why," said the one with the binoculars.

"But you still haven't said how you know that. I'm not wearing a uniform, and I'm pointing a gun at you. I know you're in the Gestapo. And the plain fact is that I'm a British spy."

"No, you're not, you're in the same line of work we are."

"Shut up, Karl," said the man with the boxer's ear.

"And what line of work would that be?"

"You know."

"Shut up, Karl. Don't you see what he's trying to do?"

"I'm your enemy, Karl. And I'm going to kill you."

"You can't."

"Yes, I can."

"You can't, because you're Reich Security Office, just like us, that's why."

Schellenberg smiled. "There, now. That wasn't so very difficult. Since you've admitted you know who I am, then you'll understand why I'm anxious to find out why you should want to follow me, an SD general."

"Guilty conscience, is it?" said the man with the ear.

"Tell you what, Karl. I'm going to count to three, and if you don't tell me what this is all about, I'm going to execute you both. Right here. Right now. One."

"Tell him, Jürgen."

"He won't shoot us, Karl."

"Two."

"Keep your mouth shut, Karl. He won't do it. He's just bluffing."

"Three."

Schellenberg squeezed the trigger, and a startling staccato burst of fire shattered the silence of the forest. The MP40 was considered an effective weapon at up to a hundred meters, but at less than ten meters it was positively deadly, and he could hardly have missed his primary target—the tougher-looking man with the boxer's ear. With the impact of each 9mm Parabellum bullet that struck him in the face and torso his body jerked and a short, feral scream escaped his bloody mouth. Then he rolled over, writhing on the ground, and a second or two later, was still.

Realizing that he was still alive, the other Gestapo man, the one called Karl, began to cross himself furiously, uttering a Hail Mary.

"Better talk to me, Karl," said Schellenberg, tightening his grip on the MP40's plastic handle. "Or would you like me to count to three again?"

"It was the chief's direct order."

"Müller?"

Karl nodded. "He's trying to find out how far these peace negotiations of Himmler's have gone. If it's just Dr. Kersten, or if you're involved, too."

"I see," said Schellenberg.

Things were a lot clearer to him now. In August of '42, there had been a discussion involving himself, Himmler, and Himmler's chiropractor, Dr. Felix Kersten, concerning how a peace with the Allies might be negotiated. The discussion had stalled pending the failed attempt to remove von Ribbentrop—who was perceived to be an obstacle to a diplomatic peace—from his post as Reich foreign minister. But Schellenberg was completely unaware of any current peace negotiations.

"Do you mean to say that there are peace negotiations taking place right now?"

"Yes. Dr. Kersten is in Stockholm, talking to the Americans."

"And is *he* under surveillance, too?"

"Probably. I don't know."

"What about Himmler?"

"We were told to follow you. I'm afraid that's all I know."

"From where does Müller get this information?"

"I don't know."

"Take a guess."

"All right. The splash around Prinz Albrechtstrasse is that there is someone in Himmler's own office at the Ministry of the Interior who's been throwing his voice in our direction. But I don't know his name. Really I don't."

Schellenberg nodded. "I believe you."

"Thank God."

His mind was racing. There would have to be an investigation into the murder of the Gestapo man, of course. Müller would welcome a chance to embarrass him, and more important, Himmler. Unless . . .

"Have you got a radio in your car?"

"Yes."

"Did you radio your last position?"

"We haven't reported anything since we stopped outside the Ka-De-We."

There it was, then. He was in the clear. But only if he was prepared to act decisively, now and without hesitation.

Even as the logic of it presented itself clearly to Schellenberg's mind, he squeezed the trigger. And as he machine-gunned the second Gestapo man, in cold blood, Schellenberg felt that, finally, he had a kind of answer to the question that had often haunted him in the company of his more murderous colleagues. Two bodies now lay dead on the ground in front of him. Two murders hardly compared with Sandberger's 65,000 or Janssen's 33,000, but it could hardly be denied that the second murder had felt easier than the first.

With shaking hands, Schellenberg lit a cigarette and smoked it greedily, giving himself up to the soothingly toxic, alkaloid effect of the nicotine in the tobacco. With nerves somewhat steadied, he walked back to his car and took a large mouthful of schnapps from a little Wilhelmine silver hip flask he kept in the glove box. Then he drove slowly back to the Berkaerstrasse.

V

THURSDAY, OCTOBER 7, 1943,
LONDON

MY JOURNEY FROM NEW YORK to London would have left Ulysses looking for a couple of aspirin. Eight hours after leaving LaGuardia Airport at 8.00 A.M. on Tuesday the fifth, I had only traveled as far as Botwood, Newfoundland, where the U.S. Navy Coronado flying boat stopped to refuel. At 5:30 P.M., the four-engine plane was back in the air and heading east across the Atlantic like an outsized goose flying the wrong way for winter.

There were three other passengers: a British general named Turner; Joel Beinart, a USAAC colonel from Albuquerque; and John Wooldridge, a naval commander from Delaware, all three of them tight-lipped men whose demeanor seemed to indicate it wasn't just walls that had ears but the fuselage of a transatlantic aircraft as well. Not that I was feeling very gabby myself. For much of the journey, I read the Katyn files given to me by the president, which put the kibosh on any conversation.

The Wehrmacht file on Katyn had come via Allen Dulles from the OSS office in Berne. It was the most exhaustively detailed of the files, but I wondered how Dulles had come by it. In my mind's eye I pictured some blond, blue-eyed *Übermensch* from the German embassy in Bern just turning up at the OSS office one day and handing over the file as if it were nothing more important than the Swiss daily newspapers. Or had Dulles met up with his opposite number in the Abwehr for a glass of hot wine in the bar of the Hotel Schweizerhof? If either of these two scenarios were true, then it

73

seemed to imply a degree of cooperation between Dulles and German intelligence that I found intriguing.

An astonishing number of photographs accompanied the findings of the so-called International Committee. Assembled by the Germans, it included the professor of pathology and anatomy at Zagreb University, Ljudevit Jurak, and several Allied officers who were German POWs. It was obvious that the Nazis hoped to exploit the massacre to drive a wedge between the Soviet Union and its Western allies. And, whatever happened, it was impossible to see how, after the war, the British or the Americans could ask the people of Poland to live in peace with the Russians. That possibility seemed no more likely than the chief rabbi of Poland asking Hitler and Himmler to come over for a Passover drink and a couple of hands of whist.

At Katyn there had been a systematic attempt by the Russians to liquidate the national leaders of Polish independence. And it was clear to me that Stalin, no less than Hitler, had wanted to reduce Poland to the level of a subject state within his empire. Just as important, however, he had wanted revenge on the Poles for the defeat they had inflicted on the Red Army and on its commander—Stalin himself—at the Battle of Lvov in July 1920.

I had witnessed the Russian hatred of the Poles at first hand and in circumstances that even now, more than five years later, I still found troubling. No, "troubling" didn't really cover it; potentially dangerous was more like it. To have one skeleton in my OSS locker was a misfortune, but to have two looked like a serious predicament.

The Coronado gave a lurch as we hit some turbulence, and the naval commander groaned.

"Don't worry about that," said the USAAC colonel. "Try to think of an air pocket as something to catch the plane rather than to trip it up."

"Would anyone care for a drink?" asked the British general. He was wearing breeches, tall riding boots with buckles, and a thick belted tunic that looked as if it had been tailored before the year

1900. A woolly-bear caterpillar clung tenaciously to his upper lip underneath a hooked nose. With fine, peaceful, well-manicured hands, the general threw open a large and well-provisioned hamper basket and took out a flat pint of bonded bourbon. A minute later the four of us were libating the benevolence of the gods of transatlantic air travel.

"Is this your first time in London?" asked the general, offering me a shoe-sized sandwich from a shoebox-sized tin.

"I was there before the war. At the time I was thinking of going up to Cambridge to do a doctorate in philosophy."

"And did you? Go up to Cambridge?"

"No, I went to Vienna instead."

The general's Wellington-sized nose wrinkled with disbelief. "Vienna? Good God. What on earth possessed you to do that?"

I shrugged. "At the time it seemed like the place to be." And added, "I also had some family there."

After that the general regarded me somewhat as if I might be a Nazi spy. Or a relative of the Führer perhaps. Hitler may have been the leader of Germany, but the general didn't look as if he had forgotten Hitler had been born in Austria and had spent much of his young adult life knocking around Vienna. If I had said I had shared rooms at Wittenberg with Faustus he could not have regarded me with more suspicion, and we fell silent.

Arriving in Vienna at the age of just twenty-three, my Sheldon Travelling Fellowship supplemented by a very generous allowance from my mother's even richer aunt, the Baroness von Bingen, not to mention the use of her very elegant apartment in the city's exclusive Prinz Eugen Strasse, I had been almost immediately involved with the Vienna Circle—then the intellectual center of liberal European philosophy and notable for its opposition to the prevailing metaphysical and idealist trend of German philosophy. Which is just another way of saying that all of us were the self-annointed apostles of Einstein and relativity theory.

Moritz Schlick, my near neighbor in Vienna and the Vienna Circle's leader, had invited me to join the group. The circle's aim was to make philosophy more scientific, and while I had found it hard to feel much in common with them—several of the circle's members were theoretical physicists, about as easy to talk to as men from Mars—it soon became clear that just to be involved with philosophy and the Vienna Circle was in itself a political act. The Nazis were set on the persecution of all those who didn't agree with them, including the Vienna Circle, quite a few of whom were Jews. And after the election of the pro-Nazi Engelbert Dollfuss as chancellor of Austria, I decided to join the Communist Party. It was a party to which I belonged until the long, hot, and, for me, promiscuous summer of 1938.

By then I was living and lecturing in Berlin, where I was engaged in an affair with a Polish aristocrat, the Princess Elena Pontiatowska. She was a close friend of Christiane Lundgren, a UFA film studio actress who was herself sleeping with Josef Goebbels. Through Christiane I ended up meeting Goebbels socially on several occasions and, because of my Communist Party membership, of which neither Goebbels nor the princess was aware (nor, for that matter, did they know anything of my being half Jewish), it was not long before I found myself approached by the Russian People's Commissariat for Internal Affairs, the NKVD, and asked if I would spy on the German minister.

The idea of spying on the Nazis held considerable appeal. It was already clear there was going to be another European war. I told myself I would be doing my anti-Fascist bit in the way others had done during the Spanish Civil War. And so I agreed to report on any conversations I had with Goebbels. But after the Munich agreement in September of 1938, I became more actively involved. I agreed to accept an invitation to join the Abwehr, the military intelligence wing of the German army, with a view to supplying more detailed information to the NKVD.

In order to magnify my informal standing in the Abwehr, the NKVD provided me with some information that, at the time, I thought to be harmless. Later on, I discovered, to my horror, that the NKVD had used me to give the Nazis the names of three members of the Polish Secret Service. These three agents, one of them a woman just twenty-two years of age, were subsequently arrested, tortured by the Gestapo, tried by a German People's Court, and guillotined at the notorious Plotzensee Prison in November 1938. Sickened at having been used by the Russians to rid themselves of people they regarded with no less hatred than they regarded the Germans, I severed my contacts with the NKVD, resigned my lectureship at Berlin University, and returned home to Harvard with my tail between my legs.

The plane lurched again and then seemed to wallow like a small ship in the trough of an invisible wave.

I now regarded my former membership in the German Communist Party as a youthful indiscretion. I told myself that if I was ever in Berlin or Vienna again it would be because the war was over, in which case what the OSS might think of my former political allegiances would hardly matter very much.

At last the plane landed at Shannon, where we stopped to refuel, stretch our legs, and say good-bye to the naval commander, who was to fly north to Larne in another plane to meet his new ship. The rest of us flew east to Stranraer, where I sent telegrams to some of the people I hoped to see before catching the train south to London. I even sent one to Diana back in Washington, informing her that I had arrived in Britain safely. And forty-five hours after leaving New York, I arrived at Claridge's.

Though buttressed with heavy timbers and sandbags, all building windows crisscrossed with tape to cut down on flying glass, the West End of London still looked much as I remembered it. The bomb damage was confined to the East End and the docks. The Americans I saw on leave were nearly all Air Corps, kids most of them, just as Roosevelt had said. Some didn't look old enough to be served alcohol, let alone fly a B-24 on a bombing mission to Hamburg.

Although it was comparatively early when I checked into my hotel, I decided to go straight to bed and drank a glass of scotch to help me find oblivion. I was finally drifting off to sleep when I heard the air-raid siren. I put on my dressing gown and slippers and went down to the shelter, only to find that few of the other hotel guests had bothered to do the same. Returning to my room when the all-clear sounded, I had just closed my eyes again when there was another warning; this time, walking along the landing toward the emergency stairs, I met a small, piggy-looking man wearing evening dress, with red hair, round glasses, and a large cigar. He resembled a cherub thickened with alcohol and pinched with disappointment, and was quite unperturbed by the high-pitched purr—like a heavenly choir of dead cats—of the siren.

Noting my haste, the man chuckled and said, "You must be an American. Word of advice, old boy. Don't bother going to the shelter. It's only a small air raid. Chances are that whatever bombs do get dropped will be somewhere east, along the Thames, and well away from the West End. Last month there were just five people killed by Jerry bombs in the whole of Great Britain." The man puffed his cigar happily as if signaling that five dead was as trifling as a game of semi-billiards.

"Thank you, Mr. . . . ?"

"Waugh. Evelyn Waugh."

Taking his advice, I went back to bed, downed another scotch, and, with no more disturbances, or at least none that I heard, finally slept for six hours.

When I awoke, I found that almost a dozen replies to the telegrams I had sent from Stranraer had been pushed under my door. Among all the telegrams from the diplomats and intelligence officers I hoped to see were a couple of messages from two old friends: Lord Victor Rothschild and the novelist Rosamond Lehmann, with whom I had been flirting for more than ten years. In an attempt to add some color to what was already known about Katyn, I faced a great many meetings with angry Poles and stuffy British civil servants, and so I was relying on Ros and Victor to help me enjoy myself. There was also a telegram from Diana. It read: IS IT POSSIBLE TO BE GLAD YOU'RE THERE, IF I'M NOT GLAD YOU'RE

NOT HERE? DISCUSS. That was probably Diana's idea of a philosophical question.

After a tepid English bath, a smallish English breakfast, and a thorough look through the London *Times,* I left the hotel, heading for Grosvenor Square. I spent the morning there meeting various people in the London station of the OSS. David Bruce, the station chief, was a forty-four-year-old multimillionaire who had the dubious distinction of being married to the daughter of Andrew Mellon, the U.S. steel magnate, one of the world's richest men. Several of Bruce's executive officers were no less rich, blue-blooded, or intellectually advantaged, including Russell D'Oench, the shipping heir, and Norman Pearson, a distinguished Yale professor of English. The London station of the OSS looked like an extension of Washington's Metropolitan Club.

Pearson, in charge of the OSS London Bureau's effort to counter German intelligence, was a published poet. Having sorted me out some ration coupons, he volunteered to squire me around London's intelligence community. He was a year my junior, and a little on the thin side, made thinner by the food, or rather the lack of food available in the London shops. His suit, tailored in America, was now a couple of sizes too big for him.

Pearson was good company and hardly the kind of desperado most people would have expected in an intelligence job. But this was typical of our service. Even after three months' instruction in security and espionage from the OSS training center at Catoctin Mountain, there were few of my colleagues—Ivy League lawyers and academics, like myself—who ever saw the need to behave like a military organization, or even a quasi-military one. The joke around Washington was that being an officer with the OSS was "a cellophane commission": you could see through it, but it kept the draft off. And there was no getting away from the fact that for many of the younger officers, the OSS was a bit of an adventure and an escape from the rigors of ordinary military service. Quite a few officers were insubordinate as a matter of principle, and so-called orders were often put to a vote. And yet, through all of this, the OSS held together and did some useful work. Pearson was if anything more conscientious and soldierlike than most.

Pearson took me to the headquarters of the British Secret Intelligence Service, also known as MI6, the center of British counterintelligence. They were housed at 54 Broadway Buildings, a dingy structure of makeshift offices filled with staff in dowdy-looking civilian clothes.

Pearson introduced me to some of the section officers who had prepared much of the Katyn material used by Sir Owen O'Malley, the British ambassador to the Polish government in exile. It was Major King, the officer who had evaluated the original reports, who alerted me to the fact that whatever clarity existed with regard to Katyn was about to be muddied:

"The Soviet armies under General Sokolowski and General Jermienko recaptured Smolensk just two weeks ago, on September twenty-fifth," he explained. "They retook the region of the Katyn Forest grave sites a few days later. So the exhumations the Germans had declared would take place in the autumn are now impossible. The chances are, of course, that the Russians will dig up the bodies again and produce their own report, blaming Jerry. But that's not really my patch. You'd best speak to the chaps in Section Nine. Philby handles the interpretation of all the Russian intelligence we get."

I smiled. "Kim Philby?"

"Yes. Do you know him?"

I nodded. "From before the war. When we were students, in Vienna. Where can I find him?"

"Seventh floor."

Kim Philby looked more like a master in an English public school than an officer in the SIS. He wore an old tweed jacket with leather patches on the elbows, a pair of brown corduroy trousers held up by red suspenders, a flannel shirt, and a stained silk tie. Not very tall, he looked lean and even more undernourished than Pearson, and he smelled strongly of tobacco. It was almost ten years since I had seen him but he hadn't changed very much. He still looked shifty and guarded. Seeing me standing next to his untidy desk, Philby stood, smiled uncertainly, and glanced at Pearson.

"My God, Willard Mayer. What on earth are you doing here?"

"Hello, Kim. I'm with the OSS."

"You didn't tell me you knew this chap, Norman."

"We've only just met," said Pearson.

"I'm here for a week," I explained. "Then it's back to Washington."

"Sit down. Make yourselves at home. Catherine! Could you bring us all some tea, please?"

Still smiling uncertainly, Philby surveyed me steadily.

"The last time I saw you," I said, "you were getting married. At the town hall in Vienna."

"February 1934. My God, doesn't time fly when you're enjoying yourself."

"How is Litzi?"

"Christ only knows. I haven't seen her in a long time. We're separated."

"I'm sorry."

"Don't be. We never really got on. Can't think why I married her. She was too wild, too bloody radical."

"Perhaps we all were."

"Maybe. Anyway, I have Aileen now. Two children. A girl and then a boy. And another on the way, for my sins. Are you married, Will?"

"Not so far."

"Sensible fellow. You played the field, as I recall. And usually won. So what brings you up here to the homely comforts of Section Nine?"

"Because I hear you're the Russian expert, Kim."

"Oh, I wouldn't say that." Philby lit a cigarette and, tucking one hand underneath his armpit, smoked briskly. A ten-shilling note protruded from the none-too-clean handkerchief in his breast pocket. "But we have our moments of inspiration."

The tea arrived. Philby glanced at his pocket watch, busied himself sorting out the chipped cups and saucers, and then, removing the lid, glanced inside the great brown enamelware pot, like the Mad Hatter looking for the dormouse. *Twinkle, twinkle, little bat,* I said to myself, *how I wonder what you're at.*

"I'm investigating the Katyn Forest massacre," I said. "For President Roosevelt. And I was wondering if you had any insight as to what might happen now that the Russians are in possession of that region again."

Philby shrugged and poured the tea. "I expect the Supreme Council will appoint some sort of extraordinary state commission to investigate crimes committed by the German Fascist invaders, or some nonsense like that. To prove it was all a dastardly plot cooked up by the Jerries to disturb the harmonious unity of the Allies." He picked a piece of tobacco off his lip. "Which is no more than our own foreign secretary, Mr. Eden, said in the House of Commons a while back."

"Saying it is one thing. Believing it is quite another."

"Well, you'd probably know more about that than me, old boy." He stirred his tea thoughtfully, like a man mixing paint. "But let's see, now. The Ivans will appoint a bunch of academicians and authors to the commission. Someone from the Smolensk Regional Executive. A People's Commissar for this or that. Someone from the Russian Red Cross and Red Crescent Societies. Medical chap from the Red Army, probably. That kind of thing."

I sipped the tea and found it too strong to be palatable. When they took away the pot, they'd probably use the dregs to paint a wooden fence. "Do you think the Soviets will invite anyone independent to join such a commission as you describe?"

"You put your finger right on it, Willard old boy. Independent. How is that independence to be guaranteed? The Germans have got their report. Roosevelt is going to have his. And now I expect the Russians will want theirs. I suppose people will have to make up their minds about what to believe. If you think in terms of global struggle, this kind of thing is inevitable. But whatever the rights and wrongs of the matter, the Russians are still our allies and we will have to learn to work with them if we are going to win this war."

He seemed to have finished his analysis, and I stood up and thanked him for his time.

"Anything for our American cousins."

Pearson added his thanks, and Philby said to me, "Norman is notable for being the least bewildered fellow in Grosvenor Square." He'd brightened noticeably now that I'd said I was leaving. "We do our best not to be too dry or intimidating for you American chaps, but we cannot know how we seem. That we have survived unconquered thus far is because we have let nothing affect us. Not ration cards, not German bombs, no, not even the English weather—eh, Norman?"

Leaving Pearson at Broadway Buildings, I walked back across the park, pondering the renewal of my acquaintance with Kim Philby. I had known Harold "Kim" Philby for a brief period before the war. In late 1933, just down from Cambridge, Philby had arrived in Vienna on a motorcycle. Four years younger than me and the son of a famous British explorer, Philby had thrown himself into working for Vienna's left-wing resistance, with little thought for his own safety. After nine Socialist leaders had been lynched by the Heimwehr, Austria's right-wing, pro-Nazi militia, he and I had helped to hide wanted leftists until they could be smuggled out of the country to Czechoslovakia.

While Philby and I had remained in Vienna, Otto Deutsch, a Ph.D. working for the sexologist Wilhelm Reich, not to mention the NKVD, had made several attempts to recruit the two of us to the Russian Secret Service. It was an invitation I had resisted at the time. I didn't know about Philby himself, who had returned to England with Litzi in May 1934, so that she might escape the clutches of the Heimwehr, for she had been more openly active than Kim. I had always assumed that, like myself, Philby had resisted Deutsch's invitation to join the NKVD in Vienna. But seeing him again, working for the SIS in the Russian counterintelligence section and apparently nervous at the renewal of our acquaintance, made me wonder.

Of course I could say nothing about this without drawing attention to my own background. Not that I thought it really mattered very much. If the British were, as was generally supposed by the OSS, breaking the German codes and not passing on relevant information to the Russians for fear of being asked to share all decoded German material, then, doubtless, Philby would see it as his duty to remedy such perfidious behavior toward an ally. I might even have applauded such so-called treachery. I would not have done it myself, but I might almost have approved of it being done by someone else.

Back in my hotel room, I made some notes for my Katyn report, had another tepid bath, and put on a tuxedo. By six-thirty I was in the bar at the Ritz ordering a second martini even as I was finishing my first. Saying the right thing, saying a lot less than people wanted to know, saying not very much at all, just listening—it had been a long day, and I was desperate to relax. Rosamond was just the woman to pull out the pins.

I had not seen her since the war began, and I was a little surprised that her once brown wavy hair was now gray, with a blue rinse; and yet she had lost none of her voluptuous allure. She kissed and hugged me.

"Darling," she cooed, in her soft, breathy voice. "How wonderful to see you."

"You're still as gorgeous as you always were."

"It's very sweet of you, Will, but I'm not." She touched her hair self-consciously.

I judged her to be in her early forties by now, but more beautiful than ever. She always reminded me a little of Vivien Leigh, only more womanly and sensuous. Less impetuous and much more thoughtful. Tall, pale-skinned, with a magnificent figure that belonged on a chaise longue in some artist's studio, she wore a long, silvery skirt and a purple chiffon blouse that outlined her full figure.

"I brought you some stockings," I told her. "Gold Stripe. Only I'm afraid I left them in my room at Claridge's."

"On purpose, of course. To make sure I'd come back to your hotel."

Ros was used to men throwing themselves at her feet, and she almost expected it as the price of being so beautiful, even as she did her best to play that down. This was an almost impossible task; most of the time, and wherever she was, Ros always stood out like a woman wearing a Balenciaga cocktail dress to a Sunday school picnic in Nebraska.

"Of course." I grinned.

She fingered the string of pearls around her creamy white neck as I ordered a bottle of champagne.

I offered her a cigarette and she squeezed it into a little black holder.

"You're living with a poet these days, is that right?" I leaned forward to light her cigarette and caught a whiff of some perfume that reached right down into my trouser pocket, and then some.

"That's right," she puffed. "He's gone off to visit his wife and children."

"Is he any good? As a poet, I mean?"

"Oh, yes. And terribly good-looking, too. Just like you, darling. Only I don't want to talk about him, because I'm cross with him."

"Why?"

"Because he's gone off to visit his wife and children instead of staying here in London with me, of course."

"Of course. But what happened to Wogan?"

Wogan Philipps, the Second Baron Milford, was the husband Ros had left to be with her poet.

"He's getting married again. To a fellow Communist. At least he is as soon as I've divorced him."

"I didn't know Wogan was a Communist."

"My dear, he's positively riddled with it."

"But *you're* not a Communist, are you?"

"Lord, no. I am not and never have been a political animal. Romantically inclined toward the left, but not actively. And I expect men to make *me* their abiding cause, not Hitler or Stalin. Just as I have made men mine."

"Then here's to you, sweetheart," I said. "You get my vote, every time."

After a flirtatious dinner, we walked around the corner to St. James's Place, where Victor Rothschild had a top-floor flat. A servant gave us a message that His Lordship had gone to a drinks party in Chesterfield Gardens and we should join him there.

"Shall we go?" I asked Rosamond.

"Why not? It beats going home to an empty flat in Kensington. And it's been simply ages since I went to a party."

Tomas Harris and his wife, Hilda, were a wealthy couple whose hospitality was exceeded only by their self-evident good taste. Harris was an art dealer, and many of the walls of the house in Chesterfield Gardens displayed paintings and drawings by the likes of El Greco and Goya.

"You must be Victor's American," he said, greeting me warmly. "And you must be Lady Milford. I've read all of your novels. *Dusty Answer* is one of my favorite books."

"I've just finished reading *Invitation to the Waltz*," said Hilda Harris. "I was so excited when Tom told me you might be coming. Come on, let me introduce you to some people." She took Rosamond by the elbow. "Do you know Guy Burgess?"

"Yes. Is he here?"

"Willard!"

A dark-haired and stocky but handsome man came over and greeted me, exuding an air that was part rabbinical, part tycoon, part Bolshevik, and part aristocrat. Victor Rothschild was a prophet crying in a wilderness of privilege and position. We shared a love of jazz and a mutually rosy view of science, which was easier for Victor, given that he was actually a scientist. Victor couldn't have made himself more scientific if he'd slept on a Petri dish.

"Willard, good to see you," he said, shaking my hand furiously. "Tell me, you didn't bring your saxophone, did you? Will plays a pretty mean sax, Tom."

"I didn't think it was appropriate," I said. "When you're the president's special envoy, traveling with a saxophone is a little like bringing your pool cue to an audience with the Pope."

"President's special envoy, eh? That *is* impressive."

"I think it sounds more impressive than it is. And what about you, Victor? What are you up to?"

"MI5. I run a little antisabotage outfit, X-raying Winston's cigars, that kind of thing. Technical stuff." Rothschild wagged his finger at me. "Introduce him to someone, Tom. I'll be back in ten minutes."

Watching Rothschild disappear out the drawing room door, Harris said, "He's too modest by half. From what I hear he's involved in bomb disposal. Tackling the latest German fuses and detonators. It's dangerous work." Glancing over my shoulder, Harris waved a tall, rather limp-looking man of the lean and hungry kind over toward us. "Tony, this is Willard Mayer. Willard, this is Anthony Blunt."

The man who came over had hands that more properly belonged on a delicate girl and the sort of fastidious, well-bred mouth that looked as if he'd been weaned on lemons and limes. He had an odd way of speaking that I didn't like.

"Oh, yes," said Blunt, "Kim's been telling me all about *you*." He pronounced the last word with an indecent amount of emphasis, as if affecting a kind of disapproval.

"Will?"

I turned to find Kim Philby standing behind me.

"Fancy that. I was just talking about you, Will."

"Be my guest. I'm fully insured."

"He's a friend of Victor's," Harris told Philby, moving away to greet yet another guest.

"Listen," said Philby, "thanks awfully for not dropping me in it this afternoon. For not mentioning exactly what we got up to in Vienna."

"I couldn't very well have done that. Not without dropping myself in it, too. Besides"—I flicked a match against my thumbnail and lit a cigarette—"Vienna was more than ten years ago. Things are different now. Russia is our ally, for a start."

"True," said Philby. "Although there are times when you wouldn't think so, the way we run this war."

"Speak for yourself. I'm not running anything except the length and breadth of the odd tennis court. Pretty much I do what I'm told."

"What I meant was that sometimes, when you look at the Red Army's casualties, it seems as if the Soviet Union is the only country fighting Germany. But for the existence of the eastern front, the very idea of the British and the Americans being able to mount a landing in Europe would seem preposterous."

"I was speaking to some guy in my hotel who told me that there were just five people killed in Britain during the whole of September. Can that really be true? Or was he just trying to convince me that I could leave my umbrella at home?"

"Oh, yes," said Philby, "that's perfectly true. And meanwhile the Russians are dying at a rate of something like seventy thousand a month. I've seen intelligence reports that estimate total Russian casualties at over two million. So you can see why they're so worried that we'll negotiate a separate peace and they'll end up fighting Hitler on their own. It's a fear that will hardly be assuaged by the knowledge that your president is now scrutinizing those murders in the Katyn Forest."

"I believe it's still common practice for murder to be scrutinized," I said. "It's one of the things that helps to give us the illusion that we're living in a civilized world."

"Oh, surely. But Stalin could hardly be blamed if he suspects that the Western allies might use Katyn as an excuse to postpone an invasion of Europe, at least until the Wehrmacht and the Red Army have destroyed each other."

"You seem to know a lot about what Stalin suspects, Kim."

Philby shook his head. "Intelligent guesswork. That's what this lark is all about. Thing about the Russians is, they're not hard to second-guess. Unlike Churchill. There's no telling what's going on in that man's devious mind."

"From what I gather, Churchill hasn't paid much attention to Katyn. He doesn't behave like a man who's preparing to use it as an excuse to postpone a second front."

"Perhaps not," admitted Blunt. "But there are plenty of others who would, you know? The Jew-hating brigade who think we're at war with the wrong enemy." He grabbed a glass off a passing tray and swallowed the contents in one greedy parabola. "What about Roosevelt? Do you think he would countenance it?"

Blunt smiled warmly, but I still didn't like his mouth.

Catching my frown, Philby said, "It's all right, Willard. Anthony is one of us."

"And what might that be?" I said, bristling. The proposition that Anthony Blunt was "one of us" seemed almost as offensive to me as its corollary, that I might be one of them.

"MI5. In fact, Anthony might be just the man you need to speak to about your Polish thing. The Allied governments in exile, neutral countries with diplomatic missions in London, Anthony keeps an eye on all of them, don't you, Tony?"

"If you say so, Kim," smiled Blunt.

"Well, it's no great secret," grumbled Philby.

"I can tell you this," said Blunt. "The Poles would dearly like to get their hands on a Russian who's an attaché at the Soviet embassy in Washington. Fellow named Vasily Zubilin. In 1940 he was a major in the People's Commissariat on Internal Affairs and commanded one of the execution battalions at Katyn. It seems that the Russians sent him to Washington as a reward for a good job. And to get him out of the neighborhood. And because they know he's never likely to defect. If he did, they'd simply tell your government what he did at Katyn. And then some Pole would very likely want to have him charged as a war criminal. Whatever *that* is."

"So, how do you know Victor?" Blunt asked abruptly, changing the subject.

"We share a similarly perfunctory attitude to our Jewishness," I said. "Or, in my case, and to be more accurate, my half-Jewishness. I went to his wedding to Barbara. And you?"

"Oh. Cambridge," said Blunt. "And Rosamond. You came with her, didn't you? How do you know Rosie?"

"Do stop interrogating him, Anthony," said Philby.

"It's all right," I said, although I didn't answer Blunt's question and, hearing Rosamond's distinctive laugh, I glanced around and saw her listening with much amusement as a disheveled figure held forth loudly about some boy he was trying to seduce. I was beginning to suspect that almost everyone invited to the party had been to Cambridge and was either a spy, a Communist, or a homosexual—in Anthony Blunt's case very probably all three.

Rothschild came back into the room carrying a saxophone triumphantly aloft.

"Victor." I laughed. "I think you're very probably the only man I know who could track down a spare saxophone at eleven o'clock at night." I took the sax from my old friend, who sat down at the piano, lit a cigarette, then lifted the lid.

We played for more than half an hour. Rothschild was the better musician, but it was late and people were too drunk to notice my technical shortcomings. After we had finished, Philby drew me aside.

"Very good," he said. "Very good indeed. That was quite a duo."

I shrugged and drank a glass of champagne to moisten my mouth.

"You remember Otto Deutsch, of course?" he said.

"Otto? Yes. What ever happened to him? He came to London, didn't he? After Austria went Fascist."

"He was on a ship that was sunk in the mid-Atlantic by a German submarine." Philby paused and lit a cigarette.

"Poor Otto. I didn't know."

"He tried to recruit me, you know. To the NKVD, back in Vienna."

"Really?"

"I couldn't see the point, quite frankly. I think I would have worked for them if I'd stayed on in Austria. But for Litzi's sake I had to leave. So I came back here, got a job on the *Times*. But I saw Otto again, in 1937, when he was on his way to Russia. I think he was rather lucky not to get shot in the Great Purge. Anyway, he tried to recruit me here in London, would you believe? God knows why. I mean, any information a journalist gets, he tends to pass on to his readers. I was a Communist, of course. Still am, if the truth be known, which, if it was, I'd be out of the service on my ear."

"Why are you telling me this, Kim?"

"Because I think I can trust you, old boy. And what you were saying earlier. About the idea of our side in this war negotiating a peace with Jerry."

I didn't recall saying anything much about that, but I let it go.

"I think if I ever did find out something like that, then secrecy be damned. I'd march straight round to the Soviet embassy and shove a note through the bloody letterbox. Dear Comrade Stalin, The British and Americans are selling you down the Volga. Yours sincerely, Kim Philby, MI5."

"I don't think that's going to happen."

"No? Ever hear of a chap called George Earle?"

"Yes. As a matter of fact he's one of the reasons I'm here. Earle's the president's special representative in the Balkans. He wrote an unsolicited report for FDR about the Katyn Forest massacre. He's a pal of Roosevelt's. Rich. Very rich. Like the rest of Roosevelt's pals."

"You included," chuckled Philby.

"That's my family you're talking about, Kim. Not me."

"Lord, now you sound just like Victor." He laughed. "The epicurean ascetic." Philby grabbed another glass of champagne.

I grabbed one myself and sipped it slowly this time. I wanted to cool down and stop myself from punching Philby. I excused him because he was drunk. And because I wanted to hear more about George Earle.

"Listen," he said, with the air of someone who couldn't make up his mind if he was offering up gossip or a state secret. It seemed quite possible that he didn't know the difference. "The Earle family made its money in the sugar trade. Earle dropped out of Harvard, and in 1916 he joined General Pershing's army, trying to hunt down Pancho Villa in Mexico. Then he joined the U.S. Navy and won the Navy Cross, which is how he's so thick with Roosevelt. FDR's a big navy man, right?"

I nodded. "Where are you going with this, Kim?"

Philby tapped the side of his nose. "You'll see." He lit another cigarette and then snatched it from his mouth impatiently.

"A lifelong Republican, Earle nevertheless supported Roosevelt for president in 1932. And as a reward, FDR made him his naval attaché in Ankara. Now, then. Here comes the good part. Hefty— that's our chum Earle's nickname—has a girlfriend, a Belgian dancer and part-time prostitute named Hélène, who works for us. I'm telling you all this so you'll know where some of our information is coming from.

"In May of this year, Hefty met the German ambassador in Ankara. As I'm sure you are aware, the ambassador is also the former German chancellor, Franz von Papen. According to Hélène, Hefty and von Papen conducted some secret peace negotiations. We're not quite sure if the talks were initiated by Earle or by von Papen. Either way, Earle reported back to FDR and von Papen reported back to someone in Berlin—we're not exactly sure to whom. Nothing much seemed to happen for a while. Then, just a few days ago, Earle had a meeting with an American by the name of Theodor Morde. Ever hear of him?"

"I've never heard of Theodor Morde," I said, truthfully.

"Morde's a chap who used to work for COI in Cairo before it turned into your mob, the OSS. I thought you might know him."

"I've never heard of him," I repeated.

"Morde's an American who travels on a Portuguese passport. Works for the Reader's Digest organization. The sort of fellow your mob could very easily deny. I'm sure you know the kind of thing. Anyway, this fellow Morde had a meeting with von Papen just two days ago. We've no idea what was said. Hélène isn't fucking *him*, unfortunately. But other sources seem to indicate that afterwards, Morde gave Earle some kind of document from von Papen for Roosevelt. And that, for now, is as much as we know."

Throughout Philby's discourse I felt my jaw tighten. Blunt's information about Vasily Zubilin had been surprising enough, but this was much more disturbing, and the apparent insouciance with which Philby had delivered his bombshell, so typically English, only seemed to make matters worse.

"And did you go straight round to the Soviet embassy and shove a note through the letterbox? Like you said?"

"Not yet," said Philby. "But I still might."

"What stopped you?"

"You did, as a matter of fact."

"Me?"

"Turning up in my office like that, out of the blue, after all these years. Not only that, but you turning out to be another of Roosevelt's special representatives, just like old Hefty. And I thought to myself, Don't do anything hasty, Kim. Perhaps old Willard can help you put some flesh on the story, if there is one. Stand it up, as we journalists say."

My initial sense of caution had given way to intrigue. If Philby was right, and Roosevelt really was negotiating a separate peace, then what was the point of the Big Three?

"How?"

"Oh, I dunno. Keep your ears open on Campus and around the White House, that sort of thing. A watching brief, that's all."

"And suppose I do hear something. Then what?"

"There's a pal of mine at the British embassy in Washington. Bit of an old lefty, like you and me. Name of Childs. Stephen Childs. A good solid chap but also inclined to the view that the Russians are being given the sharp end of the stick. If you did hear anything fishy, you might give him a call. Have a drink. Talk it over. Decide between yourselves what to do about it and simply act according to what your consciences dictate. As for me . . ." Philby shrugged. "I shall have to see what more can be discovered through our agents in Ankara. But frankly I am not optimistic, and we shall have to see where your man Morde turns up next."

"I'm not promising anything," I said. "But I'll see what I can do. With Roosevelt. 'I'll observe his looks. I'll tent him to the quick. If he but blench, I know my course.'"

Philby was looking puzzled.

"*Hamlet*," I explained. "As a matter of fact, what did you *read* when you were up at Cambridge?"

Philby grinned. "Marx and Engels, of course."

VI

FRIDAY, OCTOBER 8, 1943, BERLIN

"IT SOUNDS TO ME as if you've been reading *Der Pimpf*," Himmler told Schellenberg. *Der Pimpf*—The Squirt—was the monthly periodical for young boys in the Hitler Youth organization. It contained a mixture of high adventure and propaganda. "Assassinate the Big Three? Are you mad? Really, Schellenberg, I'm surprised at a man of your obvious intelligence coming up with a harebrained scheme like this. What on earth made you think of such an idea?"

"You did, Herr Reichsführer."

"Me?"

"Your speech at Posen. It made quite an impression on me. You said that it's faith that wins battles, and that you didn't want pessimists in our ranks, or people who have lost their faith in the Fatherland. I thought to myself that if Skorzeny could pull off something like the rescue of Mussolini, then, perhaps, something even more daring might be achieved."

"Pessimism is one thing, Schellenberg, but reckless optimism is quite another. And so is realism. I expect realism from a man of your abilities. As we both know, Skorzeny's mission was carried out at the Führer's request. It was an absurd idea and achieved nothing of any practical use. Did you even hear me mention the name of Skorzeny at Posen? No. You did not. Normally, given enough time, I could have killed off Hitler's idea of rescuing Mussolini, in the same way that I've killed off a lot of other idiotic schemes. But he kept on and on about this one until I could see no way of avoiding it. And, my God, whoever expected the fool to succeed?"

They were in Himmler's new office at the Ministry of the Interior on Unter den Linden, next to the old Greek embassy. From the double-height first-floor windows, recently made bombproof, Schellenberg could see the Adlon Hotel and the very window of the room where he had made love to Lina the previous Saturday.

"Realism demands that we pursue peace with the Allies, not try to assassinate their leaders."

Schellenberg nodded but quietly marveled at the many contradictions that were evident in Himmler's character and conduct. The Himmler now talking peace was the very same Himmler who, on August 25, the day he had taken over from Wilhelm Frick as minister of the interior, had sentenced a government councillor to the guillotine for "defeatist talk." The councillor's execution could only have been for show, thought Schellenberg; to encourage the others. The Reichsführer's remark seemed to confirm what he had learned from the two Gestapo men he'd been obliged to murder: that Himmler was indeed conducting some kind of private peace negotiations that might leave him at the head of a post-Hitler government.

"No," said the Reichsführer. "I don't think they would take kindly to that. Not while we're trying to talk peace."

So there it was, thought Schellenberg. He'd admitted it. Of course in Himmler's arrogance it would probably never have crossed his mind that the Gestapo might properly regard this as treason. That they would actually have the audacity to spy on him, the Reichsführer-SS, would be quite unthinkable.

"You don't look surprised, Schellenberg," observed Himmler.

"That we're trying to talk peace? If you recall, Herr Reichsführer, it was I who suggested the need for an alternative strategy to end the war in August last year. At the time, I believe you told me I was being defeatist."

Schellenberg could see that Himmler hardly cared to be reminded of this. "So what's this, then?" Himmler said, brandishing the dossier containing details of Operation Long Jump, irritably. "Another alternative?"

"Exactly that, Herr Reichsführer. Another alternative. I'm afraid I wasn't aware of your own peace initiative."

"You are now. As a matter of fact, that's why I summoned you here this morning."

"I see. And is Felix Kersten involved?"

"Yes. How did you know?"

"It was a guess."

"Well, it's a damned good one." Himmler sounded irritated again.

Schellenberg shrugged apologetically, but inside he felt his stomach sink. He was all for talking peace with the Allies, but he had hardly supposed that the Gestapo could have been right about Felix Kersten: that a Finnish masseur should have been entrusted with negotiating Germany's fate seemed beyond all common sense. He didn't disagree with Gestapo Müller in that regard, anyway.

"I don't know what plans you've made for the evening," said Himmler, "but I'm afraid you'll have to cancel them. I'm sending you to Stockholm right away. My personal plane is waiting for you at Tempelhof. You'll be in Sweden by lunchtime. There's a suite booked for you at the Grand Hotel, which is where Felix will meet you."

Himmler produced a key chain from his trouser pocket and rose from his chair; he unlocked a wall-mounted Stockinger safe from which he removed a thin-looking official briefcase with a pair of handcuffs attached to the handle. "You'll have full diplomatic status, so there should be no reason for the Swedes to ask you to open this briefcase. But I'm opening it now in order to impress on you the need for absolute secrecy. There are only five people who know about this mission: the Führer, myself, von Ribbentrop, Felix Kersten, and now you. You'll need to change out of uniform, of course. You can do that when you return home to collect your passport and some clothes for your stay. Oberleutnant Wagner will escort you to the cash office, where you can collect some Swedish money." Himmler handcuffed the briefcase to Schellenberg's wrist, handed him the key, and then unbuckled the flap to reveal three white envelopes, each of them protected by several sheets of cellophane plastic, and a cigarette lighter. Schellenberg guessed that the purpose of the cellophane sheets was not to stop the envelopes from getting dirty but to enable them to burn more quickly if he needed to destroy them.

"Each letter has been written by the Führer himself," explained Himmler. "One is addressed to President Roosevelt, another to Joseph Stalin, and the third to Prime Minister Churchill. You will hand this bag to Dr. Kersten, who will put each letter into the hands of the appropriate person in Stockholm, during which time you will offer him any assistance he might require. Is that clear?"

Schellenberg clicked his heels and bowed his head obediently. "Quite clear, Herr Reichsführer. Might I be allowed to inquire as to the contents of the Führer's letters to the Big Three?"

"Even I don't know precisely what has been written," said Himmler. "But I believe that the Führer has sought a clarification of the Allied declarations regarding unconditional surrender. He wishes to find out if the Allies really do not want a negotiated peace and points out that such a demand, if it is genuine, would be unprecedented in the annals of modern war."

"So," said Schellenberg, "nothing very important, then."

Himmler smiled thinly. "I fail to see the funny side of this, Schellenberg, really I do. The future of Germany and the lives of millions of people might easily depend on the contents of this briefcase. Do you not agree?"

"Yes, Herr Reichsführer. I am sorry."

Oberleutnant Wagner escorted Schellenberg to the cash office in the ministry's basement. Not that this was necessary. Schellenberg had started his SS career at the Ministry of the Interior and knew very well where the cash office was. Fiddling his expenses had always been one of Schellenberg's major accomplishments.

"How's Colonel Tschierschky, sir?" asked Wagner. "Still got that blue BMW Roadster, has he? Just the car I'd be driving if I could afford it."

Schellenberg, who wasn't much interested in cars, grunted without much enthusiasm as the cashier counted a sizable wad of Swedish kronor onto the counter in front of him. Wagner eyed the money greedily as Schellenberg tossed the wads of cash into the briefcase still handcuffed to his wrist, and then locked it again. Together, he and Wagner walked to the front door of the ministry.

"You and Tschierschky were in a special action group, weren't you, Wagner?"

"Yes, sir."

"And before that?"

"I was a lawyer, sir. With the Criminal Police, in Munich."

Another damned lawyer. Schellenberg's nose wrinkled with distaste as he left the ministry. It was hard to believe that he himself had given up medicine to become a lawyer, of all things. He hated lawyers. It had been a mistake to try to kill all the Jews when there were still so many lawyers.

He drove back to his apartment and changed out of uniform. Then he threw some things into an overnight bag, collected his passport, and went outside. At Loesser and Wolff's on the corner of Fasanenstrasse, he bought twenty Jasmatzis and some newspapers for the flight. Then he drove to Tempelhof, where Himmler's plane was waiting. It was a Focke Wulf FW 200 Condor, the same kind of plane that Schellenberg had hoped to use in the plan to mount a bombing raid on Teheran.

Once on board he handed the crew their sealed orders and then took his seat, avoiding the Reichsführer's vast leather chair with its personal escape hatch—in the event of an emergency, the occupant had only to pull on a red lever and a door would be opened hydraulically beneath the seat, allowing him to slide out, still strapped into his seat, and then drop to the ground by parachute. But the very idea of sitting in a seat that might drop out of the plane was not, in Schellenberg's opinion, conducive to a comfortable journey. So he sat in the smaller seat opposite, the one that was usually occupied by Himmler's girlfriend, his adjutant, or his private secretary. He lit a Jasmatzi and tried to take his mind off the dangers of the flight ahead. The Reichsführer's personal Condor was probably the nearest thing Germany had to an American flying fortress, but by late 1943 the RAF was considered much too ubiquitous in German skies to risk frequent flights in it, and Himmler usually needed several cognacs to steady his nerves. Schellenberg followed suit.

Less than ten minutes later the Condor's four BMW engines were driving the plane down the runway and then into the air, with Schellenberg staring through the fifty-millimeter-thick bulletproof-glass window at the city below. From the air it was easier to see just how effective the RAF had become; there was hardly one neighborhood in the whole of Berlin that did not show some bomb damage. Another year of this, thought Schellenberg, and there wouldn't be very much of a city left for the Russians to capture.

They flew south, toward the suburb of Mariendorf, before turning west toward Zehlendorf and the Grunewald, and then north over the Olympic Stadium and the Citadel at Spandau, where some of the Reich's most important state prisoners were incarcerated. The plane climbed steadily, and when, after about thirty minutes, it had leveled out at just over 5,000 meters, one of the four-man crew came into the passenger area to bring Schellenberg some blankets.

"Tell me," said Schellenberg, "what do you think of this plane?"

The man pointed at Himmler's seat. "May I?"

"Be my guest," said Schellenberg.

"Best long-range airliner in Europe," said the man, whose name was Hoffmann. He sat down and made himself comfortable. "If not the world. I never understood why we didn't make more of these. This plane will get you to New York, nonstop, in just under twenty hours. Mind you, it's not particularly fast. Even a Short Sutherland will catch one of these and shoot it down. And God forbid a Mosquito should ever find us. But aerodynamically speaking, at least, the Condor is outstanding."

"And as a long-range bomber?"

Hoffmann shrugged dismissively. "In the beginning it was quite an effective Atlantic bomber. I sank a few ships myself before transfering to the Government Group. But as I said, it's an easy target for a fighter, even with all the armament we're carrying. If you have the element of surprise, then it's okay, I suppose. Some of the later models have search radar, which gives you a useful blind-bombing capability; or they'll have a radio-guidance installation for missiles. The range is the thing. I mean, think about it, sir. New York. This plane could bomb New York. Chances are we'd catch them napping. After all, nobody expects a bomber to come all that way. Of course it would mean getting our feet wet, but I reckon it would be worth it, don't you? I mean, just think how many we'd kill in a densely populated place like New York. Once you've got the element of surprise, you're halfway there, aren't you?"

The man reached inside his flying suit and took out a Walther PPK fitted with a noise eliminator on the barrel, which he pointed at Schellenberg. For half a moment Schellenberg thought Hoffmann was going to use the gun to make some sort of comparison, but instead the Walther stayed pointed at his chest.

"I'm afraid I'll have to ask you for that briefcase, sir," he said.

"Oh, I like the 'sir,'" said Schellenberg. He put down his glass of cognac and held up the briefcase so that it dangled from the manacle on his wrist. "You mean this briefcase? The key is on a chain in my trouser pocket. I'll have to stand up to retrieve it. If that's all right with you."

Hoffmann nodded. "Do it very carefully."

Schellenberg stood up slowly, showed the man his empty hand and then slid it carefully into his trouser pocket, pulling out a long silver key chain.

Hoffmann's grip tightened nervously on the Walther, and he licked his lips. "Now sit down and unlock the bracelet."

Schellenberg staggered back into his seat as the plane lurched a little in an air pocket; finding the key at last, he unlocked the manacle from his extended wrist.

"Now hand it over."

Schellenberg watched patiently as the man balanced the brief-case on his lap and tried the lock on the flap. "It's locked," he said quietly. "There's a different key."

Hoffmann flung the briefcase back at him. "Do it."

Schellenberg unlocked the briefcase and then handed it over again. Hoffmann nursed it on his lap for several seconds as if uncertain what to do, and then glanced inside to find only the cellophane sheets, the money, and the cigarette lighter.

"Is this all?"

"I don't know," said Schellenberg. "I haven't yet looked at the contents. My orders were merely to hand the briefcase over in Stockholm, not examine the contents."

"There has to be something more than this," insisted Hoffmann. "You're an SS general. The head of Foreign Intelligence. You wouldn't be going all the way to Stockholm aboard Himmler's private plane just to hand over some Swedish money and a cigarette lighter. You're a traitor. You're planning to betray Germany to the Allies. Himmler gave you this briefcase himself. There was something in here before the money went inside it. Something connected with what's happening in Stockholm. You must have taken it out on the way to the airport. Whatever it is, you must have it in your coat pocket or in your bag. I'll ask you to tell me where it is, and then I'll count to three. And if you don't tell me I'll shoot you. I won't kill you. Just hurt you. Sir."

"You're right, of course," said Schellenberg. "I dislike the practice of manacling a briefcase to one's wrist. Himmler's crazy idea. It's like advertising that one is carrying something valuable." He pointed at the gray Loden coat hanging in the closet behind him. "In the pocket of my overcoat there are three letters written by the Führer, addressed to each of the Big Three, declaring Germany's willingness to surrender."

"You're a liar."

"There's an easy way to prove that," said Schellenberg. "Just look in my coat. If I'm wrong, then go ahead and kill me. But if I'm right, then think about it. It's you who is the traitor, not me. It's you who will be interfering with a direct order of the Führer. I could have you shot for this."

Hoffmann smiled cynically. "Right now, it's you who stands the best chance of being shot, not me."

"True. Well, then, let me get my coat and you can make up your own mind." Schellenberg stood up.

"Stay where you are. I'll get it."

"In the right-hand pocket. There's a large manila envelope."

"I thought you said there were *three* envelopes."

"There are. Inside the manila one. Look, these are letters from the Führer, not notes from some lovesick soldier. They're in another envelope to keep them clean, of course. Roosevelt is hardly likely to look favorably on an envelope with a thumbprint on it, is he?"

Hoffmann transferred the Walther from his right hand to his left as he prepared to search Schellenberg's coat pocket. "It had better be there," he said. "Or you're a dead man."

"And how would you explain that to the rest of the crew?"

Hoffmann laughed. "I won't have to. As soon as I've got this envelope of yours, I'm going to shoot them and bail out."

Schellenberg swallowed hard, feeling as if he had been kicked in the stomach; already he was considering the preposterous fate that would surely follow his unfortunate death in an air crash somewhere over the Baltic Sea: undoubtedly he would be given a place in Himmler's ludicrous crypt for SS generals at Wewelsburg Castle, near Paderborn. Himmler would make another dreadful speech and Canaris would, perhaps, shed a crocodile tear for old times' sake. Schellenberg realized that if he wanted to avoid this sort of charade, he would have to deal with Hoffmann, who even now was sliding his hand inside Schellenberg's coat pocket.

The old tricks were still the best ones. In the early days of the war, Schellenberg had filled a whole prisoners' block at the Sachsenhausen concentration camp with Jews from Germany's criminal underworld and set them to work producing counterfeit British currency. (The £20,000 used to pay Cicero had come straight from the printing presses at Sachsenhausen.) Among these Jews were several expert *"ganefs"*—Jewish pickpockets, whom Schellenberg had used for a number of undercover operations. One of these *ganefs*, a Mrs. Brahms, who was considered the queen of Berlin's underworld, had shown Schellenberg a good way of protecting himself from pickpockets. By pushing several needles down into the lining of the pocket, with the points toward the bottom, it was possible to slide a hand into the pocket without injury, but almost impossible to pull the hand out again without encountering the points of the needles. Mrs. Brahms called it her "rat-catcher," because the principle was the same as was used in a certain kind of rodent trap.

"There's nothing in this pocket," said Hoffmann and, pulling his hand out again, screamed out loud as a dozen sharp surgical needles pierced his flesh.

Schellenberg was out of his seat in an instant, hauling the Loden coat, still attached to Hoffmann's hand by the needle-filled pocket, over the man's head and then punching him hard, several times, in the head. Hoffmann fell back into Himmler's leather chair and swept the coat away from his face before leveling the silenced gun at Schellenberg and pulling the trigger. Schellenberg threw himself to the floor of the aircraft as the gun fired, the bullet shattering a glass in the liquor cabinet.

Still struggling with the coat and the pain in his right hand, Hoffmann wrestled himself around to take another shot at Schellenberg, who was lying immediately beside Himmler's seat, partly protected by the huge leather armrest.

Schellenberg had little time to think. He reached for the red lever beside Himmler's chair and pulled it hard. There was a loud hydraulic clanking noise, as if someone had struck the belly of the Condor with a large wrench, and then a rush of freezing-cold air, a scream, and the seat carrying Hoffmann disappeared through a large square hole in the floor. But for the strength of his grip on the red lever, Schellenberg might have fallen out of the plane, too. As half of his body dangled outside of the Condor's fuselage, he had a brief vision of seat and man separating in the air, the parachute deploying, and Hoffmann falling into the Baltic Sea.

Shocked by the freezing air, his other hand too numb with cold to get much of a hold on the lip of the open escape hatch, Schellenberg called out for help, his voice hardly audible above the rushing air and the roar of the Condor's four BMW engines. He felt himself slipping out of the aircraft as the hand clinging to the red lever grew weaker and increasingly numb by the second. His last thought was of his wife's father, Herr Grosse-Schönepauck, an insurance executive, who was going to have to pay out on the policy Schellenberg had bought, and how he would love to have seen the expression on the old man's face as he signed the check. The next moment he felt someone gripping him under the arms, hauling him back aboard the plane, and then rolling him away from the open escape hatch.

Exhausted, Schellenberg lay there for almost a minute before a blanket was laid on top of him, and one of the remaining crew, a huge fellow wearing a Luftwaffe radio/gunner's badge, helped him to sit up, and then handed him a glass of cognac.

"Here," he said, "get this down you."

The man looked grimly out of the open hatch. "And then you can tell me what happened to Hoffmann."

Schellenberg downed the brandy in one gulp and, leaning against the fuselage, glanced at his clothes, which were soaking wet and covered with grease and oil. He went into the lavatory to wash and then fetched his bag to change into the clothes that had been hiding the Führer's letters. At the same time, he gave the man, a flight sergeant, a slightly expurgated account of what had happened. When he had finished talking, the sergeant spoke.

"Hoffmann took a phone call, at Tempelhof, about thirty minutes before you arrived."

"Did he say who it was that called him?"

"No, but he looked a bit strange. After that he said very little, which was strange, too, because he was always quite a talkative fellow."

"So I noticed. Had you known him long?"

"No. He joined the Government Group only a couple of months ago, after a long stint on the Russian front. Someone pulled some strings for him, we figured. Well, we were pretty sure about that. His brother is in the Gestapo."

Schellenberg nodded. "It figures."

He drank another cognac, and took a seat at the back of the plane, as far away from the open hatch as possible; then, covering himself with as many blankets as were available, he closed his eyes.

SCHELLENBERG KNEW STOCKHOLM well and liked it. In late 1941 he had spent a lot of time in Sweden when Himmler had sent him there to encourage the dissemination of Hitler's racial ideology.

Although a neutral country, Sweden was effectively enclosed by German-held territory and secretly allowed the passage of German troops on Swedish railways. It also sold Germany more than 40 percent of her iron-ore requirements. Nevertheless, while showing a congenial face to Germany, Sweden was proud of its independence—the Nazi Party had never achieved representation in the parliament—and guarded this independence jealously. Consequently, when Schellenberg arrived at Stockholm's airport, despite his diplomatic cover, he was obliged to answer a number of questions regarding his business before being allowed into the country.

After clearing immigration, he was met by Ulrich von Geinanth, the first secretary at the German Legation and the senior representative of the SD in Stockholm.

Was it Schellenberg's suspicious imagination or had the first secretary been just a little disappointed to see him?

"Good flight?" asked von Geinanth.

"They're all good when you're not shot down by the RAF."

"Quite. How is Berlin?"

"Not so bad. No bombers this week. But they've had it pretty bad in Munich, Kassel, and Frankfurt. And last night it was Stuttgart's turn."

Asking no more questions, von Geinanth drove Schellenberg to

Stockholm's harbor area and the Grand Hotel close by the old town and the Royal Palace. Schellenberg disliked staying at the embassy and preferred the Grand, where, largely, he was left alone to take advantage of the excellent kitchens, the wine cellars, and the local whores. Having checked in, he left a message with the concierge for Dr. Kersten and then went up to his room to await the chiropractor's arrival.

After a while there was a knock at the door and, always careful of his personal security, Schellenberg answered it with a loaded Mauser hidden behind his back.

"Welcome to Sweden, Herr General," said the man at the door.

"Herr Doctor." Schellenberg stood aside and Felix Kersten entered the suite. There was, he thought, a Churchillian aspect to the doctor: of medium height, he was more than a little overweight, with a double chin and a large stomach, which had helped earn him the sobriquet Himmler's Magic Buddha.

"What's the gun for?" frowned Kersten. "This is Sweden, not the Russian front."

"Oh, you know. One can't be too careful." Schellenberg made the automatic safe and then returned it to his shoulder holster.

"Phew, it's hot in here. Would you mind if I opened a window?"

"Actually, I'd rather you didn't."

"In that case, with your permission, I'll take off my jacket." Kersten removed the coat of his three-piece blue pinstriped suit and hung it on the back of a dining chair, revealing arms and shoulders that were the size of a crocodile wrestler's—the result of more than twenty years of practice as a chiropractor and master masseur. Until 1940, when Germany had invaded the Netherlands, Kersten's most important clients had been the Dutch royal family; but thereafter his chief client (Kersten had had little choice in the matter) was the Reichsführer-SS, who now regarded the burly Finn as indispensable. At Himmler's recommendation Kersten had treated a number of other top Nazis, including von Ribbentrop, Kaltenbrunner, Dr. Robert Ley, and, on a couple of occasions, Schellenberg himself.

"How is your back, Walter?"

"Fine. It's my neck that's stiff." Schellenberg was already removing the stud from the collar of his shirt.

Kersten came around the back of his chair. "Here, let me have a look."

Massive cold fingers—like thick pork sausages—took hold of Schellenberg's slim neck and massaged it expertly. "There's a lot of tension in this neck."

"Not just my neck," murmured Schellenberg.

"Just let your head go loose for a moment." One big hand grasped Schellenberg's lower jaw and the other the top of his head, almost like a Catholic priest giving a blessing. Schellenberg felt Kersten turn his head to the left a couple of times, experimentally, like a golfer teeing up a big drive, and then much more quickly, and with greater power, twisting it hard so that Schellenberg heard and felt a click in his vertebrae that sounded like a stick breaking.

"There, that should help."

Schellenberg rolled his head around on his shoulders a couple of times, just to make sure that it was still attached to his neck. "Tell me," he said. "Does Himmler let you do that?"

"Of course."

"Then I wonder why you don't break his neck. I think I would."

"Now, why would I want to do that?"

"I can think of a million reasons. And so can you, Felix."

"Walter, he's attempting to make peace with the Allies. Surely, in that, at least, he deserves our support. What I'm doing in his name could save millions of lives."

"Possibly." Schellenberg took out a red leather Schildkraut cigarette case, a present from Lina, and offered Kersten one of his Jasmatzis. Lighting Kersten's cigarette, he was close enough to see the strange black ring around the iris in each of the chiropractor's blue eyes that lent them a strangely hypnotic aspect. This near to Kersten, it was easy enough to give credence to the rumor about his mesmeric influence on Himmler.

"Since we're talking about saving lives, Felix, might I suggest you start carrying a gun yourself."

"Me? Carry a gun? Why?"

"You have powerful friends. Among them I include myself. But, as a result of that, you also have powerful enemies. Heinrich Müller of the Gestapo, for one."

"Oh, he won't find anything on me."

"No? There are some people in Germany who might argue that meeting members of the American intelligence services is prima facie evidence you are a spy."

"I haven't met anyone from American intelligence. The only American I've met while I've been in Stockholm has been Roosevelt's special representative, Mr. Hewitt. He's a New York attorney and a diplomat, not a spy."

Schellenberg smiled. It always gave him a little thrill to present people with the evidence of their naïveté. "Abram Stevens Hewitt," he said. "Grandson of a former mayor of New York and a large contributor to the U.S. Democratic Party. Father a Boston banker. Graduate of Harvard and Oxford universities. Involved in a financial scandal involving the Ivan Kreuger Swedish Match company in 1932. Speaks fluent Swedish and German. And a member of the Office of Strategic Services since 1942. The OSS is an espionage and counterintelligence organization. Hewitt reports to the head of the Swedish station, Dr. Bruce Hopper, himself a former Harvard professor of government, and Wilko Tikander—"

"Not Wilko Tikander!" exclaimed Kersten.

"—a Finnish-American attorney from Chicago and chief of OSS operations here in Stockholm." Schellenberg paused to allow the effect of his revelations to sink in. "Felix," he added, "all I'm saying is that you need to be careful. Even if the Gestapo can't discredit you—and there's no doubt that won't be easy so long as you enjoy Himmler's confidence, which you do, obviously, since you are, as you say, here in Himmler's name—even if they can't discredit you in Himmler's eyes, they might still decide to remove you. If you know what I mean."

"You mean, kill me?"

"Yes. You have a wife and three sons. You owe it to them to be vigilant."

"They wouldn't harm them, would they?"

"No. Himmler wouldn't allow that. But here, away from Germany, there's a limit to what even Himmler can do. Do you know how to use a pistol?"

"Yes. During the war, the last war, I was in a Finnish regiment that fought the Russians."

"Then take this." Schellenberg handed him his Mauser; he had another one in his bag. "Keep it in your coat pocket, just in case. Only better not carry it around Himmler. He might think you don't like him anymore."

"Thank you, Walter. Is it loaded?"

"There's a war on, Felix. It's wise to assume that most guns are loaded."

Kersten drew heavily on his cigarette and then stubbed it out, only half-smoked. He looked unhappily at the Mauser in his big hand and then shook his head.

"I can't cure him, you know."

"Who?"

"Himmler. He thinks he's sick. But there is no cure because there's no real illness. I can only alleviate the symptoms—the headaches, the stomach convulsions. Sometimes he thinks he has cancer. There is no cancer. But mostly he thinks his symptoms are caused by overwork, or even by a poor constitution. They're not. There's nothing physically wrong with the man."

"Go on."

"I'm afraid to."

"I'm not your enemy, Felix."

Kersten nodded. "I know, but still."

"Are you saying he's mentally ill?"

"No. Yes, in a way. He's sick with guilt, Walter. He's paralyzed with horror at what he has done and at what he continues to do." Kersten shook his head.

"And is this why he has initiated these peace moves?"

"Only partly."

"Personal ambition, I suppose. He wants to take over."

"No. It's not that. He's actually much more loyal to Hitler than you might suppose, Walter."

"What, then?"

"Something terrible. A secret I cannot reveal to anyone. Something Himmler told me. I can't tell you."

Schellenberg poured them each a drink and smiled. "Now I really am intrigued. All right. Let's suppose for a minute that you're going to tell me, but only on condition that we think of someone else who could have told me. Someone other than Himmler. Now, who else could that be?" He handed Kersten a glass of apricot brandy.

Kersten thought for a moment and then said, "Morell."

Schellenberg wracked his brain for almost a minute, trying to think of a Morell with whom Kersten might be acquainted, and then felt his eyes widening with surprise.

"Not Theodor Morell."

"Yes."

"Jesus." Theodor Morell was Hitler's personal physician. "All right, if I'm ever tortured by the Gestapo, I'll say it was Morell who told me."

"I suppose I have to tell someone." Kersten shrugged and drained his cognac glass in one go. "Could I have another?"

Schellenberg fetched the bottle and refilled the Finn's glass.

"I've warned Himmler of the consequences for the German people of doing nothing about this. That's the real reason he's making these peace overtures to the Americans. He's known about this since the end of last year."

"Hitler's ill?"

"Worse than ill."

"Dying?"

"Worse than that."

"For Christ's sake, Felix, what is it?"

"Last December, at Himmler's castle near the Wolfschanze, Himmler took a thirty-page dossier from his safe and showed it to me. It was a top-secret file about Hitler's health. He asked me to read the file with a view to my treating Hitler as a patient. I read it and wished I hadn't. Dr. Morell had noted some loss of normal reflexes in Hitler that might have indicated some degeneration in the nerve fibers of the spinal cord, possibly even signs of progressive paralysis."

"Go on."

"It was Morell's opinion that this was tabes dorsalis, also known as locomotor ataxia." Kersten lit a cigarette and stared grimly at the glowing tip. "A tertiary syphilitic infection of the nerves."

"Holy Christ!" exclaimed Schellenberg. "Are you saying that the Führer has syphilis?"

"Not me, for God's sake. Not me. Morell. And this was only a suspicion. Not a complete diagnosis. For that there would have to be blood tests and an examination of Hitler's private parts."

"But if it's true?"

Kersten sighed loudly. "If it's true, then it's possible that, periodically at least, Germany may be led by someone suffering from acute paranoia."

"Periodically."

"Hitler might appear rational for most of the time, with bouts of insanity."

"Just like Nietzsche."

"Exactly so."

"Except that Nietzsche was in an asylum."

"Actually, no. He was committed to an asylum but was released into the care of his own family and eventually died at home."

"Raving."

"Yes. Raving."

"That sounds familiar."

Schellenberg collected his overnight bag off the bed and emptied the contents into the quilt. "Then let us hope that when he wrote these letters to each of the Big Three he was in a rational phase."

"So that's why you're here."

"Yes. Himmler wants you to deliver them to the appropriate government representatives."

Kersten picked up one of the three letters and turned it over in his pudgy hands as if it had been something written in Goethe's own handwriting. "To bear such a huge responsibility," he muttered. "Incredible."

Schellenberg shrugged and looked away. That Germany's future should be entrusted to the hands of a forty-five-year-old Finnish masseur seemed no less incredible to him.

"Hewitt, I suppose, for the letter to Roosevelt," said Kersten.

Schellenberg nodded vaguely; could any of the Big Three possibly treat such a bizarre overture with any seriousness?

"Madame de Kollontay, for the Soviets, of course."

He liked Kersten and had the greatest respect for him as a therapist, and yet he could not help but think that this kind of backdoor diplomacy—no, asylum-door diplomacy was more like it—was doomed to fail.

"I'm not sure about the British," murmured Kersten. "I haven't had a great deal to do with the British. Henry Denham, perhaps. Now, he *is* a spy, I think."

All of which left Schellenberg angry with Himmler. What on earth was he thinking? Was Himmler any less insane than Hitler?

"I'll ask Hewitt when I see him later this afternoon," continued Kersten. "He's a patient of mine, you know. His back pain provides a useful cover for our meetings."

How dare he, thought Schellenberg. How dare Himmler charge this simple man, of limited intellectual ability, with a mission like this and describe Schellenberg's own idea as sounding like something out of *Der Pimpf*?

Schellenberg could now see no alternative. He was going to have to try again to sell Himmler on his plan to assassinate the Big Three. And perhaps there was something in Nietzsche that might help. He was no philosopher, but he remembered enough of what he had read of Nietzsche to know that Himmler would appreciate his florid tone. There was a phrase in Nietzsche's book about morals that seemed appropriate. About how only rare superior individuals—the noble ones, the Übermenschen, yes, Himmler loved that particular word—could rise above all moral distinctions to achieve a heroic life of truly human worth. Something like that, perhaps, might help sell Himmler on his plan. And after Himmler, Hitler, too. Hitler would be easy. Himmler was the harder sell. After Himmler, Hitler would be a piece of cake.

VII

Friday, October 15, 1943, Washington, D.C.

I PULLED THE LAST PAGE off the typewriter carriage, separated it from the carbon copy, added it to the pile of typewritten pages, and then read the report through from start to finish. Satisfied with what I had written, I stapled the sheets together and placed them in an envelope. It was just after eleven o'clock. I thought that if I took the report straight over to the White House first thing in the morning, the president might add it to his next evening's reading. And going into the hallways I placed the envelope containing the report inside my briefcase.

A moment or two later Diana came through the front door using the key I had given her to do exactly that. She had her own place up in Chevy Chase to which I had a key, and this arrangement made us feel like a really modern couple with a healthy sex life and a pet dog. I just hadn't gotten around to buying the pet dog yet. Mostly she came to my place because it was a little nearer the center of Washington, such as it is.

She shook out her umbrella and set it in the hall stand. She was wearing a navy blue suit with gold buttons and a white blouse inside it that was low enough to remind me of one of the reasons I was attracted to her. I was grown up enough to understand the principle behind this kind of adolescent fascination. I just didn't know why I was still such a sucker for it. Her blond hair made her look like a minor goddess, and on it she wore a broad-brimmed hat that might have been stolen from a Catholic priest, always assuming they'd gone over to wearing pink hats instead of red ones that season. I pitied the people behind her in the movie theater. That was, if she really had been to a movie. She smelled of cigarettes and perfume and alcohol, which is a combination my nose found almost irresistible. But it hardly seemed appropriate for someone who had spent her evening with Don Ameche. Unless she really had spent her evening with Don Ameche. Which might have explained everything.

"How was the movie?" I enquired.

She took a couple of Grand Inquistor's pins out of her hat and placed them and it on the hall table.

"You'd have hated it."

"I don't know. I like Gene Tierney."

"Hell looked nice."

"Somehow I've always thought it would."

She walked into the drawing room and helped herself to a cigarette from a silver box.

"Where's it playing?" I asked. "Maybe I'll go and see it."

"I told you. You'd have hated it."

"And I said I liked Gene Tierney. So maybe I'll go and see it."

She lit her cigarette irritably and walked over to a chair where the *Post* had been tossed earlier that evening. "It's in there somewhere," she said.

"Actually, I know where it's playing. I just wanted to see if you did."

"What are you driving at?"

"Only that you don't look or smell like someone who's been to a movie with some girlfriends."

"All right. I didn't go to the movies. Satisfied?"

I smiled. "Perfectly." I picked up my empty glass, took it into the kitchen, washed and dried it, came back into the drawing room, and put it away in the cabinet. I think I even managed to whistle a few bars of some jaunty Irish air. Diana hadn't budged. She was still standing there, arms folded across her chest and, but for the cigarette in her well-manicured hand, she looked like the school principal awaiting an explanation. That was what impressed me. The speed with which she managed to turn things around so that I was the one who was at fault.

Diana gave me another irritated glance. "Aren't you going to ask me who I was with?"

"No."

"So you're not bothered who I was with."

"Maybe I just don't want to know." I hadn't meant to start anything. I wasn't exactly a model of fidelity myself.

"I guess that's what bothers me the most. That you're not bothered." She smiled bitterly and shook her head, as if disappointed in me.

"I didn't say I wasn't bothered. I said I didn't want to know. Look, it's okay. Forget I ever mentioned it. Let's go to bed." I took her hand. But she took it back.

"If you cared for me, you'd at least act as if you were jealous, even if you weren't."

That's the true genius of women. Most of them could give Sun Tzu an object lesson in how attack is the best form of defense. I had caught her out in a lie and already I was the one who was being made to feel I had let her down.

"I do care for you. Of course I care for you. Only I thought we were beyond acting like a couple of characters in a play by Shakespeare. Jealousy is just the pain of injured pride."

"It always comes back to you, doesn't it?" She shook her head. "You're a clever man, Will, but you're wrong. That's not what jealousy is at all. It's not the pain of injured pride. It's the pain of injured *love*. There's a big difference. Only, for you I think pride and love are one and the same. Because you couldn't ever love a woman more than you love yourself."

She leaned forward to kiss me and for a moment I thought that everything was going to be all right. But then the kiss landed, chastely on my cheek, and it was as if she were saying good-bye. The next moment she was back in the hall, collecting her umbrella, and her pins, and her hat. That was the first time, when she walked out the door, leaving the key on the hall table, that I realized I loved her.

VIII
Monday, October 18, 1943,
Rastenburg, East Prussia

The road took them through an area of small lakes and thick forest. It was here, in 1915, that Hindenburg had dealt the Russian army a crushing blow, killing 56,000 men and capturing 100,000 in a winter battle from which the tsar's army never recovered. Before 1939, the area had been a favorite destination for boating enthusiasts; by 1943 there was no sign of any activity on the lakes.

Walter Schellenberg leaned back in the rear seat of the speeding open-topped, armor-plated Mercedes and shifted his gaze from the back of Oberleutnant Ulrich Wagner's head to the tightly woven canopy of trees overhead. Even on a bright October's afternoon like this one the forest made the road as dark as something out of the Brothers Grimm; and that protected the Wolfschanze from being seen from the air. Which was the reason the Führer had chosen to locate his Wolf's Lair headquarters in this godforsaken place. And yet, despite the continued pretense that the area concealed nothing more important than a chemical plant, it seemed not only certain that the Allies knew of the Lair's existence but also that their bombers had the range to attack it. As recently as October 9, 352 heavy bombers of the USAAC had struck at targets just 150 kilometers away that included the Arado plants at Anklam, the Focke Wulf airframe plant at Marienburg, and the U-boat yards at Danzig. Was it actually possible, Schellenberg asked himself, that the Allies could no more contemplate killing Hitler than Himmler could?

The Reichsführer-SS, sitting next to Schellenberg, removed his glasses and, cleaning them with a monogrammed cloth, took a deep and lusty breath of the forest air. "You can't beat this East Prussian air," he said.

Schellenberg smiled thinly. After a three-hour flight from Berlin, during which they had been buzzed by an RAF Mosquito and bounced around like a shuttlecock by some turbulence over Landsberg, his appreciation of East Prussian air was less than wholehearted. Thinking that he might improve the hollow feeling in his stomach if he ate something—so close to a meeting with the Führer, he didn't dare to touch the flask of schnapps he had in his briefcase—Schellenberg removed a packet of cheese sandwiches from his coat pocket and offered one to Himmler, who seemed on the verge of taking it, then thought better of it. Schellenberg had to look away for a moment for fear the Reichsführer would see him smiling and know that he was recalling an occasion, years before, during the invasion of Poland, when Himmler and Wolff, having helped themselves to several of Schellenberg's sandwiches, had discovered, too late, that they were moldy. His fledgling career in the SD had almost ended right then and there as, between roadside retches, Himmler and his aide had accused the junior officer of trying to poison them.

Himmler's eyes narrowed. "I don't know why you're eating those now," he said. "There will be lunch at the Wolfschanze."

"Perhaps, but I'm always too nervous to eat when I'm with the Führer."

"I can understand that," conceded Himmler. "It's quite a thing to sit beside the most remarkable man in the world. It's easy to forget something as mundane as food when you're listening to the Führer."

Schellenberg might have added that his own appetite was also curbed by the Führer's revolting table manners, for unlike most people, who lifted their cutlery to their mouths, the Führer kept the arm which held his spoon or fork flat on the table and brought his mouth down to his plate. He even drank tea from a saucer, like a dog.

"I need to pee," said Himmler. "Stop the car."

The big Mercedes drew to the side of the road, and the car following behind, carrying Himmler's secretary, Dr. Brandt, and his adjutant, von Dem Bach, drew up alongside.

"Is anything the matter, Herr Reichsführer?" Brandt enquired of his boss, who was already marching through the trees and fiddling with the fly buttons of his riding breeches.

"Nothing's the matter," said Himmler. "I need to pee, that's all."

Schellenberg stepped out of the car, lit a cigarette, and then offered one to von Dem Bach's aide.

"Where are you from, Oberleutnant?" he asked, walking in vaguely the same direction as Himmler.

"From Bonn, sir," said Wagner.

"Oh? I was at Bonn University."

"Really, sir? I didn't know." Von Dem Bach's aide took a long drag on his cigarette. "I was at Ludwig-Maximilians University, in Munich."

"And you studied law, I suppose."

"Yes, sir, how did you know?"

Schellenberg smiled. "Same as me. I wanted to be a lawyer for one of those big companies in the Ruhr. I suppose I rather fancied myself as a big-shot industrialist. Instead I was recruited into the SD by two of my professors. The SD has been my life. I was in the SD before I was even a party member."

They came closer to Himmler, who seemed to be having a problem undoing his last fly button, and Schellenberg turned back to the car, with Wagner following.

The gunshot, almost deafening in the woods, felled Oberleutnant Wagner as if his bones had turned to jelly. Instinctively Schellenberg took one pace away and then another as Himmler advanced on Wagner. Staring down at his victim with forensic interest, his chinless face trembled with a mixture of horror and excitement. To Schellenberg's disgust, the Walther PPK in the Reichsführer's hand was made of gold, and as Himmler held it at arm's length once again to deliver the coup de grâce, he could see Himmler's name inscribed on the slide.

"I took no pleasure in that," Himmler said. "But he betrayed me. He betrayed you, Walter."

Almost casually, Brandt and von Dem Bach walked over to inspect Wagner's body. Himmler started to holster his weapon. "I took no pleasure in that," he repeated. "But it had to be done."

"Wait, Herr Reichsführer," Schellenberg called out, for it was plain Himmler was trying to holster a weapon that was cocked and ready to fire. He took hold of Himmler's trembling, clammy hand and removed the pistol from his grip. "You need to lower your hammer—thus, sir." And holding his thumb over the hammer, Schellenberg squeezed the trigger lightly and then eased the hammer forward against the firing pin, before working the safety catch. "To make your pistol safe. Otherwise you might blow your toe off, sir. I've seen it happen."

"Yes, yes, of course. Thank you, Schellenberg." Himmler swallowed uncomfortably. "I never shot anyone before."

"No, Herr Reichsführer," said Schellenberg. "It's not a pleasant thing to have to do."

He glanced down at Wagner, shook his head, and lit another cigarette, reflecting that there were many worse ways to get it if you had been stupid enough to incur the wrath of Heinrich Himmler. When you had seen Russian POWs doing hard labor in the quarry at Mauthausen you knew that for a fact. Following the attempt on Schellenberg's life in Himmler's private plane, a discreet investigation had revealed Ulrich Wagner had been the only one who could have telephoned Hoffmann at Tempelhof Airport and alerted him that there was something in Schellenberg's briefcase that had a bearing on the secret peace negotiations being conducted by Felix Kersten. As soon as Wagner had seen the Swedish currency on the cashier's desk in the Ministry of the Interior, he would have known Schellenberg's destination. And then there was the fact that before joining Himmler's personal staff, Wagner had worked in Munich for the Criminal Police Council at a time when the senior police counselor had been Heinrich Müller, now chief of the Gestapo. It seemed that Ulrich Wagner had been Müller's spy on Himmler's personal staff for years. Not that there was any real proof of Müller's direct involvement. Besides, Himmler had no wish to bring formal charges against the Gestapo chief; that would be to risk exposing the complete history of Kersten's peace negotiations, about which the Führer was, perhaps, still unaware.

"What shall we do with the body?" asked Brandt.

"Leave it," said Himmler. "Let the beasts of the forest have him. We shall see if Müller's Gestapo is equal to the task of finding him here."

"So close to the Wolfschanze?" Schellenberg asked. "It's probably the last place they'll think of looking."

"So much the better," sneered Himmler, and led the way back to the car.

They drove on and reached a turnpike barrier across the road. It was manned by four SS men. All four recognized the Reichsführer but went through the motions of checking his identity, asking for SS paybooks and Führer visitor chits. Their papers were examined again at a second checkpoint, and the duty officer in the guardhouse telephoned ahead and then told Himmler that his party would be met by the Führer's ADC at the Tea House. Waving the car through into Security Zone 2, the officer smiled politely and administered his usual warning before giving the Hitler salute.

"If your car breaks down, sound the horn and we'll come and get you. Above all else, stay with the car and don't ever leave the road. This whole area is mined and observed by hidden marksmen who have strict orders to shoot anyone who strays from the road."

They drove on until a barbed-wire fence and a few buildings came into view. Some had grass growing on their flat roofs; some were covered with camouflage nets to help hide them from reconnaissance planes. It was only after a third checkpoint that the car finally reached Restricted 1, which was the most secure zone of the three.

Anyone seeing R1 for the first time would have compared the Führer's Prussian HQ to a small town. Covering an area of 250 hectares and made up of 870 buildings—most of them private concrete bunkers for various party leaders—R1 at the Wolfschanze included a power station, a water supply, and an air-purification installation. The Führer HQ was an impressive-looking redoubt, although to Schellenberg's more sybaritic sensibilities it was difficult to see why anyone would have wanted to stay more than one night in such a place, let alone the six hundred nights Hitler had spent there since July 1941.

Himmler's party left their cars parked inside the gate and walked toward the Tea House, a wooden Hansel-and-Gretel sort of building opposite the bunkers of Generals Keitel and Jodl, where the General Staff took their meals, when they were not obliged to dine with the Führer. Inside, the Tea House was plainly furnished with a dull bouclé carpet, several leather armchairs, and a few tables. But for the presence of several officers awaiting their arrival, it might have passed for a common room in a Roman Catholic seminary. Among the waiting officers were two of Hitler's personal adjutants, SS-Gruppenführer Julius Schaub and Gruppenführer Albert Bormann. Schaub, the chief of the adjutants, was a clerkish, mild-mannered man who wore spectacles and managed to look like Himmler's elder brother; both his feet had been injured in the Great War and he used a pair of crutches to get about the FHQ. Albert Bormann was the younger brother of Martin Bormann, Hitler's private secretary and the man who controlled everything that happened at the Wolfschanze. He was also his elder sibling's bitter rival.

"How are things in Berlin?" Schaub asked.

"There was a bombing raid last night," Schellenberg answered. "Nothing much. Eight Mosquitoes, I believe."

Schaub nodded politely. "We tend not to mention bombing raids to the Führer. It only depresses him. Unless of course he asks about them specifically. Which he won't."

"I have better news, I think," said Himmler, who had recovered a bit of his former color since murdering his subordinate. "Last night we shot down a Wellington over Aachen. The five thousandth Bomber Command aircraft shot down since the start of the war. Remarkable, is it not? Five thousand."

"Please tell the Führer," said Schaub.

"I intend to."

"Yes. Five thousand. That will cheer him up."

"How is he?"

"Concerned about the situation in the Crimea," said Schaub. "And in Kiev. General Manstein thinks Kiev is more important. But the Führer favors the Crimea."

"Can we offer you gentlemen any refreshment?" Albert Bormann asked. "A drink, perhaps?"

"No, thank you," said Himmler, answering for himself and Schellenberg, who had been about to ask for a coffee. "We're quite all right for now."

They left the Tea Room and headed further into the FHQ, where all was bustle and activity. There was a lot of construction work under way—to increase the strength of existing bunkers and to construct new ones. Polish workers trudged by with barrow loads of cement; others shouldered planks of wood. Schellenberg reflected that security was being defeated by the very effort being made to increase it. Any one of the hundreds of laborers who were at work in Restricted 1 could have smuggled a bomb into the Wolf's Lair. Not to mention the General Staff in attendance, who had no great love for Adolf Hitler, not since Stalingrad, anyway. While it was customary to leave hats, belts, and pistols on a rack outside the Führer Bunker, briefcases were permitted, and no one ever searched these. His own briefcase contained a second pistol and the plans for Operation Long Jump, and had not been examined since his arrival in Rastenburg. It might easily have also contained a hand grenade or a bomb.

The Führer Bunker was one hundred meters north of the Tea House. As they neared it, Schellenberg continued to dwell on the security system at Rastenburg. How might one have set an assassination in motion? A bomb would be the best way, there could be no doubt about that. Like every other bunker at the Wolfschanze, the Führer Bunker was aboveground, with no tunnels or secret passages. To offset this, it was covered with at least four or five meters of steel-reinforced concrete. Most important of all, there were no windows. This meant that the blast of any bomb detonating inside Hitler's bunker would have nowhere to go but inward, actually creating a more lethal effect than had the building been made of wood.

An Alsatian bitch gamboled up to Himmler, its tail wagging amiably, prompting the Reichsführer to stop and greet the animal like an old friend. "It's Blondi," he said, patting Hitler's dog on the head and prompting Schellenberg to glance around for her master.

"We're looking for a boyfriend for Blondi," said Albert Bormann. "The Führer wants Blondi to have some puppies."

"Puppies, eh? I hope I can have one. I should like to have one of Blondi's puppies," Himmler said.

"I think it's safe to assume that everyone would," said a short, stocky man with round shoulders and a bull neck, who had just arrived on the scene. It was Martin Bormann, which meant the Führer could not be far away. Hearing heels clicking to attention, Schellenberg looked to the left and saw Hitler coming toward them through the trees. "Everyone would like a puppy from the most famous dog in the world."

Schellenberg jumped to attention, extending his right arm straight in front of him as, with slow steps, Hitler approached, his own arm partially raised. The Führer was wearing black trousers, a simple open-necked field-gray uniform jacket that revealed a white shirt and tie, and a soft, rather misshapen officer's cap that had been chosen for comfort as opposed to style. On the left breast pocket of his tunic he wore an Iron Cross First Class, won during the Great War, together with the black ribbon denoting someone who had been wounded, and a gold party badge.

"Himmler. Schellenberg—good to see you again, Walter," he said, speaking in the soft Austrian accent Schellenberg knew so well from the wireless.

"And you, my Führer."

"Himmler tells me that you have a plan that will win us the war."

"Perhaps when you've had a chance to study my memorandum, you'll agree with him, my Führer."

"Oh, I hate written reports. I can't stand them. If it was up to these officers of mine, I'd never stop reading. Official papers on this, official papers on that. I tell you, Schellenberg, I've no time for paper. But let a man speak and I'll soon let you know what's what. Men are my books—eh, Himmler?"

"You can read us all quite fluently, my Führer."

"So we'll go inside and you can tell me everything, and then I'll tell you what I think."

Hitler, gesturing toward the Führer Bunker, placed another peppermint lozenge in his mouth and, walking beside Schellenberg, started to chat aimlessly.

"I walk a lot in these woods. It's one of the few places I can walk freely. In my youth I used to dream of vast spaces like this, and I suppose life has enabled me to give the dream reality. I should prefer to walk in Berlin, of course. Around the Reichstag. I always liked that building. People said I was responsible for its being burned down, but that's nonsense. No one who knows me could say I had anything to do with that. Paul Wallot wasn't a bad architect at all. Speer doesn't like him, but that's no disqualification. Anyway, I walk here in these northern forests like that fellow in Nietzsche's unreadable book—*Zarathustra*. I walk because I feel like a prisoner in these dugouts and my spirit needs space to roam around."

Walking along, listening to the Führer talk, Schellenberg smiled and nodded, thinking that any small talk he might offer could only injure his chances of selling Hitler on the idea of Operation Long Jump.

They entered the Führer Bunker, and Schellenberg followed Hitler, Bormann, and Himmler to the left, into a large room dominated by a map table. The Führer sat down on one of the half-dozen easy chairs by the empty fireplace and motioned Schellenberg to join him. Hitler disliked heat, and Schellenberg always came away from a meeting with the Führer blue with cold. While he waited for Himmler, Schaub, and the two Bormanns to be seated, Schellenberg took a closer look at his Führer, attempting to discern any sign of tabes dorsalis or tertiary syphilis. It was true, Hitler looked much older than a man of fifty-four years and seemed quite sparing in his gestures and the movement of his hands; there was, however, a compelling sense of physical force about the man, and Schellenberg did not feel Hitler was on the edge of physical collapse. Certainly he was under tremendous pressure, but the pale face, the globular eyes, and the faraway look of a sleepwalker—or a holy man—that Schellenberg had observed when he had last been to the Wolfschanze, seemed quite unchanged. It had never been possible to look at this morbid, quasi-mad Dostoyevskian figure and think of him as you would have of any ordinary man, but Schellenberg saw no real reason to suppose that Hitler was on the verge of total insanity.

His thoughts were interrupted as Hitler turned to him and asked him to begin. Schellenberg described the plan he had already sold to Himmler as a backup plan in case the peace negotiations, initiated by the delivery of the Führer's letters to the Big Three, did not bear fruit. By now, any kinks in Operation Long Jump had been ironed out, and it was eminently practicable. Though Schellenberg did not say as much to Hitler, von Holten-Pflug had returned from Vinnica to report that a team of one hundred Ukrainians were now, with the agreement of General Schimana, a unit within the Galicia Division of the Waffen-SS. All of them had parachute experience and were highly aggressive, fired up by the prospect of assassinating Marshal Stalin. Keeping Hitler in the dark about their true ethnic origin did not worry Schellenberg. He assumed that if the mission failed, the Russians would want to keep it quiet that fellow countrymen had been involved; and if it succeeded, then their origins would hardly matter. So Schellenberg left it that they were all SS volunteers from the Galicia Division.

Hitler listened, interrupting the briefing only rarely. But when Schellenberg mentioned Roosevelt's name, he leaned forward in his chair and clasped his hands together in one fist, as if throttling the president's invisible figure.

"Roosevelt is nothing more than a repulsive Freemason," he said. "For that reason alone all the churches in America should rise up against him, for he is moved by principles that are quite at odds with those of the religion he professes to believe in. Actually, the noise he made at his last press conference—that nasal way he has of speaking—was typically Hebraic. Did you hear him boast that he has noble Jewish blood in his veins? Noble Jewish blood! Ha! He certainly behaves like some pettifogging Jew. In my opinion his brain is every bit as sick as his body."

Martin Bormann and Himmler laughed and nodded their assent, and, warming to his theme, Hitler carried on:

"Roosevelt is the living proof that there is no race in the world that is stupider than the Americans. And, as for his wife, well, it's quite clear from her Negroid appearance that the woman is a half-caste. If anyone ever needed a warning of the menace half-castes pose to civilized society, Eleanor Roosevelt is it."

Hitler sank back in his armchair, wrapping his arms about him like a shawl. Then he nodded to Schellenberg to continue. But a minute or two later he was delivering his own idiosyncratic opinions of Stalin and Churchill:

"Stalin is one of the most extraordinary figures in world history. Quite extraordinary. Have you ever heard him give a speech?" Hitler shook his head. "Terrible. The man owes nothing to rhetoric, that much is certain. And if von Ribbentrop is to be believed, he has no social graces whatsoever. He is half-man, half-beast. He is never able to leave the Kremlin, but governs thanks to a bureaucracy that acts on his every nod and gesture. He cares nothing for his people. Not a thing. Indeed, I quite believe he hates the Russian people as much as I do. How else could he be so profligate with their lives? That makes Stalin a man who demands our unconditional respect as a war leader." Hitler smiled. "In a way I should be almost sorry to see him dead, because, I must admit, he's a hell of a fellow. Schellenberg's quite right, though. If anything were to happen to him, the whole of Asia would collapse. As it was formed, so it will disintegrate.

"Now, Churchill—he's quite a different story. I never yet met an Englishman who didn't speak of Churchill with disapproval. The Duke of Windsor, Lord Halifax, Sir Neville Henderson, even that idiot with the umbrella, Neville Chamberlain—all of them were of the opinion that Churchill was not only off his head but a complete bounder, to boot. Absolutely amoral. It's all you would expect of a journalist, I suppose. Say anything, do anything just to keep in the fight when any fool could have seen—can still see—that England should make peace. Not just to save England, but to save the whole of Europe from Bolshevism. It did Churchill a huge amount of harm in his own party when he went to Moscow. The Tories were furious about it and treated him like a pariah when he came back. And who can blame them? It will be the same story in Teheran. Shaking hands with Stalin? They'll love that back in England. He'd better wear gloves, that's all I can say."

By now Schellenberg was dying for a smoke and impatient to carry on outlining his plan, but Hitler wasn't yet finished with Churchill.

"I look at him and I can't help but agree with Goethe that smoking makes one stupid. Oh, it's all right for some old fellow— whether he smokes or not doesn't matter in the least. But nicotine is a drug, and for people like us, whose brains are on the rack of responsibility day and night, there's no excuse for this repulsive habit. What would become of me, and of Germany, if I drank and smoked half as much as that creature Churchill?"

"It doesn't bear thinking of, my Führer," said Himmler.

With that the tirade ended and Schellenberg was, at last, allowed to continue. But when he reached the part that involved the Kashgai tribesmen of northern Iran, Hitler interrupted him once again, only this time he was laughing.

"To think that I'm a religious figure in the Muslim world. Did you know that Arabs are including my name in their prayers? Among these Persians I shall probably become a great khan. I'd like to go there when the world is at peace again. I'll begin by spending a few weeks in some sheikh's palace. Of course, they'll have to spare me from their meat. I won't ever eat their mutton. Instead, I shall fall back on their harems. But I've always liked Islam. I can understand people being enthusiastic about the paradise of Mahomet, with all those virgins awaiting the faithful. Not like the wishy-washy heaven that the Christians talk about."

He stopped suddenly, and Schellenberg was finally able to finish outlining Operation Long Jump. Almost perversely, it was now that Hitler chose silence. From the breast pocket of his field jacket, he took out a cheap nickel-framed pair of reading glasses and glanced over the main points of Schellenberg's memorandum, sniffing loudly and sucking more of the peppermint lozenges he was so fond of. Then, removing his glasses, he yawned, making no attempt to cover his mouth or to excuse himself, and said: "This is a good plan, Schellenberg. Bold, imaginative. I like that. To win a war you need men who are bold and imaginative." He nodded. "It was you who went to Stockholm with the letters, was it not? To see this Finnish fellow of Himmler's."

"Yes, my Führer."

"And yet you bring me this plan. Operation Long Jump. Why?"

"It's always a good idea to have a plan in place in case another falls through. That's my job, sir. That's the essence of intelligence. To prepare for all eventualities. Suppose the Big Three don't agree to your peace proposals? Suppose they don't even answer your letters? Better to have my men on the ground in Iran."

Hitler nodded. "I can't tell you everything that's happening, Schellenberg. Not even you. But I think you might be right. Of course we could always do nothing and hope that the conference will be a disaster on its own terms. That might well happen, because it's quite clear the early sympathy that existed between the British and the Americans is not blooming. I tell you, there's a considerable amount of antipathy on the part of the British toward the Americans, and the only man among them who loves America unconditionally is himself half American—Roosevelt's poodle, Winston Churchill. This conference in Teheran is going to last for days." Hitler grinned. "That is, if your men don't kill them all." Hitler laughed and slapped his right thigh. "Yes, it will last for days. Like the last one, in Canada, between Churchill and Roosevelt. And now that Stalin's on board, things will last even longer. I mean, it's only too easy to imagine how enormous their difficulties must appear to them. The Red Army's huge losses, the prospect of a European invasion, millions of lives in the balance. Believe me, gentlemen, it will require nothing short of a miracle to harness the British, the Americans, the Russians, and the Chinese to the common yoke of winning a war. History teaches us that coalitions rarely work, for there always comes a point where one nation balks at making sacrifices for the sake of another.

"The Americans are an unpredictable lot, and, frankly, they haven't much stomach for any kind of sacrifice, which of course explains their tardiness in becoming involved in this war—and the last one, for that matter. In a tight corner, they're just as likely to break as stand the course. The British are infinitely more courageous, there's no comparison. How the Americans have the nerve to cast aspersions on the British after all that they have endured is almost incomprehensible. As for the Russians, well, their powers of resistance are quite inimitable.

"I won't be surprised if this conference collapses under the weight of the discord that exists among the Allies. Stalin and Churchill hate each other, that much is certain. The interesting thing will be to see how Roosevelt and Stalin hit it off. I suspect, if only from his speeches, that Roosevelt will behave like a whore for Stalin, trying to seduce the old bastard. Stalin, I'm sure, will just sit there, waiting to see just how far Roosevelt will go to charm him. Meanwhile Churchill's waiting on the sidelines seething, like some cuckolded husband watching his stupid wife make a spectacle of herself but unable to say anything out of fear she'll leave him." Hitler slapped his thigh again. "By God, I'd like to be there to see it."

His eyes narrowing, Hitler gave Schellenberg a shrewd look. "You're as clever as Heydrich," he said. "I don't know if you're as ruthless, but you're certainly as clever." He smacked Schellenberg's memo with the back of his hand. "And there is no doubt that this is a clever plan."

Abruptly, Hitler stood up, prompting everyone else to do the same. "I'll give you my decision after lunch."

The meeting adjourned to the dining room, where several members of the General Staff joined them. Throughout the meal they were treated to more of Hitler's monologues. Hitler ate quickly and with little finesse: a corn on the cob to start, over which he poured almost a cupful of melted butter, no main course, and then a huge plate of hot pancakes with raisins and sweet syrup. Schellenberg felt sick just looking at Hitler's menu choices and struggled to finish the Wiener schnitzel that he himself had ordered.

After lunch Hitler invited Schellenberg to walk with him, and the two men made a circuit of Restricted 1, Hitler pointing out the swimming pool, the cinema, the barbershop—he was very proud that they had "enticed" Wollenhaupt, the barber from Berlin's Hotel Kaiserhof, to cut the hair of the General Staff at the Wolf-schanze—and the bunkers of Göring, Speer, and Martin Bormann. "There's even a cemetery," said Hitler. "Just to the south of here, across the main road. Yes, we've got pretty much everything we might need."

Schellenberg didn't ask who was buried in the cemetery. Even for an intelligence chief there were some things it was better not to know. Finally Hitler came to the point.

"I admire your plan. It's like something from a book by Karl May. Have you ever read any books by Karl May?"

"Not since I was a boy."

"Never be ashamed of that, Schellenberg. When I was a boy, Karl May's books had a tremendous influence on me. Now, listen. I want you to go ahead with your plan, in the way that you suggested. Yes, send your team into Persia, but do nothing without authorization from me or Himmler. Is that clear?"

"Perfectly, my Führer."

"Good. They're to do nothing unless I give you the go-ahead. Meanwhile, I will tell Himmler and Göring that Operation Long Jump gets top priority. Is that understood?"

"Yes, sir. Thank you, sir."

"One more thing, Schellenberg. Be careful of Himmler and Kaltenbrunner. Perhaps a man of your resources needn't worry too much about Kaltenbrunner. But Himmler—you'll have to watch out for him, that's for sure. Watch out that he doesn't get jealous of you in the same way he got jealous of Heydrich. And you remember what happened to him. It was too bad, really, what happened, but inevitable, I suppose, given all the circumstances. Heydrich was too ambitious, and I'm afraid he paid the price for that."

Schellenberg listened, trying to contain his astonishment, for the Führer seemed to be suggesting that far from being murdered by Czech partisans, somehow Himmler had had a hand in Heydrich's assassination.

"So be careful of Himmler, yes. But also be careful of Admiral Canaris. He's not the old fool the Gestapo make him out to be. All of us can still learn a great deal from that old fox. You mark my words, the Abwehr still has the capacity to surprise us."

IX

TUESDAY, OCTOBER 19, 1943,
ZOSSEN, GERMANY

ADMIRAL CANARIS was feeling the cold. It wasn't that he had just returned from Madrid the previous day and found the Abwehr's gasproof gray-green bunker at Army Field Headquarters in Zossen, about thirty kilometers south of Berlin, to be damp and inadequately heated. No, it wasn't that at all, for unlike most of the senior figures in the Nazi hierarchy, he was something of a Spartan and cared little for his own comfort. At the Abwehr's offices on Tirpitz Ufer, an elegant four-story building near Berlin's Landwehr Canal, he had often slept on a camp bed and still thought nothing of doing without a meal so that his two wirehaired dachshunds, Seppel and Kasper, might have fresh meat.

No, the cold Canaris was feeling had more to do with the intelligence failures of his own organization and, as a corollary, the knowledge that he seemed to have lost the ear of the Führer.

The Abwehr was Germany's oldest secret service and had existed since the time of Frederick the Great. The word *Abwehr* translates as "defense" but was taken to apply to military intelligence in general, and the so-called Ausland Abwehr, or foreign intelligence department (the AA) in particular. Reporting directly to the High Command of the German army, the AA had, so far, resisted absorption by Kaltenbrunner's Reich Security Office, the RSHA; but Canaris wondered for how much longer he could maintain that independence in the face of recent failures.

The first came in 1942. An operation, code-named Pastorius, had landed eight AA spies in the United States. Things went disastrously wrong when two members of the team betrayed the others to the FBI. Six good men went to the electric chair in August 1942, and Roosevelt had not only confirmed their death sentences but reportedly joked about it, expressing his regret that the District of Columbia did not hang its capital prisoners. That disaster had been followed quickly by the AA's failure to detect the Red Army's buildup of troops in the Stalingrad area, and a third gross failure came when it was taken unawares by the Anglo-American landings in North Africa, in November 1942. Meanwhile, elaborate and expensive undertakings aimed at fomenting anti-British uprisings in India, South Africa, and Afghanistan, as well as anti-Soviet revolts in the Caucasus, had all come to naught. The most recent disaster came in April 1943, when two senior members of the AA were arrested by the Gestapo for malfeasance, currency offenses, and undermining the war effort. It was only thanks to Himmler (and, it was strongly rumored, the Führer himself) that Admiral Canaris had managed to avoid a more serious charge and to retain control of his near discredited department.

Discredited perhaps, but the AA was not without an extensive network of spies, many of them working in the Reich's diplomatic missions abroad as well as in von Ribbentrop's Foreign Ministry on the Wilhelmstrasse. As a result, Canaris knew all about Agent Cicero and the forthcoming Big Three Conference in Teheran, although nothing at all of Schellenberg's Operation Long Jump. He also knew the substantive part of a secret conversation that had taken place at the Wolfschanze more than a week before between Hitler and Himmler. This morning, he had summoned to the bunker he now treated as home only those officers from the AA and the Wehrmacht whom he regarded as above suspicion. The topic was assassination.

His office was furnished and decorated in much the same fashion as the office on Tirpitz Ufer had been: a small desk, a larger table, a few chairs, a clothes locker, and a safe; on his desk stood a model of the light cruiser *Dresden*, on which he had served during the Great War, and a bronze trio of three wise monkeys; on the walls were a Japanese painting of a grinning demon, Conrad Hommel's full-length portrait of the Führer—the canine-minded Canaris always thought it made Hitler look like a little dog—and a picture of General Franco. Canaris was well aware that this was an odd juxtaposition of portraits: despite Franco's fascism and Spain's civil war debt to Germany, he and Hitler disliked each other intensely; Canaris, on the other hand, had nothing but the greatest warmth and admiration for the people of Spain and their leader, having spent a great deal of time in the country before the war.

The admiral stood holding one of the dachshunds as the meeting convened. He was a small man, just five foot three, with silver hair, and quite round shouldered, which lent him an unmilitary bearing. Wearing a naval uniform and surrounded by much younger, taller officers, Canaris looked more like a village schoolmaster waiting for his class to settle down behind their desks.

He put his dog on the floor, took a seat at the head of the table, and immediately lit a large Gildemann cigar. Last to enter the bunker with its steep A-shaped roof (so designed so that bombs would slide off) was "Benti" von Bentivegni, an equally diminutive officer who was of Italian descent, but whose monocle and stiff manner marked him out as an almost archetypal Prussian.

"Close the door, Benti," said Canaris, who disliked the way every time someone entered the bunker the wind blew a handful of leaves in through the steel door. Dead leaves were all over the carpet and were easily mistaken for dog turds, so that Canaris was constantly thinking that Seppel and Kasper had disgraced themselves. "And come sit down."

Bentivegni sat and began fixing a cigarette into an amber holder. Canaris pressed a button underneath the table to summon the orderly. The next moment the internal door to one of the connecting tunnels opened and a corporal stepped into the room, carrying a tray bearing a coffeepot and several cups and saucers.

"I don't believe it," said Colonel Freytag von Loringhoven, his keen nostrils already sucking in the aroma. Food at the Zossen mess was poor, consisting almost exclusively of field rations and ersatz coffee; for most of the officers around the table, who were more used to dining at the Adlon or the Café Kranzler, it was just another reason to hate Zossen and the Army Field HQ, code-named Zeppelin. "Coffee. Real coffee."

"I brought it back from Madrid," said Canaris. "As well as some other provisions which I have given to the cook. I've asked him to prepare a special meal for us." Canaris liked good food and was something of a cook himself. There had been a time, before the war, when the admiral had even cooked dinner for Heydrich and his wife at his house in Dolle-Strasse.

"No one could accuse you, Herr Admiral, of not looking after your men," said Colonel Hansen, savoring the coffee in his cup.

"Don't tell anyone," said Canaris. "This really is top secret."

"And how is Madrid?" asked von Bentivegni. As head of Section III he was especially concerned with the AA's infiltration of the Spanish intelligence service.

"The Spanish government is under pressure from the Americans to stop their exports to us of wolfram and to expel all German agents."

"And what does Franco say about that?"

"I didn't actually get to see the general," admitted Canaris. "But I saw Vigon." General Juan Vigon was the chief of the Spanish general staff. "And I saw the new foreign minister, Count Jordana, too. I was obliged to point out the number of occasions on which the Abwehr and the Spanish police have acted in concert against Allied and anti-Franco resistance groups."

Canaris continued describing the diplomatic aspects of his visit, even describing the strategic importance of wolfram as a material for manufacturing bomb electrodes, until the orderly had finished serving the coffee and left the room. As soon as the door was closed, Canaris came to the main point of the meeting.

"While I was in Spain I had a chance to speak to Diego. For the benefit of our colleagues in the Wehrmacht, Diego is the name of a successful Argentinian businessman who is also our top agent in South America."

"Our top lady-killer, too," observed Colonel Hansen, who, as head of Section I, was responsible for radio and courier links with all the Abwehr's agents abroad. "I've never known a fellow quite so successful with the ladies."

Canaris, who had little interest in ladies these days, did not mind Hansen's interruption; he welcomed any opportunity for levity at Zossen, where the atmosphere was becoming increasingly desperate.

"Diego?" von Loringhoven said.

"Diego is his code name," he explained. "Since the Pastorius experience we only use code names. None of us has forgotten the executions of six good men in June. We try not to mention names in the Abwehr. No, not even the name of the man we are planning to kill in Teheran. From here on I shall only refer to him by his operational code name, Wotan."

Canaris paused for a moment, to relight his cigar, before continuing: "Now, then. Diego was in Washington only a few days ago, where he met Harvard. Harvard is the Abwehr's last important spy in Washington and an agent we have been using since 1940, when he was a rich man in his own right, owning a decent-sized chemical company. When an investment went badly wrong for him, the Abwehr was able to pay off his debts, refinance the company, and buy lots of defense shares in his name. I tell you this so you will understand that his loyalty is to Germany and the Abwehr, rather than National Socialism.

"At the beginning of the war we encouraged Harvard to become a member of the American Ordnance Association, a pro-defense lobby with close ties to the War Department. As a result he receives a great many War Department press releases and is well-known around Washington, with lots of friends in the Senate and Roosevelt's cabinet. Since 1942 he has, to all intents and purposes, been the owner of a house in Acapulco, where he has often entertained senators who have been totally unaware that the place is full of hidden microphones. Harvard's main usefulness has been in reporting Washington gossip, but occasionally he has also been able, on an informal basis, to recruit people who are sympathetic to our cause.

"One such is a man, code-named Brutus, who will be accompanying President Roosevelt on his forthcoming visits to Cairo and Teheran for the Big Three Conference. I need not remind you that this is extremely timely. Fate has presented us with an opportunity that might otherwise have taken months, perhaps years to prepare. Think of it, gentlemen. Our own man, inside Stalin's own conference room at the Russian embassy in Teheran, and armed quite legitimately. In my opinion, the very simplicity of such a plan is its best guarantee. As you all know, I have always taken the view that a lone assassin stands the best chance of success in the killing of any head of state. With all the NKVD security apparatus that Comrade Beria will undoubtedly deploy, it seems highly unlikely that Wotan will be suspecting an assassination to come from this particular quarter."

"Is Wotan to be shot, then?" asked Hansen.

"No, he is to be poisoned," said Canaris. "With strychnine."

Von Loringhoven, a Balt who had grown up in Imperial Russia and trained with the Latvian army before transferring to the Wehrmacht, shook his head. As someone who had recently served as the intelligence officer with a unit of pro-German Cossacks on the eastern front, he was quite used to seeing men so consumed with hatred that they were prepared to betray their own country and to kill their own kind. But Brutus seemed harder to understand. "So what's in it for him?" he asked bluntly. "How do we know he will do it?"

"He's a patriot," replied Canaris. "A German-American, born in Danzig, who would like to see a swift end to this war. With honor for Germany. If he fails to kill Wotan with poison, he will shoot him."

"And he's prepared to give his own life for this? The Russians will shoot him if he's caught. Or worse."

"I don't see how else this undertaking is to be carried out, Baron," said Canaris.

"Nor do I," observed von Bentivegni.

"It's one thing saying it," said von Loringhoven. "But it's something else to do it."

"Successful assassinations have nearly always involved men acting on their own who were prepared to sacrifice their own lives for a cause they believed in. Gavrilo Princip when he killed the Archduke Ferdinand. John Wilkes Booth when he killed Lincoln. And the fellow who murdered President McKinley in 1901." Canaris had made a close study of presidential assassinations. "Leon Czolgosz. One man with the will to act decisively, can change history. That much is certain."

"Then I have another question," said von Loringhoven. "For all of us. Are we all satisfied that in this murder there is honor for the Abwehr and for the Wehrmacht? I should like to know that, please. To me, poison is not the action of honorable men. What will history say of men who plotted to poison Wotan? That's what I should like to know."

"It's a fair question," said Canaris. "At the risk of sounding like the Führer, my own opinion is this. That we might never get a better chance than this one. Also, that if we are successful, then such an operation could only restore the reputation of the Abwehr in Germany. Just think of the look on all their faces when they learn what has happened. The people who wrote us off. Himmler and Müller. That bastard Kaltenbrunner. We'll show them what the Abwehr is capable of. Not to mention the people of Germany. If this conference succeeds, Stalin, Churchill, and Roosevelt will have succeeded in stripping this country of every shred of honor."

Von Loringhoven still looked unconvinced. So Canaris spoke again.

"Do we need to remind ourselves why we have set this plan into motion? In January, at Casablanca, President Roosevelt made a speech demanding the unconditional surrender of Germany. A speech that our sources inside the British secret intelligence service have assured us even Sir Stewart Menzies, my opposite number, regarded as disastrous. Gentlemen, there is only one other example of unconditional surrender in recorded history: the ultimatum that the Romans gave the Carthaginians in the Third Punic War. The Carthaginians rejected it and the Romans felt this justified razing Carthage to the ground—something they had intended to do in the first place. Roosevelt has backed us into a corner with his demand for unconditional surrender. History will say that he gave us no choice in the matter but to act as we have done. Germany demands that we do this. And for me that is enough. That is always enough. If Brutus succeeds, then the Allies will undoubtedly negotiate."

Von Loringhoven nodded. "Very well," he said. "I am convinced."

Everyone else at the table nodded firmly.

Canaris sipped his coffee and leaned back from the table. Staring at the ash on his cigar, he said, "I have thought long and hard about a code name for this operation. And you will not be surprised that I have chosen 'Decisive Stroke.' Because I think we can all agree that the assassination of Wotan is what this will be. Perhaps the most decisive stroke in the history of modern warfare."

X

SUNDAY, OCTOBER 31—
MONDAY, NOVEMBER 1, 1943,
WASHINGTON, D.C.

THORNTON COLE disliked homosexuals. Not loudly. He just disliked them for what he imagined were moral reasons and, when homosexuals worked for the government, for security reasons, too. He thought they might be blackmailed. Cole headed up the German desk at the State Department and had admired Sumner Welles as a farsighted internationalist, much to be preferred to the elderly and unimaginative Cordell Hull. But now, following the resignation of the assistant secretary of state and the rumors about Welles's homosexuality, Cole had felt obliged to revise his good opinion of Welles—the more so when, upon recalling his own meetings with the man, he fancied that he might once have been the object of a pass.

Like Welles, Thornton Cole had been a Grottie—a graduate of Groton. Another well-connected Grottie, Willard Mayer, had introduced Cole to Welles, and after that, at Welles's instigation, the two men had met a couple of times at Washington's Metropolitan Club. Cole had been flattered by the older man's attention, and even what now looked to be a clumsy pass had not set off alarm bells. It had happened a few years back, also at the Metropolitan. Welles had had too much to drink and in the course of the evening had compared Cole's profile to that of Michelangelo's *David,* adding, "Of course I can't answer how your body compares, but your head is certainly as handsome as David's." Sumner Welles was married, with children, and Thornton Cole had been of the opinion that the assistant secretary of state's words were merely maladroit and certainly not evidence of any sexual attraction. Now, of course, the re-mark looked very different. This realization upset Thornton Cole quite disproportionately, and, reasoning that Welles was hardly likely to be the only homosexual in the State Department, he had written down the names of the other men he suspected of being secretly queer: Lawrence Duggins (Welles's former deputy), Alger Hiss, who was assistant to Stanley Hornbech, the State Department's political adviser in charge of Far Eastern affairs, and David Melon, who worked for Cole on the German desk. Cole resolved to keep tabs on each of them. He focused first on his own deputy, and the nascent idea that he might uncover a whole nest of fags in State began to take hold of his imagination when he discovered that Melon was friendly with a man named Lovell White. Cole added White's name to his list when he found that the two men occasionally spent the night together at White's elegant Georgetown home. White, a flamboyant dresser and Washington wit, was a member of the American Ordnance Association, a pro-defense lobby with close ties to the War Department. Friendly with several senators and congressmen, White frequently invited the great and the good to his house in Acapulco and seemed to know everyone in government. The question was, how many of *them* were homosexuals, too? Thornton Cole made it his mission to find out.

It was usually only on weekends that Cole found the time to indulge his peculiar hobby. Unmarried, but conducting an affair with another man's wife, he was used to loitering in dark doorways and watching someone's house from a parked car. This particular Sunday, an unseasonably warm night and hardly like any Halloween he could recall, Cole followed Lovell White to the Hamilton Hotel, which overlooked Franklin Park, a notorious meeting place for homosexuals.

In the bar of the hotel, Cole had spied Lovell White deep in conversation with a man whose face, if not his name, Cole remembered as someone he had once or twice seen around Henry Stimson, the secretary of war. Another potential homosexual in the War Department was better than he had expected, and, debating how next to proceed—should he contact Hoover at the FBI?—Thornton Cole wandered into the park itself, to contemplate his next move.

But while Lovell White's liaison was illicit, it was not illicit in a homosexual way. Lovell White was indeed a homosexual, but the man with him was no invert but Brutus. White, an experienced agent, had already noticed that he was being followed and had detailed Agent Diego, whose real name was Anastasio Pereira, the Abwehr's South American agent, to watch his back. Pereira had seen Thornton Cole follow White from the spy's home in Georgetown and, realizing that the identity of Brutus might now be compromised, he tailed Cole into Franklin Park and approached him, asking for a light.

Despite his Hooverish interest in uncovering homosexuals in government, Cole was quite unaware of the park's reputation and regarded Pereira's approach without alarm.

"It's a fine evening," Pereira observed, catching up with Cole. "At least it would be if I didn't think my wife was in that hotel with another man."

"I'm sorry to hear that."

"Not as sorry as they're going to be when I surprise them."

Cole smiled thinly. "And what are you going to do?"

"Kill them both."

"You're joking."

Pereira shrugged. "What would you do?"

"I don't know."

"Where I come from there is no other way." By now Pereira was satisfied of two things: that Cole was alone and that he was not a cop or an FBI agent. Everything about Thornton Cole looked tailor-made, and his long, thin hands were not those of a policeman—perhaps a musician's or an academic's. Whoever this man was, he was certainly not a professional. "I am from Argentina." In the darkness, Pereira retrieved a switchblade from his coat pocket and snapped it open. "And there we stab a man who screws your wife."

Even as he uttered the words, Pereira plunged the knife into Cole's body just beneath the sternum. It was an expert blow delivered by a man who'd killed before with a knife, and it penetrated Cole's heart. He was dead before he hit the ground.

Pereira dragged the body into some bushes, wiped his knife on the dead man's coat, and pocketed his wallet. Then he lifted the hand that had inflicted the lethal wound to inspect his sleeve and, finding some blood on the cuff of his shirt, slipped off his jacket for a moment and rolled up his sleeve. After this, he put his jacket back on and walked back to the distinguished Renaissance Revival building that was the Hamilton Hotel. As he entered, he passed Brutus on his way out. The two men ignored each other. In the light of the lobby Pereira checked himself for bloodstains and, finding none, wandered down to the bar where he knew Lovell White would be waiting for him.

Pereira, dark and handsome, could not have looked less like the short, fat, balding man with glasses who, seeing the Argentinean appear in the hotel bar, waved a waiter toward him and ordered two dry martinis. From the expression on Pereira's face, he judged that he might need one.

"Well?" asked White as Pereira sat down.

"You were right. You *were* being followed."

"Did he see me with our friend?"

"Yes, he saw you both. I'm certain of it."

"Shit. That's fixed us."

"Relax. Everything is fixed."

"Fixed? What do you mean, fixed?"

"The man who followed you is now dead. That's what I mean."

"Dead? Where? Jesus Christ. Who was he?"

Pereira picked up the *Washington Post* from the banquette where Lovell White was sitting and perused the front page coolly. "So, Il Duce is believed to be in Italy again," he said.

"Never mind that for now," whispered White. "What do you mean, he's dead?"

"No, he's in Italy. It says so right here, my friend."

Lovell White grimaced and looked away. Sometimes Pereira was just a little too relaxed for his own good; but he knew there was no point in hurrying the Argentinean; he would explain only when he was good and ready. The waiter came back with the drinks, and Pereira drank his in two large gulps.

"I need another," he said.

"Here, have mine. I don't want it. And you look like you need it."

Pereira nodded. "I followed him across to the park and stabbed him. Don't worry. He's tucked up for the night in some bushes. I don't think anyone will find him until morning."

"Well, who the hell was he?"

Pereira placed Thornton Cole's wallet on the table. "You tell me," he said.

White snatched the wallet off the table and opened it on his lap. A moment or two passed as he examined the contents. "Jesus Christ, I know this guy," he said at last.

"Knew," said Pereira, beginning his second martini.

"He's from the State Department."

"I didn't think he was a cop." Pereira took out a gold cigarette case and lit a Fleetwood. "Too Ivy League to be a cop."

White rubbed his fleshy chin nervously. "I wonder if he was on to us. If he told anyone else about me."

"I don't think so. He was on his own."

"How can you be sure about that?"

"Do you think I'd be sitting here now if he were working with someone else?" said Pereira.

"No, I guess not." White shook his head. "I don't get it. Why would Thornton Cole be following me?"

"Perhaps he was queer for you."

"Very funny."

"I wasn't joking."

"The question is, what are we going to do about this?"

"Do?" Pereira grinned. "I think I've done everything that can be done, don't you?"

"Oh, no. No, no, no. You don't just murder someone from the U.S. State Department and expect it to be treated like an ordinary street killing. There will be a major inquiry. In which case it's possible the Metro police might find something that will explain why Cole was tailing me." He nodded thoughtfully. "On the other hand, maybe there's a way we can close down this investigation before it even gets started. To cripple an inquiry from the very outset."

"Is there such a way?"

White stood up. "Finish that drink and show me where you left the body. We have to make this look like the real thing. To dress the set, so to speak."

The two men walked out of the hotel.

"So why do queers come here and not somewhere else?"

"They have to go somewhere," said White. "But maybe they come here for sentimental reasons. Frances Hodgson Burnett, the author of *Little Lord Fauntleroy*, used to live just off this square. But the truth is, I don't know. Who knows how these things get started?"

Pereira showed him where Thornton Cole's body was hidden, and for a moment White stared at the corpse with something close to fascination. He had never before seen a dead body, and in the darkness Cole looked hardly dead at all.

"Come on," urged Pereira. "Do whatever the fuck you're going to do and let's get out of here."

"All right." He pocketed the money from Cole's wallet and tossed it on the ground beside the body. Then he took a book of matches and a ticket from Rigg's Turkish Bath on Fifteenth and G Streets from his own vest pocket and slipped them into Cole's pockets. The matchbook was from a private club in Glover Park and, like the Turkish bath, was well-known to the police as a haunt of Washington's homosexual community.

Bending over the body, he undid Cole's fly buttons.

"What the hell are you doing?" hissed Pereira.

"Just keep a look out and shut up." White pulled the dead man's penis out of his pants. "I know what I'm doing. This kind of thing happens all the time, believe me. And I already told you about the reputation of this park. By the time I've finished here, this is going to be one investigation they're going to want to keep very quiet."

White undid his own fly buttons. The way he saw it, Thornton Cole's murder was going to make the Sumner Welles scandal look like a Sunday school picnic.

Taking out his own penis, he began to masturbate.

THE OSS OCCUPIED a complex of four redbrick buildings at 2430 E Street, on the corner of Twenty-third Street and the Foggy Bottom bank of the Potomac River. When the OSS had moved into the E Street building, they discovered two dozen monkeys—medical research subjects—that the National Institutes of Health had left behind, and this had prompted Radio Berlin to remark that FDR had a team working for him that included fifty professors, twenty monkeys, and a staff of Jewish scribblers.

At the time I didn't think the Germans were so very far from the truth. I was impressed that they should have known as much about the OSS as evidently they did. Especially the bit about the monkeys.

Further along E Street a brewery lent the air a strong, pungent smell that prompted me to remember all that was sour in my life. I was one of Roosevelt's Jewish scribblers. The only trouble was I felt like one of the monkeys. A monkey deprived of a tree to swing in and without a banana.

I had tried telephoning Diana on a number of occasions but her maid, Bessie, said she wouldn't take my calls. Once, in an effort to trick her into coming to the phone, I even pretended to be one of her decorating clients, but by then Bessie was easily able to recognize my voice. Her friends avoided me, too, as if I had caused her some hurt, and not the other way around. Soon, I took to driving by her house in Chevy Chase at all hours of the day and night, but Diana's car was never there. What made things worse was that she still hadn't given me any kind of explanation for her behavior to me. The injustice of what had happened seemed almost as hard to bear as the heartache. My situation began to feel hopeless. But there seemed to be nothing else that I could do for the moment and, after all, there was still a war on. I had a job to do.

In fact it wasn't much of a job. I wished that when Allen Dulles had gone off to Switzerland to head up the OSS office in Berne, I had gone with him. But for a fever, I might have. Instead of which I remained behind in Washington, distracted by memories of Diana, and chafing under the leadership of Donovan's number two, Otto Doering.

Now that my report on the Katyn Forest massacre had been turned in to the president, I had settled back to my original job. I was spending some of my time devising a plan for finding the German spy who had reported on the existence of those twenty monkeys. I was sure he was based in Washington, and I had planted a number of false facts with several different local organizations before carefully monitoring which of these was reported on Radio Berlin or appeared in a speech by some leading Nazi. So far, I had narrowed the search to someone in the War Department.

Some of my time was spent compiling personal data on the leading figures in the Third Reich. This could be very personal indeed, such as the rumor that SD chief Walter Schellenberg was screwing the widow of his old boss, Reinhard Heydrich; or that Heinrich Himmler was obsessed with spiritualism; and what exactly had happened after Hitler had been treated for hysterical blindness by a psychiatrist at a military hospital in 1918.

But most of the time I worked on setting up an American-supported German resistance movement. Unfortunately it had turned out that several members of this popular front were German Communists, and this had brought them, and to some extent me, under the scrutiny of the FBI. So when two mugs wearing cheap shiny suits and carrying short-barreled .38s where their hearts ought to have been presented themselves in front of my desk that Monday afternoon, I assumed the worst.

"Professor Willard Mayer?"

"Look," I said, "if you've come to ask me more questions about Karl Frank and the Popular Front, I'm afraid there's nothing more I can add to what you Feds already know."

One of the men shook his head and took out some ID in his

leatherlike sixteen-ounce paw. As I leaned in to take a squint at it, I caught the rank smell of sweat on his frayed shirt and the liquor on his breath. He was too grimy for FBI, I realized. Too grimy and all too human. He had a face ingrained with disbelief and a belly like the heavy bag at Stillman's. I could have hit him all day and he'd still have been blowing smoke rings from the cheap cigar in the corner of his mouth.

"We're not Feds," he said. "We're from the Metro Police Department, First Precinct on Fourth Street. I'm Lieutenant Flaherty and this is Sergeant Crooks. We're here to ask you about Thornton Cole."

"Thornton Cole? Last time I looked he was working for the State Department."

"Last time?" said Flaherty. "When was that?"

"A month ago. Maybe longer."

"What did he do there?" asked Crooks. The sergeant was smaller than his lieutenant, but not much. His green eyes were quicker, perhaps more skeptical, too, and when they narrowed I felt their shoemaker's awl effect on the front of my head.

"He worked at the German desk. Analyzing German newspapers, propaganda, intelligence—anything that might aid our understanding of what the Germans are thinking. Basically the same thing I do here."

"Is that how you come to know him well?"

"I wouldn't say we know each other all that well. We don't send each other a card at Christmas, if that's what you mean. Look, Lieutenant, what's this about?"

Flaherty pressed his belly hard as if he might have an ulcer. It wasn't enough to gain my sympathy.

"Any idea what Cole gets up to in his private life?"

"'Gets up to'? No, I have no idea. For all I know he has a hammock above his desk and a private life that's built around a stamp collection. As I said, our acquaintance is limited to work. Now and then I'll send something his way, and now and then he'll send something to me. Usually it arrives in a nice big brown envelope with the words 'Top Secret' printed on the corner, just so that I know not to leave it on the bus. It's that and the occasional hello at the Metropolitan Club."

"What kind of 'something' did you send each other?"

I smiled a patient sort of smile, but I was beginning to feel like Flaherty's ulcer. "Gentlemen. I'm sure you could beat it out of me in sixty seconds flat, but you must know that his work, like mine, is classified. I'd need the permission of my superiors to answer that question. Assuming you could find one of my superiors. It's a little early for some of the white-shoe boys that run this place. I'd like to be of assistance. But right now you're asking the wrong questions. If I knew what this was about, then I might be able to provide some answers you could exercise your pencils on."

"Thornton Cole was found dead early this morning," said Lieutenant Flaherty. "In Franklin Park. He'd been murdered. Stabbed once through the heart."

Funny thing: whereas I merely *felt* that I had been stabbed through the heart, Thornton Cole really *had* been. The poor bastard. I tried to convince myself that I almost envied him, but it didn't work. Diana had been right about that much, anyway. I did love myself—at least enough not to want to be dead on her account.

"Frankly, the case looks open-and-shut," said Crooks. "But we have to go through the motions. I mean the guy had been robbed, and—"

"We went to his house," said Flaherty, interrupting Crooks quickly. "On Seventeenth Street? We found your name in his address book."

"Oh, right." I lit a cigarette. "So what did you do, open it at random? The address book. What happened to A through L?"

"We divided it up into four sections," said Flaherty.

"Fair enough. But surely the people at State would have a better idea of what he was up to than me."

"The thing is, nearly all his superiors are in Moscow," said Crooks. "With Cordell Hull. The secretary of state is attending some kind of conference there with the British and the Chinese."

I shrugged. "I rather doubt his murder could be related to anything he was working on. I mean, his work was secret, but it wasn't at all hazardous. I don't think."

The two detectives nodded. "That's what we thought," said Crooks.

"We just came from H Street," said Flaherty. "Someone at the Metropolitan Club said you once introduced Cole to Sumner Welles. Is that right?"

"That was quite a while ago. And I fail to see the relevance."

Flaherty took off his hat and rubbed his head. "It's probably not relevant at all. We're just trying to build a picture of the kind of society in which the late Mr. Cole moved. What sort of a man was he?"

I shrugged. "Intelligent. Good German speaker. Hardworking."

"Any idea why he wasn't married?"

"No. But I don't see what that could tell you. I'm not married, either," I replied. Nor likely to be, I told myself.

"Any idea what he might have been doing in Franklin Park, sometime around midnight?"

"I really can't imagine. It was a warm night. And it was Halloween. Maybe that's relevant."

"A trick-or-treat that went wrong?" Crooks shook his head and smiled. "That's some trick you're suggesting. A knife through the heart."

"I don't know that I'm suggesting anything, gentlemen. But there were some high spirits in evidence around town last night."

"How do you mean, high spirits?"

"Didn't you see the paper? Someone smashed the nose off the Statue of Justice."

"Is that a fact?"

"I can't see how they might be connected. But, then, I'm not a detective. Although it seems to me that if I were, I'd probably look to try and connect the unusual, and to rob unusual things of their isolation, so to speak. Isn't that the essence of detective work? The search for a sense of meaning? A truth concealed? A truth that exists behind the facade? The idea that something can be known?"

Flaherty looked at Crooks, uncomprehending.

"I have no idea what you're talking about, sir," he said.

"Forgive me," I shrugged. "It's my job to think counternaturally, so to speak. To challenge various presuppositions and beliefs and to question certain assumptions and perceptions. You think you're looking for answers, but the truth is that really you're just looking for the right question. As I said before."

Flaherty lit a cigarette and winced as tobacco smoke flooded his eye momentarily.

"Did he have any hobbies you know of?" asked the detective.

"Hobbies? I don't know. No, wait. I seem to recollect he was very fond of the works of Sir Arthur Conan Doyle." When the two cops looked blankly back at me, I added, "Sherlock Holmes?"

"Oh, right, Sherlock Holmes. I listened to it last night," confessed Flaherty. "On WOL?" He smiled. "Solving a murder is easy when you're Sherlock Holmes. But it's not so easy when you're just a Washington cop."

"Yes," I said. "I can believe that."

Flaherty handed me his card.

"If you think of anything."

I nodded, resisting the temptation to tell him that I was a philosopher and that I thought of things all the time. I only wished I could have thought of a way of persuading Diana to take me back.

XI

WEDNESDAY, NOVEMBER 10, 1943,
WASHINGTON, D.C.

WHEN I ARRIVED at the White House that evening, I was again sent to wait in the Red Room. I was beginning to feel quite at home there, although blue might have suited my mood a little better. I tried not to look at the picture of the lady above the fireplace, the one who reminded me of Diana.

There was a matronly briskness about Mrs. Tully that surprised me, given the comparatively late hour, and even on the thick rugs and runners, the heels of her shoes sounded like a drumbeat. Smelling lightly of cologne and wearing a neat gray dress, she looked as if she had just started her day's duties. I resisted the temptation to tease her again. A lot of the playfulness had gone out of me of late.

I found Roosevelt making cocktails, carefully stirring the martini jug with a long-handled spoon.

"I've been looking forward to this, Professor."

"Me, too, sir."

"I went to the airport today, to greet Mr. Hull on his return from Moscow. It's a courtesy usually reserved only for visiting heads of state. Everyone is wondering why I did that. The fact is I wanted to make him feel and look important before I make him look and feel quite the opposite."

Roosevelt handed me a martini and, holding the jug between his thighs, wheeled himself over to the sofa, where I was now seated. We toasted each other silently. I didn't like the president's way with a martini any more now than before, but it was full of alcohol and that was all that really mattered.

Encouraged by the president's confidential manner, I felt bold enough to make an observation. "You sound like you're planning to fire him, sir."

"Not fire. Just neglect. Hurt his pride a little. That kind of thing. I expect you've heard of the coming Big Three summit. Stalin and Churchill will bring their two foreign ministers, of course. But not me. I'm taking Harry Hopkins. Mr. Hull is going to stay behind and clean up his own backyard. At least that's what I'm going to tell him. Moscow was Hull's big chance at real diplomacy, and he fucked it up. That joint four-power declaration about unconditional surrender and trials for war criminals? Window dressing. I didn't send Hull all that way to state the obvious. I wanted a meeting with Stalin at Basra. Know where that is?"

I had an idea Basra was more likely to be in the Middle East than in Wyoming, but exactly where in the Middle East I couldn't say. The geography of sand dunes and wadis was never my strongest subject.

"It's in Iraq. The good thing about Basra is that I could have gotten to it by ship. There's a constitutional requirement that the president should not be away from Washington for longer than ten days. Hull's job was to try and make Uncle Joe understand that. But he screwed up. Welles could have done it. He was a real diplomat. But Hull." Roosevelt shook his head. "He understands the Tennessee timber business and not much else. Born in a log cabin, you know. Nothing wrong with that, mind. In fact, I had hoped his being a kind of American peasant would help him find some common ground with Stalin, only it didn't work out that way. Stalin may be a peasant, but he's a fucking clever peasant and I needed someone clever to deal with him. So now I have to go somewhere else for the Big Three, and I'm pretty pissed about it, I can tell you. Now I'm going to have to go by ship *and* by air."

Roosevelt sipped his martini, and then licked his lips with satisfaction.

"You heard about this fellow Thornton Cole and what happened to him, I suppose?" he asked.

"That he'd been murdered? Yes, sir." I frowned as I failed to see what Roosevelt was driving at.

"I see you don't know the whole story."

"I guess not."

"Know what a Florence test is?"

"No, sir."

"It's something the forensic boys do, to test for seminal fluid. It seems that Thornton Cole's trousers were covered in semen."

I suddenly realized what the Metro police had been driving at with their questions about me introducing Sumner Welles to Cole at the Metropolitan Club. They must have suspected me of being involved in some kind of ring of Washington sissies. I had known several homosexual men in my time, mostly in Berlin and Vienna, and even one or two in New York. I held nothing against them just as long as they didn't try to hold anything against me. What a man did in the privacy of his own circle of hell was no business of mine. At the same time, I could hardly believe what I was hearing. It was true what I had told the Metro police. I hadn't known Thornton Cole all that well. But I wouldn't ever have guessed that he was a homosexual any more than I was one myself.

"I made sure I was the first one to tell Hull all about it," said Roosevelt, gleefully. "In the car, on the way back from the airport. You should have seen his face. It was priceless, just priceless. That's what I meant when I said he should stay home and clean up his own backyard." Roosevelt laughed cruelly. "The son of a bitch."

I tried not to look shocked, but I could not help but feel a little taken aback at this display of presidential vindictiveness.

Roosevelt lit a cigarette and finally came to the point of my presence. "I read your report," he said. "It was refreshingly pragmatic. For a philosopher, you're quite the Realpolitiker."

"Isn't that the proper job of the intelligence officer? To separate the politics of reality from a policy founded upon the principles of justice and morality? And philosophically speaking, Mr. President, I can't see much at all that's wrong with that."

"You'll make a logical positivist out of me yet, Professor."

Roosevelt grinned. "But only in private. Realpolitik is like homosexuality. Best when it's practiced behind closed doors." Roosevelt sipped his cocktail. "Tell me something. Have you got a girlfriend?"

I tried to contain my irritation.

"Are you asking me if I'm homosexual, Mr. President?" I said through gritted teeth. "Because if you are, the answer is no. I'm not. And as a matter of fact I don't have a girlfriend. But I did, until quite recently."

"I don't care what a man does in private. But when it becomes public it's a different matter. You see how sex becomes the purest kind of Realpolitik there is?"

I lit a cigarette. I had a strong sense that the president was leading me somewhere a long way from Katyn Forest.

"Professor Mayer? I want you to come to the Big Three with me. As I told you, I'm taking Harry Hopkins instead of Hull. I guess you know that Harry's been living here at the White House since 1940. There isn't a man in Washington I trust more. He's been with me through thick and thin, since '32. But Harry has a problem. He gets sick. Much of his stomach was cut away because of cancer, and that makes it difficult for him to absorb protein.

"So I want you to understudy Harry and be ready to step into his shoes if he should become ill. Only I don't want Harry to know about it. You understand? It will be our dirty little secret. People will ask why you're along for the ride, and you'll have to tell them to mind their own damned business. That will only make them more curious, of course, so we'll have to devise some sort of official position for you. Executive officer to General Donovan, or something. But what do you say? Will you come?"

A trip to somewhere warm sounded nice, especially now that I was sleeping alone. And leaving Washington, going somewhere far away, might just help to bring Diana to her senses.

"Of course, sir. It would be an honor and a privilege. When do we leave?"

"Friday. It's short notice, I know. You'll need to get some shots. Yellow fever, typhoid, things like that. And we'll be away for quite a while. At least another month. In Cairo we'll hook up with Donovan. Meet the British and the Chinese. Then go on somewhere else for the conference with Stalin. I can't tell you where that is yet. Only that it's not Basra, more's the pity."

"I like a little mystery in my life."

"I know you won't be insulted if I say I hope I don't have need of your counsel while we're away. However, there's something I'd like your opinion on right now."

"Anything, Mr. President."

Roosevelt stubbed out his cigarette, screwed another Camel into his holder, and lit it quickly, before fetching some papers from underneath a bronze ship's steering clock on the untidy-looking desk.

"Your boss is inclined to be an enthusiast of all kinds of intelligence," said Roosevelt. "Of whatever character and provenance. And quite regardless of appearances and the diplomatic niceties. Now, as you know, I strongly hold the view that the Russians are the key to the defeat of Germany. As soon as we came into this war, I decreed that there was to be no spying on the Russians, and on the whole we've stuck to that. More or less. However, this past February the War Department's Military Intelligence Division, G-2, started examining Soviet diplomatic cablegrams in order to prove, or disprove, a persistent rumor we had been hearing that the Russians have been negotiating a separate peace with the Nazis."

Roosevelt refilled our glasses. After two, the anesthetic effect of the gin kicked in and the president's martinis didn't taste half bad.

"In an effort to scotch the rumor, we managed to establish our own source in the Soviet embassy. And what has since become clear is that the Russians have a network of spies working right here in Washington. For example, here are a number of memos Donovan's sent me that relate to tidbits of information we've had."

Roosevelt adjusted the pince-nez on the bridge of his long nose, glanced over the memos he was holding, and then handed one to me.

"This first memo from Donovan speaks about a British intercept regarding an NKVD agent working here called 'Nick'; and another one called 'Needle.' Apparently they had a meeting here in

Washington just last week." Roosevelt handed me another of Donovan's memoranda. "This one talks about someone called 'Söhnchen' meeting an American called 'Croesus.' And in this one we have someone called 'Fogel' handing over some information to 'Bibi.'"

Another log shifted noisily on the fire. This time it sounded a lot like my own doom.

"Your boss and G-2 think that this puts a completely different complexion on my original executive order about spying on Russia," continued Roosevelt. "After all, if they're spying on us, it kind of makes us look like chumps if we don't try to find out more—for example, from those cablegrams between Moscow and Amtorg, the Soviet Trade Mission in New York, they've been examining. Not that they've had much luck, because the Soviets are using a two-part ciphering system that G-2 has regarded as unbreakable. Until now, that is. A week or two ago, in Cairo, Bill Donovan got hold of some Soviet duplicate onetime pads. And now he wants my permission to go ahead and decode all the recent radio traffic that we've been able to intercept. The code name for these signals intercepts is Bride."

"And you want my opinion regarding what, exactly, sir?"

"Do I let the original executive order stand, or should I let G-2 and your General Donovan run with this?"

"Can I speak frankly, Mr. President? And in confidence?"

"Of course."

I chose my words carefully. "I just wonder if we would be having this conversation at all if the Bride material related to British signals traffic. The Soviets are also our allies, after all. They might be a little pissed at us if they found out."

"Wait a minute. Are you suggesting that the British are spying on us, too?"

"I don't know that I would call it spying, exactly, sir. But they do act on the wish to know more than we tell them."

"I call that spying," frowned Roosevelt.

"Whatever you call it, sir, it happens. It's the same with the Russians. I think the reality is that the Soviets are just as nervous that we will make a separate peace with the Germans as we are that they will do the same. Especially in the wake of the Katyn Forest massacre."

"That's a fair point."

"And another thing," I said, gathering confidence. "Even while we speak, there are Russians here in Washington quite legitimately to learn about the equipment we're sending them as lend-lease. It's hard to know what they could spy on that we aren't already prepared to tell them."

Roosevelt remained silent, and I realized that if there *were* secrets, he wasn't likely to confirm or deny this.

"Besides, isn't the point of your meeting with Stalin to demonstrate your goodwill toward each other?"

"Of course it is."

"Then suppose they found out we were spying on them? Analyzing their signals traffic. Ahead of the Big Three. How would that look?"

"That, of course, is my major concern. It would ruin everything."

"Frankly, sir, I can't imagine why you're even contemplating it. But there is another factor that perhaps you might not be aware of. Only I shouldn't like General Donovan to know I told you."

"This conversation never took place," said Roosevelt.

"The most vital intelligence sources are the decrypted transcripts known as Magic and Ultra."

"I couldn't comment on that, either," said Roosevelt.

"Those are controlled by General Strong, as chief of Military Intelligence. Strong keeps Donovan and the OSS from seeing Magic and Ultra, and this rankles with Donovan. To get himself included in the loop, he needs to have something that Strong wants. Something to trade. And it sounds to me that these Soviet codebooks might be the answer to his problem. A quid pro quo.

"Now, as you know, Mr. President, Bill Donovan's a great Anglophile, but he's also a great Russophobe; and, under the influence of the British, the general holds that preventing the domination of Europe by Russia is almost as important as the defeat of Germany. He wrote a paper on the subject for the Joint Chiefs at the Quebec Conference. It's my own impression that the general is only paying lip service to the need for cordial relations with the Russians. Really, I wouldn't be at all surprised if he is already looking for several other ways of circumventing your ban concerning intelligence operations against the Soviet Union."

"Do you know that for a fact?"

"Let's just say I have my suspicions. Under the lend-lease agreement, we're building some oil refineries in Russia. It's my strong impression that several of the employees, including the chief engineer, are also working for the OSS."

"I see."

"Look, sir, I'm not saying the general isn't loyal. Nor am I saying for a minute that the OSS is a renegade organization. It isn't. But everyone knows that Wild Bill has a tendency to be a little . . . overzealous."

Roosevelt uttered a laconic laugh. "Don't I know it."

In all normal circumstances I had already said more than enough, but the plain fact was that I had been rattled by the sight of the intelligence memorandum I still held in my hand, specifically by two of the code names that appeared on it. "Rattled" didn't really cover the way I was feeling. "Rattled" implied that the doors were still attached to the jalopy that was my life, yet I knew they had just been torn off by the ghost of my own past.

Croesus had been the code name the NKVD had given to me back in Berlin when I had reported to them about my conversations with Goebbels. That might just have been a coincidence, only it looked less so in conjunction with the other name, Söhnchen. A German word of endearment meaning "sonny" or "sonny-boy," Söhnchen had been the name that Otto Deutsch, the NKVD's man in Vienna, had called Kim Philby in the winter of 1933–34, when both he and I had helped Austria's Communists to fight the Heimwehr. I had a terrible feeling that the reported meeting between Croesus and Söhnchen, dated the week commencing October 4, 1943—that could hardly be a coincidence, either—

related to the conversation I had had myself with Kim Philby at the house of Tomas Harris, in London.

If I had had more time to think about it I might have drunk the rest of the martini straight from the jug and then laid my head on the fire. Instead, somehow, I kept on talking.

"Perhaps," I heard myself suggest, "if the president were to order the general to return the codebooks to the Russians, at the Big Three Conference itself, then the Russians might view such a gesture as an act of good faith."

"Yes, they might just do that," admitted Roosevelt.

I took a deep breath, trying to allay the chill feeling of sickness that was still in my stomach. If the president didn't go for my idea, there was a strong chance the Bride material might be decoded and eventually reveal the identity of Croesus. It would hardly matter to the FBI that I was no longer working for the NKVD. Nor would it matter that the spying I had done for them had been carried out against the Nazis. The plain fact of having spied for the Russians at all would be enough when seen alongside my former Communist Party membership. Enough to persuade them to tie me up and throw me in the river to see if I might float.

I had very little to lose by urging the matter further. I helped myself to another martini.

"It might even be an opportunity to give them some other stuff, too," I said smoothly. "Miniature cameras, microdot manufacturing systems, even some German intelligence relating to Soviet ciphers which troops have captured in Italy. To help bring them into line."

"Yes. I like your thinking. But not Ultra. Nor, I think, Magic. If the Russians ever did make another nonaggression pact with the Nazis, we might regret that." Roosevelt chuckled. "But, my God, I'd love to see Donovan's face when he reads this particular executive order."

I breathed a sigh of relief and drained my glass, drunk with my small triumph. "So you'll order Donovan to give the Soviets those codebooks back?"

The president grinned and toasted me silently with an empty

glass. "It'll serve that son of a bitch right for trying to creep around my orders."

A little later I went out to my car and got into it. I was feeling halfway drunk, so I wound down the windows and drove slowly back to Kalorama Heights. When I parked in my driveway, I cut the motor and sat for a few moments, looking at the house but not really seeing anything. In my mind's eye I was standing behind Franklin Roosevelt as he shook Marshal Stalin by the hand.

XII

Thursday, November 11, 1943,
Washington, D.C.

As soon as I arrived at the Campus that Thursday morning, Doering telephoned asking me to see him in his office.

Otto Doering was everything Bill Donovan was not: patient, conservative, sedentary, and studious, the deputy director of the OSS hardly looked like the kind of man who had once worked as a horse wrangler. Doering was not a popular man at the Campus, but I respected his sharp legal mind and organizational abilities and, early on, I had formed the strong impression that Doering must have been an excellent and formidable attorney. Which is to say that I pretty much hated his guts.

When I found Doering I was surprised to discover the deputy director was with General Strong from G-2. Another army officer I didn't recognize was also in attendance.

"Gentlemen, this is Major Willard Mayer. Willard? I think you've met General Strong."

I nodded and shook hands with a slim, smooth-faced man—another lawyer, this one a professor of law at West Point. Nicknamed King George on account of his grand manner, it was correctly supposed that General George Strong had begun his military career fighting the Ute Indians.

"And this is Colonel Carter Clarke, from the Army's Special Branch."

Clarke was a younger but heavier man, with cold blue eyes and a pug's broken face. The silvery gray hair that grew off the top of his head seemed to have taken fright at the brutish ideas that were concealed in the thick skull underneath. I didn't doubt that if Strong had told him to lead a cavalry charge on a renegade Indian village, he would have drawn his saber and performed his duty without a thought.

I kept on nodding, but the feeling of relief I had enjoyed on leaving the White House the previous evening was already turning to concern: the Army's Special Branch supervised the Signals Intelligence Service at Arlington Hall, in the northern suburbs of Washington. I wondered if the presence of these two hard-assed soldiers was linked to my earlier conversation with the president regarding Bride and Donovan's Russian codebooks.

"Congratulations," said the general, smiling stiffly. "I hear you're going to be General Donovan's executive officer at the Big Three."

"Thank you, sir," I said, sitting down.

"Yes, congratulations," Doering said coolly.

I guessed Doering had little or no idea why I of all people should have been ordered to attend the conference; but he could hardly admit as much in front of General Strong and Colonel Clarke. Despite the presence of the two army officers in Doering's office, there was no love lost between G-2 and the OSS.

"What, precisely are your orders, Major?" inquired the general.

"Sir, I'm to join the USS *Iowa* at Point Lookout tomorrow afternoon and to await further instructions from General Donovan in Cairo."

"I understand the president asked for you personally," said Strong. "Any idea why?"

"I'm afraid you'll have to ask the president that, General. I just do what I'm told."

I watched Strong shift uncomfortably in his chair and exchange an exasperated glance with Clarke. Strong was probably wishing he could have treated me like a Ute Indian who was off the reservation.

"All right, Major," Clarke said. "Let's try this on for size. Are you able to shed some light on why the president has ordered us to provide some technical assistance to Soviet military intelligence?

Portable microfilm sets, some intelligence captured from the Germans in Italy relating to Soviet ciphers, that kind of thing. Do you have an idea what might have put this notion into his head?"

"I believe the president is very concerned that the Big Three Conference should be a success, sir. When I saw him last night, in connection with a report he had asked me to write regarding the Katyn Forest massacre, he indicated he was considering a number of initiatives designed to gain the trust of the Soviets. Although he mentioned nothing specific, I imagine this technical assistance you describe is part of one of those initiatives."

"And what is your opinion of the wisdom of extending this kind of help to the Soviets?" asked Strong.

"Is the general asking for my personal opinion?"

"He is," said Strong and lit a hand-rolled cigarette made of a rather barbarous and pungent tobacco.

It seemed obvious that Strong greatly resented the very idea of the United States returning Donovan's captured Soviet intelligence codebooks before he had a chance to use them on the Bride material. It seemed equally obvious that it was in my best interests to try to dissemble a little, in an attempt to gain the general's trust, just in case Strong and Doering were planning some sort of scheme to circumvent the president's orders.

"Then, frankly, I have my doubts, sir. It seems to me that defeating the Nazis will leave a power vacuum in Europe, and unless we are extremely careful, it might be filled by the Soviet Union. I think the families of more than four thousand Polish officers massacred by the NKVD in the Katyn Forest might legitimately argue that the Russians are not much better than the Nazis. Whatever we give the Soviets now in the way of intelligence-gathering might easily end up being used against us."

I was just regurgitating Donovan's Quebec paper for the Joint Chiefs; given the enduring enmity that existed between the general and the chief of the OSS, it was highly unlikely that Strong would have read Donovan's paper himself. With the general nodding thoughtfully, I pressed on.

"It's my opinion that we should maintain the greatest possible vigilance concerning Russian capabilities and intentions. Only, I don't see how that's possible so long as the president continues to forbid intelligence operations against the Soviet Union. If defeating the Nazis is the only thing we achieve in Europe, I don't think it's too much of an exaggeration to say that we will have lost the war."

I shrugged.

"You asked me for my personal opinion. As I said, my discussions with the president centered on a report I prepared concerning the Katyn Forest massacre."

"Yes, of course," said General Strong. "A terrible business. Nevertheless, we simply can't ignore the wishes of the president regarding his own intelligence initiative vis-à-vis the Soviets. And since you're going to see Donovan, and Donovan is going to meet General Fitin of the NKVD at the Big Three, it's probably best that he puts this technical assistance the president wants us to afford the Soviets into the hands of Fitin personally. In other words, when you go aboard the *Iowa* tomorrow, Major, we want you to take with you a package you're to give Donovan when you see him in Cairo."

"Very well, sir."

"Naturally," said Doering, sounding rather paternal, "you're to take special care of this package. After all, we don't want this equipment falling into the wrong hands."

"Of course," I said.

"That's why we came down here," explained Strong. "To impress upon you the need for strict security in this matter."

"I don't think you can get more secure than the biggest battleship ever built."

Doering stood and, from behind his desk, picked up a navy blue grained-leather suitcase and placed it beside my chair. Glancing down, I saw the initials WJD underneath the handle. It was Donovan's case. "You're to give this to General Donovan," said Doering. "Everything he needs for the Russians is inside it."

"Is it locked?" I asked.

"Yes. I have one key, and General Donovan has the other."

"Then I guess that's everything. If you don't mind, sir, I'm going to take the rest of the day off. I have to pack a suitcase of my own."

I picked up the case and left Doering's office congratulating myself that at least I would not have to encounter the deputy director's cold, humorless face for another five or six weeks.

Downstairs I tidied my desk, said a few good-byes, and then walked out of the Campus. Placing the case in the trunk of my car, I sat in the driver's seat and contemplated my next move. Not for a moment did I accept Strong's account of what was inside Donovan's case. From the weight of it, there had to be more than just a few rolls of microfilm, some miniature cameras, and a microdot manufacturing system. And why hadn't they given me a key? The only possible answer was that there was something else in the case that they did not want me, and, by extension, the president, to know about. Unless, of course, I was already under suspicion and the whole business with the case was just a trap.

I decided it was imperative I saw what was in the case before I handed it over to Donovan in Cairo. There was only one thing to do.

I started the car and drove to Eighteenth Street, close to the millionaire mansions on Massachusetts Avenue. I parked outside Candey's Hardware Store, a curiously narrow little place below a custom tailor's shop set amid a row of tall town houses.

Opening the car trunk, I inspected the locks on the case carefully. The quality of the luggage and the manufacturer's mark, "LV," indicated it was a Louis Vuitton, likely bought in Paris or London. Rehearsing my story, I removed the case, closed the trunk, and went inside.

I would have recognized Candey's blindfolded, just from the smell. Chunk glue, birdseed, hardware cloth, Mason jars full of paint, mineral spirits, and alcohol dispensed from fifty-five-gallon drums made Candey's as distinctive as a beauty parlor selling just one brand of perfume. It was also the place where almost everyone in government went to get tools sharpened and keys cut.

I placed Donovan's case on the long wooden counter in front of a white-haired clerk who looked as if he'd been there when the store opened in 1891.

"Was there something in particular?" he asked, his teeth hanging a couple of tendrils of saliva from top to bottom lip, like paperhanger's glue.

"I've just come back from London," I explained. "Which is where I bought this case. Just as I was leaving town we were bombed and somehow I managed to mislay my keys. It's a rather expensive case and I'm reluctant to break it open. Can you open it for me? I mean, without breaking the locks?"

The clerk gave me the once-over, and deciding that I hardly looked like a thief in my tailor-made gray flannel suit, he shouted back into the shop.

"Bill? We've got a gentlemen here who needs you to open a suitcase."

Another clerk came along the counter. This one was wearing a bow tie, an apron, armlets to protect the sleeves of his shirt, and enough hair oil to grease every pair of hedge shears on the wall behind him. He let me repeat my explanation and then regarded me with slow disbelief. Outside a streetcar roared past the narrow window, causing a temporary eclipse inside the shop. When the daylight returned I saw that he was inspecting the locks.

"Nice-looking piece of luggage. I can see why you don't want to break the locks." He nodded and began to experiment with various types of key.

Fifteen minutes later I was leaving the store with a new set of keys for Donovan's case. I drove north to Kalorama Heights.

As soon as I was through the door I hoisted the case onto the dining table and, using the new keys, opened the lid. Inside the blue-moiré-silk-lined suitcase were several rolls of film, some camera equipment, and a large parcel wrapped in brown paper. I fetched a magnifying glass from my study and examined the parcel carefully, checking to see if there was anything about the paper in the way it had been wrapped that might tip off Donovan that it had been opened. Only when I was thoroughly satisfied there was not, did I carefully peel away the Scotch tape and unwrap the parcel.

There were ten files, all of them from the Signals Intelligence Service at Arlington Hall, and containing dated, enciphered Soviet telegrams sent and received by Amtorg—the Soviet trading agency—and several diplomats in the Soviet Embassy. All of the files were labeled BRIDE: TOP SECRET. A letter from a Colonel Cooke explained in detail what I had already guessed.

FROM: LT COLONEL EARLE F. COOKE
B BRANCH/CRYPTANALYTIC
U.S. ARMY SIGNALS INTELLIGENCE SERVICE
ARLINGTON HALL STATION
4000 LEE BOULEVARD
ARLINGTON, VIRGINIA.

TO: GENERAL W.J. DONOVAN,
OSS, CAIRO

November 11, 1943
Re: BRIDE

Dear General Donovan,

I understand from General Strong and Colonel Clarke in G-2, that we have a short window of opportunity to make use of the Soviet onetime cipher you have in your possession before you are obliged to comply with the President's wish that the same onetime pad be returned to General Fitin of the NKVD. In order to take full advantage of this window I am enclosing copies of all intercepts for you to loan to General Stawell of the British SOE in Cairo, together with the onetime pad, with a view to his people being able to decipher the BRIDE intercepts.

As you know, Lieutenant Hallock has recently demonstrated that the Soviets are making extensive use of duplicate key pages assembled in onetime pad books and that even a single duplication of a onetime pad cipher might render Soviet traffic vulnerable to decryption.

Until now we have regarded the cipher used by the Amtorg as most complicated, possessing the greatest secrecy of any within our knowledge; and it is hoped that even in the limited amount of time available to us the British crypto-analysts might make some headway with BRIDE. They should be apprised of the following information: 1] there appear to be several variants of the Soviet onetime pad cipher; and 2] the Soviets may be using a two-stage encoding procedure, encrypting a message from a separate codebook, and then again with the pad.

It may be that the decryption of BRIDE, and of Soviet signals traffic in general, becomes a long-term project; at the very least, a wider dissemination of this material is to be welcomed if BRIDE is ever to be properly understood and used. But any decryption will provide investigative leads for the FBI as the identities of cover names in BRIDE traffic become more obvious. I am informed by the FBI here in Washington that they are already following up new information that the agent known as Söhnchen has a wife named Lizzie.

Yours sincerely,
Earle F. Cooke,
Lt. Colonel Commanding B Branch

I took a deep breath and read the letter again, slightly astonished that G-2, SIS, and the OSS were all prepared to disobey the spirit, if not perhaps the letter, of a presidential order regarding spying on the Russians. I asked myself what Roosevelt would have said if he had become aware of Cooke's letter, and then decided that it was as likely as not that Roosevelt knew about it anyway. I had already formed the impression that saying one thing and then doing another seemed fairly typical of FDR. He might even have authorized this particular intelligence initiative against the Soviet Union.

That scared me. Spies of any shade were taking a big risk in America.

I read the letter a third time. They had already managed to determine that Söhnchen had a wife named Lizzie. Mrs. Philby was not called Lizzie, but Litzi, and since Philby wasn't an American, the FBI effort would, very probably, not get very far. That was good. And Colonel Cooke had written that he was cautious about the chances of successfully decrypting Bride. That was good, too. But the letter worried me all the same.

I rewrapped the parcel carefully and considered my options. Losing the case was out of the question; besides, that would only draw attention to me. Indeed, if they already had suspicions about me, losing the case would only confirm them.

I returned the parcel to the leather suitcase and then relocked it before placing it beside the front door. Then I went upstairs to pack my own bag, telling myself that I might easily be robbed in Cairo. Failing that, I might perhaps rely on British red tape and bureaucracy to slow things down a little, perhaps even frustrate them completely. It wasn't much to rely on. But for the moment it was all the hope I had. But I also had to admit there was a part of me that didn't care.

Later that same evening I drank too much and got out the part of me that didn't care and had a closer look at it. Underneath the bright lights of my living room it didn't look nearly so blasé. Which was how it came to me that I should write Diana a letter before I crossed the Atlantic again, just in case a German submarine decided to gather me to the Lord.

As love letters go, it wasn't Cyrano de Bergerac, but it was not bad for someone as out of practice at writing that kind of thing as I was. The last time I had dipped a pen in a bottle of blind adoration before applying the nib to some finely laid notepaper I'd been about nineteen years old and in my first year at Harvard. I don't remember the girl's name, or what happened to her, except to say that she never replied.

I sat down at my desk and let my heart run around the room naked for a while so I could describe how this looked as accurately as possible. Then I picked up my best pen and started to write.

Probably I played up the secrecy and danger of the mission ahead of me more than I should have, but the part about how stupid I thought I had been and how much I cared for Diana read accurately enough. I wondered that I hadn't thought of writing to her before. I might even have used the word "love" once or twice. More if you counted the corny little poem I started, finished, and then tossed in the wastepaper basket. Lastly, I put a three-cent picture of the president on the envelope, just to remind her of the exalted circles in which I was moving these days.

I laid my letter to Diana on the hall table with a note to Michael asking him to post it first thing in the morning. Ten minutes later I crumpled up the note and tossed it in the wastepaper basket alongside my crummy attempt at a love poem. I had decided that I would post the letter myself on my way to Hampton Roads the next day. Finally, I tossed the letter on the front seat of my car and drove up to Chevy Chase, intending to put it in her mailbox so that she might read it over breakfast and realize the justice of giving me a second chance.

It was raining by the time I got to the little town of Chevy Chase and the 1920s-vintage colonial where Diana lived. By now I had convinced myself to forget about the letter. If her car was there I was going to ring her doorbell, throw myself on her mercy and my knees, and ask Diana to marry me. In a church, if she wanted. With witnesses present to make sure we both meant it.

I parked on the street and, ignoring the rain, walked toward the verandah, trying not to make a mountain out of the molehill-shaped Nash coupe that was in the driveway behind Diana's ruby red Packard Eight. A dim light burned behind the plush velvet curtains in her drawing room window, and as I approached the house I could hear the sound of music. It was easy, unhurried music. The sort of music you like to have in a seraglio when you don't want to listen to anything except someone else breathing softly in your ear.

I stood on the verandah and, forcing myself to play the Peeping Tom, looked in through a fissure in the curtains. Neither of the two people lying on the rug in front of the fire saw me. They were too busy doing what two people do when they have decided to see just how far they can throw their clothes across the room. Doing what I'd done myself on that same rug just a few weeks before. And the way they were doing it, it looked as if it was going to be a while before Diana was free to listen to my proposal of marriage.

Suddenly I seemed ridiculous to myself. Especially the notion about asking her to marry me. It was quite obvious to me that the very idea of marrying me couldn't have been further from her mind. With no other idea in my head I returned to my car and, for quite a while, just sat there trying but failing to detach my mind from what was happening on that rug. Half of me hoped that the man would come out so that I could get a better look at him. I even constructed a little scene that had me facing them both down, but the more I thought about that, the uglier it seemed. And as the dawn came up I took the envelope, placed it in her mailbox, and drove quietly away.

XIII

Friday, November 12—
Sunday, November 14, 1943,
Point Lookout

I HAD MISSED THE BOAT. Leaning on the hood of my car, I smoked a cigarette and looked out at the waters off the southernmost point of Maryland's Western Shore where the USS *Iowa* was now no more than a trail of smoke on the burnished horizon. It was hardly my fault; the *Iowa* had sailed early. Or so the pierman had told me.

I was still pondering my next move when a couple of black Hudsons rolled up and discharged four tough-looking men with nervous eyes and tight lips. They were wearing dark suits, hats, and ties that matched their less than sunny dispositions.

I threw aside my cigarette and straightened up. So this was how the FBI arrested you. They got you to drive seventy miles out of Washington on a wild-goose chase and then, when you were waiting somewhere quiet, they picked you up without any fuss. True, I had a gun in my shoulder holster, but there was less chance of my using it to resist arrest than there was of my not being able to complete the crossword puzzle in the *Post*.

"Professor Mayer," one of the men asked, with a voice that contained no inflection. He had a hard, neat, well-kept face, like the picket fence in front of the American Horticultural Society. He tried to put a smile in his blue eyes but it came off looking sarcastic.

"Yes," I said, bracing myself. I almost held my wrists out in front of me.

"Could I see some identification, please, sir?" While he waited, he pulled his finger until the knuckle cracked.

I took out my wallet. I was sure they were about to inspect Donovan's suitcase and inform me I had failed to notice something concealed in the wrapping of the parcel that would prove I had opened it.

The man looked at my ID card and then handed it to one of his colleagues; finally he produced his own ID. To my surprise, he was a U.S. Treasury Agent—not from the FBI at all.

"I'm Agent Rowley," he said. "From the Presidential Secret Service detail. We've come to escort you on board ship."

Relieved that I was not going to be arrested, I laughed and waved my hand at the empty dock. "That I'd like to see, Agent Rowley. The boat is gone."

Agent Rowley managed a sort of smile. His four teeth were small and sharp and far apart. I could see why he hadn't put his mouth into the smile before. "I'm sorry about that, Professor. The *Iowa* had to off-load oil to allow her draft to make it up the Chesapeake. So now she's gone on to Hampton Roads to take on more fuel. I'm afraid you'd left home before we had a chance to inform you this morning."

It was true. I'd left just before eight o'clock that morning. After my romantic evening in Chevy Chase, I'd made an early start. Which was easy enough, given that I hadn't actually gone to bed.

"But that's on the other side of the bay. Is there another boat to take us there?"

"I'm afraid not, sir. We're going to have to drive. One of these agents will take your car back to Washington. If you don't mind, sir, we'll hold on to your identity card for now. It'll make things easier for us supernumeraries when we go on board the *Iowa*."

"You're going, too?"

"Four of us. Ahead of the president, who's going aboard after midnight. The boss is an old Navy man and he's kind of superstitious. Friday-night sailings are bad luck."

"I'm not so crazy about them myself."

Three hours later we passed through a naval security checkpoint and were directed to the quay where the *Iowa* was to be found. All of us fell silent as, turning onto the quay, we caught our first sight of the *Iowa*'s distinctive clipper bow and, behind it, the forecastle and fire-control tower that rose a hundred feet above a deck, bristling with gun batteries. But the height of the *Iowa*'s superstructure looked compact compared to its enormous nine-hundred-foot length, which, together with the 212,000-horsepower engines, gave the battleship its high speed.

Alongside the battleship, last-minute stores and other supernumerary passengers were going aboard under the watchful eyes of a group of armed sailors. A couple of tugs spewing smoke were attaching lines alongside the crocodile's nose that was the bow. Above all these, on three different decks, sailors leaned on rails observing the comings and goings below. As I walked up the port gangway underneath the massive antiaircraft battery, I felt as if I had arrived in an oceangoing shanty town built of armored steel. A strong smell of oil filled my nostrils, and somewhere above the primary conning position flue gases were venting noisily into the gray November sky. The ship felt alive.

At the end of the gangway, one of the Secret Service agents was already handing over my bags and my ID to a waiting officer. Consulting a clipboard, he ticked a sheet of paper and then waved another sailor toward me.

"Welcome aboard, sir," the sailor said, collecting my bags. He had the kind of Brooklyn mutt's face you got in a choir, but only if the choir was in Sing Sing. "If you'll follow me I'll show you to your quarters. Please watch your step—the deck is a little wet—and your head."

The sailor led me along a passageway. "We got you in a wardroom one level below the flag and signal bridge. Just so you can remember where that is, that's underneath the main battery detector and behind the second uptake."

"Uptake?"

"Funnel. If you get lost, just ask for the second uptake 4A. Four A is the forty-millimeter magazine."

"That's a comforting thought." I ducked to follow him through a doorway.

"Don't you worry, sir. The face armor on this ship is seventeen inches thick, which means the *Iowa* is meant to go in harm's way and take that shit."

We ducked through another doorway, and somewhere behind us a heavy door clanged shut. I was counting myself lucky that I didn't suffer from claustrophobia.

"Up here, sir," the sailor said, heading up a flight of stairs. "In there you got the head. You'll be messing forward of here, sir, with the other supernumeraries, in the captain's pantry. That's in front of the first uptake, underneath the secondary battery detector. Meals are 0800, 1200, and 2000. If you want to throw up, I advise you to do it in the head and not over the side. On this ship someone's liable to get a face full if you go puking in the wrong place."

Mutt-face put my bags down in front of a polished wooden door and knocked hard. "You're sharing with another gentleman, sir."

"Come," said a voice.

The sailor opened the door and, saluting out of habit, left me to make my own introduction.

I put my head into the cabin and saw a face I recognized, a guy from the State Department named Ted Schmidt.

"Willard Mayer, isn't it?" said Schmidt, rising from a narrow-looking bunk and advancing to shake my hand. "The philosopher."

"And you're on the Russian desk at State. Ted Schmidt."

Schmidt was a pudgy man with dark curly hair, thick horn-rimmed glasses, and eyebrows to match. I had known him briefly at Harvard and recalled a slightly thinner man with a good sense of humor and a taste for expensive wine. He was smiling, only the smile didn't sit right beside the sadness in his twitching, bloodshot eyes, the patches of stubble he'd missed with his Rolls, and the liquor on his breath. Two o'clock in the afternoon was a little early to be hitting the cabin bottle, even for a star-crossed lover like me. He was wearing a pair of corduroy trousers, a thick checked shirt, and a pair of English brogue shoes. In his hand was an unlit nickel cigar. Apart from what he was wearing, he looked and sounded like almost anybody you might see at State. He sounded like a character in a novel by Edith Wharton.

"Welcome to second class. I suspect there are better cabins than this one. And I know there are worse ones." Schmidt picked up Donovan's blue leather suitcase and brought it into the wardroom. "Nice luggage. Did you steal it?" Seeing me frown, he pointed to the initials WJD.

"It belongs to General Donovan. I'm taking it to Cairo for him." I threw my own case onto the bed and closed the door.

"There's another guy from State, fellow named Weitz, John Weitz, who's somewhere ahead of the chimney stack. By the look of it, he's sleeping in a closet. There's just me and him, from State. We're along to translate what the Rooskies are saying. Not that I think we'll even get near the table. Harriman's flying into Cairo from Moscow with his own guy. Fellow named Bohlen. So Weitz and I are on the bench, I think. Until Bohlen breaks his neck or fumbles the ball. The State Department's in pretty bad odor right now."

"So I hear."

"And you? What's your function on this little mystery tour?"

"Liaison officer from General Donovan to the president."

"Sounds suitably vague. Not that anyone's saying very much at all. Even the crew don't know where we're going. They know it's somewhere important. And that some VIPs are coming aboard. Did that sailor give you the crap about the effectiveness of our armor?"

"As a matter of fact he did. I imagine the purser on the *Titanic* gave his passengers the same spiel."

"You better believe it." Schmidt laughed scornfully and lit the cigar. It stunk up the room as if he'd put a match to a skunk. "I haven't met a sailor yet who understands the principle guiding the *Iowa*'s immune zone. Put simply, our armor is compromised by the effective range of our guns. We have to get in closer to a target to use them, and the closer we get, the more likely it is that a shell will cause some real damage.

"Then there are the torpedoes. German torpedoes, that is, not ours. The kraut fish are more powerful than the *Iowa*'s designers allowed for. Oh, I'm not saying we're at risk or anything. But a direct hit is a direct hit, and no amount of armor is going to stop the effect of that. So the next time you hear some guy blowing off about the impregnability of this ship, ask him why the crews manning those gun turrets carry derringers in their boots."

"Why *do* they carry derringers in their boots?" I asked. I didn't imagine it was because they played a lot of poker.

"Take a look inside one of those turrets and you'll understand. It takes quite a while to get out of one. They probably figure that it would be better to shoot themselves than be drowned like rats."

"I can understand that."

"Me, I have a real fear of drowning," admitted Schmidt. "I can't even swim, and I don't mind admitting that this voyage fills me with a sense of foreboding. My brother was a sailor. He was drowned on the *Yorktown*, at the Battle of Midway." Schmidt smiled nervously. "I guess that's why the subject preoccupies me so much."

"You won't drown," I said, and showed Schmidt one of the two automatics I was carrying. "If necessary, I'll shoot you myself."

"That's very American of you."

"Don't mention it. It's the least I can do for a Harvard man."

Schmidt opened a small locker by his bed. "I'd say that calls for a drink, wouldn't you?" He produced a bottle of Mount Vernon rye and poured two glasses. Handing one to me, he said, "Here's to not drowning and not getting blown up by a torpedo."

I raised my glass. "And to the Big Three."

I really don't remember much more about the rest of that day except that Schmidt and I got as stiff as a couple of cigar-store Indians. That made me feel a lot better about what I'd seen on Diana's rug the night before, which is to say, I stopped feeling very much at all. Schmidt probably drank about twice as much as I did. For one thing it was his liquor we were drinking. For another, I figured he'd had a lot more practice. He put the stuff down his throat with no more thought than if it had come straight out of a cow.

There was no fanfare for the president's arrival on board the *Iowa*. Waking early the next morning, we discovered that the ship was already under way, and since it seemed highly unlikely that the *Iowa* would have left Hampton Roads without him, we concluded that Roosevelt must have joined the ship sometime during the night.

Donning thick coats and ignoring our hangovers, we went up onto the first superstructure deck to catch sight of the *Iowa* and its escort of three destroyers at sea. It was a raw, cold morning and the wind off the rough-looking sea quickly sharpened our appetites. We went forward in search of breakfast. In the captain's mess, we found several of the Joint Chiefs and Harry Hopkins already at the table under the restless eyes of four Secret Service agents at the next table.

A cadaverous man in his early fifties, and clearly sick from cancer—a disease that had also killed his wife and father—Hopkins glanced up from his neglected ham and eggs and nodded affably our way. "Good morning," he said pleasantly as Generals Marshal and Arnold continued their impenetrable conversation.

"Good morning, sir."

Seeing Hopkins in the flesh—what little there was of it—drove home the strangeness of a man not in uniform and with no official position in Roosevelt's administration playing such an important role in our forthcoming mission. Beyond the fact that he was from Sioux City, Iowa, and had been secretary of commerce, I knew very little about the man who had been living in what had been Lincoln's study at the White House for more than three years. I'd seen men with thinner arms and faces, but only on a pirate's flag. The cuffs of his shirt had almost swallowed up his hands. His salt-and-pepper hair was as dry and lifeless as the front lawn of a bankrupt tenant farm in Oklahoma. Shadowy dark eyes full of pain gave the impression he had been stabbed just under the heart. A cynic might have suggested that Roosevelt kept Hopkins around to make himself appear electably healthy.

Given the president's brief, that I should understudy this frail, scrappy-looking man, I was hoping to get a chance to know him better during our voyage; but Hopkins was way ahead of me.

"Which one of you two boys is Professor Mayer?" he asked. "The philosopher."

"Me, sir."

"I read your book," he said, and smiled. His teeth looked so even, I wondered if they might be false. "I can't say that I understood all of it. I was never much of a scholar. But I found it . . ." He paused. "Very energetic. And I can see why it would appeal to other philosophers to have a philosopher telling them all how important they are."

"In that respect, at least," I said, "philosophers are no different from politicians."

"You're probably right," and he smiled again. "Sit down, Professor." He shifted his smile to Schmidt. "You, too, son. Help yourself to some coffee."

We sat. The coffee was surprisingly good and very welcome.

"Coming back to your book for a moment," said Hopkins. "It seems to me that while your approach is generally right, your details are wrong. I'm not a philosopher, but I'm a pretty good gin rummy player and, well, the mistake you make is to assume that every card you hold that doesn't look as though it might make a meld is deadwood. Your deadwood might make the other fellow a sequence, or a group, and therefore you might be ill advised to discard it. Do you see what I'm saying?"

"Maybe that's true," I said. Then, embracing Hopkins's metaphor, I continued. "But there has to be some deadwood or you couldn't discard. And if you can't discard, you can't complete your turn. I like your analogy, sir, but I think it helps my position more than yours."

"Then I guess you should go ahead and knock," grinned Hopkins. He finished his coffee. "I take it you play the game. Gin rummy?"

Ted Schmidt shook his head. "Just bridge," he said.

"Oh, that's too sophisticated for a country boy like me."

"I play," I said.

"Thought you did. Well, good. We'll have a game later on."

Hopkins stood, nodded courteously, and left the mess. A minute or two later, the two generals followed, accompanied by Agent Rowley, leaving Schmidt and me alone with the three remaining Secret Service men. A minute or two later, Schmidt excused himself. He looked as if he was going to throw up.

In their cheap dark suits, the three agents stuck out like a trio of gooseberries among all the uniforms and the Sloppy Joes like Schmidt and me. Underneath the White House veneer, they were just cops with better manners and sharper razors. In the cramped conditions of the ship, they seemed boxed in and unmanned. Thick-ribbed, urgent, puissant, they had the look of men who needed to ride on the running board of a presidential limousine and investigate suspicious open windows in order to give their lives meaning, in the same way that I required a good book and a Mozart quartet.

"What exactly does a philosopher do?" asked one of them. "If you don't mind me asking." The man tossed a packet of Kools onto the table and leaned back in his chair.

I picked up my coffee cup, went over to their table, and sat down. One of the other agents tamped his pipe with a biscuit-colored thumb and stared at me with dumb insolence.

"There are three kinds of questions in life," I told the man. "There's the how-does-fire-work kind of question." I picked up one of his cigarettes, put a flame to it, snapped the lighter shut, and then shook the rest of his cigarettes onto the table. "Then there's the how-many-cigarettes-do-you-have-left kind of question. Ten take away one equals nine, right? Most of the questions you can ask in life will fall into one of those two boxes. Empirical or formal.

"And the questions that don't? They're the philosophical ones. Like, 'What is morality?' Philosophy begins when you don't know where to look for an answer. You say to yourself, What kind of question is this, and what kind of answer am I looking for? And is it possible that I might be able to slot this question into one of the other two boxes after all? That, my friend, is what a philosopher does."

The three agents looked at one another with skeptical expressions and restrained smiles on their faces. But the Secret Service agent hadn't finished quite yet with our oceangoing Socratic dialogue. "So what about morality?" he asked. "The morality of killing someone in wartime, for instance. Better still, the morality of killing Hitler. Morality tells you that murder is wrong, right? But suppose it was Hitler. And suppose you had the chance to kill Hitler and save thousands, perhaps millions of people."

"You ask me, Stalin's just as bad as Hitler," said one of the other agents.

"Only, here's the thing," continued the man. "You're not allowed to kill him with a pistol. You gotta do it with a blade, or maybe your bare hands. What do you do then, huh? I mean everything tells you to kill him, right? To kill him, no matter what."

"You kill the son of a bitch," said the third man.

"I'm trying to ask a philosophical question here," insisted the first man.

"A philosopher can't tell you what to do," I told him. "He can only explain the issues and values that are involved. But in the end, it's up to you to decide what's right. Choices such as the one you describe can be difficult."

"Then, with all due respect, sir," said the agent, "philosophy doesn't sound like it's any damned use to anyone."

"It won't give you absolution. If that's what you want, you need to see a priest. But for what it's worth, if it was me and I had the chance to kill Hitler with a blade or my bare hands, hell, I'd do it."

Utilitarianism, pure and simple? The greatest happiness of the greatest number? I almost managed to convince myself. But not them. And noticing their enduring skepticism, I changed the subject, asking them their names. The one who had asked me what philosophy was made the introductions. Blond, blue-eyed, with a small scar on one cheek, he looked like a member of a German dueling society.

"The guy with the pipe is Jim Qualter. My name is John Pawlikowski. And the tall one is Wally Rauff."

I pricked up my ears as I heard that last name. Walter Rauff was also the name of the Gestapo commander in Milan. But the agent didn't look like he'd have welcomed the information.

THAT SAME EVENING I found myself invited up to the captain's cabin to play gin rummy with Hopkins, General Arnold, and the president. Outside the cabin, Agent Rauff sat on a chair reading Kurt Kruger's *I Was Hitler's Doctor.* He glanced up as I appeared and, without saying anything, reached over and opened the door.

The ship's captain, a man named John L. McCrea, was FDR's former naval aide and a good friend. He had turned over his own cabin to the president. A number of alterations had been made to suit the man in the wheelchair. An elevator had been installed so that FDR could move easily from one deck to another. Ramps had been built over the coaxials and other deck obstructions. A new bath had been installed, and the mirror lowered to enable the president to shave while he was in his chair.

Roosevelt's valet, Arthur Prettyman, had brought a number of items to help make McCrea's largish but Spartan cabin a presidential home away from home. Not the least of these were FDR's favorite reclining chair and some china and silver from the White House. Later, Hopkins told me that Prettyman had also brought along the president's deep-sea fishing gear and several Walt Disney movies, including *Snow White and the Seven Dwarves* and *Pinocchio,* which was Roosevelt's personal favorite.

A proper card table had been erected, and the president, wearing old trousers, a thick fishing shirt, and a hunting vest containing cigarettes and the long-stemmed matches he favored, was already shuffling the cards.

"Come on in, Professor, and take a seat," he said. "Arthur?" FDR turned to his black valet. "Get Professor Mayer a martini, would you, please?"

Prettyman nodded silently and retired to the rear of the cabin to prepare my cocktail. I hoped he hadn't borrowed the recipe from the president.

"Did you bring some money to lose?" asked the president. "The stakes are ten cents a point. And I'm feeling lucky tonight."

I thought it best not to mention that I had learned to count cards at Harvard. I had once written a small paper on probability theory as a generalization of Aristotelian logic. I wondered what the laws of etiquette were on taking money from the president of the United States in a card game.

"You've met Harry," said FDR. "This is General Arnold."

I nodded at the chief of the American Air Corps, a largish, smug-looking man who, for all his extra size, seemed not much healthier than Hopkins: sweat was pouring from his brow and his color was not good.

"How are your quarters?" Arnold asked politely.

"Fine, sir. Thank you."

"Hap hates the sea—don't you, Hap?" said Hopkins, sitting down at the card table and pouring himself a glass of Saratoga Springs water. "Hates the sea and hates ships. I'll deal first if you like, Mr. President."

"Beats swimming, I guess," growled Arnold.

"So what do you think of my ship?" FDR asked me.

"Very impressive." I took the drink from Prettyman's silver tray and sipped it cautiously. For once, it was perfect. "I'm almost sorry that I'm not going to see all these guns in action."

"I don't see why you shouldn't see them in action," said Roosevelt. "Come to think of it, a display of firepower might be good for morale. Let the crew know what kind of navy Hitler was fool enough to declare war on. What do you think, Harry?"

"You're the navy man, Mr. President, not me. If I had a stomach I might look as bad as Hap here."

"That true, Hap? Are you belly sick?"

"I'm fine, sir," Arnold said gruffly.

Hopkins dealt the cards.

"I think the professor's given me a good idea," said FDR, picking up his hand and starting to sort it. "We'll see how the *Iowa* can defend itself against an air attack. Shall I go first?"

FDR took the turned-up card and placed another on the discard pile.

The very next moment an enormous explosion rocked the ship and, seconds later, the door burst open to reveal Agent Rauff, gun in hand. "Are you okay, Mr. President?" he gasped.

"I'm fine, Wally," Roosevelt said coolly.

Then, over the loudspeaker mounted in the corner of the cabin came the warning. "General stations. General stations. This is not a drill. Repeat, this is not a drill."

"What the hell's going on?" said Arnold.

"Sounds like we're under attack," said Roosevelt, not even looking up from his cards. "A submarine, perhaps."

"Then I'd guess we'd better stay in here and out of the way," said Arnold. "Let McCrea do his job." Unperturbed, he drew a card from the stock pile and placed one on top of the discards.

Thinking I could hardly do less than General Arnold, I followed suit and found I could already make a sequence of four hearts.

"Go and find out what's happening, Wally," FDR told Rauff. "And for Christ's sake, put that fucking gun away. This is a battleship, not Dodge City."

"Yes, sir," said Rauff, and holstering his weapon, he went out of the cabin to find Captain McCrea. The president took the five of spades I had just discarded and put down a diamond. "Thank you, Professor," he muttered.

Arnold put down the spade I needed to make a group, which prompted me to count my three remaining cards. I might have knocked as soon as I had picked up Arnold's card but by now I had guessed what the president was doing and, holding my remaining spade, I discarded a club and decided to hang on for gin. I felt anything but calm. Somewhere, a submarine might already have fired a second torpedo that even now was speeding inexorably toward the *Iowa*, but there was no sign of fear in Roosevelt's demeanor. Any tension in the president's face had to do with the card he had just drawn. Part of me wanted to put on a life vest; instead, I waited for Arnold to take his turn, and then picked up a card.

A moment later the door opened and Captain McCrea entered the cabin and stood to attention, although his uniform looked as if it might have managed this feat on its own. With his shiny shoes, shiny smile, shiny hair, shiny eyes, and shiny fingernails, McCrea was straight out of the box.

"Well, John," said FDR, "are we under attack?"

"No, sir. A depth charge fell off the stern of one of our escort destroyers and detonated in the rough sea."

"How the fuck is that possible?"

"It's a little hard to say for sure, sir, while we're maintaining radio silence for security reasons. But I would imagine someone didn't set a safety the proper way."

"Which ship was it?"

"The *Willie D. Porter* just flashed a signal to say it was them."

"Jesus Christ, John, isn't that the ship that backed into another ship while the *Iowa* was leaving Norfolk?"

"That's right. Admiral King's none too pleased about it, I can tell you."

"I bet he's not," laughed Arnold.

"By the way, John," Roosevelt said. "I've decided I'd like to see this ship demonstrate its firepower."

"Maybe you could use the *Willie D.* for practice," said Arnold.

"Ernie King would probably agree with you," continued Roosevelt. "How about tomorrow morning, John?"

"Yes, sir," grinned McCrea. "I'll organize a display you won't ever forget."

"Since we're not actually under attack," said Arnold, "could we get back to the game?"

But as soon as McCrea had left the cabin, I knocked and spread my cards on the table. "Gin," I said.

"I've got a better idea," said FDR. "We'll attach Willard to one of those weather balloons."

An hour later, when I was more than fifty points ahead, Captain

McCrea returned to inform the president that the convoy was stopping to search for a man overboard from the *Willie D*. Roosevelt looked grimly at the darkness outside the porthole and sighed. "Poor bastard. The man overboard, I mean. Hell of a night to fall overboard."

"Look on the bright side," suggested Hopkins. "Maybe it's the guy who fucked up with the depth charge. Saves a court-martial."

"Gentlemen," said Roosevelt. "I think we had better conclude our game. Somehow it doesn't seem right for us to continue playing gin rummy when a man on this convoy is missing and presumably drowned."

With the game over, I returned to my cabin to find Ted Schmidt lying on his bunk, apparently insensible, but still holding the neck of the now empty bottle of Mount Vernon rye. I removed the bottle from Schmidt's pudgy fingers and covered him with a blanket, wondering if his drinking was habitual or occasioned by fear of being abroad on the ocean in a battleship.

The next morning I left Schmidt to sleep it off and returned to "Presidential Country" to watch the barrage display from the flag bridge reserved for Roosevelt's use during the voyage. Admirals Leahy, King, and McIntire (FDR's physician) were already on the bridge, and we were soon joined by Generals Arnold, Marshall, Somervell, Deane, and George, as well as some diplomatic personnel I didn't recognize. Last to arrive were Agents Rowley, Rauff, and Pawlikowski, Rear Admiral Wilson Brown, Harry Hopkins, John McCloy, the assistant secretary of war, Arthur Prettyman, and the president himself. He wore a regulation navy cape with velvet collar and braid frogs and a jaunty little hat with the brim turned up. He looked like a bookmaker going to his first opera.

"Good morning, gentlemen," Roosevelt said brightly. He lit a cigarette and glanced over the rail at the secondary battery detector and the gunfire control station below. "Looks like we picked a nice day for it."

The ship was just east of Bermuda on a moderate sea with pleasant weather. I was only feeling a little seasick. I trained my binoculars on the escort destroyers. The *Iowa* had been making twenty-five knots, but the three smaller destroyers—the *Cogswell,* the *Young,* and the *Willie D. Porter*—had found the pace hard going. I overheard Rear Admiral Brown telling the president that the *Willie D.* had lost power in one of its boilers.

"She's not what you would call a lucky ship, is she?" observed the president.

Hearing a loud metallic clunking noise, I glanced down to see, immediately beneath me, one of the *Iowa*'s nineteen 40-millimeter guns being loaded. A little further to my right, in front of the first uptake, a sailor was manning one of the ship's sixty 20-millimeter guns. The weather balloons were launched and a minute or so later, when these had achieved a sufficient altitude, the antiaircraft batteries began to fire. If I'd been deaf, I think I would still have complained about the noise. As it was, I was too busy covering my ears with both hands and remained that way until the last of the balloons had been hit, or had drifted out of range toward the escort destroyers. It was then I noticed something unusual to starboard and turned toward Admiral King, a tall, slim-looking man who resembled a healthier version of Harry Hopkins.

"The *Willie D. Porter* appears to be signaling, sir," I said, when the noise had finally abated.

King trained his binoculars on the flashing light and frowned as he tried to decipher the Morse code.

"What do they say, Ernie?" asked the president.

I had already read the message. The training at Catoctin Mountain had perhaps been better than I remembered. "They're telling us to go into reverse at full speed."

"That can't be right."

"Sir, that's what they're signaling," I insisted.

"Doesn't make sense," muttered King. "What the hell does that idiot think he's playing at now?"

A second or two later all became frighteningly clear. On the underside of the flag bridge, immediately beneath our feet, an enormous public-address system burst loudly to life. *"Torpedo on the starboard quarter. This is not a drill. This is not a drill. Torpedo on the star-board quarter.*"

"Jesus Christ!" yelled King.

Roosevelt turned to the Negro valet standing behind him. "Wheel me over to starboard, Arthur," he said with the air of a man asking for a mirror to see himself in a new suit. "I want to take a look for myself."

Meanwhile Agent Rowley drew his pistol and leaned over the side of the flag bridge as if to shoot the torpedo. I might have laughed if the possibility of being hit amidships and sunk had not seemed so likely. Suddenly the previous evening's predicament of the *Porter's* man overboard seemed more immediate. Just how long could a man survive in the waters of the Atlantic Ocean? Half an hour? Ten minutes? Probably less than that if he was seated in a wheelchair.

The *Iowa*, taking evasive maneuvers, increased speed and began turning to port and, a long minute later, an enormous explosion threw up a mountain of water behind the battleship. The ship see-sawed underfoot as if Archimedes had sat down in his bath and then got up again to answer the phone, and I felt the spray hit my face hard.

"Did you see that?" exclaimed the president. "Did you see that? It went straight by us. Couldn't have been more than three hundred yards off our starboard side. My God, that was exciting. I wonder if it's one sub or several."

As a display of sangfroid, it ranked close to Jeanne d'Arc asking her executioner for a light.

"If it's several, we're screwed," King said grimly and stormed his way to the bulkhead door, only to find Captain McCrea appearing on the flag deck in front of him.

"You're not going to believe this, Admiral," said McCrea. "It was the *Willie D.* that fired on us."

Even as Captain McCrea spoke, the *Iowa's* big 16-inch guns were turning ominously in the direction of the *Willie D.*

"Commander Walter broke radio silence to warn us about the

fish," continued McCrea. "I've ordered our guns to take aim at them just in case this is some kind of assassination plot."

"Jesus Christ," snarled King, and, taking off his cap, he rubbed his bald head with exasperation. Meanwhile, Generals Arnold and Marshal were making a hard job of not smirking at the now obvious discomfort of their rival service. "That fucking idiot."

"What are your orders, sir?"

"I'll tell you what my goddamn orders are," said King. "Order the commander of the *Porter* to detach his fucking ship from the escort and make all speed for Bermuda. There, he is to place his ship and his whole fucking crew under close arrest pending a full inquiry into what just happened here today, and a possible court-martial. And you can tell Lieutenant Commander Walter personally from me that I consider him the worst fucking naval officer commanding a ship I've come across in more than forty years of service."

King turned toward the president and replaced his cap. "Mr. President. On behalf of the navy, I should like to offer you my apologies, sir, for what has happened. But I can assure you that I intend to get to the bottom of this incident."

"I think we *all* nearly got to the bottom," Marshall said to Arnold. "The bottom of the ocean."

Back in the cabin I found Ted Schmidt sitting crapulously on the edge of his bunk, wearing his life vest and clutching a new bottle of rye. What do you do with a drunken sailor, I asked myself wearily. Giving him a taste of the bosun's rope end, shaving his belly with a rusty razor, and even putting him in bed with the captain's daughter were, all of them, solutions that came musically to mind.

"What's happening?" hiccuped Schmidt. "I heard firing. Are we under attack?"

"Only by our own side," I offered, and explained what had happened.

"Thank God." Schmidt collapsed back on his bunk. "It would be just my luck on top of everything else that's happened to get killed by my own side."

I took the bottle from Schmidt and poured myself a drink. After the cold air of the flying bridge I needed something warm inside of me. "Would you care to talk about it?"

Schmidt shook his head, miserably.

"Look, Ted, this has got to stop. Getting tight is one thing. Getting shit-faced is quite another. Maybe the Russians at the Big Three will forgive you smelling like a bootlegger's glove, but I don't think the president will. What you need is a shave and a shower to scrub the sideboard off your breath. Every time you whistle I swear I'm halfway up Mount Vernon. After that, we'll go find you a cup of strong coffee and some fresh air. Come on. I'll hold your toilet bag."

"Maybe you're right."

"Sure I'm right. If this were dry land, I'd feel duty bound to smack you in the mouth and confine you to your cabin. But since this is a ship, we'll say that you're seasick. That's a perfectly respectable thing to be at sea. Besides, there are men, sober men, in command of destroyers, who are more incapable than you, Ted."

When Schmidt had cleaned himself up and changed his clothes, we went forward. Only one man was in the mess when we got there. He was a lean, athletic-looking man wearing a Yale bow tie, a V-necked pullover, and half-moon glasses. There was a knife-edge crease to his gray flannels. His hair was short and silvery, and in his hand was a book as thick as a car tire. It was titled *The Fountainhead*. He had a distant manner and seemed to view our arrival with all the enthusiasm of a courtier finding a dog turd inside the gates of the Forbidden City. Schmidt introduced him.

"This is John Weitz," he said.

I nodded, smiling affably, but hardly liking this man at all. Weitz nodded back and sent up a small puff of smoke as if signaling that he wasn't particularly friendly. Meanwhile, a mess attendant announced that he would fetch a fresh pot of coffee.

"John's the other Russian specialist they've sent from State," added Schmidt.

It was a remark that provoked some indignation in John Weitz. The first, I was to learn, of a lot more where that had come from.

"Can you believe that?" Weitz said to me. "*Can* you? The most important diplomatic event of the century and just two of us from the State Department."

Having already learned Harry Hopkins's low opinion of State, I could believe it only too easily. And John Weitz seemed hardly the type to restore the reputation of the department in the eyes of Hopkins.

"It seems to me," said Schmidt, "that the president has a dog but wants to wag the tail himself."

Weitz nodded, angrily. This show of agreement between the two Russian specialists did not, however, extend to how the Soviet Union ought to be treated as an ally of the United States, and it wasn't long before a heated discussion was under way. I kept out of it for the most part, not because I disliked political arguments but because it seemed to me there was something personal about this particular argument. Something that wasn't quite explained by the simple fact that John Weitz was a shit.

"It sticks in my throat that the president is going to shake Stalin's hand," Weitz confessed.

"Why the hell shouldn't the president shake Stalin's hand?" Schmidt asked. "The Russians are our allies, for Christ's sake. That's what you do when you've made an alliance. You shake hands on it."

"And it doesn't bother you that Stalin signed the death warrant on ten thousand Polish officers? Some ally." Weitz relit his pipe, but before the still hungover Schmidt could answer, he added, "Some ally, one that tries to make a separate peace with Germany. That's the only reason there hasn't been a Big Three before now."

"Nonsense." Schmidt was rubbing his eyes furiously.

"Is it? The Russian ambassador to Stockholm, Madame de Kollontay, has been practically sleeping with von Ribbentrop's representative, Peter Kleist, since the beginning of the year."

Schmidt looked at Weitz with contempt. "Bullshit."

"I don't think you understand the Russian mentality at all," Weitz continued. "Let's not forget that the Ivans have made a separate peace with the Germans before. In 1918, and again in 1939."

"Maybe that's true," said Schmidt, "but things are very different now. The Russians have every reason to trust us."

"Hey, I'm not saying they can't trust *us,*" laughed Weitz. "The question is, can we trust *them?*"

"We promised Stalin a second front in 1942, and again in 1943, and look where we are now. There won't be a second front before August of next year. How many more Red Army soldiers will die before then? A million? Stalin can be forgiven for thinking that he's fighting this war by himself."

"All the more reason, then, for him to negotiate a separate peace," insisted Weitz. "It's hard to imagine any country being able to sustain losses like that and want to go on fighting."

"I might agree with you if the Red Army had lost the initiative. But they haven't."

Even as the two men argued, I had thought of a better reason why Stalin might just have been inclined to sue for peace: his greatest fear was not the Germans but the Russians themselves. He must have been terrified that his own army would mutiny against the appalling conditions and high casualties, just as it had in 1917. Stalin knew he was sitting on a powder keg. And yet what choice did he have?

John Weitz could only see the Soviet Union as a potential aggressor. "You mark my words," he said. "Stalin is coming to this Big Three with a shopping list of countries he thinks he can occupy permanently without a shot being fired. And Poland is at the top of the list. If he thought that Hitler would agree to those demands, believe me, he'd make a deal with him even while he was shaking FDR's hand. You ask me, we should let them both bleed white. Let the Nazis and Communists kill each other off and then pick up the pieces."

By now the argument had grown very bad-tempered. And personal, too.

"Hell, it's no wonder the Russians don't trust us with bastards like you around," yelled Schmidt.

"I think I'd rather be a bastard than an apologist for a murdering swine like Stalin. Who knows? Maybe you're worse than that, Ted. You wouldn't be the first fellow traveler at State."

Schmidt stood up abruptly, his fists clenched and his soft, clean-shaven face quivering with anger. For a moment I thought that he would strike Weitz, and I and the two mess attendants who were on duty had to move quickly to intervene before actual blows were exchanged.

"You heard what he called me," Schmidt protested to me.

"Looks like I hit a nerve," grinned Weitz.

"Maybe you should shut up," I suggested.

"And maybe you should be more careful about the company you keep," replied Weitz.

"That's good coming from you, you faggot," said Schmidt.

Given the situation in the State Department—Sumner Welles, and then Thornton Cole—this was not an insult that John Weitz was likely to let pass, and before either I or the mess attendants could prevent him, he had punched Ted Schmidt hard on the nose—hard enough to make his nose bleed. He would have punched Schmidt again, too, but for the intervention of myself and one of the mess attendants.

"I'm going to kill him," he yelled, repeating the threat several times.

"I'd like to see you try, you faggot," grinned Schmidt, wiping his bleeding nose with his handkerchief.

The noise of this fracas brought Agents Rauff and Pawlikowski into the mess as Schmidt and Weitz continued to abuse and threaten each other.

"If you two gentlemen are supposed to be diplomats," said Pawlikowski, pushing Weitz up against the cabin wall when he tried to hit Schmidt again, "then God help us all."

Rauff looked at Schmidt and then at me. "I think you'd better get him out of here," he said. "Before the president or any of the Joint Chiefs come in here."

"Good advice," I said, and took a firm hold of Schmidt's arm and moved him smoothly toward the mess room door. "Come on, Ted," I said. "He's right. We don't want the president seeing this. Let's go back to the quarters."

"He called me a faggot," was the last thing I heard from Weitz as I closed the door behind us.

When we were back in the cabin, Schmidt sat down on his bunk and reached for his bottle.

"Don't you think you've had enough of that stuff?" I snapped. "What the hell's the matter with you, anyway? And why on earth did you call Weitz a faggot?"

Schmidt shook his head and laughed. "I just wanted to get to him. Stick some mud on that Fascist bastard. People around State are kind of nervous about the possibility of there being some kind of organized pansy hunt. God forbid they should ever find a queer who's also a Communist. They'd probably lynch him from the top of the Washington Monument."

I had to admit there was some truth in that.

Schmidt was silent for a minute. Then he said, "Are you married, Willard?"

This struck a nerve as I remembered how the president and perhaps the Metro police had asked me the same thing.

"What, are you going to call *me* a faggot, too? Is that it?"

Schmidt looked pained. "Good Lord, no." He shook his head. "I was just asking."

"No, I'm not fucking married." I shook my head bitterly. "I had a girl. A really nice girl. A girl I should have married. And now— well, now she's gone. I'm not exactly sure why or even how, but I blew it." I shrugged. "I miss her a lot. More than I thought possible."

"I see." Schmidt nodded. "Then we're in the same boat."

"Not for much longer if you carry on like you did just now. They'll put you off at the next desert island."

Schmidt smiled, his pudgy face a mixture of sympathy and irony. I didn't much care for the sympathy, but the irony looked interesting.

"You don't understand," he said, taking off his glasses and cleaning them furiously. "The day before I came on this ship, my wife, Debbie, told me that she was going to leave me." He swallowed hard and chipped me another twitching smile. It landed right on top of the large bag of self-pity I'd been carrying ever since coming on board the *Iowa*.

"I'm sorry." I sat down and poured us both a drink. Short of fetching the ship's chaplain, it seemed like the proper thing to do. "Did she say why?"

"She's been having an affair. I guess if I'm honest, I knew she was up to something. She was always out somewhere. I didn't want to ask, you know? In case my worst suspicions were confirmed. And now they are."

He took the drink and stared at it as if he knew it wasn't the answer. So I lit a cigarette and fed it between Schmidt's lips.

"Do you know the other guy?"

"I did know him." He smiled sheepishly as he caught my eye registering his use of past tense. "It's a little more complicated than you might suppose. But I have to tell someone, I guess. Can you keep this to yourself, Willard?"

"Of course. You have my word."

Schmidt swallowed the drink and then took a suicidally long drag on his cigarette.

"The other man is dead." He smiled bitterly and added, "She's leaving me for a dead man, Willard. Can you beat that?"

I shook my head. I couldn't even get near to beating it. I didn't even know the name of the guy I'd seen with Diana on the rug in her living room.

Schmidt snorted with laughter and then wiped tears from his eyes. "Not just any dead man, mind you. No, she had to pick the most infamous dead man in Washington."

I frowned as I tried to figure out who Ted Schmidt could have been referring to. There was only one infamous dead man in Washington I could think of whom Ted Schmidt might have known. "Jesus, Ted, you don't mean Thornton Cole."

Schmidt nodded. "I do mean Thornton Cole."

"But wasn't he . . . ?"

"That's what the Metro police said. I did some checking. They're working on the assumption that Cole went to Franklin Park to have sex with a male prostitute, who then robbed and murdered him. But you can take it from me, Thornton Cole was certainly not homosexual."

"And you know that for sure?"

"Debbie is carrying his baby. I know *that* for sure. We hadn't made love in a very long time. Cole is the father, all right. It's all in the letter she wrote me the day before I got on this stinking tub."

"You say you haven't told anyone else about this."

Schmidt shook his head. "No one else knows. Except you."

"Well, don't you think you should tell someone? The police?"

"Oh, sure. I want everyone in Washington to know that another man was fucking my wife. Yes, good idea, Willard. Like I said, I only just found out about it myself. And who am I going to tell? The captain?"

"You're right. There's never a cop around when you need one." I shrugged. "How about the Secret Service?"

"Then what? We're maintaining radio silence, remember?"

"You're going to have to tell someone. A man was murdered, Ted. If the Metro cops knew Cole was having an affair with your wife, they could hardly treat the murder as some kind of pansy thing. There must be more to it than that."

Schmidt laughed. "Sure. Maybe they'll think it was domestic. That *I* killed him. Have you thought about that? I tell them what I know and the next thing, I'm a suspect. I'm not so sure Debbie doesn't think *I* had something to do with it, anyway. Because I would have killed him if I'd had the opportunity, not to mention the guts. I can just see it. I tell those guys and I'll find myself arrested the minute I step off this ship." He shook his head. "Secret Service, FBI. I don't trust any of these bastards. The only reason I'm talking to you is because we knew each other at Harvard. Sort of." Schmidt brought the glass up to his lips before he realized he'd already drunk the contents. "I'm not a drunk, Willard. I don't normally drink. But what else do you do in a case like this?"

"Don't ask me. I'm a stranger here myself." I poured us both another. What the hell, I thought, we were brothers in suffering.

"Besides, there's another reason I don't want the Secret Service and the FBI crawling all over my life. Something John Weitz said."

"Oh, forget him."

"I've always sympathized with the Communist movement, Will. Ever since Harvard. I guess that does make me a sort of fellow traveler, just like he said."

"It's one thing to sympathize and quite another to belong," I told him firmly. He may have outranked me in human suffering, but I wasn't going to let him outrank me in political radicalism. "You never belonged to the Communist Party, did you?"

"No, of course not. I never had the guts to join."

"Then you've got nothing to worry about. Since Pearl, we're *all* fellow travelers. That's the only decent line to take. That's what this Big Three is all about. John Weitz needs to remember that. I don't think FDR would appreciate some of the things he said in the mess just now. And I happen to know for a fact that your views about the Soviet Union are pretty much in accordance with the president's."

"Thanks, Willard."

"You know, some of the president's Secret Service detail. They're not so bad."

"You really think I should tell them what I know?"

"Yes. Let me tell you why. Thornton Cole worked on the German desk, right?"

Schmidt nodded. "I didn't know him well, but by all accounts he was pretty good at his job."

"Have you considered the possibility that there's a security aspect to this whole story? Maybe he found out something that was connected to his German work at State. Could be that's what got him killed."

"You mean, like a German spy?"

"Why not? A year ago the FBI picked up eight German spies in New York. The Long Island spy ring? But there must be others. That's one of the things that keeps Hoover in a job."

"I never thought of that."

"In which case, and I hate to say this, but it's just possible that Debbie might be in some danger, too. Perhaps she knows something. Something about Thornton Cole. Something that could get her killed." I shrugged. "Assuming you don't actually want her dead, that is."

"I still love her, Will."

"Yeah. I know what that feels like."

"So which one of the agents do you think I should speak to? I mean, you've spoken to some of them, right?"

I thought about my previous day's conversation on the subject of "What is philosophy?"

"I don't know. Agent Rauff seems quite intelligent," I said, recalling one of their names. And then another. "Pawlikowski isn't such a bad guy."

"For a Polack," laughed Schmidt.

"You got something against Polacks?" I asked.

"Me, I'm German, like you," replied Schmidt. "We've got something against nearly everyone."

XIV

MONDAY, NOVEMBER 15, 1943,

THE ATLANTIC OCEAN

WHEN I AWOKE the next morning, I was surprised to find that Ted Schmidt was already up and gone from the cabin.

After a shower and a shave, I went along to the mess room, expecting to find him enjoying a plate of ham and eggs. I was disquieted for a moment at not finding him there, but told myself it was a big ship and Schmidt was probably up on deck, clearing his head in the fresh air. Disquiet turned to concern when, after a leisurely breakfast and a walk with Harry Hopkins on deck, I returned to the cabin to find Schmidt was still not there. I began a one-man search that included everything from the pilot's house to the first-aid room and the main deck, fore and aft. Then I went to tell Captain McCrea that Ted Schmidt was missing.

McCrea, a career navy officer from Michigan who had seen action during the First World War, was also a lawyer and possessed of a lawyer's cool head.

"I ought to add that he'd been drinking, quite heavily. So it's just possible that he's sleeping it off in some quiet corner of the ship I don't know about."

The captain heard me out with the air of a defense attorney listening to a particularly implausible story offered by his client, and then ordered his executive officer to organize an immediate search of the ship.

"Can I help?" I offered.

Containing his now very evident dislike of me, McCrea shook his head.

"It might be best if you waited in your cabin, just in case he shows up there. Which I'm sure he will. This is a big ship. I get lost myself sometimes."

I went back to my cabin and lay down on my bunk, trying not to dwell on the thought that was uppermost in my mind: the vague possibility that Schmidt might have committed suicide. On a ship where the men manning the guns carried derringers to avoid being drowned like rats in their gun turrets, love and jealousy might have seemed rather old-fashioned, unmanly reasons for killing yourself. But I could hardly deny their devastating effect on poor Ted Schmidt. And while I had already rejected the idea of self-slaughter for myself, I didn't know him well enough to assess whether he was the type to kill himself. Assuming that there was such a thing as a type.

Restless, I got up and searched Schmidt's luggage for a clue as to what might have happened. Some kind of note or letter was usually considered customary. There was a letter. But it wasn't from Ted. Inside a brown leather address book, I found the letter from Schmidt's wife, Debbie, telling Ted about her affair with Thornton Cole and informing him that she was leaving him. I pocketed the letter, intending to give it to Captain McCrea if the search failed to find Schmidt on board.

Just before midday, when the search had been going on for almost two hours, there was a knock at the door and a sailor came in and saluted. He looked about twelve years old.

"The captain's compliments, sir. He'd like you to join him in his cabin."

"Right away," I said and, grabbing my coat, followed the young sailor forward. "No sign of Mr. Schmidt, I assume?"

But the boy merely shrugged and said he didn't know.

I found the captain with the chief petty officer and Agents Qualter, Rowley, Rauff, and Pawlikowski. Their somber expressions told me the worst. McCrea cleared his throat and rose slightly on his well-polished toes as he spoke.

"We've searched the Big Stick from bow to stern and there's no sign of him. It's even money Schmidt went overboard."

"Are we stopping the ship? I mean, if he *has* gone overboard, we ought to search for him, the way we did for the sailor on the *Willie D.*"

The captain and the CPO exchange a weary look.

"When did you last see Mr. Schmidt?" asked McCrea.

"Around ten o'clock last night. I turned in immediately after dinner. What with all this sea air, I was bushed. And a little drunk, probably. Schmidt was probably a little drunk, too. I think I heard him go out of the cabin at around eleven. I assumed he'd gone to the head. I didn't hear him come back."

McCrea nodded. "That would fit. The chief petty officer here had a conversation with Mr. Schmidt at around 2320 hours."

"There was alcohol on the gentleman's breath," said the CPO. "But he didn't seem drunk to me. He wanted me to direct him to the Secret Service's quarters."

"Only he never arrived," said Rauff.

"You're aware that alcohol is forbidden on this vessel," said McCrea.

"Yes. I think the president is aware of it, too. And I had several drinks with him the night before last."

McCrea nodded patiently. "All right. Let's say, just for the sake of argument, that he went into the water around midnight. That's twelve hours ago. Since then we've sailed almost three hundred miles. Even if we turned around and went back to look for him, it would be hopeless. There's no way he would survive in the Atlantic Ocean for twenty-four hours. I'm afraid the man is dead."

I let out a long sigh. "Poor Ted. His brother was on the *Yorktown,* you know. He drowned, too." Even as I spoke, I recalled Schmidt telling me how, as a corollary of his brother's death, he had a horror of drowning. This hardly seemed to make it likely that Schmidt would have thrown himself overboard. If he had wanted to commit suicide, surely he would have found some other way. He might have taken my pistol, for example, and shot himself. After all, he had seen where I left my gun. "But I don't think he would have jumped. He was scared of drowning."

"Have you any idea what Schmidt wanted to speak to the Secret Service about?" asked McCrea.

I was quite sure that Schmidt would never have jumped overboard. And if he wasn't on the ship, then there were only two other possibilities. That he had fallen overboard while drunk. Or that someone had pushed him, in which case it might be better to say as little as possible, and nothing at all about Schmidt's wife and Thornton Cole.

"I have no idea," I said.

"The CPO tells me that there was an altercation in the mess room yesterday. Involving Mr. Schmidt and Mr. Weitz, from the State Department. One of the mess attendants said they came to blows. And that you were there."

"Yes. They were having a discussion about our relations with the Soviet Union. It turned into an argument, in the way these things do sometimes. Mr. Schmidt spoke in favor of our Russian ally, and Mr. Weitz took the opposite position. But I wouldn't think it was uncommon for officials from State to hold very different views on that particular subject. Especially now that the president is going to shake Marshal Stalin's hand at the Big Three."

"I'm amazed that you say that," said McCrea. "These men were diplomats. Surely it's unusual for two diplomats to come to blows over such a thing."

"In normal circumstances I might agree with you, Captain. But things are perhaps different when you're on a warship in the middle of the Atlantic. We all have to live cheek by jowl with people whose opinions we can't get away from. People, I might add, who don't live their lives according to military discipline."

McCrea nodded. "That's true."

"Let me ask you a straight question, Professor," said Agent Rauff. "If Schmidt had encountered Mr. Weitz again. Last night, for example. Do you think it's possible they might have come to blows?"

Clearly Rauff was already thinking that John Weitz was made to order for the rap.

"Yes, it's possible. But I certainly don't think John Weitz is the type to throw a man overboard who has disagreed with him about something, if that's what you were driving at."

I found myself accompanied back to my cabin by two of the Secret Service agents.

"I take your point about a man who's frightened of drowning not wanting to throw himself overboard," Rauff told me. "So maybe someone else did."

"It crossed my mind," I admitted.

"In which case, it's possible the president is also at risk. So I'm afraid we'll need to take a look through the dead man's things. Just in case there's a note, or something."

"Help yourself." I opened the door and pointed at Schmidt's bunk. "That was his bunk. And those are his bags. But I already looked for a note. There isn't one."

With little or no space in the cabin, I waited in the doorway while the search proceeded, which gave me an opportunity to take a closer look at the two agents while they went about their business.

"You must have been nice and snug in here," observed Rauff. He was dark, with hollow, lazy eyes and a rather wolfish grin, and a face that was heavily pockmarked, as if he had once had a bad case of chicken pox.

"We're in with three other guys," explained Pawlikowski. "Up forward on the second deck, right underneath one of those sixteen-inch gun turrets. There's a power handling platform that keeps the turret supplied with shells. And we can hear it pretty much all the time, since they're always running exercises. Even at night. You wouldn't believe the noise. But in here, a man can hear himself think." He looked up from the open bag in front of him and turned to face me. "You must have talked a lot."

"When we weren't reading, or asleep."

Pawlikowski hoisted another bag onto my bunk and began to search it. He looked as if he might have boxed a bit: his jaw was as square as the signet ring on one of his thick fingers. A two-dollar traveling chess set protruded from one of his jacket pockets and he tried, unsuccessfully, to stifle a yawn as he went about his business.

"Are you in charge of the White House detail?" I asked Rauff.

"Only on board this ship. The man in charge the rest of the time is Mike Reilly. Only he's in North Africa right now, awaiting our arrival on Saturday."

"So, what's it like, guarding the president?" I asked Pawlikowski.

Pawlikowski shrugged. "Me, I'm new at this. I was guarding someone else before the boss. John McCloy at the War Department." He nodded his head at Rauff. "Ask him."

"It's not like anything I know," said Rauff. "And I've been on the job since before the war. Back in 1935 we had nine men guarding FDR. Today it's more like seventy. You see, the boss is extra vulnerable, him being in a chair and all. He just can't duck like any normal person. One time, in Erie, Pennsylvania, someone threw a rubber knife at him. We didn't know it was rubber at the time, of course. Anyway it hit the boss square on the chest. Now if that had been a real knife, it might have killed him. And none of us saw it coming. Except the boss. But he couldn't get out of the way."

"You need eyes in the back of your head in this job," added Pawlikowski. "That's for sure. Even on a United States warship. Can you believe those pricks on the *Willie D.*?"

"Yes, what was the story?" I said. "I never did hear a proper explanation of what happened there."

Pawlikowski snorted with laughter. "Goddamned idiot captain decided to take advantage of the president's little fireworks display to use the *Iowa* as the target in a training exercise. The torpedo firing was only supposed to be simulated but someone managed to shoot off a live one. King is furious about it. Apparently it's the first time in naval history that an entire ship and its crew have been placed under arrest." Pawlikowski removed two bottles of Mount Vernon rye from the bottom of Schmidt's bag and shook his head. "This fellow came well prepared, didn't he?"

"Maybe that's why he was looking for me last night," laughed Rauff. "To invite me for a drink."

Pawlikowski started to replace the dead man's things, including the two bottles, in his bag. "There's nothing in here to give us any clues," he said. I stepped out of the doorway to let him pass and saw that the chess set was in his hand. Seeing my eyes on it, he said, "Do you play?"

"Not really," I lied.

"Good. Then I stand half a chance of beating you."

"All right. But later on, okay?"

"Sure. Whenever you say."

"John Weitz," said Rauff. "How well do you know him?"

"I don't know him at all," I said.

"Well, if you don't mind me saying so, you were kind of quick to defend him, weren't you? I mean, we both heard Mr. Weitz say he was going to kill Schmidt."

"I think that was just heat of the moment, don't you?"

"Maybe so. But I'm kind of curious to know why you chose to defend him like that. Is it an Ivy League thing, do you think?"

"I suppose I did answer a bit automatically." I shrugged. "It might have been an Ivy League thing, as you call it. I'm sorry."

"He probably had nothing to do with it," said Pawlikowski. "But we do have to ask, you know? If someone did kill Mr. Schmidt, then that someone could kill again, you know?"

"On the other hand," said Agent Rauff, "maybe it was just an accident. Maybe Mr. Schmidt went up on the main deck and got hit by a freak wave, you know? It gets kind of rough up there sometimes." He shrugged. "Drunk. Up on the bows in a strong sea. At night. Who knows what might have happened?"

I nodded, anxious to be rid of them now. I was still thinking about Ted Schmidt. I stayed in my cabin and thought about him for the rest of the day. Nobody knocked on my door. Nobody told me he had been found in some forgotten corner of the ship.

XV

WEDNESDAY, NOVEMBER 17, 1943,

THE ATLANTIC OCEAN

BELOW TURRET ONE, with its triple 16-inch battery, I stood on the main deck watching the bows of the Big Stick's hull slip through the white-capped sea. I turned my back on the freshening breeze for a moment, placed a cigarette between lips rimed with ocean salt, and, behind the windbreak of my coat collar, took a light from the Dunhill.

Paying little or no attention to me, sailors worked steadily on the slowly moving deck, swabbing its sun-bleached wooden planks, setting antiaircraft batteries, stowing ropes, shifting ordnance, or just sitting on the pelican hook stoppers that secured the anchor chain, enjoying their smokes and bottles of Coca-Cola from the soda fountain in the enlisted mess. At a mile or two's distance, the destroyer escort broke the horizon, while high above me, atop the main conning tower, the air-search radar antenna kept on turning in a monotonous circle.

Somewhere a bell rang and several smaller gun turrets turned to starboard, lethally erect, like the gum-chewing, wisecracking, sex-starved sailors that manned them, reminding me that this was a place bereft of females. And one female in particular. For a moment I wondered what she was doing, and then I remembered what I had seen through the window of her living room.

Feeling the cold now, I went forward to the primary conning tower and met John Weitz coming along the corridor outside my cabin. He was wearing the same Yale bow tie under a pea jacket that looked a size too big for him and carrying a brown paper parcel under his arm. He smiled nervously, and for a moment I thought he would walk by without saying anything. Then he stopped and, moving his weight uncomfortably from one leg to the other, tried to look apologetic, only it came out shifty.

"My laundry," he said, awkwardly lifting the parcel. "I got kind of lost on my way back to my cabin."

I nodded. "You certainly did," I said. "The laundry room is at the back of the ship. I believe the people who know about these things call it the stern."

"Listen," continued Weitz, "I'm awfully sorry about what happened to Ted. I feel pretty dreadful about it. Especially in view of what I said."

"You mean about wanting to kill him?"

Weitz closed his eyes for a moment, and then nodded. "Naturally I didn't mean any of it."

"Naturally. All of us say things sometimes we don't really mean. Cruel things, stupid things, reckless things. Saying things we don't really mean is one of the things that makes conversation so interesting. Something like this happens, it just reminds us to be more careful the next time we open our big mouths. That's all."

Despite what I had said to the Secret Service, John Weitz was near the top of my list of potential murderers. If someone had pushed Ted off the boat, then John Weitz looked as good a suspect as anyone else. The bow tie certainly didn't help his case in my eyes.

Weitz stretched his lips back from his teeth. "Yes, I suppose you're right." He tried again for a little absolution.

"I feel pretty bad about it, all the same. There was no need for me to say what I said. Calling him a fellow traveler like that."

"Yes, that was unnecessary," I said. "It's a horrible phrase. And under the present circumstances you might just as well call the president a fellow traveler."

Weitz winced again. "That doesn't seem so very far-fetched to me," he said. "I'm a Republican. I didn't vote for Roosevelt."

"So you're the one."

He would not be drawn into another argument. "The worst part of it is that Captain McCrea has asked me to write to his wife." He sighed. "Since I'm the only other guy on this ship from State."

"I see. Did you know him well?"

"That's the thing. No, I didn't. We were colleagues, but never close."

There was no movie theater on the *Iowa*. There was no radio in my room. And I didn't much like the book I was reading. I decided to let out some line and play with him a little more.

"I'm not surprised. Since that Sumner Welles business in the summer, it doesn't pay to be too close to anyone in the State Department. Especially on a crowded ship like this one."

"Meaning?"

I shook my head. "You were telling me how you and Ted weren't intimate friends."

"He was a Russian affairs analyst. And I'm a linguist. As well as Russian, I speak Byelorussian and Georgian."

"That explains everything."

"Does it?"

"No. Actually, I'm puzzled. How is it that you don't actually like Russians and come to speak these languages?"

"My mother is a White Russian émigré," he explained. "She left St. Petersburg before the revolution and went to live in Berlin, where she met my father, a German-American."

"Then we have something in common. I'm German-American, too." I smiled. "We should find some leather shorts and drink some beer sometime."

Weitz smiled. He must have thought I was joking.

"One of those damned Secret Service men virtually accused me of being a German spy. The Polack."

"You must mean Pawlikowski."

"That's him. Pawlikowksi. Son of a bitch."

"So that's what Pawlikowski means. I wondered." I shook my head. "They're all kind of jumpy since the *Willie D.* incident."

"Oh, that. That's history. I was just speaking to the guy in the laundry." He pointed his thumb back over his shoulder, up the gangway, in the wrong direction. I leaned against the wall and looked over his shoulder as if the laundry really had been where he was pointing. What was he doing so far from his own cabin, up forward, and equally far from the laundry, which was near the stern?

"It seems there's a German sub operating in this area. Two of our escort destroyers picked up a German broadcast right in this area. At 0200 this morning."

"That's curious."

"Curious? It's damned alarming, that's what it is. Apparently they're going nuts about it up on the bridge."

"No, I meant in a kind of why-didn't-the-dog-bark sense."

"I don't understand."

"Never mind. Look, I'll write to Ted Schmidt's widow, if you like."

"Would you? I'd appreciate it. It's kind of hard to write to a guy's wife when you never really liked him, you know."

"Are you married?"

His eyes flickered. "No."

"Me neither. Ted wasn't a bad guy, you know."

"No, I suppose not."

I stepped into my cabin and closed the door behind me. I stood perfectly still, or as still as I could manage with the swell that was under my feet. The minute I saw dry land again I was going to kneel down and kiss it, like it was Ithaca and my middle name was Odysseus. I didn't remove my coat. I was too busy trying to decide if someone other than me had been in there. The door was not locked. Santini, the sailor who brought me a cup of coffee in the morning, might have come in and dusted some, I supposed. Or could Weitz have come in and searched it while I was up on deck? Not that he would have found anything of importance. Donovan's suitcase remained locked. And Debbie Schmidt's letter to her husband, detailing her affair with Thornton Cole, was safely in my pocket. None of this concerned me unduly. It was what Weitz had said about the German sub in the area that really interested me now.

Leaving the cabin again, I went to look for Captain McCrea and found him on the bridge, behind turret two, with his phone talker and watch officer. "I wonder if I might have a word with you, Captain. In private."

"I'm a little busy right now," he said, hardly looking at me.

"It might be important," I said.

McCrea let out a tutting, matronly sort of sigh, as if I had told him I'd thrown up on my bedroom slippers, and led me back through the control room and into the corridor beyond. "All right, Professor. What is it?"

"Forgive me, Captain, but I'm curious about this submarine."

He sighed again. It was bed for me with no supper if I wasn't careful.

"What about it?"

"It's my understanding that our two escort destroyers picked up a German broadcast in the area at around 0200 hours this morning."

McCrea stiffened perceptibly. "That's right."

"I don't mean to be impertinent," I said, enjoying my impertinence, "but it was my understanding that the *Iowa* is equipped with the very latest sonar and radar technology."

"It is," he said, inspecting his shiny fingernails. Probably he had a young sailor polish them and the ship's brass every morning at six bells.

"Which makes me wonder why it was that the *Iowa* did not pick up the same broadcast?"

McCrea glanced over his shoulder and then ushered me into the head. As he closed the door behind him, I toyed with the idea of saying that he had made a mistake, that I wasn't one of the pansies and cookie pushers employed by the State Department he'd heard about from FDR and Harry Hopkins. Instead I kept my mouth shut and waited.

"I'll be frank with you, Professor," he said. "It seems that the radio seaman on duty at the time left his post without authorization. The man has been disciplined and I consider that the matter is now closed. In view of what happened with the *Willie D. Porter*, I decided that confidence in this voyage would best be served if the incident was not mentioned to the president or the Joint Chiefs."

"I'm sure you're right, Captain," I grinned. "And you have my word that I won't mention it to anyone. Most of all to Admiral King. All the same, I'd like to satisfy myself with one or two questions I have regarding what happened."

"Such as?"

"I'd like to speak to the radio seaman who left his post."

"May I ask why?"

"I'm a specialist in German intelligence, Captain. It's my job to scratch an itch when I get one. I'm sure you understand. So if you could send the man in question along to the radio transmitter room? Don't bother to escort me there. I know the way."

McCrea could see the ace sticking out of my sleeve. And there was nothing he could do about it. The last thing he wanted was Admiral King hearing about this latest incident. His voice dropped a couple of fathoms.

"Very well. I trust that you'll keep me informed of your observations."

"Of course, sir. Be my pleasure."

McCrea nodded curtly and returned to the bridge.

I went along to the RT room and knocked at the door. Entering, I explained my mission to the radio communications officer on duty, a twenty-five-year-old lieutenant named Cubitt. Tall, swivel-eyed, with a wooden sort of expression—which is to say no expression at all—a sharp nose, pale skin, and a woman's red lips, he looked like Pinocchio's smarter brother. But only just.

The lieutenant was on the point of asking me to leave when the telephone rang. He answered it and I overheard McCrea ordering him to cooperate with "the asshole" and, when "the son of a bitch" was through, to come and tell him what I had wanted to know.

I smiled at one of the two radio seamen who were in the room with Cubitt. Each man sat in a swivel bucket seat in front of one of six operating positions and was wearing headphones and a microphone around his neck. It was like a hotel switchboard. As well as a set of bookshelves, I could see a safe where I guessed the code-books were stored, and a large battery cabinet.

"Loud, isn't it?" I said when Captain McCrea had finished speaking to the lieutenant. "The telephone, I mean. I could hear every word." I looked more closely at the phone, which was made by Western Electric. "About how many of these are there on board a ship of this size?"

"About two thousand, sir," the lieutenant replied, trying to contain a stammer that was accompanied by a fit of blinking.

I whistled quietly. "That's a lot of phones. And all this equipment." I waved my hand at more than a dozen receivers and transmitters. "What do we have here? Talk between ships, ship-to-shore, direction-finding equipment, transmitters, receivers, all on different frequencies, am I right?"

"Yes, sir."

"All right, Lieutenant, let's talk about submarines. German submarines."

"Sir, the North Atlantic is ringed with a network of radio direction-finding stations. Using Adcock direction-finding antennae—"

"Spare me the textbook tour. I'm talking about German subs in the immediate vicinity. What happens? How do all these toys function to keep us safe?"

"Operators listen in on assigned frequencies. These frequencies are listed in numbered sets called a 'series.' The U-boats tend not to change their frequencies very often. On hearing a U-boat transmission, the intercepting operator presses a foot pedal, which activates his microphone. He then shouts a coded warning to other ships in the convoy to tune in to the intercepted frequency. Bearings are then obtained, at which point the idea is to chase down the bearing and take countermeasures."

I nodded. His succinct explanation had earned a nod at least. "Those countermeasures being depth charges and other assorted fireworks. I see. And did any of this take place last night?"

Lieutenant Cubitt's swivel eyes swiveled like they were on gyroscopes.

"Um . . . up to a point."

"Explain, please."

"Sir, our destroyer escort ships picked up a transmission on a key. You know, Morse code. They started to get a bearing, but before a fix could be obtained the signal stopped. So they tried to get a handle on the U-boat's own homing beacon, but nothing doing there, either. That's not uncommon; the homing beacon diffuses quite rapidly."

"Am I correct in thinking that had this RT room been manned, you would have been able to triangulate the bearing and get a fix on the U-boat?"

"Yes, sir. Only, the radio seaman on duty at the time, Radio Seaman Norton, had left his post without orders."

"Why did he do that?"

"I don't know, sir."

"Let me put it another way. What was his explanation?"

"He claims that there was a telephone call from me, summoning him urgently to the radar room."

"Strange, don't you think, Lieutenant, that he should have been summoned away at that particular moment?"

"In point of fact, it was just before the first transmission was picked up on the key."

"Exactly what bearings were obtained for the U-boat, before the signal stopped?"

Lieutenant Cubitt showed me a map. "Here are the two escort destroyers, the *Iowa*, and the bearings, sir," he said.

"These bearings would seem to indicate that the U-boat was in the immediate vicinity of the *Iowa*."

"Yes, sir."

"In which case I can quite understand why the captain wanted this kept quiet. On the face of it, we've had a lucky escape."

Cubitt's stammer kicked in again. So did the blinking eyelids and the swiveling eyeballs.

"Take your time, Lieutenant," I told him gently.

"A U-boat would be ill-advised to attack three warships in close formation, sir. That would be to risk being destroyed. They're after much easier prey. Merchant shipping, mostly. That doesn't fight back."

"Worth the risk, I'd have thought."

"Sir?"

"A chance to kill the president and the Joint Chiefs. That is, if one of our own escort destroyers doesn't do it first."

One of the radio seamen thought that was pretty funny.

There was a knock at the door of the RT room and a small, slim, pale man with blond hair and a hunted, furtive look came in and saluted smartly. He wasn't much older than twenty, but there were some worry lines on his forehead that looked like the grille on a Chevrolet. Someone had been giving the boy a hard time.

"This is Radio Seaman Norton, sir," said Cubitt. "Norton, this is Major Mayer. From Intelligence. He has one or two questions for you."

I lit a cigarette and offered one to Norton. He shook his head. "Don't smoke," he said.

"Last night at 0200 you were the only man on duty," I said. "Is that standard practice? To have just one man on duty?"

"No, sir. Normally there would be two of us on the night watch. But just before we came on duty, Curtis went sick. Food poisoning, it looks like."

"Tell me about the telephone call you claim you received."

"The man on the phone said he was Lieutenant Cubitt, sir. Honest. I'm not making this up. Maybe one of the guys was winding me up, I don't know, but it sounded just like him. What with the stammer and—" Norton stopped speaking and glanced at the lieutenant. "Sorry, sir."

"Go on," I told him.

"Whoever it was ordered me to report immediately to the radar room. So I did."

"You left your post," said Cubitt. "Contrary to orders. But for you we might have got a fix on that sub. Instead of which, it's still out there."

Norton grimaced with the pain of his guilt and nodded.

"Radio Seaman Norton," I said. "I'd like you to take me to the radar room."

"What—*now*, sir?"

"Yes, now."

Norton glanced at Cubitt, who shrugged and then nodded.

"Follow me, please, sir," Norton said and hurried to comply with my request.

It took us the best part of six minutes to get down to the main deck, walk aft of the second uptake, and then climb several stairs to the rear conning tower, where, underneath the main battery director, the radar room was located.

"And now, if you don't mind," I said, "I'd like you to lead me back to the radio transmitter room."

Norton gave me a look.

"It's important," I added.

"Very well, sir."

Arriving back at the RT room, I glanced at my watch.

"Was the radio room empty upon your return here?"

"Yes, sir. You do believe me, don't you?"

"Yes, I believe you." I opened the door and sat down opposite the transmitting key, which wasn't much more than a piece of black Bakelite about the size of a small doorknob attached to a metal plate screwed to the operator's desk. "Which transmitter does this use?" I asked Cubitt.

The lieutenant pointed to the largest piece of equipment in the room, a black box measuring almost six feet high and two and a half feet wide, and on which a small sign was attached that said PLEASE DO NOT TOUCH.

"This," said Cubitt, "is the TBL. A low-frequency, high-frequency transmitter. It's used exclusively to provide ship-to-ship communications." He frowned. "That's odd."

"What is?"

"It's switched on."

"Is that unusual?"

"Yes. We're supposed to be observing radio silence. If we wanted to contact the destroyer escort in an emergency we'd use the TBS. That's Talk Between Ships." He touched the TBL. "It's warm, too. It must have been on all night." Cubitt looked at the other three men in the room. "Anyone know why this is switched on?"

The three radio seamen, including Norton, shook their heads.

I stared closely at the Westinghouse-made TBL. "Lieutenant, what band is this on?"

Cubitt leaned in close to check the dial, and I caught the smell of something nice on his hair. It made a pleasant change from sweat and body odor.

"Six hundred meters, sir. That's what it should be on. All our coastal defenses use the six-hundred-meter band."

"How hard would it be to retune this to another waveband?" I asked no one in particular.

"All of this stuff is a bitch to retune," said Radio Seaman Norton, who seemed to have woken up to the fact that I was on his side. "That's why we got the sign."

"Pity," I said.

"How's that?" asked Cubitt.

"Only that it makes my theory a little harder to sustain."

"And what theory is that, sir?"

I grinned and looked around for an ashtray. Norton grabbed one and held it in front of me. It wasn't so much of a theory as a strong possibility. Probably I should have kept this to myself, but I wanted to help the boy they'd accused of neglecting his duty.

"That we have a German spy aboard this ship." I shrugged off their loud guffaws. But Norton wasn't laughing. "You see, the destroyer escort didn't intercept a signal being broadcast from a U-boat but from the *Iowa* itself. A broadcast being made by the same person who lured Seaman Norton off to the radar room. It takes about twelve minutes to go there and come back here."

"Longer in the dark, sir," Norton added helpfully. "You kind of have to watch your footing on those stairs at night. Especially in a sea like last night."

"Then call it fifteen minutes. More than enough time to broadcast a short message, I'd have thought."

"But to what?" asked Cubitt. "A U-boat?"

"There's nothing to stop the krauts tuning in to that six-hundred-meter waveband, sir," offered one of the other radio seamen. "The U-boats used to do that a lot when we first got into the war, before we cottoned on to the fact that they were doing it and started to send our signals in code. They sank an awful lot of shipping that way."

"So if a German spy did send a signal from here on the six-hundred-meter waveband," I said, "the signal could have been picked up anywhere between here and the United States. By another ship. By a German U-boat. By our coastal defenses. Possibly even by another German spy tuning in to the six-hundred-meter waveband in Washington, D.C."

"Yes, sir," said the seaman. "That's about the size of it."

There was a long silence as the men in the radio room faced up to the logic of what I had established.

"A German spy, huh?" sighed Cubitt. "The captain is going to love that."

Friday, November 19—
Saturday, November 20, 1943,
the Atlantic Ocean

The atmosphere around Roosevelt grew a lot more tense—certainly among the members of his Secret Service detail—when my idea about a German spy aboard the *Iowa* became more generally known.

On one particular occasion, however, the defensive posture assumed by FDR's bodyguards seemed to go beyond what was reasonable. The morning of the nineteenth, the *Iowa* sighted the fourth escort group; it comprised the light cruiser *Brooklyn* and five destroyers, two of them American and three British. While watching the new escort group through binoculars on the flag bridge, FDR's cape blew off. A young seaman fetching the cape off the air-search antenna had climbed up to return it to the president, only to find himself wrestled to the deck by Agents Pawlikowski and Rowley, guns drawn and faces contorted with alarm.

"For Christ's sake," yelled Admiral King, "are you two guys too dumb to see that the boy was only fetching the president his cape?"

That was the moment when Captain McCrea turned on me. "This is all your fault," he hissed at me. "I blame you and your loose talk about German spies for this."

It was a nice sentiment. I went back to my cabin, filled a glass with scotch, stood in front of the mirror, and toasted myself silently. "Here's to the satisfaction of being right," I told myself.

After that I kept to my cabin, rereading the books I had brought and drinking up much of what remained of Ted Schmidt's supply of Mount Vernon. I even wrote the letter of condolence to his widow, and then rewrote it when I was sober, editing out all the stuff about how his last words had been about her. But that didn't make any difference. It still left me feeling depressed as hell. I couldn't help but let my mind's eye picture Debbie Schmidt reading it and then, in my romantic little scenario, flagellating herself over the way she had behaved toward him. A psychiatrist would probably have told me I had in fact written another letter to Diana.

The State Department would certainly have forwarded the letter to Mrs. Schmidt. But thinking to speed its journey home by writing Schmidt's home address on the envelope, I searched his bag, looking for his address book, only to discover it was missing. For a brief stupid moment, I considered reporting the theft to the captain, and then rejected the idea. McCrea would hardly have thanked me for alleging that yet another crime had been committed aboard his precious battleship.

It was just my luck that whoever had stolen Ted Schmidt's address book should have ignored Donovan's Louis Vuitton suitcase containing all those Bride intercepts.

But who had taken the address book? After all, what good was a State Department employee's address book in the middle of the Atlantic Ocean? It looked even less useful now that we were about to land in North Africa.

At 1800 hours the combined task group reached a point about twenty miles west of Cape Spartel, not far from Tangier. All the ships went to general quarters, for now we were in range of enemy attack from the air. The voyage was almost over.

The *Iowa* and its escort group were due to come through the Straits of Gibraltar at night, under a blackout. That had been the intention, but powerful Spanish searchlights had managed to mark the ship out, providing a very easy target for any German submarines that might have been in the area. I've never liked cruises very much. But we were lucky.

The ship finally anchored at Oran, where Mike Reilly, the head of the White House Secret Service detail, came aboard to supervise the president's disembarkation. With the ship's entire crew mustered on deck, FDR was lifted into a motorized whaleboat on the port side of the ship and then lowered into the water, whereupon his boat came around to the gangway and Harry Hopkins and the Secret Service climbed in alongside their beaming president.

I had expected to want to kiss dry land when once again I was standing upon it. Instead, I almost fell on it. It felt strange to be on land, and I lurched unsteadily as my legs, used to compensating for the movement of a ship's deck underneath my feet, adjusted suddenly to being on solid ground. But it's also possible I was just a little drunk.

There was hardly time to look around Algeria's second-largest city and its busy port, where infamously the British had bombed the French navy, before a U.S. Army sergeant with a Wiener schnitzel ear and a nose like a bicycle saddle asked me for my name. When I gave it to him he handed me a slip of paper showing two numbers, and directed John Weitz and me to the car that, as a part of the presidential motorcade, would transport us fifty miles to the United States Army airstrip at La Senia.

It was nine o'clock in the morning and the air was already as warm as a Louisiana bread oven. I took off my coat and fanned myself with my hat. The boat landing was thick with the oily exhausts of U.S. Military Police motorcycles as they revved loudly, impatient to escort the presidential party through the streets of the thousand-year-old city. It looked like a proper seaport with a castle and a church, and reminded me of a coastal town in the south of France. I imagined that was the way the French liked it. The only trouble was that there were three-quarters of a million Algerian Arabs living in it. The place looked friendly enough. But then, we weren't French.

John Weitz and I found our car. The American MP driver saluted and handed us some American newspapers, a letter for Weitz, and a telegram for me that made my heart leap like a cat for a moment. The driver was the eager type, keen to show us how well he could drive a car along an empty desert road. Red-haired, red-faced, and red-eyed, as if he had been drinking. He hadn't. It was the wind and the sand. Algeria seemed to have a monopoly on wind and sand. Red looked over our shoulders and told us that as soon as Mr. Schmidt showed up we could be on our way.

"He won't be joining us," I said. "I'm afraid he's dead."

"That's too bad," said Red. "What should I do with this, sir?" The MP showed me the telegram for Ted Schmidt.

"You can give that to me," I told him. "And I have a letter for his widow that I'd like you to post for me."

I climbed into the back of the car, alongside Weitz.

"Thanks again for doing that," said Weitz. "Writing that letter to Schmidt's wife. I really appreciate it."

"No problem."

I waited until the motorcade was under way before opening my own telegram. The optimist in me had hoped it might have been from Diana. But it was from Donovan, informing me that I should make contact with a Major Poole, the OSS man in Tunis, at the Café M'Rabet, that same afternoon.

Schmidt's telegram was from the State Department. It was dated the previous day, Friday, November 19, and I read it through several times. Ted Schmidt's widow had been killed in a car accident on Thursday afternoon.

The streets of Oran were lined with U.S. Army soldiers who came to attention as the motorcade swept through. The Algerians standing behind them waved hospitably at the most powerful man in the world, apparently, and his escort. I hardly noticed. The news that both of the people who had been in a position to shed more light on the murder of Thornton Cole were dead preoccupied me.

"Bad news?" asked Weitz.

"It seems that Ted's widow was involved in a traffic accident the day before yesterday."

"Oh, God. Is she okay?"

"She's dead."

"That's terrible. What a terrible tragedy." Weitz shook his head. "Did they have children?"

"No."

"That's something, I suppose."

I leaned forward to speak to Red. "There's no need to send that letter I gave you," I told him. "The one for Mr. Schmidt's widow? It seems she met with a fatal car accident."

"That's a rare coincidence," observed Red.

"Yes, it is," I said thoughtfully.

This coincidence might be less of a coincidence than it seemed. Debbie Schmidt's accident may not have been an accident at all. She, too, might have been killed to ensure silence regarding Cole's true sexual predilection. Which could have meant that I was very possibly the only person alive who knew that Thornton Cole had not been murdered in the scandalous way the Metro Police had believed.

At La Senia Airport half a dozen American C-54s were lined up to fly us the 653 miles to Tunis. And it was only then, as I saw everyone on the airstrip, that I realized just how large the U.S. delegation really was, for many more had joined it since our arrival in Oran. The Joint Chiefs, their liaison officers, military attachés, Secret Service men—all were lining up to board the planes. The delegation was set to get even bigger when yet more diplomats joined it in Tunis and Cairo.

To my surprise, I found myself assigned to the first plane, along with the president, Mike Reilly, the president's personal bodyguard, and Harry Hopkins, whom I sat next to.

Reilly was a smooth-faced, dark-haired man, with hooded eyes and the hard look of a former bootlegger. He came from Montana, but it might just as well have been Connemara, with a touch of the Spanish Armada. He wore a double-breasted, nicely cut flannel suit and was never very far from Roosevelt's right ear, into which he would sometimes whisper something important. He had dropped out of George Washington, where he had studied law, to work for the Farm Credit Administration, investigating cases of fraudulent lending agencies. Reilly transferred to the Secret Service in 1935, and in that capacity had always worked at the White House. This I learned from Harry Hopkins while we waited in the plane for Reilly and one of the other agents to carry Roosevelt bodily up the aircraft steps. Once the president was aboard, the doors were closed and the C-54 began to taxi up the runway.

"Did you know that there's a town called Oran in the state of Iowa?" Hopkins asked me as the four Pratt & Whitney engines revved louder. "That's my home state. Ever been to Sioux City, Professor? Don't go. That's my advice. There's nothing there. My father was from Bangor, Maine, and he went west to look for gold. Never found any. He became a harness maker instead. You know anything about horses?"

I shook my head again.

"Keep it that way. Unpredictable animals. Dad got his leg broke by a runaway team in Chicago. Best thing that ever happened to him. He sued the freight-line owners for ten thousand dollars and bought a harness shop with the proceeds, in a place called Grinnell, Iowa. Don't ask me why he went there. He hated the place. But we buried him there just the same."

I smiled, and for the first time I saw why FDR liked having Hopkins around; in addition to a dry sense of humor, which the president seemed to share, there was something very commonsensical about Harry Hopkins.

Three and a half hours after leaving La Senia we reached El Aounia Airfield, about twelve miles northeast of Tunis. It was less than eight months since Allied forces had inflicted a decisive defeat on Rommel in the area, and wrecked aircraft still littered the ground on both sides of the runway. It was an unnerving sight to behold from the vantage point of a plane that had yet to land safely, even if the wrecks *were* German planes.

The president's C-54 was met by his two sons, Elliott and Franklin Junior. Franklin Roosevelt Jr.'s ship, the USS *Myrant*, had suffered bomb damage at Palermo and was undergoing repairs at Gibraltar. At least that was the story they had put out. Meanwhile, Elliott Roosevelt commanded a photo-reconnaissance squadron that was stationed in the area.

We drove through the ruins of the ancient city of Carthage, destroyed by the Romans in 146 B.C., to Tunis, where, next to the Zitouna, the city's largest mosque, FDR and his immediate party were staying in the famous Casa Blanca. Formerly the seat of the Tunisian government, the Casa Blanca was currently being used by General Eisenhower as his operational headquarters. Vacating the Casa Blanca for the duration of the president's stay, Eisenhower, together with Hopkins and the rest of us, was accommodated in La Marsa, about twenty minutes outside the city center, in a beachfront French colonial house, a great wedding cake of a place with enormous and ornate blue doors.

The city of Tunis was bigger than I had imagined, and I thought it neither very Arab nor very African. Nor, for that matter, very French, either. After a short nap, I took a quick look at the famous souk and the mosque, and then sought out the Café M'Rabet, where I was to meet the OSS man in Tunis.

Ridgeway Poole had a Ph.D. in classical archaeology from Princeton and, already the author of one book on Hannibal and the Punic Wars, he had jumped at the chance of working for the OSS just a few miles from Carthage. He had been stationed in Tunis for just three months, working under vice-consular cover, but he knew the area very well, having worked on an important prewar excavation of the Antonine thermal baths. Fluent in Arabic and French, he seemed entirely at home in the cool interior of the café, sitting on a little platform, shoes off, smoking a sweet-smelling water pipe and sipping Arab tea.

"Sit down," he said. "Take off your shoes. Have some tea." Poole waved a waiter toward us and ordered without waiting for me to agree. "Pity you're not here very long," he said.

"Yes, isn't it?" I said, trying to conceal my lack of enthusiasm for the second large North African town I'd seen that day.

"Donovan's reserved you a room at Shepheard's Hotel, in Cairo, which, all being well, is where he will meet you for lunch tomorrow. Lucky you. I wouldn't mind a weekend at Shepheard's myself."

"Have you any idea how long we're going to be there?"

"Donovan said at least four or five days."

"I've an old girlfriend in Cairo. I wonder if I might be able to send her a telegram."

"No problem. I can fix that for you."

"I'd also like to get a message back to Washington."

"A girl in every port, eh?"

"Actually this is a message to the Campus. I was hoping that someone there might be able to check out the circumstances of a death." I told Poole about Ted Schmidt's disappearance and his wife's death in a traffic accident.

"All right. I'll see what I can organize. All part of the service. So, what are your plans? Care to make a night of it? I'd be happy to show you the ruins. Couple of clubs I know."

"I'd like to, really. But there's a dinner tonight at La Mersa. Harry Hopkins's son and the two Roosevelt boys and their fathers. It seems I'm invited."

"That blowhard Elliott's been talking about nothing else these past few days. 'Idiot Roosevelt' we call him. He's been fucking some British WAC while his wing has been stationed here. That's okay to do if you're a nobody like me, and I've certainly had my moments since I got here. But you can't expect to get away with that kind of thing when your pa is the president of the United States and you've got a wife and three kids back home."

"Yeah, well, the sons of famous fathers. Listen, there's one more favor you could do for me. Only I'm kind of behind with what's been happening in Germany. I was wondering if you knew of a shortwave radio receiver I might listen to. In private. Preferably through a set of headphones—just in case anyone thinks I'm a German spy."

"I can do better than that," said Poole. "That is, if you don't mind driving about ten miles into the desert."

In Ridgeway Poole's dusty-looking Peugeot 202 we drove north out of the city on the Bizerte Road, through military cemeteries and fields piled high with broken ordnance and ammunition dumps. Overhead, flights of the American Eighth Air Force rumbled through the sky like rusty dragonflies on their way to bomb targets in Italy.

Nearer Protville, which was our destination, Poole explained that he had lots of friends in the American First Antisubmarine Squadron, which was stationed in a building formerly occupied by the Luftwaffe. "They've got a German radio," he said. "And it's in perfect working order. A real beauty. The radio officer is a pal of mine from before the war. I don't imagine he'll mind you using it. Here we are."

Poole pointed out four RAF Bristol Beaufighters and about ten USAAC B-24s. Operating as part of the Northwest African Coastal Air Force, it was the task of the B-24s to seek out and destroy enemy submarines between Sicily and Naples and west of Sardinia, and to fly escort for Allied shipping convoys. We found the squadron in a jubilant mood. One of the B-24s had shot down a long-range Focke Wulf 200 and, even now, a navy patrol was out searching the Gulf of Hammamet for the Germans who had bailed out.

"A 200," I remarked, when Poole had finished making the introductions. "That's a strange plane to be operating this far south."

"You're right," said Lieutenant Spitz. "Mostly they operate as maritime patrol airplanes over Salerno, but this one must have strayed off course. Anyway, we're pretty excited about it, what with the president coming here this afternoon."

"The president's coming here? I didn't know."

"FDR's son, Elliott—his recon squad is stationed here. When you guys drove up we thought you were the advance party."

Even as Spitz was speaking, a truck carrying more than a dozen MPs hove into view, and then another.

"This looks like them now," said Poole.

"I'll see that they don't bother you," said Spitz, and he showed us into a small white building where the radio room was housed, then left us with Sergeant Miller, the radio operator.

"We have a Tornister Empfanger B," Miller said proudly. "And the ultimate German receiver, the E52b Köln. The frequency range is selected by the oblong control to the left of the indicator." Miller plugged in some headphones and switched on the E52. "But it's already tuned in to Radio Berlin, so all you gotta do is listen." He handed me the phones.

I thanked him and sat down. Glancing at my watch, I put on the headphones, thinking I might just catch the next German news broadcast. Poole and Miller went outside to watch the deployment of MPs.

During the Atlantic voyage of the *Iowa,* the *Washington Times-Herald* had published the rumor that an international conference of major importance was about to be held in Cairo, and I wanted to find out if these rumors were being reported on German radio. I was hardly surprised to discover that they were, and in detail. Not only was Radio Berlin reporting that Churchill and Roosevelt planned to meet General Chiang Kai-shek in Cairo, but also that a conference of the Big Three, "to decide on military plans of great magnitude against Germany," would take place at another location in the Middle East immediately afterward. On the face of it, I could hardly imagine that the Cairo conference could now proceed safely. And the Big Three conference now looked about as secret as a Hollywood divorce. Mike Reilly might as well have sent a press release to Hedda Hopper.

I kept on listening, hoping to learn more, turning up the volume as, for a moment, the signal from Radio Berlin seemed to fade away. Or at least, that was my intention. But somehow I managed to feed the German-speaking voice straight through the main loudspeaker. At almost full volume, it sounded like a speech at a Nuremberg party rally.

Panicking a little as I realized what I had done, I whipped off the headphones and tried to flick the switch that would cut the speaker. All I managed to do was find yet another pretuned German-language frequency. I jumped up and closed the open window quickly before trying, a second time, to switch off the radio. I was still examining the front of the Telefunken set when the door burst open and two U.S. Military Policemen stormed into the radio room and leveled their carbines at my head. I raised my hands instinctively.

"Turn it off," yelled one of the policemen, a sergeant with a face of weathered brown brick.

"I don't know how."

The policeman worked the bolt on his carbine so that it was ready to fire. "Mister, you've got five seconds to turn it off or you're a dead man."

"I'm an American intelligence officer," I yelled back at him. "It's my fucking job to monitor German radio broadcasts."

"And it's my job to protect the president's ass from German assassins," said the sergeant. "So turn off the goddamn radio."

I turned to face the radio, suddenly aware of the very real danger I was in. "Friendly fire" they called it, when your own side killed you. Which probably didn't make it feel any better. I was about to experiment with another switch on the German radio when the MP said, "And don't try to signal to anyone, either."

I shook my head and, hardly certain of what I was doing, stood back from the radio, still keeping my hands up. I don't have any excuse for this kind of cowardly behavior except to say that sometimes I get a little nervous when there's a dumb, trigger-happy Okie pointing a loaded rifle at my head. I'd seen the metal hole at the end of the wooden part. It looked like the Washington Street traffic tunnel.

"*You* try to turn it off," I yelled. "This isn't my radio and I don't know how."

The MP sergeant spat copiously onto the dirt floor, took a step forward, and fired, twice, at the radio, which ended the German broadcast, forever.

"Now why didn't I think of that?" I said. "Shoot the radio. Let me find you a German newspaper and you can shoot that, too."

"You're under arrest, mister," said the MP, and, grabbing hold of one of my wrists, he handcuffed me roughly.

"Do they train you boys to think when you're standing up?" I asked.

The two MPs frog-marched me outside the radio hut toward a group of jeeps that were now parked in the middle of the airbase. In the distance, surrounded by more MPs and oblivious of what had just happened, the president was inspecting Colonel Roosevelt's recon squadron. But as we neared the first group of jeeps, I saw Agents Rauff and Pawlikowski throw down their cigarettes and walk toward us.

"Tell these two clowns to uncuff me," I told them.

"We caught this guy using a German radio," said the MP who had fired the two shots.

"He makes it sound like I was telling Hitler the president's telephone number."

"Maybe you were at that," sneered the sergeant.

"I was monitoring a German news broadcast. On a shortwave receiver. I was not transmitting a message. As an OSS officer that's my job."

"Show us," Rauff told the MP, and, still handcuffed, I found myself marched roughly back into the radio hut.

"This is a German radio, all right," said Rauff, examining the equipment. "Be easy to send a message to Berlin on this."

"Not anymore," I said. "Not since Davy Crockett here put a couple of bullets into it. Listen, Rauff, there's a radio operator somewhere around here named Miller. And a lieutenant named Spitz. I expect they're on the other side of the airfield getting a look at the president. They'll tell you that the Germans left all this equipment behind when they pulled out. And as I was trying to explain to these two a minute ago, one of my jobs is to monitor German radio broadcasts. That is a proper function of intelligence, which is something I imagine still has relevance in the world of the Secret Service."

"Oh, yes," said Rauff. "Which is how I come to be thinking that it is a hell of coincidence that it should be you who suggested a German spy was sending radio messages from the *Iowa*."

"Hey, that's right," agreed Pawlikowski, lighting a Kool. "It *was* him, wasn't it? Might be a good way of covering up the fact he's the German spy. Like a double bluff."

Liking his theory a lot, Rauff added, "And let's not forget that fellow Schmidt. He shared a cabin on the *Iowa* with you, didn't he? Could be he found out that you were a German spy and was about to tell us. Except that you killed him first."

"Listen to me," I said. "According to the German news broadcast

I just heard, the Germans know all about this Cairo conference. And it sounds to me like they've got some pretty good ideas about the one after that. Now, if I were a Luftwaffe commander in North Italy with fifty Junkers 88 bombers at my disposal, I would already be planning to bomb Mena House in Cairo. Yes, that's right. Mena House. The Germans even know that that's where the conference is going to be held. Under the circumstances, it would seem that even an elementary level of prudence demands a change of location. So why don't you tell that to Hopkins and we'll see what he has to say about all this?"

Rauff searched me and found my automatic. "Well, well, the prof is concealing some iron here."

"That's standard issue for all OSS officers. Surely you must know that."

"I'd say you've got some explaining to do, Prof," said Rauff. "And I'm not talking about the meaning of life."

"The meaning of life? Tsk, tsk, Agent Rauff. You've been reading a book again."

XVII

SATURDAY, NOVEMBER 20—
SUNDAY, NOVEMBER 21, 1943,
TUNIS—CAIRO

IT WAS MIKE REILLY, the head of the White House Secret Service detail, who decided that I was telling the truth. But it took him a lot of frowning and several fingernails to arrive at the conclusion that if I really had been a German agent then I'd had ample opportunity to take a pop at Roosevelt while I was on the *Iowa;* or in the president's study back in Washington. I was beginning to see why the U.S. Treasury wanted to keep the service a secret. It wouldn't have done to let the Germans know that the president's safety depended on cheeseheads like Rauff and Pawlikowski.

"I'm sorry about that, Prof," Reilly told me when his two men had gone. "But they're paid to be overzealous."

"I understand. So am I."

We were meeting on Saturday evening in the magnificent dining room at La Mersa. As soon as Rauff and Pawlikowski left for La Casa Blanca, Reilly had the Joint Chiefs join us, and I told them what I had heard on Radio Berlin.

"Is this confirmed?" asked Admiral Leahy, who was FDR's personal representative on the Joint Chiefs.

"Yes, sir," said Reilly. "I took the liberty of radioing the American legation in Cairo and was told that while they had no knowledge of what the Germans were broadcasting, the president's imminent arrival in Cairo is an open secret. They would be very surprised if the Germans didn't know about it."

"So what are the British saying?" General Marshall asked. "This is supposed to be their sphere of influence."

"They're saying that eight squadrons of fighter aircraft have been concentrated in Cairo for the protection of the president and Mr. Churchill," said Reilly. "And that there are more than a hundred antiaircraft guns on the ground, to say nothing of three infantry battalions."

"And Churchill? What's his opinion?" asked Admiral King.

"Mr. Churchill is still en route from Malta aboard the HMS *Renown*," Reilly said. "He's not due in Alexandria until tomorrow."

"And Eisenhower?"

"General Eisenhower is well aware that security in Cairo has not been the best, sir."

"That's a considerable understatement," General Arnold said.

"If you remember, it was Ike who proposed the conference be moved to Malta."

"No, Mike, Malta's no good," Arnold answered. "There are no decent hotels in Malta."

This was the kind of diplomacy I could understand. Good hotels made for good foreign policy.

"There's no decent food and not much water," Leahy added.

My mind was made up. I didn't want to go to Malta any more than Arnold.

"Maybe we're making too much of this," said Arnold. "Okay, the secret's out. We were aware of that on the *Iowa*. All that's changed is that we know for sure that the krauts are in on the secret. If they were planning a surprise bomber attack, then they'd hardly tell the world on Berlin Radio that they know all about the conference. I mean, that would just put us on our guard. No, they'd say nothing at all about it."

"What do you think, Prof?" asked Reilly

"I think General Arnold makes a good point. But at the very least, we should be even more vigilant. Deploy a couple of night-fighter squadrons north of Cairo. Bring in some more armored cars. More troops."

"Makes sense," agreed Leahy. "What else?"

"Since the two principal targets are the president and Mr.

Churchill, perhaps we ought to leave the final decision to them. A short delay in the departure for Cairo might be a good idea, just to give them time for an exchange of telegrams."

"Mike? What do you think?"

"It couldn't do any harm to stay here another day," agreed Reilly. "And it might be better if the president flew at night."

"That's true," said Arnold. "There would be no need for a fighter escort at night."

"How about this?" I said. "All the Joint Chiefs to fly on Sunday morning, six A.M., as scheduled. But the president doesn't fly until late Sunday evening, which means he wouldn't arrive in Cairo until Monday morning. In other words, we fool the world into believing the president is arriving in Cairo at lunchtime on Sunday, when in fact he won't be there for another twenty hours. That way, if the Germans were to mount an attack, then the president would be safe."

"Let me get this straight," said General Marshall. "Are you proposing to use the Joint Chiefs as decoys?" The cavernous dining room at La Mersa seemed to give his words an extra resonance.

"That's right, sir, yes."

"I like it," said Reilly.

"You would," growled King.

"My suggestion has another advantage," I added.

"What do you want us to do now?" asked Arnold. "Put up some smoke for German bombers?"

"No, sir. I was thinking that when you all arrived in Cairo, who better than yourselves to evaluate the security situation on the ground for the president? If you get there and decide that the situation warrants a change of location, you could direct the president somewhere else. Alexandria, for example. After all, that's where Churchill is due to arrive tomorrow morning. And I'm told there are some excellent hotels in Alexandria."

"I don't like Alexandria," said General Marshall. "It's a hundred miles nearer to Crete, and the last I heard, there were thirty thousand German paratroopers on Crete. Not to mention, the Luft-waffe."

"Yes, sir, but the Luftwaffe on Crete is mostly all fighters, not bombers," I said. This was the advantage of being a specialist in German intelligence. I did at least know what I was talking about. "And they're short of fuel. Of course, we could always choose Khar-toum. But the logistics of moving everyone in Cairo a thousand miles to the south might be too much to contemplate."

"Damn right they are," muttered King.

"There are no good hotels in Khartoum, in any event. I'm not sure there are even any bad ones."

I found myself beginning to warm to Arnold.

"Gentlemen," said Marshall. "I think we'll just have to hope that for once British defenses are as good as they say they are."

I WENT BACK to La Mersa, had a shower, and checked my mail. There wasn't any. Poole wanted me to see four of the local sights. Two of the local sights were named Leila and Amel, the other two were called Muna and Widad. But I'd had enough excitement for one day. Besides, I could hardly have looked in my shaving mirror and told myself I was in love with Diana with some Tunisian broad's lipstick on my shirt collar. So I had a lousy dinner and went to bed early, although, as things turned out, I was not alone.

Early on the morning of Sunday, November 21, I awoke, with a couple of flea bites. It was a bad start. And when I looked in my shaving mirror I didn't feel I had gained very much from declining Ridgeway Poole's offer of hospitality. Awakening with a couple of Tunisian girls had to be better than awakening with a couple of flea bites. Things always look a lot different in the morning.

At six A.M. I accompanied the Joint Chiefs on one of the C-54s leaving the airfield of El Aounia. Ahead of us lay a five-and-a-half-hour flight to Cairo. I was pleased to discover that none of the president's Secret Service agents were on our plane. The last thing I wanted was to endure the further scrutiny of Agents Rauff and Paw-likowski.

APPROACHING CAIRO from the west, we enjoyed a spectacular view of the Pyramids before putting down at an RAF airfield in the western desert. Minutes later, the RAF were driving the Joint Chiefs and their liaison officers to the Mena House hotel, near the Pyramids at Giza. I was driven to Shepheard's Hotel in the center of Cairo.

"*Imshi,*" yelled my driver, or, as often, "Fuck off," as he steered the little Austin Seven between ancient-looking Thorneycroft buses, nervous flocks of sheep, cruelly laden asses, and other impatient drivers.

"From America, sir?" asked the driver. He was a blue-eyed, hatchet-faced man, as lean as a garden hose, and by the look of things, just as wet. Sweat rolled out of his wavy short black hair, down his thin white neck, and underneath his khaki shirt collar, to join a large damp patch between his shoulder blades.

"Yes. And you?"

"Manchester, England, sir. I used to dream of being somewhere hot, sir. And then I came here. Did you ever see such a bloody place, sir? Bloody chaos, that's what it is."

"Seen much action?"

"None since I've been here. At least not from the bloody Germans. You'll see the antiaircraft searchlights at night, but there's little chance of any bombers coming this far south. Not since the summer. By the way, sir, the name is Coogan, sir. Corporal Frank Coogan, and I'll be your regular driver while you're here in Cairo."

"Nice to meet you, Frank."

At last Coogan turned down a side street and I caught my first sight of the famous Shepheard's Hotel, an ungainly building at whose large front terrace dozens of British and American officers were seated. Coogan pulled up, waved away an Arab guide wearing a bright red tarboosh, and, collecting my cases off the luggage rack, led the way inside.

Battling my way through officers of all ranks and races, prosperous Levantine businessmen, and several dubious-looking women, I presented myself at the reception desk and glanced around at the Moorish-style hall with its vast pillars, thick and lotus-shaped, and the grand staircase that swept upward, flanked by two tall caryatids of ebony. It was like being on the set of a film by Cecil B. DeMille.

There were three messages for me: one from Donovan, suggesting that we meet for a drink in the hotel's long bar at three o'clock; an invitation for dinner the following evening from my old friend, the Princess Elena Pontiatowska, at her house in Garden City; and a letter from Diana.

I dismissed Coogan, and, thinking I might try one last time to lose Donovan's case, I let the hotel manager organize its delivery to my hotel room. But fifteen minutes later, I was safely ensconced in my suite with all my bags, including Donovan's. Throwing open the shutters and the windows, I stepped onto the balcony and surveyed the rooftops and the street below. There was no doubt about it: Donovan had done me proud; I could not have chosen better myself.

I put off reading Diana's letter for as long as I could, the way you do when you're afraid of finding out a truth. I even smoked a cigarette while I contemplated it from a safe distance. Then I read it. Several times. And there was one passage in her letter to which I paid particular attention.

You mentioned the injustice of my walking out on you as I did and avoiding you these last few days. I'm afraid I was and still am very angry with you, Willard. The person with whom I had spent that evening, when I was supposed to be at the movies, was an old friend of mine, Barbara Charisse. I don't think you've ever met her, but she has heard of you and, recently, she had been in London. She's also an old friend of Lord Victor Rothschild, whom I believe you do know. It seemed she had been at a party you were also at, and had heard from some pansy that while you were in London you were sleeping with someone called Rosamond Lehmann. Normally I wouldn't mind, but it irritated me the way you quizzed me about whether I'd seen that film or not, and your unspoken assumption that you had occupied the moral high ground by not asking me about it further. And I thought to myself, Fuck you, mister. Fuck you, for making me feel like I was the betrayer. So, since you ask, I find that I haven't really changed that opinion. I also find that I'm not likely to change it, either.

Fuck you, Willard.

I folded Diana's letter up and put it in my breast pocket, right next to the aching hole where my heart had been. A few minutes before three o'clock, I went down to the lobby. Outside on the hotel terrace someone was playing a piano, badly, while the lobby was buzzing loudly with conversations, mostly in English. I went into the Long Bar, forbidden to ladies, and glanced around as a group of slightly drunk British officers clapped their hands loudly for service and shouted Arabic words they mistakenly believed would summon a waiter.

Almost immediately I saw Donovan, seated with his back to a pillar and sweating profusely in a white tropical suit that was maybe a size too small for his retired football player's physique.

Approaching the silver-haired figure, I reviewed all of the prejudices I was likely to encounter with this sixty-year-old Hoover Republican, this millionaire lawyer, Irish Catholic decorated war hero. To my certain knowledge, the general had been away from Washington since July, first visiting his son—a lieutenant who was aide to Admiral Hall in Algiers—then in Sicily, then in Quebec, and, for the most part of October and November, in Cairo, trying to foment an anti-Nazi revolution in Hungary and the Balkans.

"Good afternoon, General." Even as I shook Donovan's strong hand and sat down, he was catching the waiter's eye, stubbing out his cigarette, and checking the time on the gold pocket watch he'd pulled from his vest.

"I like a man who is punctual," said Donovan. "God knows that isn't easy in this country. How was the voyage? And how is the president?"

I told him about the *Willie D.* incident and mentioned my suspicions regarding the disappearance of Ted Schmidt and the death of his wife back in Washington. "It's my opinion that there was a German spy aboard the *Iowa*," I said. "And that having killed Schmidt, he radioed someone in the States to do the same to Mrs. Schmidt. I think someone wanted to make sure that an investigation into Cole's murder was closed down as quickly as possible, and the Welles scandal made this easy. But my guess is that Cole was on to a German spy. Possibly the same German spy who was aboard the *Iowa*."

"That makes some sense."

"I asked Ridgeway Poole if he could radio the Campus and find out some more about Mrs. Schmidt's accident."

Donovan winced a little, and I remembered, too late, that he hated Washington's nickname for the OSS HQ almost as much as he hated his own. The "Wild Bill" cognomen by which he was known referred to the Donovan who had won the Distinguished Service Cross in 1918. These days, the general preferred to project a more sober, responsible image than that of the dauntless battlefield hero. Personally, I didn't like heroes very much. Especially when they were officers. And whenever I looked at Donovan I wondered how many men in his platoon his heroism had got killed.

"I wouldn't worry too much about German spies if I were you," Donovan said as the waiter came over at last. He ordered a lemonade.

My jaw dropped. For a moment, I was too astonished at what the general had just said to order anything at all. I asked for a beer and, when the waiter had gone, an explanation.

"We're at war with the Germans," I said. "German intelligence is my special field. I'm supposed to be a liaison officer between you and the president. Why would I *not* worry about German spies? Especially if one were so close to the president and might already have murdered someone."

"Because I happen to know that the last thing the Germans want right now is to kill President Roosevelt," answered Donovan. "For the last few weeks, my man in Ankara has been conducting talks with Franz von Papen, the German ambassador. Von Papen is in touch with leading figures in the German government and army, with a view to negotiating a separate peace between the Germans and the Western allies."

"Does the president know about this?"

"Of course he does. Goddamn it, do you think I'd do something like this on my own initiative? FDR has an election in 1944, and I'd say the last thing he wants is to send a million American boys into battle unless he absolutely has to."

"But what about 'unconditional surrender'?"

Donovan shrugged. "A bargaining ploy, designed to bring Hitler to his senses."

"And the Russians, what about them?"

"Our intelligence indicates that they've been making their own peace feelers, in Stockholm."

I shook my head in disbelief. "Then what's the point of all this Big Three stuff?"

Donovan straightened his right leg, painfully. "Peace negotiations take time," he said. "Especially when they're being conducted in secret. Besides, they could easily fail. What's more, we think Sextant One and Sextant Two will help to keep the Germans focused."

Sextant One was the official code name of the Cairo Conference, and I presumed Sextant Two referred to the Big Three Conference itself.

"I guess that explains a lot," I said, although, in truth, I wasn't quite sure exactly what it did explain. It explained why the Joint Chiefs had not been more worried about coming to Cairo. But none of that explained why the Schmidts were dead. Unless, of course, Ted Schmidt really had thrown himself over the side of the boat, and Debbie Schmidt had met a genuine traffic accident.

At the same time, I was aware that even if a separate peace negotiation was being pursued with one German faction, there were probably others, the fanatics, still intent on winning the war, whatever the cost.

One thing was clear, at any rate. Kim Philby had been right to be concerned about American peace moves in Ankara. Donovan had just given me the high-level confirmation Philby had been looking for; that the Americans really were of a mind to sell out the Russians. But who could I tell? A Russian at Sextant Two, wherever that might be? That hardly seemed practical. And what of the Russians themselves? Was it really possible, as Donovan had said, that they, too, were trying to negotiate a separate peace, in Stockholm?

Our drinks arrived. Caring nothing for Donovan's opinion now, I wished I had asked for a double brandy. I lit a cigarette. I could taste the ash even as I smoked it. I felt certain that there was something important Donovan was not telling me. But what? Was it possible that the secret peace negotiations with the Germans were making better progress than Donovan had seemed to indicate?

"So where is Sextant Two to be held?" Seeing Donovan hesitate, I added, "Or am I going to have to tune in to Radio Berlin to find out?"

"I heard about what happened." Donovan smiled. "One of those Secret Service idiots contacted me on the radio to check out your bona fides. A guy named Pawlikowski. As if one of my own people could be a spy."

I smiled politely and wondered what Donovan would say if he ever did find out that I had once spied for the NKVD.

"In which case you won't mind telling me where Sextant Two is going to take place."

"The Joint Chiefs are kind of itchy about the security situation here in Cairo," said Donovan. "Everybody knows that the president and Churchill are here. But it wouldn't do to let too many people in on the location for our next port of call."

"But you're going to tell *me*, aren't you?"

Donovan nodded. "It's Teheran."

I pulled a face. "You can't be serious."

"Of course I am. Why? What do you mean?"

"Whose brilliant idea was that? Iran is the most pro-German country in the Middle East, that's why. The Joint Chiefs must be crazy."

"I had no idea that your knowledge of German affairs extended so far east," observed Donovan.

"Look, sir, the British invaded Iran, or Persia as it was then, to protect Russia's back door. They deposed the last shah and put his son in his place. The Iranians hate the British and they hate the Russians. I don't think there's a worse place for a Big Three Conference." I laughed with disbelief. "Teheran is full of Nazi agents."

Donovan shrugged. "I believe it was Stalin's choice."

"There's a Pan-Iranian neo-Nazi movement, and according to our sources, two of the ex-shah's brothers were in Germany a while ago to enlist Hitler's help in getting rid of the British."

Donovan continued to look unperturbed. "There are thirty thousand American troops in Iran and God knows how many British and Russians. I'd say that's more than enough to ensure the security of the Big Three."

"And there are three-quarters of a million Iranians who live in Teheran. Very few of whom are on our side in this war. As for the tribesmen in the north of the country, they're pro-Nazi to a man. If that's Stalin's idea of security, then he must have a screw loose."

"From what I've heard, he has. But don't worry about it. All the leading pro-German leaders have been arrested."

"I hope you're right, sir."

"Teheran's as safe as we are here in Shepheard's," insisted Donovan.

I glanced around the Long Bar. It was true, there were so many British and American uniforms I could easily have believed I was back in London.

"So relax," said Donovan. "See the sights. Enjoy yourself. They won't need you very much at Mena House. Not unless you speak Chinese. Besides. I've got a job for you while you're here. You brought that suitcase from General Strong?"

My heart sank. "Yes, sir. It's up in my room."

"Good. Tomorrow, we'll take a ride over to Rustum Buildings. That's where the Special Operations executive and British intelligence have their headquarters in Cairo. The sooner we get started on that Bride material, the better."

XVIII
MONDAY, NOVEMBER 22, 1943,
VINNICA, UKRAINE

THE GERMAN ARMY had hoped that withdrawing forces to the western bank of the Dnieper would provide them a respite from the Red Army, but Stalin had other ideas. Almost as soon as the withdrawal was completed, with enormous loss of life, he ordered his soldiers to attack. By November 6, Hoth's Fourth Panzerarmee had been forced out of Kiev, and likewise the armor the Germans had concentrated on Zhitomir, a town eighty kilometers west of Kiev, with the aim of counterattacking the Russians. There was little appetite among German soldiers for a new offensive. The courage of the Wehrmacht was undiminished, but it was only those few reinforcements who had arrived from Germany and who lacked all experience of the Russian winter who were fanatical enough to believe that the war in Russia could still be won. Deeply demoralized, poorly equipped, and inadequately supplied, Germany's soldiers—far from home in a vast and inhospitable country, and lacking any overall battle plan—faced an army that grew stronger every day, and for whom retreat now seemed impossible.

Of all the problems that faced Manstein's army, none was greater than Hitler's vacillating leadership: just as the counterattack on Kiev seemed ready, Hitler ordered his armor south, to defend the Crimea, leaving Zhitomir to be captured by the Red Army. It was recaptured by the 58th Panzerkorps on November 17, but long before then the headquarters for Operation Long Jump had been shifted seventy-five kilometers south, to the village of Strizhavka.

Strizhavka was the location of Hitler's Wehrwolf Headquarters and close to Vinnica, a largish Ukrainian city with several cathedrals, a smaller, more parochial version of Kiev. The city was the center of a Jew Free Zone ruled by the Reichkommisariat of the Ukraine, the Vinnica Oblast. Some 200,000 Jews from Vinnica and the surrounding areas—some from as far afield as Bessarabia and northern Bukovina—had been murdered at the local brickworks and in the Pyatnychany Forest. Every one of Strizhavka's 227 Jews had been "evacuated" before Hitler's Ukrainian headquarters were built. Death, it was said by the local people, was a way of life in the Vinnica Oblast.

Even as Schellenberg was driven from the airport to the country house on the edge of the Yuzhny Bug River, where the Special Section from Friedenthal was now stationed, an execution was taking place at a gibbet erected in the main square of Vinnica. Six terrorists from the Trostyarets partisans were seated on the edge of a truck with nooses around their necks—seated because they had been brutally tortured and none of them was able to stand.

"Do you want to watch, Herr General?" asked the SS sergeant driving the surprisingly luxurious Horch that had fetched Schellenberg from the airport.

"Good God, no."

"It's just that these are the bastards who murdered and mutilated some friends of mine. All we found were their heads. Four of them. They were in a box with the word 'shit' painted on it."

Schellenberg sighed. "Get out and watch, if you must," he sighed impatiently.

The sergeant left Schellenberg alone in the back of the car. He lit a cigarette and placed his pistol on the seat beside him, just in case the partisans had any friends ready to attempt a revenge attack or carry out a robbery—the trunk of the car contained a box of gold he had brought from Berlin to reward the Kashgai tribesmen of northern Iran. He even removed his cap to make his rank seem less obvious, and, turning up the collar of his leather coat, tried to stay warm. Outside the car it wasn't much above freezing, and a layer of damp fog hung over the town, chilling his bones and penetrating the distributor on the execution truck, which appeared to be having some trouble starting. Schellenberg laughed scornfully and shook his head. Serves the army right for trying to make a show of it, he thought; better to shoot a man and have done with it instead of this performance. Himmler would not have agreed with him, of course. Himmler was all for making an example of the victims of Reich justice. Which probably explained why, after Hitler, he was the most hated man in Europe. Not that he seemed to be aware of the loathing with which he was held, even in Germany. And it seemed ludicrous to Schellenberg that the Reichsführer-SS should ever have believed that the Allies might choose to make a peace with him instead of Hitler. There was no doubt in Schellenberg's mind; at some stage, Himmler would have to be removed.

It wasn't just the Reichsführer's lack of realism, or his continuing, debilitating loyalty to the Führer that offended Schellenberg's scheming mind. It was also his apparent prevarication. Even now, Himmler wanted Operation Long Jump to proceed only as far as parachuting the team into Iran; the final order—if it ever came—to assassinate the Big Three was to be withheld until the last possible minute, much to Schellenberg's irritation. He and Himmler had argued about it the day before his departure.

"It's a pretty tall order," he had told Himmler. "To parachute those men into Iran and then risk not being able to communicate with them."

"Nevertheless, those are my orders, Schellenberg. Unless they receive a clear order from me or the Führer, the mission is not to proceed. Is that quite clear?"

"It's a good plan," insisted Schellenberg. "Perhaps the best plan we've got right now."

"That is your opinion. The Führer and I have agreed to your plan thus far only in order to keep our options open."

"It's asking a lot of men to risk their lives going all that way for an operation that might be scratched at the last moment."

"They are SS. They have taken an oath of obedience to me and the Führer. They'll damn well do what they're told, Schellenberg, and so will you." Himmler's eyes narrowed suspiciously. "I hope these are SS men, Schellenberg. Waffen-SS, Fourteenth Grenadiers, Galicia Division, I think you told me. I should take a very dim view of you and this whole operation if I ever found out that your team was composed largely of Zeppelin volunteers. Ukrainian nationalist cadres. I trust you haven't forgotten my speech at Posen."

"No, Herr Reichsführer, I haven't forgotten that."

That was another reason Himmler had to be removed, thought Schellenberg. All those Ukrainian volunteers who, with the exception of a dozen German officers and NCOs, now made up the Special Section. If Operation Long Jump was a success, then no one would ever mention that the team had not actually been German—no one in Germany, at least. But if the operation failed and Himmler ever found out about their true origins, things might go quite badly for him.

Lina Heydrich had agreed. She hated Himmler even more than her late husband had, especially now that Schellenberg had told her how he suspected the Reichsführer of having been complicit in her husband's murder. Lina's hatred had hardly been softened by the death of her ten-year-old son, Klaus, on October 24, in a traffic accident in Prague: the boy had been knocked down and killed by a truck in the gateway of the Jungfern-Breschau Castle in Prague.

"I wrote to Himmler asking that Klaus be excused from the Hitler Youth," she had said. "Remember how I told you I would? But Himmler replied that Klaus's father wouldn't have wanted him to leave the youth movement and that the boy should remain. That's why he was in Prague. He was there on an outing with the Hitler Youth. I never liked it there, when Reinhard was running the Bohemian Protectorate. And Klaus should never have gone back. Not after what happened to his father in Prague. And, by the way, I made some inquiries about Reinhard's death. You were right, Walter. It was Himmler's own doctor who treated Reinhard after the attack in Prague. The drugs he used were experimental and should not have been administered."

Lina so hated Himmler, she even suggested how Schellenberg might bring about his downfall.

"You must go to Rastenburg and see Martin Bormann," she said. "You must tell him all about Himmler's secret peace negotiations with the Russians. Bormann will know how to bring the evidence before the Führer."

The comforts provided by Lina seemed a long way off now, waiting in the cold for an execution to proceed in the main square in Vinnica. At last the truck's engine turned over, and as it moved slowly away, the six partisans were left dangling from their gibbet. Schellenberg looked away in disgust and turned his mind to Operation Long Jump. If it succeeded and the Big Three were killed, surely the Allies would make peace. But until then he would have to try to facilitate Himmler's removal, as Lina had urged. From Vinnica, he planned to fly to Rastenburg and, on the pretext of informing Hitler that Long Jump was ready to go ahead, would talk to Bormann.

But Lina had offered yet more advice on how he might protect himself against Himmler. "Those Ukrainians in your Special Section," she had said. "The Zeppelin volunteers. You'd better make sure that if any of them do make it back from Persia, they don't ever talk."

She was right, of course, and the more he thought about her advice, the more he realized that whatever the outcome in Teheran, all of the Ukrainians would have to disappear. It wasn't just Himmler who might decide to make an issue out of Long Jump. It might also be the Allies. He now thought it best if there were as few witnesses as possible who could ever speak about what he had set into motion.

His driver finally returned to the car. "Thank you, sir," he said, starting the engine. "That meant a lot, to see those Popovs get their just deserts. Those heads that were in the box, you see. My friends. The Popovs cut off their noses, ears, and lips before they beheaded them. Can you imagine it?"

"I'd rather not, if you don't mind, Sergeant," said Schellenberg. "Now get a fucking move on, I'm freezing."

They drove north along a road busy with German traffic: SMG

machine-gun carriers, Pumas, 37-millimeter PAKs, some SdKfz troop carriers, and, most reassuring to Schellenberg, who was not used to being quite so close to the front line, a column of Panzer tanks—with its excellent armor and 88-millimeter gun, the Panzer was probably the best tank in the world. If only there had been more of them. If only they didn't guzzle so damn much fuel. If only . . .

The country house where Schellenberg's Special Section was headquartered looked like something from a Chekhov play. Surrounded with cherry trees and a forest of shrubs, the whitewashed wooden house was large and beautiful, with a big verandah and a high mansard roof. As soon as Schellenberg was inside warming himself in front of the fire and enjoying a cup of hot coffee, von Holten-Pflug asked Captain Oster to assemble his men in the ballroom, and under a magnificent chandelier, Schellenberg stood in the center of the room to address more than a hundred men. Among his audience were eighty Ukrainians, twelve German officers and NCOs, and twenty-four Luftwaffe officers who were to fly a combination of transport and bombing missions. It was the first time that any of them, with the exception of von Holten-Pflug and Captain Oster, had been informed of their target.

"Gentlemen," said Schellenberg. "During the last few weeks you have all been training for Operation Franz. I have to tell you now that Operation Franz has been canceled."

At this there was a loud groan from the men. Schellenberg raised his voice to make himself heard.

"The fact is, the name Operation Franz has always been a fiction. The task that lies before you is to be called Operation Long Jump. You will still be parachuted into Iran. But your target was never a railway. You have a different target, a target of great historical importance. Perhaps the most important in history. If you succeed, you will win the war. And that is no exaggeration, believe me.

"This morning, via our communications center in Ankara, I received a message from Wannsee. It came from one of our agents in Cairo. The message confirmed that today, November twenty-second, 1943, at nine thirty-five A.M. local time, Franklin Roosevelt landed in

Egypt. He will remain there in talks with Winston Churchill and General Chiang Kai-shek for the rest of the week. It's our reliable information that Roosevelt and Churchill will fly from Cairo to Teheran for talks with Stalin, on Sunday, November twenty-eighth. Tuesday, the thirtieth, is the British prime minister's birthday, and we expect the British to throw a party at their embassy in Teheran. We intend to make sure that Germany sends a gift to Mr. Churchill. A gift that Marshal Stalin and President Roosevelt will be able to share in."

At this there was a roar of approval.

"Ninety-five men will leave here today in two Junkers 290s. After a refueling stop in the Crimea, you will continue on to Iran. Half of you will be dropped near Qazvin and referred to hereafter as North Team. The other half will be dropped near the holy city of Qom and be known as South Team. Both teams will be met by friendly Kashgai tribesmen with trucks. They will transport you to your respective targets. All of you will be wearing Russian uniforms. South Team will travel to the Russian army airfield at Gale Morghe, west of Teheran, where, at seven o'clock that evening, you will destroy the enemy's radar installation. Once that is accomplished, you will radio North Team, who will be staying at a safe house in Teheran's bazaar, about half a mile from the British embassy. North Team will confirm to the Luftwaffe that the targets are in the embassy, and a squadron of four Focke Wulf 200s, each equipped with two radio-controlled missiles, will attack. These planes will be vulnerable to fighter attack, so you can see the importance of knocking out the radar. The enemy will put fighters up, but in the dark it will be like looking for a needle in a haystack. As soon as the missiles are launched and the embassy destroyed, North Team will mount an attack and kill any survivors. After the operation is completed, each team will be collected by the Iranian underground movement and transported across the border into neutral Turkey.

"I know many of you will welcome a chance to kill Stalin. But by killing Roosevelt and Churchill as well, you will be hastening the end of this war. Of course, it won't be nearly as easy as I've made it sound. Perhaps some of you are wondering what kind of a fool would dream up a plan like this. Well, I am that fool. And since many of you are Ukrainians, I'd like to remind you of an old Ukrainian saying: *Ne takiy ya durniy yak ty mudriy!* Schellenberg waited a moment for the laughter among the Zeppelin volunteers to subside a little before supplying the German translation: I am not as stupid as you are smart.

"And because you are smart," he added, "you will succeed. Because you are smart you will win. Because you are smart you will come home."

IT WAS TIME to go to the airport to see off the two parachute teams. Schellenberg rode with von Holten-Pflug, who was to command South Team, Captain Oster, who was to command North Team, and an ex-NKVD officer named Vladimir Shkvarzev, who was in charge of the Ukrainians. Shkvarzev was a heavyset, brutal-looking man with an eye patch and several gold teeth—most of his own had been kicked out by the Gestapo. But Schellenberg had no doubt of Shkvarzev's loyalty. The Ukrainian knew what would happen to him if ever he was recaptured by the NKVD. The Gestapo were clever like that. They had forced Shkvarzev to torture some of his own comrades to death with a butcher's knife before releasing other prisoners so that they could return to their own lines and denounce Shkvarzev to the NKVD as a Gestapo stooge. And when at the airport Schellenberg wished him and his Ukrainians good luck, the ex-NKVD man had smiled wryly.

"There's another Ukrainian saying you might like to bear in mind, Herr General," said Shkvarzev. "*Shchastya vysyt na tonenki nytci a bida na hrusim motuzi.* Roughly translated it means, Good luck hangs by a thread, but bad luck on a thick rope." Shkvarzev made a gesture as if clutching a noose around his neck and, still smiling horribly, got out of the car and walked toward one of the planes.

"Don't worry about Shkvarzev," said Oster. "He's a damn good fighter. They all are. They were at Cherkassy, and before that Belgorod. I saw them in action. They're a fearsome lot, I can tell you."

"I heard it was pretty bad there," said Schellenberg, offering the two senior German officers some cigarettes from the extra packets of Hannovers he had brought from Berlin.

Oster laughed bitterly. "Everywhere's bad," he said. "But I fear the worst is yet to come. Not least the cold. It was ten below last night. One of our NCOs, a fellow posted from Italy a month or two ago, was complaining about it, and we all just laughed. By January the glass will be down to fifty below."

"It will be warmer in Persia," said Schellenberg. "I can promise you that."

"Let's hope it's not too hot," said Oster.

"I wish we knew that this wasn't all a dreadful waste of time," objected von Holten-Pflug, lighting his cigarette. "I don't fancy just sitting around with these Kashgai tribesmen and waiting for some fucking wrestler to work up the courage to betray us to the Allies. I hope there's plenty of gold in that box you brought with you from Berlin. Because I'm sure we're going to need it."

"Himmler was quite immovable on the subject, I'm afraid," said Schellenberg. "You're to wait until you hear the old shah's name on the Radio Berlin news broadcast before proceeding with the plan."

SCHELLENBERG WATCHED the planes take off and wondered if he would ever see von Holten-Pflug or Oster again. He rather doubted it. Even if they did manage to kill the Big Three, the Allies would probably turn Persia upside down to find the assassins. Not so bad if the British or the Americans caught them, perhaps. Not so good if they were picked up by the Russians.

That afternoon, on the plane to Rastenburg, Schellenberg slept better than he had in a long time. There were no air-raid warnings at ten thousand feet, just the dull, monotonous, almost hypnotic roar of the Focke Wulf Condor's four BMW engines. Hoffmann's attempt to kill him on the flight to Stockholm was already a distant memory, and, wearing a thick lambskin flying suit and swaddled in blankets against the altitude and the November cold, Schellenberg did not awake until they were on the ground at Weischnuren Airfield, after a three-hour, 500-mile flight. He felt refreshed and hungry, and for once he was actually looking forward to his meeting with the Führer. Not to mention his dinner.

But first there was his meeting with Martin Bormann.

Schellenberg met with the Führer's personal secretary at his home, less than one hundred yards from his master's. It was always hard to explain just where Bormann had sprung from. For eight years, between 1933 and 1941, he had been nearly invisible, the right-hand man to Rudolf Hess; and it was only after the Deputy Führer's abortive peace mission to England in May 1941 that Bormann had started to make himself indispensable to Hitler—first as head of the Reich Chancellery, then as head of the Party Secretariat, and finally as Hitler's personal secretary. And yet he and Hitler were old friends, the two men having known each other since 1926. Hitler had been a witness at Bormann's wedding and was also godfather to Bormann's eldest son.

Schellenberg knew Bormann better on paper, from the details in a secret file in his safe, than in the flesh. Not that anyone apart from the Führer knew Bormann particularly well. But Schellenberg had all the dirt anyone would ever need on Bormann: about the murder he had committed in 1923, for example. Bormann had killed his own former elementary school teacher, a man named Walther Kadow. Then a member of the Freikorps (which was the Nazi SA's predecessor in all but name), Bormann had been arrested for the murder and sentenced to just one year in jail, having successfully maintained the defense that Kadow had betrayed the Nazi martyr Leo Schlageter to the French occupation authorities in the Ruhr. Only Schellenberg and Bormann himself knew the truth of the matter: that Bormann and Kadow had been rivals for the affections of a woman, and a Jewish woman at that.

Schellenberg also knew of how rich Bormann had made himself. How he had embezzled millions of reichmarks through his control of the Adolf Hitler Endowment Fund, which received money from German industry. Schellenberg even possessed evidence that Bormann had been skimming money from the royalties of Germany's number-one bestselling book, *Mein Kampf*. And not even Göring had managed to pillage as many art objects from occupied countries in Eastern Europe as Martin Bormann. In his office safe in Berlin, Schellenberg had a letter from Rahn & Bodmer, Zurich's oldest private bank, setting out the full extent of Bormann's private holdings. It was one of the young intelligence chief's many insurance policies, and on the few occasions he had been obliged to deal with Bormann, it always gave him a pleasant feeling to know that he was relatively invulnerable to Bormann's malign influence. Schellenberg even thought he had an explanation for just how it was that Bormann had managed to make himself so indispensable to the Führer. He believed Bormann was what Bormann's own father had been, and for that matter what the bull-necked bullying Bormann most resembled in the world: a regimental sergeant-major. Hitler had only ever been a corporal, and it was only natural that the sort of man with whom he should have felt completely comfortable was, temperamentally at least, a senior NCO.

"So," said Bormann, ushering them both to some armchairs in front of a blazing log fire. Unlike his master, Bormann liked a fire. "How are things on the front?"

"They could be better," said Schellenberg with what he thought was enormous understatement.

"Russians," sneered Bormann. "They're like rats. There's no end to them. How can you defeat an enemy that doesn't seem to give a fuck for his own casualties? They just keep coming, don't they? The subhuman bastards. Like the Mongol hordes. They're the complete opposite of the Jews. The Jews just roll over and die. But the Slavs are something else. Walter, there are times when I think that if you want to understand the true nature of this world you have to go to the Russian front. It's a struggle for life, like something out of Darwin, I think. Not that your boss would agree with me there." Bormann snorted with contempt. "According to Himmler, this earth is a sort of fairy land. All that crap about the spirit world and Buddhism. Jesus, Walter, how do you stand it?"

"As a matter of fact, Martin, that's what I wanted to talk to you about. Himmler."

"You know what Himmler's problem is? He thinks too much. That and the fact that he's an auto-whatsit. Self-taught."

"Autodidact."

"Precisely. He's read too much shit, that's all. Educated himself with no real discipline. He's the living proof that education is a danger. I always say that every educated person is a future enemy. Me, I do my very utmost to live and act in such a manner that the Führer should remain satisfied with me. Whether I shall always be able to do so is an open question. But the key to success is to take your lead from the Führer. To read what he reads."

"How is the Führer?"

"He's always quite cheerful, you know. No, really. Cheerful with all his heart. Especially when he's having tea with his friends, or when he's playing with his dogs. You would think he hadn't a care in the world. Hard to believe, I know, but it's true. Anyway, you'll see for yourself."

All the time he talked to Schellenberg, Bormann clutched a small black leather notebook in which he took down all the Führer's queries and orders. During meals with Hitler, Bormann was forever making notes that might result in a reprimand for one officer, or a death sentence for another. Not for nothing was Bormann regarded as the most powerful man in Germany, after Hitler. At the same time, the impression gained by Schellenberg on the few occasions he had been in the Führer's presence was that, not infrequently, Bormann passed on as firm orders from Hitler what were really no more than casual dinner-table remarks, or, worse, Bormann's own ideas to serve his personal ends.

"But," said Bormann, "you wanted to talk about Himmler, didn't you?" He opened the notebook to reveal a pencil that was as short and stubby as one of his own fingers: the impression of a butcher about to write down some housewife's order might have made Schellenberg smile, but for the obvious dangers of what he was doing.

"Doubtless you are aware that it was me who took the Führer's letters to Stockholm," said Schellenberg.

Bormann nodded.

"And that I have a good idea of the nature of those letters."

Bormann kept on nodding.

"What you are not aware of, perhaps, is that Reichsführer Himmler has also been feeling out the Allies with a view to a change of regime. Following a meeting in the Reich Ministry of the Interior on August twenty-sixth, an old acquaintance of Himmler's, Carl Langbehn, traveled to Berne to meet Allen Dulles, the station head for the American intelligence service."

At last, Bormann started writing.

"Is he the chiropractor?"

"No, that's someone else. Langbehn is a lawyer. I believe his daughter goes to school with Himmler's daughter, on the Wal-chensee. You may even remember that it was Langbehn who of-fered to defend the Communist leader, Ernst Torgler, at the time of the Reichstag fire. Now, I have a spy within the Free French in Switzerland, and thanks to him I am in possession of a copy of a telegram, sent to London, which says, and I quote, 'Himmler's lawyer confirms the hopelessness of Germany's military and politi-cal situation and has arrived to put out peace feelers.' Naturally I will furnish you with all the documentary evidence you need of the Reichsführer's treason in this matter. I did not act until I was quite sure, you understand. You do not go up against Himmler unless you are sure."

"You were just as sure when you went up against von Ribbentrop, weren't you?" objected Bormann. "And yet you failed to deliver his head."

"True. But it was Himmler who saved *his* neck. The only person who could save Himmler's neck is Hitler."

"Go on."

"For a while now it has seemed to me that by offering to seize power from the Führer and negotiate a peace, and in exchange for their approval to continue the war against the Soviet Union,

Himmler entertains hopes of some kind of personal absolution from Britain and America."

"And what is you own opinion of that, Walter? Of continuing the war against the Soviet Union?"

"Insanity. At all costs we must make peace with the Russians. My own intelligence sources suggest that Stalin's greatest fear is that the Red Army will mutiny because of the appalling casualties it is sustaining. If we make peace with the Russians before next spring, we will have nothing to fear from the Americans and the British. They would hardly risk a second front if Russia was out of the war. Himmler's plan shows no understanding of the political practicalities here, Martin. Next year is an election year for Roosevelt. It would be suicide for him to go into an election while the United States Army incurs the kind of casualties now being received by the Red Army in order to liberate Europe. Which they would if Russia were no longer a belligerent."

Martin Bormann was still nodding, but he had stopped writing, and his reaction had hardly been what Schellenberg had expected. Bormann hated Himmler, and Schellenberg thought he ought to have looked more obviously pleased at having just been handed the means of destroying his greatest enemy.

No less puzzling to Schellenberg was Hitler's own demeanor. Over dinner that night, Hitler seemed in such excellent spirits that Schellenberg was quite certain Bormann could not have told him of Himmler's treachery. When Hitler left the table for coffee in his drawing room, Bormann slipped outside for a quick cigarette, and Schellenberg followed.

"Have you told him?"

"Yes," said Bormann. "I told him."

"Are you sure?"

"What kind of idiot do you take me for? Of course I'm sure."

"Then I don't understand. I still remember the Führer's reaction six months ago, in Vinnica, when there was news about a heavy bombing raid in Nuremberg. How angry he was with Göring."

Bormann laughed. "Yes, I remember that, too. It was great to watch, wasn't it? The fat bastard's been a bad smell around here ever since."

"Then why isn't Hitler angry? After twenty years of friendship. Why isn't he furious with Himmler?"

Bormann shrugged.

"Unless." Schellenberg threw his own cigarette onto the ground and stamped on it. "Of course. It's the only possible explanation. The Führer has had a reply to at least one of those letters I took to Stockholm. That's why Himmler's not been arrested, isn't it? Because the Führer doesn't want anything to interfere with these secret peace negotiations. And because Himmler now has the perfect alibi for what he's been doing all these months."

Bormann looked up at the freezing black Prussian sky and blew out a long column of cigarette smoke, as if trying to blot out the moon. For a moment or two he said nothing; then, stamping his feet against the cold, he nodded.

"You're a clever man, Walter. But there are things happening right now to which you can't be a party. Secret things. On the diplomatic front. Himmler and von Ribbentrop are in the driver's seat, for the moment at least. The time will inevitably come when Himmler will have to be dealt with. The Führer recognizes this. And until then, your loyalty has been noted." Bormann took a last drag from his cigarette and flicked the butt into the trees. "Besides, you're our ace in the hole, remember? You and your team of cutthroats and murderers in Iran. If Hitler's peace comes to nothing, then we are going to have need of your Operation Long Jump after all."

"I see," said Schellenberg gloomily.

"I wouldn't worry too much if I were you. If things work out, then the war will be over by Christmas. And if they don't, well, that's good, too. I mean, the Big Three, they'll hardly be expecting us to try to kill them while we're still exchanging love letters, will they?"

"No, I suppose not."

They returned to the dinner table, where they found themselves jeered by Hitler.

"Here they are. The nicotine addicts. You know something?" Hitler had turned to address his other dinner guests, who included some of the General Staff and a couple of stenographers. "As soon as peace has returned I'm going to abolish the soldier's tobacco ration. We can make better use of our foreign currency than squandering it on imports of poison. I've a good mind even to make smoking illegal in our public buildings. So many men I've known have died of excessive use of tobacco. My father, first of all. Eckhart. Troost. It will be your turn, Schellenberg, if you don't quit soon. Not many people know it, but I'm ashamed to confess that I used to be a smoker myself. This was thirty years ago, mind you, when I was living in Vienna. I was living on milk, dry bread, and forty cigarettes a day. Can you imagine it? Forty. Well, one day I worked out that I was spending as much as thirty kreuzers a day on cigarettes, but that for just five kreuzers I could have some butter on my bread." Hitler chuckled at the memory of his time in Vienna. "Well, as soon as I had worked that out I threw my cigarettes into the Danube, and ever since that day I've never smoked again."

Schellenberg stifled a yawn and glanced, surreptitiously, at his watch as Hitler complained about all the cigarette burns he had found in the carpets and on the furniture at the Reich Chancellery. Then Hitler abruptly returned to the subject of peace, or at least his own peculiar idea of peace.

"As I see it, we have two goals from any peace that is negotiated," he said. "First, we must avoid paying any war indemnities. Each country must bear its own costs. With this achieved, we can reduce our war debt from two trillion to a hundred billion marks a year. I want us to become the only belligerent of this war to be free of our war debts within ten years and to be in a position to concentrate on rebuilding our armed forces. Because, as a general principle, a peace that lasts more than twenty-five years is harmful to a nation. Peoples, like individuals, sometimes need regenerating by a little bloodletting.

"My second goal is that we leave our successors some problems to solve. If we don't, then they'll have nothing to do but sleep. That's why we must resist disarmament at all costs. So we can leave our successors with the means to solve their problems. But peace can only result from a natural order. And the condition of this order is that there is a hierarchy among nations. Any peace that doesn't recognize this is doomed to failure.

"Of course, it's Jewry that always destroys this order. It's the Jew who would try to destroy these negotiations, but for the fact that we still hold the fate of about three million Jews in our hands. Roosevelt, who is in thrall to the Jewish vote in America, will not risk the destruction of what remains of Europe's Jewry. I tell you this: that race of criminals will be wiped out in Europe if the Allies don't make a peace. They know it. And I know it. If for some reason they don't make peace, it will only be because they recognize the truth of what I have always said: that the discovery of the Jewish virus is one of the greatest revelations that has taken place in the twentieth century. Yes, the world will only regain its strength and health by eliminating the Jew.

"If the Allies fail to make a peace with us, it will only be because they want to see the removal of this Jewish problem as much as we do. It's going to be interesting to see what happens."

XIX

MONDAY, NOVEMBER 22, 1943, CAIRO

THE HEADQUARTERS OF SOE—British military intelligence in Cairo—was a supposedly secret location on Rostom Street that every taxi driver and street waif in the city seemed to know as "the secret building," much to the irritation of those who worked there. Since the battle of El Alamein, it was the most important military building in Cairo. It was located in a large and ornate block of apartments right next door to the American legation and only a stone's throw from "Grey Pillars," the British GHQ.

The area outside Rostom Buildings was surrounded with checkpoints, barbed wire, and dozens of soldiers. Inside, the atmosphere was of a busy department store. It was here that the whole military effort in the Balkans was centered, most of it related to finding safe places in Yugoslavia where the new missions could be deployed.

"Of course, they're much more formal than we are," explained General Donovan as he and I climbed the stairs behind a young lieutenant escorting us up to the office of the SOE's operational commander. "But I think you'll see some similarities. They're mostly academics, like us. Not much regular army. Soldiers are probably not bright enough for this outfit. The fellow who's nominally in charge, General Stawell, is a good example. He has absolutely no experience of running a secret organization. Which is why we're seeing his number two, Lieutenant Colonel Powell. Quite an interesting fellow, this Powell. I think you'll like him. Like you, he was a professor before the war. Of Greek, at the University of Sydney."

"Is he Australian?"

"Good grief, no, he's as English as they come. Stiff as a board to look at. But as bright as new paint."

Carrying Donovan's Louis Vuitton suitcase, I trudged up the steps like a man ascending the scaffold.

Colonel Enoch Powell was a curious man. Donovan and I looked like a pair of wilted wedding cakes in our white tropical suits, but unlike his two junior officers and in spite of the heat, Powell was wearing full service dress: a collar and tie, long trousers (not the more usual shorts), tunic, and Sam Browne belts.

Donovan made the introduction. Noting my quizzical look, Powell felt moved to explain his appearance in a reedy, almost musical voice that spoke sentences as precise as any Mozart concerto.

"It's a curious fact but I find that wearing full uniform keeps up my morale," Powell explained. "By temperament I am something of a Spartan, you see." Powell lit a pipe and sat down. "I wonder. Are you the Willard Mayer who wrote *On Being Empirical*?"

I said I was.

"In many ways it was an admirable philosophical work," said Powell. "But quite wrong. I hope you will forgive me when I opine that your chapter on ethics was the most puerile piece of logic I have ever read. Sheer casuistry."

"Well, Colonel," I said, "I am an Athenian by temperament. I doubt that an Athenian and a Spartan are ever destined to agree about very much."

"We shall see," smiled Powell.

"Besides, I was describing not a first-order ethical theory but a theory of the logic of moral language."

"Indeed so. I merely question your implied assertion that our moral and aesthetic convictions are separable from our empirical beliefs."

Donovan cleared his throat, loudly, to stifle this philosophical debate before it could really get started. "Gentlemen," he said. "If I could ask you to postpone this debate until another time."

"By all means," agreed Powell. "I should like a chance to debate you, Professor Mayer. Perhaps over dinner this evening? At the Gezira Sporting Club?"

"I'm sorry but I have a prior engagement. Another time, perhaps."

"Then let us talk of your Russian transcripts," said Powell. "I'm sorry to tell you this, but cipherenes are in rather short supply right now."

"Cipherenes?" frowned Donovan.

"Cipherists, if you prefer," allowed the colonel. "Or even decipherers. Either way, there is a huge backlog of important signals traffic that has yet to be decoded. German signals to which, perforce, a greater degree of urgency is due. They are our own bread and butter, General Donovan. Since we are not yet at war with the Soviet Union, but with Germany, I am afraid that I cannot grant your material a greater priority, with or without the facility of a Russian codebook. You do understand, gentlemen?"

I breathed a sigh of relief. "Yes, I understand, perfectly," I told him.

"However," added Colonel Powell, "our Major Deakin believes he may have a somewhat unorthodox solution to your problem." Powell turned to one of the two majors who were sitting on either side of him. "Major Deakin taught history at Wadham College, Oxford," added Powell, as if this were some kind of recommendation for the British major's solution to our problem.

Major Deakin was a tall, genial man with a dark, clipped mustache and a wry sort of smile. He was handsome in a second-feature movie kind of way, except that he had a long scar over one eye. He picked a piece of tobacco off his tongue and smiled awkwardly. "Colonel Guy Tamplin would have been your best bet, of course," he said. "He used to be a banker in the Baltic states and was an expert on all things Russian. Unfortunately, he's dead. Heart attack, most probably, although there's a lot of guff going around that he was poisoned. Poison was one of Guy's pigeons, you see, for using on Jerry. It's Guy's death that has left us a bit shorthanded on the deciphering side of things."

Donovan nodded patiently, hoping that Major Deakin was about to come to the point.

"Anyway, it's my understanding that you, Professor Mayer, speak fluent German."

"That's right."

"All right. A couple of days ago one of your B-24s with an anti-submarine squadron in Tunis shot down a long-range Focke Wulf over the Gulf of Hammamet and picked up a German officer swimming for it. It's possibly because he's so keen not to be taken for a spy that he's actually being quite talkative. Claims that until recently he was working for the Wehrmacht War Crimes Bureau in the Ukraine."

At the mention of war crimes in the Ukraine I felt my ears prick up.

"I'm not sure how that helps us," Donovan said stiffly.

"Before joining the Jerry War Crimes Bureau, this chap claims he was a signals and intelligence officer, on the Russian front. The chances are he might know something about Russian codes. Well, put simply, my idea is this. That we persuade the Jerry to see if he can shed some light on deciphering Bride."

"What makes you think he'll cooperate?" I said.

"As I said, he's rather keen that we don't think he's a spy. In case we should decide to shoot him. He's not a bad egg, really. Quite intelligent. Major Max Reichleitner's his name. I reckon we could play him a little. What do you Americans call it? 'Good cop, bad cop'?"

"I'll scare him with talk of a firing squad, and you, Professor Mayer, you can do your friendly American thing. Sweeten him up with some cigarettes and chocolate and a promise to square me. I'm sure you know the kind of thing I'm talking about."

"Where is he now?" asked Donovan.

"Sitting in a cell at number ten," said Deakin.

"Can we meet him right away?" asked Donovan. "There's not much time before we have to hand these onetime pads over to the Russians."

"Yes, by all means," said Powell. "See to it, will you, Deakin?"

Donovan stood up and I followed, collecting the suitcase as I left the office.

Outside Rostom Buildings, Donovan said good-bye to me, much to my relief.

"You go on with Major Deakin," he said. "I've got to get over to Mena House for a lunch with the president. Good luck with your kraut. And keep me posted on your progress. Remember, we've got just five days before we have to hand these onetime pads back to the Russians."

He handed me a large manila envelope containing the Russian codebooks. I smiled thinly. But Donovan was too busy looking around for his staff car to notice the probably insubordinate look on my face. Deakin noticed it. Deakin noticed a lot. I decided it was probably why he was in intelligence.

"Don't worry, sir," Deakin told Donovan. "I'm sure the professor and I can crack it."

Once Donovan was gone, Deakin lit a pipe and indicated the way. "It's not far," he said. "Just around the corner. Bit of luck really. That we didn't have time to send him back to BTE last night."

"What and where is BTE?"

"British Troops in Egypt. They're in the Citadel. Bit of a hike getting over there, so those prisoners we do get for interrogation, we try to do it here. In Garden City. I say, can I help you with that case?"

"No, it's okay. This is my cross. I can manage it."

"You know, it's a lucky break, you turning up like this, Professor."

"Please. Willard."

"My name's Bill," said Deakin. "Pleased to meet you. Actually, we've met before. In London about six weeks ago. I was with SIS before joining SOE. I'm a pal of Norman Pearson's. Professor Pearson? The Yale professor of English? The two of you breezed into Broadway Buildings one afternoon while I was there and had a chat with old Kim Philby."

"Yes, of course. I'm sorry I didn't remember. I met a lot of people on that trip. It's kind of hard to remember all of them."

"Anyway, as I was saying, it's a lucky break, your turning up like this. I mean, your having been the president's special representative and whatnot."

"That was then, Bill. Now I'm just a liaison officer between Donovan and FDR. That's code, you know. For house parlormaid, assistant stage manager, and general dogsbody. I'm not even required to go to the Cairo Conference."

"Yes, but you know the president. That's the point. And you are an accredited member of his delegation."

"That's what it says on my security pass."

"So I was rather hoping you might help me at the same time as I help you. It's rather strange, really. You and Major Reichleitner both having been investigating the Katyn Forest massacre for your respective governments."

"Yes, that is a coincidence."

"Of course, that's what he was doing *then*. He has told us quite a bit about himself, but he won't tell us what he was doing so close to Tunis. Where he was going. What his mission was. At first he said he was on his way to Ankara when his plane hit some bad weather and they were forced to go south around it. Which was when he was shot down by your people. Only we checked the weather reports and conditions over the south of Europe and the northern Med were perfect that day. When I said as much to our Jerry—and this is where you come in—he went all stiff on me and told me that it was imperative he speak to someone close to President Roosevelt. That he had an important message he could put only into the hands of a member of FDR's delegation. So, as you can see, it's a stroke of luck your needing our help, too. Once he's got whatever it is off his chest, I don't see how he can fail to cooperate with your request."

"Yes, that is good news."

"If you don't mind, we'll play it the way I outlined it. I'll wear the black hat and you can wear the white one."

"I get the picture."

Grey Pillars was a stately-looking building at number 10 Tolombat Street. British officers called it "number ten," but it was better known to almost everyone in Cairo as Grey Pillars, because of the four Corinthian colonnades that enclosed its stately foyer. It was the headquarters of the British army in Egypt, although GHQ had long outgrown the original building and now occupied the whole street. Beyond the glass doors, things were less like a military HQ and more like a large Swiss bank, probably because Assicurazoni, a Trieste-based insurance company, had occupied the building before the British.

Deakin led the way down a plain marble staircase to a makeshift series of prison cells guarded by a bespectacled lance corporal reading a copy of *Saucy Snips*. Seeing Major Deakin, he hurriedly put the obscene magazine aside, snatched off his glasses, and sprang to attention. Despite a large fan on the ceiling, the heat in the cell area was almost unbearable.

"How's our Jerry?" asked Deakin.

"Claims he's sick, sir. Wants the khazi all the time." The khazi was a British army term for lavatory.

"I do hope you're taking him, Corporal. He is an officer, you know. And, as it happens, a damned important one right now."

"Yes, sir. Don't you worry about the Jerry, sir. I'll look after him."

The lance corporal unlocked the cell door and there, on an iron bedstead, wearing just his underwear, lay the German officer, apparently none the worse for his recent experiences. Major Reichleitner was a heavy-looking man with shortish fair hair and cornflower blue eyes. His jaw was as big as a sandbag, and his lips were thick and pink. He reminded me a little of Hermann Göring, the Reich's air marshal. Seeing his two visitors, he swung his legs off the bed. They were pink, with lots of short fair hair, like a breeding pair of Chester White pigs. They didn't smell much better, either. He nodded affably.

I leaned against the cell wall and listened patiently as Deakin spoke in a coarse, chewed-up, oatmeal kind of German. Probably it was the kind of German that the Holy Roman Emperor Charles V employed when he was famously speaking to his horse. Only the

French spoke worse German than the English. I lit a cigarette and waited for a verb.

"This is Major Willard Mayer. He is with American intelligence, the OSS. He has come to Cairo as part of President Roosevelt's delegation. But previously, when I met him in London, he was the president's special representative."

For all of the lance corporal's assurances about Major Reichleitner's welfare, I thought he could have used a shave and a comb. There was a burn mark on one cheek, presumably received when his plane had been shot down, and it lent a belligerent cast to his face.

"What can I do for you, Major?" I asked.

"I've no wish to insult you, Major Mayer," Reichleitner said. "But have you any way of proving you are what he says you are?"

I showed Reichleitner the Cairo Security pass given to me at the airport. "Do you speak English?"

"A little." Reichleitner handed me back my pass.

"So what's this all about?"

"Have you heard of the massacre in the Katyn Forest?" asked Reichleitner.

"Of course."

"I was part of the investigating team," said Reichleitner.

"Then I've read your report," I said, and explained the circumstances of my having been appointed FDR's special representative. "Is that what you wanted to talk about?"

"No. Not directly, anyway. Something similar. Murder on a massive scale."

"Well, that's worth some cigarettes, at least." I handed Reichleitner a cigarette and lit it, before tossing him the packet. Then we all sat down at the table as if we were about to play a game of cards.

"Your report was very thorough," I told him. "For what it's worth, I agreed with your conclusion. That, on this particular occasion at least, the German army was not responsible for mass murder."

"Your German is very good," said the major.

"It should be. My mother always read fairy tales to me in German."

"Is she German?"

"Kind of. You know, the American kind." I threaded my cigarette between my lips and sat back in my chair, my hands in the pockets of my trousers. "You were telling me a story yourself, weren't you?"

"The suitcase you found when I was picked up," Reichleitner said to Deakin. "Where is it, please?"

Deakin stood up and shouted through the judas hole. Reichleitner said nothing until the case was open on the table in front of him. It was empty.

"The clothes that were in here are at the laundry," explained Deakin.

"Yes, I know. The lance corporal explained. Have you a penknife, please?"

This time Deakin hesitated.

Reichleitner shook his head and smiled. "It's all right, Major. I give you my word as a German officer, I will not attack you with it."

"We've already cut the lining," said Deakin, handing over the knife he used on his pipe.

"It has a double lining," said Reichleitner. He unfolded the blade of Deakin's knife and levered it inside the leather lid. "Also, you have to know where to make the cut. This has been stitched in with very fine wire. With one cut you might remove the first lining, but not the leather underneath."

It took Reichleitner several minutes to remove the leather lid of his suitcase. He laid it flat upon the desk and then opened it like a large portfolio to reveal a waterproof package containing several neat piles of paper and a small roll of photographs.

"Very clever," said Deakin.

"No," said Reichleitner. "You were careless, that's all." He made one pile of pages out of the several smaller ones and then pushed the documents toward me.

"After Katyn Forest," he said, "this was the next investigation. Hardly as thorough, but just as shocking. It relates to a place in Russia called Beketovka. The largest POW camp for German soldiers captured at Stalingrad. The conditions described here apply in all Soviet POW camps for German soldiers. Except those for the SS. For the SS things are much worse. Please, read this file. Several men died to bring the information and these pictures out of Russia. I shan't detain you with the precise figures now, gentlemen. Instead I shall merely give you one statistic. Of the two hundred fifty thousand Germans captured after the surrender at Stalingrad, about ninety percent are now dead from cold, starvation, neglect, or just plain murder. My mission here is simple. To deliver this file to your president with a question. If the deaths of twenty-seven thousand Poles are not enough for you to break off your alliance with the Soviet Union, then what about the deaths of two hundred and twenty-five thousand German prisoners?"

"Only four thousand Poles have been found. So far."

"There were other graves," said Reichleitner. "In truth we had no time to examine all of them. However, our intelligence sources in Russia have indicated that this may be only the tip of the iceberg. Of the million or more Poles deported in 1941, perhaps as many as a third of them are now dead, with many more unaccounted for in Soviet labor camps."

"Bloody hell," breathed Deakin. "You can't be serious."

"Had I not seen what I have seen, then I might have agreed with you, Major Deakin," said Reichleitner. "Look, this is what I know. But what I suspect is much, much worse. There are terrible things that Germany has done, too. Dreadful things to the Jews in Eastern Europe. But we are your enemy. The Russians are your friends. Your allies. And if you do and say nothing of these things, you will be as bad as them, for you will be condoning what they have done."

Deakin looked at me. "These figures he mentions, they're impossible, surely."

"I don't think so."

"But three hundred thousand Poles?"

"Men, women, and children," said Reichleitner.

"It doesn't bear thinking of."

Reichleitner threw himself down on his bed. "Well, I have done my duty. Everything is explained in the file. I can tell you no more than you may read for yourselves."

Deakin tapped the bowl of his pipe against the heel of his hand and, catching my eye, nodded.

"Actually there's quite a lot you haven't told us, Major," he said. "Such as who sent you on this mission. And who you were to make contact with when you arrived in Cairo. You don't expect us to believe that you were going to make your way to the American legation and hand this dossier over to the president in person. To whom were you intending to entrust this?"

"Good point," I said.

"You might not be a spy yourself, but the person with whom you were supposed to make contact in Cairo almost certainly is."

"I was sent on this mission by Reichsführer Himmler," admitted Reichleitner. "My orders were to check in to Shepheard's Hotel posing as a Polish officer. I speak Polish and English. Better English than I led you to believe earlier. And I'm afraid that I was planning to do exactly as you have said. To deliver the dossier to the American legation. Number twenty-four Nabatat Street, is it not? Here in Garden City."

Deakin threw a nod in my direction. "That's the address, all right."

"I was to place the dossier in a parcel marked for the attention of your American minister, Alexander Kirk. I had a covering letter addressed to Mr. Kirk, but I lost that when I bailed out, along with my Polish passport."

"Very convenient," said Deakin.

Reichleitner shrugged. "Can you think of a better way to deliver a dossier into the hands of the Americans than simply to hand it in at the legation? I *know* Cairo. I was often here before the war. So why would I need a contact? A contact might only have compromised me and my mission."

"A contact might help you to escape from Egypt," I suggested.

"That's not so difficult, with money."

"He had several hundred pounds on him when we picked him up," explained Deakin.

"A ninety-minute train ride to Alexandria," said Reichleitner. "Then a ship to Jaffa, in Palestine. From there it's easy enough to get passage for Syria and then Turkey. I'm often in Ankara."

"Nevertheless, I still think we will have to try you as a spy," said Deakin.

"What?" Reichleitner leaped off the bed and pointed to the papers he had brought from Germany. "I came to bring you information, not to spy. What kind of spy brings papers and film with him? Answer me that?"

"These might be forgeries," said Deakin. "Disinformation designed to drive a wedge between us and our Russian allies. We call that sabotage. Same as blowing up an oil refinery or an officers' mess."

"Sabotage? But that's idiotic."

Deakin collected the Beketovka papers from the table. "These will have to be evaluated. And if they don't check out, you could find yourself facing a firing squad."

The German closed his eyes and groaned. "But this is preposterous," he said.

"Major Deakin," I said, laying my hand on the German's papers. "I wonder if I might be allowed to speak to Major Reichleitner alone for a moment? It's all right. I don't think the major will try to injure me, will you, Major?"

Reichleitner sighed and shook his head.

"All right," said Deakin. "If you're sure." He knocked on the door to summon the lance corporal, and a moment or two later Reichleitner and I were alone.

"I don't feel so good," groaned the German.

I helped myself from the packet of cigarettes I had given the major. "I can get you some medicine when I leave this cell. If you like."

Major Reichleitner nodded. "It's my stomach."

"I'm told everyone gets stomach trouble in this country. So far

I've been lucky, I guess. But then, I don't think you can catch much from cigarettes and scotch."

"I don't know if it's something I ate, or just nerves. Do you think that English idiot really means to charge me with spying?"

"I could probably persuade him not to. If you were to do me a small favor."

It was a dangerous game I had decided to play. But now that I had met Major Reichleitner, it was a game I felt I could control. I had decided that it would be better to know what the Bride material actually contained, rather than live in fear of mere possibility. If Reichleitner did manage to decode Bride, I'd decide what to do about it afterward. Controlling a man like Reichleitner, a prisoner of war, with the aid of some cigarettes and scotch and some medicine would be a lot easier than trying to deal with an Allied officer in SOE.

"What kind of a favor?" The German frowned suspiciously. "Look here, if it's information you want, there's nothing I can tell you. I can't imagine that the work of the German War Crimes Bureau is of much interest to American intelligence."

"It's my understanding from Deakin that before joining the bureau you were with a signals and communications battalion on the eastern front."

"That's right. At Heinrich East, the Regimental HQ in Smolensk. My God, it seems like a hundred years ago."

"Why did they assign you to the Katyn Forest massacre?"

"For one thing, my languages. I speak Russian and Polish. My mother is Russo-Polish. And for another, before joining the army I was a detective in Vienna. Cryptology was always a sort of hobby of mine."

"A few minutes ago—what you were saying about the Russians. I didn't want to say anything in front of Deakin, but there are an awful lot of Americans who believe that Russia is the enemy, not Germany. My boss in the OSS, for one. He hates the Bolsheviks. So much so that he's set up a secret section inside the OSS to spy on the Russians. A while ago, we started monitoring Soviet signals traffic in Washington. It seems that our ally is spying on us."

The German shrugged. "When you lie down with dogs, you catch fleas."

"More recently, we came into possession of some Soviet onetime cipher pads. For political reasons, it's been decided we'll have to return these ciphers to the Russians. But until this happens my boss wants to make whatever use of them he can, in the hope that we might get some idea as to the identity of these Russian spies in Washington. The British aren't being of much help. Frankly, they're overstretched just trying to deal with German signals. But it occurred to me that you might have had some experience with Russian ciphers because of your work on the eastern front. And given your obvious and quite understandable desire to drive a wedge between us and the Russians, I wondered if you would like to cast your eye over what we've got."

"And in return you'll persuade Deakin to drop these spying charges, is that it?"

"Yes."

Reichleitner took one of the cigarettes, lit it, and regarded me through narrowed eyes. "Did you bring the material with you?" he asked.

"It's outside."

He glanced away for a moment and then shrugged. "It might give me something to do. You have no idea how boring it is in here. And a few creature comforts would be appreciated. Some more of these American cigarettes. Some decent food. Some beer. Some wine, perhaps."

"All right."

"And don't forget that medicine. My stomach feels like there's a family of rats living in it."

"I'll see what I can do."

"But I'll tell you frankly, five days is hardly enough time. Even with the codebooks. Cryptologically speaking, the Popovs take no chances. With most systems, operators bow to convenience, because total encipherment takes time. But the Popovs are slavish in their adherence to security. And my guess is that you're not going to end up with a plaintext message. The chances are there will be lots of code names for this and that."

Reichleitner watched me for a moment and I watched him back. Then he broke off, helping himself to another cigarette.

"Luckily for you, I know what a lot of these code names mean. For example, when you see the word 'luggage' it means 'mail.' 'Novator' means 'secret agent'; and 'Sparta' means 'Russia.' That kind of thing. So we'll see what we can see."

I stood up and offered him my hand. "Sounds like we've got a deal," I said.

From Grey Pillars, I caught a taxi and ordered the driver to take me back to Shepheard's Hotel. As I sat back in the car, a large cockroach crawled across its carpeted dashboard, and I realized the driver was either wholly oblivious of or utterly indifferent to the presence of the shiny brown insect. One way or the other, it seemed to say something about the country I was in.

AT SEVEN, bathed and dressed for dinner, I came downstairs to find Corporal Coogan waiting with the car in front of the hotel, as arranged. We drove south, back to Garden City, which, despite being where the British GHQ and SOE were located, was still Cairo's most fashionable residential district.

A series of narrow winding streets that changed names at vague intervals, and in which it was not uncommon to end up exactly where you started, led to lush gardens in which sat several large white stucco mansions. Some of these might be better described as palaces. Which seemed only appropriate, given that I had been invited to dinner by a princess.

I got there early, since I guessed we had a lot of catching up to do.

Elena's house, next to what had been the Italian legation on Harass Street, was made of white stone in the French Mediterranean style, with large continuous balconies and French windows that would have let in a sphinx or two. A wrought-iron fence enclosed a large garden dominated by a stately mango tree, which was surrounded by purple and red bougainvillea.

The gate was opened by a tall man wearing a white djellaba and a red tarboosh. He directed me along a path to some steps leading up to a large terrace, where one or two figures were already milling about with cocktails in their hands. It was a hot, sticky night. The air felt like warm molasses. All the lights in the house were burning, and flaming torches illuminated the path that led from the gate to the front door, where another man in a long white robe held a tray with drinks.

I picked up a glass heavy with champagne and mounted the steps. At the top was Elena, dripping with diamonds and wearing a low-cut lilac cocktail dress, her long blond hair piled ornately on top of her head. Seeing her again, it was a little hard to believe that, for a while at least, I had shared a bed with this woman.

"Willy darling."

"You remembered my middle name."

"How lovely to see you again. The cleverest man I ever knew."

She made it sound as if I had been dead for a while. And perhaps I had, at that. Certainly since leaving Washington I had felt like a man without a future. For the first time in more than a week, I found myself smiling. I made a heroic effort to keep my eyes on her face.

"And you. Look at you. Still the most beautiful woman in the room."

She hit me playfully on the shoulder with a little fan. "Now, you know there aren't any other women here. Not yet."

"Actually I hadn't really noticed. Not since the moment I laid eyes on you."

That was what Elena did. She dazzled. Men, of course. I had never met a woman who liked her. And I couldn't blame them. Elena would have been stiff competition for Delilah. In any room, she was always the brightest thing in it. Naturally, this meant there were always lots of moths around her flame. I could see a few of them floating around on the terrace. Most of the moths were wearing British uniforms.

Elena hugged me fondly and, taking me by the elbow, hustled me off the terrace into an enormous drawing room furnished in an opulent Second Empire style with just a touch of the Levantine. The Count of Monte Cristo would not have looked at all out of place there with the daughter of Ali Pasha, the Princess Haydée. There were hookahs and tapestries and Orientalist oils by Frederick Goodall showing harem scenes and slave markets, all of which gave the room a sort of stage-sexiness. We sat down on a long French Empire sofa.

"I want you all to myself before the other guests arrive. So you can tell me what you have been doing. God, it's wonderful to see you again, darling. Now, look here, I know about the book. I even tried to read it, only I couldn't understand a word. You're not married?"

"No, I'm not married."

She seemed to read something between the frown lines appearing on my forehead.

"Marriage isn't for you, Willy darling. Not with your looks and your sex drive. Take it from someone who's been there. Freddy was a wonderful husband in many ways, but he was exactly like you in that department. Couldn't keep his hands off other men's wives, which is why he's no longer alive."

Five years had passed since I had last seen Elena. After I left Berlin, she had gone to Cairo as the wife of a very rich Egyptian banker, a Copt named Rashdi, who managed to get himself shot dead during a card game in 1941. Bill Deakin had told me that Elena was famous in Cairo, and this was hardly surprising. He also told me she was keen to do her bit for the Allies, and regularly threw soirées for SOE officers whenever they were on leave. Elena's parties were almost as famous as she was.

"So, what are you doing in Cairo? I assume you've something to do with the conference."

I told Elena I was in the OSS, serving as the president's liaison officer, and that I'd been Roosevelt's special representative in London investigating the Katyn Forest massacre. Elena's father, Prince Peter Pontiatowski, and his family had been forced to leave their family estates in the Kresy—the Polish northeast—during the Russo-Polish war in 1920. Their lands had never been recovered. As a result, Elena didn't care much for the Russians.

"There are lots of Polish officers coming tonight, and you'll find nearly all of them knew someone who was murdered at Katyn," she said. "I must get some of them to tell you about what really happened in Poland. They'll be so pleased to meet an American who knows something about what happened in Poland. Most of your countrymen don't, you know. They don't know, and I think they don't care."

There was a Baroque marble statue on a table depicting some ancient Greek hero who was being attacked by a lion that had its teeth planted very firmly in his bare ass. It looked uncomfortable. And for a moment I saw myself at the dinner table having my skinny Yankee ass similarly chewed by some disgruntled Polish officer.

"Actually, Elena," I said, "I'd rather you didn't mention my working for the president."

"I'll try, darling. But you know me. I'm hopeless with secrets. I tell all the boys who come here, 'Don't tell me anything.' I can't keep a secret to save my life. I've been an inveterate gossip ever since school. Remember what the little doctor said to me once?"

I knew she was referring to Josef Goebbels, whom we'd both known well in Berlin.

"'I have two ways of releasing information to the world,'" she said, speaking German and imitating perfectly Goebbels's impeccable, professorial, High German accent. "'I can leave a memorandum on the desk of my secretary at the Leopold Palace. Or I can tell Princess Elena Pontiatowska something in complete confidence.'"

I laughed. I remembered the occasion when Goebbels had said it, not least because the same night I had slept with Elena for the first time. "Yes, that's right. I remember."

"I do miss him sometimes," she sighed. "I think he was the only Nazi I ever really liked."

"He was certainly the cleverest Nazi *I* ever knew," I admitted.

She sighed. "I suppose I had better go back and join my other guests."

"It's your party."

"You don't understand what it's like, darling. Entertaining the troops like this. They all fancy their bloody chances. Especially the count."

"The count?"

"My Polish SOE colonel, Wlazyslaw Pulnarowicz. Carpathian Rifle Brigade. He's liable to challenge you to a duel if he sees me talking to you like this."

"So why do you bother doing it? Entertain the troops." I laughed. "Jesus, I make you sound like Bob Hope. Is Pepsodent paying for this party?"

"I do it for morale, of course. The British are very keen on morale." She stood up. "Come on. Let me introduce you to some people."

She took me by the arm again and led me back onto the terrace, where several British and Polish officers now eyed me suspiciously. There were other women at the party by now, but I didn't pay them any attention. I just meekly followed Elena around the terrace as she introduced me to one person and then another. And I made her laugh. Just like we were back in Berlin.

Eventually we went in to dinner. I was seated between Elena and her Polish colonel, who seemed none too pleased that I had usurped his position on Elena's right-hand side. He was a striking man with dark hair, a longish chin, a Fairbanks mustache, and a beautiful speaking voice that seemed quite unaffected by the harsh-smelling tobacco he rolled in his neat little cigarettes. I smiled at him a few times, and when I wasn't speaking to Elena, I even tried to make conversation. The colonel's replies were mostly monosyllabic; once or twice he didn't even bother to reply at all. Instead he just busied himself sawing at a piece of chicken as if it were a German's throat. Or mine. He wasn't the only Pole at the dinner table. Just the least friendly. There were eighteen guests, of whom at least five other officers present, not including Colonel Pulnarowicz, wore the shoulder patches of the Polish army. They were much more talkative. Not least because Elena seemed to have a limitless supply of excellent wines and spirits. There was even some vodka from the famous Lancut distillery in Poland.

Toward the end of the meal I lit us both cigarettes and asked her how it was that there were so many Poles in Egypt.

"After the Russians invaded Poland," she said, "many Poles were deported to the southern Soviet republics. Then, after Germany attacked Russia, the Russians set many Poles free in Iran and Iraq. Most joined the Polish army of General Anders to fight the Nazis. Here, in the North African theater, the Polish army was commanded by General Sikorski. But, as you know, relations between the Poles and the Russians collapsed with the discovery of the bodies in the Katyn Forest. Sikorski demanded that the Red Cross be allowed to investigate the site. In response, Stalin broke off all relations with the Polish army. A few months ago, Sikorski himself died in a plane crash. An accident, it was said. But there isn't a Pole in North Africa and Egypt who doesn't think he was murdered by Stalin's NKVD."

A captain on Elena's left was also Polish. Overhearing her, he added some comments of his own. These left me in no doubt that Elena had let the cat out of the bag as far as my report on the Katyn Forest massacre for FDR was concerned, despite my having asked her not to.

"She's right," he said. "There isn't a Pole in North Africa who trusts Stalin. Please tell Roosevelt that when you're compiling your report. Tell him that when you get to Teheran."

I shrugged. "Perhaps you know more than I do," I told him.

"That the Big Three Conference will be in Teheran?" He

laughed. Captain Skomorowski was a large man, with dark hair and a nose as sharp as a draftsman's favorite pencil. Every few minutes he would remove his glasses and wipe away the moisture that had collected on the lenses from the heat generated by his large red face. He laughed again. "This is no big secret."

"Easy to see why," I said pointedly.

"Darling, it's true," said Elena. "*Everyone* in Cairo knows about Teheran."

Elena's colonel laughed with contempt as he saw the look of surprise in my eyes. I was beginning to dislike him almost as much as he seemed to dislike me.

"Oh, yes," he said. "We know all about the Big Three in Teheran. And, by the way, that's another city full of displaced Poles. More than twenty thousand of them, for your information. There are so many Poles in Teheran, and in such disadvantaged conditions, that the Persians have even accused our people of spreading typhoid in the city. Imagine that. I wonder if you can."

"Right now I'm still trying to imagine why a colonel would be so free with this kind of information across the dinner table," I said stiffly. "Haven't you heard? Walls have ears. Although I'm beginning to think that walls in Poland have tongues instead."

"What do you Americans know about Poland?" he asked, ignoring my rebuke. "Have you ever been to Poland?"

"The last I heard it was full of Germans."

"We shall suppose that means no." The colonel snorted with derision and looked around at his fellow officers. "This makes him the ideal sort of person to be writing a report for the president of the United States about Katyn. Another stupid American who doesn't know anything about Poland."

"Wlazyslaw, that's enough," said Elena.

"Everyone knows that Roosevelt and Churchill are going to sell Poland out," persisted Skomorowski.

"Surely you can't believe that," I told him. "Britain and France went to war for the sake of Poland."

"Maybe so," said Colonel Pulnarowicz. His eyes widened. "But will it be Britain and France that throw the Germans out of Poland, or will it be the Russians? For us, there's nothing to draw between them, the Russians and the Germans. That's what the Americans don't, or won't, understand. Nobody can see the Russians giving up Poland if the Red Army reoccupies it. Will Roosevelt persuade Stalin to return land for which the Red Army has sacrificed so many men? I think I can hear Stalin laughing about that one now."

"After the war is over," a third Polish officer pitched in, "I believe it will be discovered that Stalin was much worse than Hitler. Hitler is only trying to wipe out the Jews. But Stalin is trying to eliminate whole classes of people. Not just the bourgeoisie and the aristocracy, but the peasant class, as well. Millions have died in the Ukraine. If I had to choose between Hitler and Stalin, I'd choose Hitler every time. Stalin is the father of lies. By comparison, Hitler is a mere apprentice."

"Roosevelt and Churchill will sell us down the river," said Skomorowski. "That's what we're fighting for. Two knives in the back."

"I don't think that's true," I said. "I know Franklin Roosevelt. He is a decent, honorable man. He is not the kind of man to sell anyone out."

My heart was hardly in this argument. I could not help but recollect my own conversation on the subject with the president. His words hadn't exactly suggested a man who felt any obligation to protect the interests of Poland. Roosevelt had sounded more like someone intent on appeasing Stalin, in much the same way as the former British prime minister, Neville Chamberlain, had appeased Hitler.

"This report you are compiling," said Pulnarowicz. He lit one of his little cigarettes and exhaled smoke in my face. It looked thoughtless rather than deliberate. But that was just how it looked. "Does it mean the Americans are going to pay any more attention to what happened at Katyn than the British?"

I hardly felt like telling him that my completed report was already buried on the president's direct order, exactly as the colonel had suspected it would be.

"I'm just compiling a report. It's not my job to formulate policy."

"If you're compiling a report, then what are you doing here in Cairo?" demanded Skomorowski.

"You're Polish. I'm speaking to you, aren't I?" I grinned at him. "I'd hate to have missed the opportunity to meet all of you tonight. Besides, I don't have to be in Washington to write a report." I paused. "Not that I feel at all obliged to explain myself in this company."

Skomorowski shrugged. "Or is it that by taking your time in making your report, you give Roosevelt a very valuable opportunity for delay?"

"Is Katyn even on the agenda for the Big Three at Teheran?" asked Pulnarowicz. "Will they even talk about it?"

"I really don't know what is on the agenda at Teheran," I said truthfully. "But even if I did, I certainly wouldn't discuss it with you. Security is hardly best served by this kind of conversation."

"You heard the princess," said Pulnarowicz. "It's all over the city."

Elena squeezed my arm. "Willy darling, if you stay here for any length of time, you'll recognize how true that is. It really is impossible to keep a secret in Cairo."

"So I see," I said pointedly. All the same, I found it hard to be cross with her. It was my fault for not remembering what a tremendous gossip she was.

"Not that Poland exists, anyway," Colonel Pulnarowicz added, smiling bitterly. "Not anymore. Not since January, when Stalin declared that all Polish citizens were to be treated as Soviet citizens. It's said that this was because he wanted the Poles to have the same rights as Soviet citizens."

"The same right to be shot without trial," said Skomorowski. "The same right to be deported to a labor camp. The same right to be starved to death."

Everyone laughed. It was obviously a set piece that the two Polish officers had performed together before.

"The key to this whole problem is Stalin himself," said Skomorowski. "If Stalin were removed, the whole edifice of Soviet communism would collapse. That's the only way forward I can see. As long as Stalin remains alive, we will never have a free and democratic Poland. He should be assassinated. I'll do it myself if I ever get half a chance."

There was a long silence. Even Captain Skomorowski seemed to recognize that he had gone too far. Removing his glasses, he began to wipe them again.

"Well, I don't know," said Major Sernberg. "Really I don't."

"You'll have to excuse Captain Skomorowski," Pulnarowicz told the major. "He was in Moscow when Russian troops marched into Poland and for a while he was a guest of the NKVD. In the Lubyanka Prison. And then in one of their labor camps. At Solovki. He knows all about Soviet hospitality, don't you, Josef?"

"I think," said Elena, getting up from the table, "that this conversation has gone far enough."

We listened to one of the British officers play the piano after that. This did little to improve anyone's spirits. Just before midnight, Elena's servants stopped serving alcohol. And gradually she was able to shoo her guests away. I would have left, too, but she asked me to stay on for a while, to talk about old times. Our old times. Which sounded just fine. So I went outside and told Coogan that I was staying on for a while and after that I would probably walk home.

"Be careful, sir," he told me.

"I'll be all right," I said. "I have my pistol."

"If you were thinking of going anywhere on your own, sir, then the nicest chorus girls in Cairo are at Madame Badia's, sir. There's a belly dancer called Tahia Carioca who's first rate, if you like that sort of thing."

"No, thanks."

"Or if you was with a lady, sir, there's a new place on the Mena Road, on the way to the Pyramids. The Auberge des Pyramides, it's called. Opened in the summer. Very flash. Young King Farouk goes there a lot, so it must be good on account of how that boy knows how to enjoy himself."

I grinned. "Coogan. Go home."

Back in the house, the servants had disappeared, the way good servants do when they're not wanted anymore. Elena made us some mint tea, just to prove that she could still boil a kettle, and then showed me back into the drawing room.

"Where do you find these guys?" I was feeling kind of sore about the way the evening had gone so far.

"Wlazyslaw can be quite charming sometimes," she said. "But I'll admit, tonight was not one of those occasions."

"Just sitting next to him made me want to look for some life insurance."

"He was jealous of you, that's all."

"'He was jealous, that's all'? Elena, a guy like that gets jealous, you're liable to end up with a pillow over your face. And me taking an early-morning plunge in the Nile."

She sipped her tea from a glass, snuggled up next to me on the sofa, and crossed her legs, carelessly.

"Did you ever do this with him?"

"Now who's jealous?"

"That means yes. In which case no wonder he's pissed. If you were my girl, I'd be pissed myself."

"I'm nobody's 'girl,' Willy. He knows that. Anyway, whatever happened between me and Wlazyslaw happened right here on this sofa. He's never seen the wallpaper in my bedroom. Nobody has. Not since Freddy died."

"That's a long time to spend on the sofa. Even in Egypt."

"Isn't it? A long time." She sighed, and for a moment we were both silent. "Why did you leave Berlin?"

"I'm half-Jewish, remember?"

"Yes, but the Nazis didn't know that."

"Maybe so, but *I* did. It took a while for my Jewish half to wrestle my Catholic half to the floor. Longer than it should have, perhaps."

"So it wasn't me."

I shrugged. "But for you, I'd probably have left a lot earlier. It's all your fault."

"It sounds like you're going to punish me."

"Right now I'm having a lot of fun thinking about it."

For a moment Elena's eyes grew more distant, as if she were trying to visualize something important. "What's she like? The girl in Washington."

"Did I mention a girl anywhere?"

"Not specifically. But I can tell that there is one. I always could with you."

"All right. There is and there isn't. Not anymore."

"Sounds like Wlazyslaw."

"We got further than the sofa."

"What happened?"

"She wanted me to care when I was pretending not to."

"Sounds complicated."

"Not really."

"Tell me about it. And don't think you have to make a joke about it. I can see it still hurts."

"Is it that obvious?"

"Only when I look in your eyes."

So I told her about Diana. Everything there was. Including my betrayal of her. It took a while, but when I had finished I felt better. I had lifted something from my shoulders. Like a couple of hundred tons of self-pity. It helped that she kissed me, of course. For quite a long time. The way old friends do sometimes. But for now, we kept it to the sofa.

"Do you want to stay?" she asked at about two A.M. "There are plenty of spare rooms."

"Thanks, but I have to get back to my hotel. In case there are any messages from my boss."

"Would you like Ahmed to take you in the car?"

"No, thanks, I'll walk. It will feel nice to put one foot in front of the other without breaking into a sweat."

"Tomorrow evening," she said. "Let's do something."

"Something sounds good," I said.

"Come around seven."

I WALKED NORTH, with the Nile and the British embassy on my left. In front of the embassy, British soldiers stood in sentry boxes looking slightly embarrassed at the size and grandeur of the building, a great white wedding cake of a place set in lush green gardens that looked as big as, and a lot nicer than, Buckingham Palace. For a while it seemed that a dark green sedan was following me. But after I had crossed the road, close to the Cairo Museum of Antiquities, and walked east along Aldo Street toward Opera Square, I looked back and saw that it had gone.

Not that I felt at all nervous. Cairo was still wide awake. Despite the late hour, shops remained open, clinging on to life like moss-covered shellfish in some ancient aquarium, their shabby owners surveying me with a mixture of amusement and toothless fascination. Old men in turbans dozed on street corners. Families sat in gutters and talked and pointed at me. And from an open window in a building, what sounded like a party was under way: rhythmic hand-clapping and women ululating like a war party of Cherokee Indians. Dogs barked, trams whined, car horns blared. That night, Cairo seemed like the most magical city on earth.

I walked past Groppi's, the Turf Club, and Sha'ar Hashmayim— Heaven's Gate, the largest synagogue in Cairo and instantly recognizable from the Hebrew inscriptions on the wall. The black sky above my head was swept by the cones of searchlights, hunting for German bombers that would never come. In Opera Square, near Shepheard's, neon lights advertised the existence of Madame Badia's Opera Casino. I looked at the place, remembered Coogan, and smiled. I thought I saw a man in a tropical suit step smartly sideways into a shop doorway.

Curious to see if I was being followed, I retraced my steps a few yards, but was forced to make a retreat when I encountered a whole posse of fly-whisk sellers, shoe-shine boys, flower sellers, and unshaven men selling razor blades (mostly used), at the edge of the open-air movie theater in Ezbekiah Gardens. There was a movie showing. Or rather, it was just ending, and I found myself walking against a human current made up of hundreds of people on their way out of the gardens.

I had removed my jacket to walk home. And now I dropped it on the grass. As I bent down to retrieve it I felt and heard a smallish object zip over my head. It sounded like a thick rubber band flying through the air and then striking something. I straightened up again and found myself face-to-face with an Egyptian wearing a tarboosh and a surprised expression on his face. His mouth was wide open as if he had been trying to catch the largish red fly that was crawling on his forehead. Almost immediately he dropped onto his knees in front of me, and then collapsed onto the ground. I glanced down and the red fly seemed to settle on the man's head; then I saw that it was not a fly at all, but a very distinct hole from which six small leglike threads of blood were now running. The man had been shot between the eyes.

I knew that the shot had been meant for me. I put my hand in the specially tailored pocket of my tux and on the grip of the little .32-caliber hammerless Colt they had given us at Catoctin Mountain for evening wear. I was ready to put a hole through the lining if I saw what I was looking for. A man with a silencer on the end of a small-caliber pocket pistol like my own. At the same time, I walked quickly away from the body, which no one had yet noticed belonged to a dead man. Cairo wasn't the kind of place where it was uncommon for people to lie on the ground. Even dead ones.

I walked back toward Shepheard's Hotel, my tux jacket wrapped around my hand like a large black bandage, my finger on the trigger of the little Colt. Ahead of me I saw a man walking almost as quickly. He was wearing a beige tropical suit, a straw hat, and two-tone wingtips. I couldn't see his face, but as he went by a shop window, I saw that he had a newspaper in his hand. Or rather he had a newspaper folded over his hand, and pressed close to his chest, like a bath towel. He didn't run. But he was on his toes, and I knew that this was my man.

I wanted to shout after him but guessed that this would only have made him run or draw his fire. I had no idea what he was going to do. I didn't expect him to run smartly up the red-carpeted steps of my own hotel, neatly sidestepping the man who had been there all day working a dirty postcard pitch. The street hawker had his reputation to consider. He wasn't about to be sidestepped so easily again. Not when he had a living to make. As soon as I neared the edge of the red carpet, he saw me and calculated my likely route. Wheeling around, he held up his obscene wares in front of my face and brought me to a standstill, using his malodorous body to block me first one way and then the other. The third time he did it, I swore and pushed him roughly out of my way, which earned me a mild rebuke from a British officer sitting behind the safety of the brass rail on the terrace.

Entering the lobby of the hotel, I glanced around and saw that my quarry was nowhere in sight. I went to the desk. The clerk sprang to my assistance, smiling handsomely.

"Did you see a man come in here a second ago? A European, about thirty, beige suit, panama hat, brown-and-white shoes? Carrying a folded newspaper."

The desk clerk shrugged and shook his head. "I'm sorry, sir, no. But there is a message for you, Professor Mayer."

"All right. Thanks."

I checked the bar. I checked the Long Bar. I checked the dining room. I even checked the men's room off the lobby. But there was no sign of the man with the newspaper. I went outside and back down the steps. The man with the postcards saw me and backed away nervously. I smiled and apologized and handed him a fistful of the greaseproof paper he called money. He grinned back at me, with absolute forgiveness. I had made his evening. He had sold another stupid American some dirty postcards.

XX
TUESDAY, NOVEMBER 23, 1943,
CAIRO

COOGAN PICKED ME UP from Shepheard's at eight-fifteen and we drove west. There were police milling about in Ezbekiah Gardens. With the green grass, and the men in their white uniforms, it looked more like a game of cricket than a murder investigation, and was probably just as baffling.

"Shot right between the eyes, so he was, about two-thirty last night, just after the pictures was finished," said Coogan. "Local businessman, apparently. Nobody saw or heard a thing, of course. And the police don't know anything. But that's not very surprising." He laughed. "The police never know anything in Cairo. There are five million people live in Cairo. Finding a murderer in this city is like trying to find a needle in a haystack."

There were a number of reasons I had decided that it was best to keep my mouth shut about what had happened the previous night. One was that I didn't think FDR, Hopkins, or Donovan would have welcomed any member of the American delegation getting involved with the local police. Another was that after my run-in with the Secret Service in Tunis, I wanted to keep a low profile. But the main reason I had kept silent was that I had no evidence for what I now believed: that the attempt on my life was connected with the death of Ted Schmidt. Ted's killer must surely have reasoned that suspicions would have been raised by another death aboard the *Iowa*. Killing me in Cairo would have been a lot easier than trying to kill me on the ship.

We drove across the English Bridge, and then south, toward Giza. Cairo's city buildings gave way to mud-brick villages, strong-smelling canals, and fields recently harvested of their beans. We passed the university and the Cairo Zoo, as well as a caravanserai of domesticated animals on the Giza Road: donkeys adorned with blue beads to ward off the evil eye, nervous flocks of sheep, scrawny horses that pulled ancient open-topped carriages, the gharries that plied the tourist trade all over Cairo, and, once or twice, camels carrying so many palm branches they looked like Birnam Wood come to Dunsinane. It would have been a colorful scene except for the flat white light that lay on the city like a layer of dust, draining the color out of almost everything. I felt a little drained myself. Being shot at wasn't good for my plumbing. But then again maybe that was just Cairo.

Mena House stood a stone's throw from the Pyramids. The former hunting lodge of the Egyptian khedive, it was now a luxurious hotel where Churchill, Roosevelt, and Chiang Kai-shek were meeting. The whole area bustled with troops, armored cars, tanks, and antiaircraft guns, and the strictest cordons guarded all of the approaches to the hotel and its extensive grounds.

Mena House looked very different from Shepheard's. Surrounded by lawns and palm trees and shrubberies, only the Great Pyramid spoiled the view. From the outside, it resembled some grand movie star's Hollywood mansion. I preferred the more cosmopolitan atmosphere of Shepheard's. But it was easy to see why the British military had favored a conference at Mena House. With just the desert and a few pyramids for neighbors, the former hunting lodge was easily defended. Not that the Western allies were taking any chances. There were four antiaircraft positions on the lawns, and truckloads of British and American troops, stiff with boredom and parked in the cool shade of some breezy palm trees. Everyone looked as if they were praying for a plague of locusts, just so that they might have something to practice shooting at.

I got out of the car and stepped onto a long verandah. The several steps leading up to the front door were equipped with a ramp, and inside the hotel's cool interior were yet more ramps to accommodate Roosevelt's wheelchair.

An officer at the front desk directed me to Hopkins's office, and I walked through the hotel with its fine Mashrabia wooden screens, blue tiles and mosaics, and brass-embossed wooden doors. But for the large fireplaces, which added an English touch to the decor, everything looked very Egyptian. As I sauntered down a long corridor, a small man in a white linen suit came out of a room and then walked toward me. The man was wearing a gray hat, a gray summer-weight suit, and smoking a very large cigar. It took less than a moment to register that this was Winston Churchill. The prime minister growled a "Good morning" at me as he passed.

"Good morning, Prime Minister," I said, surprised that he would have bothered speaking to me at all.

I hurried on down the corridor and found Harry Hopkins in a room that had the air of a seraglio, with arabesque arches, more Mashrabia screens, and brass lamps. But instead of some grande odalisque, or even a small one, Hopkins was with Mike Reilly and another, patrician-looking man I half recognized.

"Professor Mayer," said Hopkins, smiling warmly. "There you are." I was still a couple of minutes early, but he sounded as if they were about to send out a search party. "This is Chip Bohlen, from State. He came with Averell Harriman, from the embassy in Moscow. Mr. Bohlen speaks fluent Russian."

"That's going to come in handy," I said, shaking Bohlen's outstretched hand.

"Chip here's been defending State against me," grinned Hopkins. "Explaining all the handicaps that State Department officials have to put up with. By the way, it seems he knew your friend Ted Schmidt and his wife."

"I still can't believe he's dead. Or Debbie, for that matter. I went to their wedding," Bohlen said.

"Then you knew them well," I said.

"I knew them very well. Ted and I joined the Russian-language program at State around the same time and studied together in Paris. That's where most of our officers were sent for language study. After that we went to Estonia together, to get the sound and feel of spoken Russian, and shared an apartment for a while before he went back to Washington." Bohlen shook his head. "Mr. Hopkins says you think they were both murdered."

I tried not to look surprised. I had shared my suspicions regarding the death of Deborah Schmidt only with General Donovan and Ridgeway Poole in Tunis.

"We received a radio message for you from your people in Washington," explained Reilly. "I'm afraid that after what happened in Tunis I read it."

"You mean in case I really was a German spy?" I said.

"Something like that." Reilly grinned.

He handed me the message from the Campus. I read it quickly. There was more information about the traffic accident that had ended Debbie Schmidt's life. On Monday, October 18, she had been killed by a hit-and-run driver as she came out of Jelleff's, the ladies' store on F Street. The Georgetown apartment where the Schmidts lived had been turned over, too, and the Metro police were treating her death as suspicious.

"Why would anyone want to kill Debbie Schmidt?" asked Bohlen.

"Because Debbie Schmidt had been having an affair with someone," I explained. "That's what Ted told me, anyway. Only Ted told someone else, as well. Someone aboard the *Iowa*. I think that someone killed him. I think the murderer also tricked his way into the radio room on board the ship and sent a message back to the States. My guess is that the message contained Mrs. Schmidt's home address and a request to get rid of her."

Bohlen was frowning. "He said as much to me when he was in Moscow for the conference. That she was having an affair."

"Ted was in Moscow? With Cordell Hull?"

Bohlen nodded.

"I didn't know that."

"He was drinking a bit too much—well, it's hard not to when you're with the Soviets—and he said he had his suspicions then. He didn't say who it was. Only that I knew the man. And that it was someone in the State Department."

"Did he tell *you* who it was?" Reilly asked me.

"Yes, he did." I could see no reason now to keep any of this a secret any longer. Certainly not now that the police were involved in both Washington and Cairo. "It was Thornton Cole."

I waited for their expressions of surprise to subside. Then I said: "The fact that Deborah Schmidt was pregnant by Cole only seems to make it much less likely he could have been looking for homosexual sex when he was murdered in Franklin Park."

"I see what you mean," said Reilly.

"I'm glad someone does. I was beginning to think I just had a dirty mind. Ted and I talked this over. We both concluded that in the wake of the Sumner Welles scandal, whoever murdered Cole wanted to make sure it would be swept under the rug as quickly as possible. So the murderer made Cole's death look as if he'd been having sex with a man in a public place. Given that Cole worked on the German desk at State, it's possible he was on the trail of some kind of Washington spy ring."

"Why didn't you come forward with this information before?" demanded Reilly.

"With respect, you weren't on the ship, Mr. Reilly," said Hopkins, coming to my defense. "The professor here was hardly the most popular man on the *Iowa* when he suggested that Schmidt might have been murdered, and that there was a German spy on board."

"Besides," I said, "I could hardly be sure that whoever I told wasn't the person who killed Schmidt. In which case I might have been murdered, too." I paused a moment. "Last night I damn nearly was."

"What?" Hopkins glanced at the other two men. They looked as astonished as he did.

"Murdered."

"You don't say," he breathed.

"I *do* say. Underlined and in italics. Someone took a shot at me last night. Fortunately for me it missed. Unfortunately for someone else, it didn't. There's a body in Ezbekiah Gardens right now that should be me." I lit a cigarette and sat down in an armchair. "I figure whoever killed the Schmidts wants to kill me as well. Just in case Ted told me about Thornton Cole."

"Are the police involved?" asked Reilly.

I smiled. "Of course the police are involved. Even in Cairo they know to look for someone with a gun when they find a man lying in the park with a bullethole between his eyes." I inhaled sharply. I was almost enjoying their horror. "The police just aren't involved with me, if that's what you mean. I didn't hang around the crime scene. I tend not to when someone has fired a shot at me. With a silencer."

"A silencer?" Hopkins looked puzzled.

"You know—the little gizmo you put on the end of your gun to make it go phut phut instead of bang bang. Very useful when you want to make sure you don't disturb people while they're watching a movie." I shrugged. "There was that, and I also thought it best if the president's delegation stayed out of the picture, for now."

"You did the right thing," said Reilly.

I nodded. "At least until someone tries again. Our German agent, perhaps. If that's who it was."

"So why talk now?" asked Reilly. "To us?"

"Because neither you nor Bohlen here were on the ship, of course. Ergo, you couldn't have done it. As for Mr. Hopkins, I hardly think that the president's best friend is likely to be a German spy. I've played gin rummy with him. He's not that good a bluffer. No one in this room could possibly be involved."

Hopkins was nodding, good-humoredly.

"So what do you want us to do now?" asked Reilly. "After all, it's possible this German spy might be planning an attempt on the president's life."

"I don't think so. An assassin hardly lacked for an opportunity to kill Roosevelt when we were still on board ship. It's safe to assume that our spy has something else in mind. Perhaps—and this is only a guess—perhaps he's not an assassin at all. Perhaps the Germans want their own man in Teheran. To take the measure of the alliance. To see if there's any room for future diplomatic maneuver. I can give you all kinds of reasons if I sit here long enough."

"Do we tell the president?" Hopkins asked. "Mike?"

Mike Reilly had a look on his face that suggested he'd hit a brick wall. I kicked his thought processes aside and pressed on with my own. "For now I'd like to keep this between the four of us. Perhaps the Metro Police in D.C. will turn up something more that will help us get a lead on this guy."

"Under the circumstances, this might be a job for the FBI. What do you say, Mike?"

"I'm inclined to agree, sir."

Reilly's brain. You could almost see it jerking around in his skull, as if Hopkins had tapped it with a small reflex hammer. I smiled, trying to contain my irritation with them both.

"That's your call. But my feeling would be not to mention this to anyone until we know a little more. We wouldn't want to spook anyone. Especially the president."

"It sounds to me as though you might already suspect someone," said Reilly.

I had obviously thought about this. There was John Weitz, who had threatened to kill Ted Schmidt. And there were some of Reilly's colleagues in the Secret Service. On the night he disappeared from the *Iowa,* Schmidt had asked the chief petty officer to direct him to the Secret Service quarters. Could one of them have lured him up on deck to kill him? Disliking almost all of them, I was finding it hard to fix on one particular suspect. Agent Rauff had a name he shared with a Gestapo commander. Agent Pawlikowski looked like one of Hitler's blond beasts. And hadn't Agent Qualter expressed what seemed to be the popular view, that Stalin was as bad as Hitler? Killing Stalin, killing Roosevelt, killing the Big Three, or just trying to take the measure of the alliance—there was no shortage of possible motives for a German spy among our number.

"Maybe," I told Reilly. "Maybe not. But I'd still like to keep the lid on this for a while. In the hope that our man might reveal himself. Getting the FBI involved might prevent that from happening."

"All right," agreed Reilly. "We'll do it your way, Professor. But just in case, we'll double the detail guarding the president."

"Keep us posted, Professor," Hopkins told me as I went out the door. "If there are any developments, let us know immediately."

"If someone shoots me, you'll know I wasn't exaggerating," I told him.

I went back outside to my car. All that talk about a German spy had prompted me to recall my own secretly precarious situation. It was time I checked to see how Major Reichleitner was coming along with Donovan's Bride.

"Where to, boss?" asked Coogan.

"Grey Pillars."

I had left a five-pound note with the duty corporal to provide cigarettes, medicine, and some decent food and water for the prisoner. Entering the cell, I found the major much recovered and working diligently on Donovan's Bride material. Thanking me for the extra supplies, he told me he was making excellent progress with the signals transcripts and he might have some plaintexts to show me by the end of the week.

"Good. Sounds as though it will be just in time. We're flying to Teheran on Saturday morning."

"So it *is* Teheran. But don't they know? The place is full of German sympathizers."

I shrugged. "I tried telling them. But I'm beginning to suspect FDR thinks he walks on water."

"On water, no," said Reichleitner. "But on oil, perhaps. If they're having the conference there it's because they'll all be trying to get the shah to commit to a cheap oil price, in perpetuity."

"Maybe he can give me a good deal on a rug while he's at it."

"By the way. Did you give Roosevelt the Beketovka File?"

"Not yet." What with seeing Elena again, and being shot at, I had forgotten all about the file now lying on a table in my hotel room. "I'm still trying to get some time with the president so I can bring it to his attention."

"But you've read it yourself."

"Of course," I said, thinking I could hardly say I hadn't and still retain the German's goodwill. I resolved to try to read the file the moment I got back to Shepheard's.

"And what do you think?"

"It's shocking. I think it confirms what a lot of people in this city seem to believe already. That Stalin is as great a threat as Hitler."

Reichleitner nodded his approval. "He is. He is."

"To be honest with you, though, I'm not sure it's going to have much of an immediate influence on Roosevelt. After all, he managed to ignore all the evidence about Katyn."

"But this time the numbers are so much greater. It's evidence of a pattern of mass murder and neglect on an industrial scale. If Roosevelt can make an alliance with a man like Stalin, then there's no reason why he couldn't make a deal with Hitler himself."

I nodded uncomfortably. I wondered what Max Reichleitner would have said if I had told him what Donovan had told me: that FDR was indeed pursuing an American peace with Hitler. I told myself he wouldn't have believed a word of it.

When I got back to Shepheard's, I picked up the Beketovka File, feeling guilty about the lie I had told. I moved the armchair near the open window, but in the shade. I put a package of cigarettes on the side table next to a cold beer, my notebook, and my fountain pen. Then I dived in. It was a like diving into a dark pond to find that there was something unseen just beneath the opaque surface, like a rusty iron bedstead. The hidden object was a monograph by Heinrich Zahler. I hit my head on it. Hard.

My name is Heinrich Zahler and I was a lieutenant in the 76th Infantry Division of the German 6th Army that surrendered to the Soviets on January 31, 1943. I was born in Bremen, on March 1, 1921, but I don't expect to live to see Bremen again or, for that matter, my next birthday. I am writing now in the hope that this secretly written letter (if these writing materials are discovered, I will be executed immediately) will reach my parents. My father, Friedrich, works for the docks and harbor board in Bremerhaven, and my mother, Hannah, is a midwife at the University Hospital in Bremen. I want to tell them how very much I love them both and to abandon any hope of ever seeing me again. Death is the only escape from this, the deepest pit in hell.

Attempts to take POWs out of Stalingrad began immediately after we surrendered, when the Popovs had tired of beating us. But almost all the rolling stock was required to supply the Russian front at Rostov, and so most of us were obliged to march to the camp where we are now imprisoned. Some were loaded into cattle-trucks awaiting the arrival of a steam locomotive that never came, and after a week the cars were opened again and it was discovered that all of the men inside, some 3,000 officers and private personnel, were dead. But thousands more died of typhus, dysentery, frostbite, and wounds received in the battle before they could even leave the provisional POW camp at Stalingrad. In retrospect, they were the lucky ones.

The march to the camp that was to be our final destination took five days. We walked in all weathers, without food or water or any kind of shelter. Those who could not walk were shot or clubbed to death, or sometimes just stripped and left to freeze to death. Many thousands more died on the march here. And perhaps they were lucky, too.

This is the largest of the Russian POW camps—Camp Number 108, at Beketovka. It is what the Russians call a *katorga*. That means hard labor, low rations, and no medical attention other than that which we can provide for ourselves, which is very little. The site of the camp was formerly a school, but it is hard to believe that children could ever have been educated in such a place as this. The school was partly destroyed during the battle for Stalingrad, which means that there are no windows, no doors, and no beds; there is no roof or furniture of any kind; anything made of wood was burned long ago to provide heat for Red Army soldiers. The only fuel we have is our own dried human feces. We sleep on the floor, without blankets, huddled together for warmth in temperatures as low as -35 degrees centigrade.

When we arrived, there was no food or water, and many men died from eating snow. After two days they gave us a kind of watery bran that a horse or a dog would have ignored; even today, months after our arrival, none of us eats more than a few ounces of bread a day—if bread is what it is: this bread has more grit in it than the soles on a roadworker's boots. Sometimes, as a special treat, we boil potato peelings for soup, and whenever we can, we smoke the dust off the floor—a Russian solution to the problem of the lack of tobacco, which they call "scratch." Every morning when we pick ourselves off the floor we discover that as many as fifty of us have died during the night. A week after my arrival here I awoke to find that Sergeant Eisenhauer, a man who saved my life on more than one occasion, was dead and frozen hard to the ground, and hardly recognizable, for the rats feast on the extremities of the dead in the short time that remains before they become petrified with cold. It is not just the rats that eat human flesh in this place, however. Sometimes bodies disappear and are cooked and eaten. The cannibals among us are easily spotted by their healthier pallor and shunned by the rest of us. Otherwise, the morning always starts with bodies dragged out of the building where we sleep and, to ensure that death has not been feigned, the Popovs drive a metal spike into the skull of each corpse with a hammer. The clothes are then stripped off the body, any gold fillings removed with pliers and (for several months, until the ground unfroze) the bodies laid out on the *styena*—which is what the Popovs call the wall they have built from the naked corpses of our dead comrades.

Our guards are not soldiers, all of them are needed for the front, but the *zakone,* common criminals who were serving sentences in other labor camps and whose brutality and depravity know no limit. I believed that I had witnessed all of the evil that men were capable of inflicting upon one another during the battle for Stalingrad. That was before I came to Camp 108.

By the end of May, those of us who still remained alive at Beketovka were put to work rebuilding—first the camp itself, and then the local railway station. Winter had been bad, and many of us who survived it assumed that summer could only improve our lot—at least we would be warm. But with the summer came a heat that was no less intolerable than the cold. Worst of all were the mosquitoes. Whereas before I saw men stripped naked and forced to stand in the snow until they died (this is called *oontar paydkant*—"winter punishment"), now I see men bound naked to a tree and left to the mosquitoes until they screamed to be shot (this is called *samap paydkant*, "summer punishment"); sometimes they were shot, but mostly the mosquitoes were left to do their ghastly work, for a bullet is wasted on a German, say the zaks. In truth, however, I have seen my comrades die in all manner of revolting ways. A corporal from my own platoon was thrown into a cesspit and left to drown in excrement. His crime? He asked a zak for some water. A friend of mine, Helmut von Dorff, a lieutenant from the 6th Panzer Army, was executed for going to the assistance of a comrade who had fallen at work under the weight of the railway sleeper he was obliged to carry on his shrunken shoulder. The zaks tied von Dorff to a telegraph pole and rolled it down a steep hill into the river Volga, where, presumably, he drowned.

Punishments other than death are rare indeed, but those that do exist are unusually cruel and often fatal anyway to men severely weakened by starvation, overwork, and dysentery. One man, so emaciated from lack of food his buttocks had virtually disappeared, was beaten on the bones of his behind until they were through the skin and flesh, and he died soon afterward from infection; but for the most part, beatings are so routine they hardly count as punishment, and the zaks like to devise new ways of enforcing their idea of discipline. This was the way they punished a Luftwaffe sergeant from the 9th Flak Division: they locked him inside a coffin-shaped box in which thousands of lice had been allowed to multiply and left him there for twenty-four hours; when they removed the lid, his body had swollen up so much from his bites that they could not pry him from the box and had to break off one side of it, much to the amusement of the zaks. Here is another: a staff officer from the 371st Infantry Division—I do not remember his name—they put a long piece of rope in his mouth, like a bridle, pulled the ends over his shoulders and tied them to his wrists and ankles; they left him on his stomach like that for a whole day, without water, and he has never walked since.

Morality has no meaning in a place like this. It is a word that does not exist in Beketovka, perhaps nowhere in all of Russia. Even so, there are times when I cannot help but think that we brought these misfortunes on ourselves by invading this country. Our leaders took us here and then abandoned us. And yet I am still proud to be a German and proud of the way we have conducted ourselves. I love my Fatherland but I fear what is to come, for if the Red Army were ever to conquer Germany, who knows what sufferings might be inflicted on our kith and kin? It does not bear thinking about.

There were 50,000 of us who marched from Stalingrad to Beketovka—since then as many as 45,000 have died. I have learned from Germans transferred from other camps that in these, too, it is the same story. Those who died were the best of us for, strange as it might seem, often the strongest died first. For myself, I will not survive another winter; already I am sick. There is a rumor that I am to be sent to another camp—perhaps Camp 93 at Tyumen, in Omsk Province, or Oransky Number 74 in Gorky Province; but I don't think I will live to complete the journey.

I would write more but cannot as I fear discovery; but there is no end to what could be written about this dreadful place. To whoever is reading this, I ask you, when the opportunity presents itself, please say a prayer for those like me whose deaths in this place will go unnoticed; and for those less fortunate souls who remain alive. God bless you, dear reader. And God bless the Fatherland. I ask forgiveness of all those I have wronged. They know who they are. I do not know the date, but I think it must be late September 1943.

Heinrich Zahler
Lieutenant
76th Infantry,
Camp Number 108
Beketovka.

I went to the hotel balcony and put my face in the sun just to remind myself I was still alive. Between the jumbled rooftops and the minarets, elegantly tall palm trees swayed in the warm breeze that swept off the Nile. In the street below, the Cairo traffic was going about its reassuringly argumentative business. I took a deep breath of air and tasted gasoline, sweat, Turkish coffee, horse dung, and cigarettes. It tasted good. Beketovka seemed like a million miles away, on another planet. I couldn't think of a better antidote to Camp 108 than Cairo, with its smelly drains and its dirty postcards.

The smart thing to have done would have been to leave it alone. Not to get personally involved. Except that I was involved. So instead of doing the smart thing and lying to Reichleitner—telling him I had given the file to FDR—I decided that I had to talk to someone about what I had read. And I could think of no one better than the major himself. But first I went down to the Long Bar and asked the head barman if they had a bottle of Korn. He said they had several because there was no demand for German liquor among the British. It wasn't that the English didn't like the taste, just that they didn't know such a thing even existed. I gave the man a couple of pounds and told him to bring me a bottle and two small glasses. Then I put it inside my briefcase and had Coogan drive me back to Grey Pillars.

Major Reichleitner was at work on the ciphers. He looked a little tired. But his eyes widened when he saw the bottle.

"My God, Fürst Bismarck," he said. "I don't believe it."

I produced the two glasses, placed them on the table, and filled each to the brim. We toasted each other silently and then drained the glass. The German mixed-grain liquor slipped into my body as if it had been something that belonged there, like my own heart and my lungs. I sat down on the bed and lit us both a cigarette.

"I owe you an apology, Major."

"Oh? How's that?"

"Earlier on, when I told you I'd read the Beketovka File, that was a lie. I hadn't read it at all. But I've read it now."

"I see," said Reichleitner. He looked a little uncertain of where this conversation was now headed. I wasn't sure myself. I refilled his glass. This time he sniffed it carefully, several times, before emptying the spirits down his throat.

I produced the Beketovka File from my briefcase and laid it on the table next to the bottle of Korn.

"My father is a German Jew," I told him. "Born in Berlin, but brought up and educated in the United States. My mother comes from an old German family. Her father was the Baron von Dorff, who also went to live in the United States, to seek his fortune. Or at least to make another. He left behind a sister and two brothers. One of them had a son, my mother's cousin. Friedrich von Dorff. We all spent one Christmas together in Berlin. Many years ago.

"When the war started, Friedrich's son, Helmut, joined the cavalry. The Sixth Panzer Army, Sixteenth Division. With General Hube. The battering ram of the Panzer Corps. In August 1942 they crossed the Don, heading for Stalingrad. I thought he had been killed there. Until this afternoon, that is, when I read Heinrich Zahler's account of life in Camp Number 108, at Beketovka. If you can call it life."

I picked up the relevant page and read from it aloud.

"Your mother's cousin's son," said Reichleitner.

I nodded. "I know a second cousin doesn't sound like very much of a reason to be affected. But we were a close family. And I remember Helmut von Dorff extremely well. He was just a boy when I knew him. Not more than ten or twelve years old, I suppose. A beautiful boy. Gentle, well read, thoughtful, interested in philosophy." I shrugged. "As I said, I had thought he was dead already. So it seems strange to read about him now. And horrible, of course, to learn the mean and degrading circumstances of his death."

"Then we are enemies no more," said Reichleitner.

He took the bottle by the neck and filled our glasses himself. We toasted each other again.

"I just wanted you to know. So that you can be sure I will do everything I can to make sure that the president reads this."

"Thank you," said Reichleitner. He smiled sadly. "This is good stuff. Where did you get it?"

"Shepheard's Hotel."

"Ah, Shepheard's. I wish I were there now."

"After the war perhaps you will be."

"You know, I was thinking. I never saw Hitler. Not close up, anyway. But in Teheran, you'll probably get to see Stalin. Up close. As close as I am now, perhaps."

"Perhaps."

"I envy you that opportunity. A chance to look him in the eye and see what kind of man he is. If he's the monster I imagine him to be."

"Do you think he *is* a monster?"

"I tell you honestly," said Major Reichleitner. "I think I'm more afraid that he might seem just like you or me. An ordinary man."

I left Major Reichleitner with the bottle and the cigarettes to continue working on the ciphers.

Outside Grey Pillars, I found myself feeling light-headed. Light-headed but heavy of spirit. Diana Vandervelden seemed almost as far away from me as Beketovka. Which was a pity, as the battery inside my chest was needing the kind of boost that only the company of a good friend could provide. A good female friend who still cared for me a little, perhaps. So I bought some flowers and walked round to Elena's house. We had arranged to meet that evening.

Elena's butler, Hossein, asked me to wait in the drawing room until his mistress was awake, explaining she always slept for a couple of hours in the afternoon. But I had the distinct impression that she was not alone. There was a certain masculine smell in the air. A smell like American cigarettes, Old Spice, and brilliantine. On the sofa was the October edition of *Jumbo Comics*, featuring Sheena Queen of the Jungle, which hadn't been there the previous evening. I flicked through the comic book while I waited. Sheena had large breasts and wore a fetching sort of loincloth made from leopard skin. For killing panthers and riding elephants, Sheena's outfit looked like a good choice. But you needed something different when your prey had just two legs. Elena knew that. And when, eventually, she came into the drawing room, she was dressed in something much more practical. She was wearing a white silk dressing gown underneath which she was practically naked. Which was fine if she really had been sleeping. A lot of people sleep naked. A few of them even do it alone. Not that she felt any pressing need to explain herself.

"What a nice surprise," she said.

"I'm a bit early," I said. "But I was in the area. So, I thought I'd drop by." I brandished the magazine as evidence. "I hope I'm not interrupting something."

She took the magazine from my hand, glanced at it, and then tossed it aside. "One of the boys from last night must have left it."

"That's what I thought."

We sat down on the sofa. Elena crossed her legs, affording me a fine curving view of her upper thigh.

"Light me a cigarette, will you, darling?"

I lit us each one and concentrated on the little matching silk slipper that was holding on to the end of her perfect toes.

"I called your hotel this morning, but they said you'd already gone out."

"Oh?"

"Yes. I wanted to see that you were all right. Last night, just after you'd left, I went up to bed and as I was drawing the curtains in my room, I saw a car parked on the corner. And a man standing beside it."

"What kind of car?" I asked.

"Dark green. Alfa Romeo sports sedan."

"Uh-huh."

"I had the strange idea that the driver was Wlazyslaw Pulnarowicz. I mean, it looked very much like the colonel. Except for the fact that he wasn't wearing his uniform. And he owns a white BMW."

"I see. What was he wearing? This man you saw."

Elena shrugged and played with her cigarette.

"The light wasn't good. But I think he was wearing a light brown suit and spat shoes. You know, white, with a dark toe."

"How about a hat?"

She shrugged. "Yes. A Panama. He was holding it in his hands."

I thought for a moment about the man who had shot at me. "When you first talked about the colonel, you said he was the old-fashioned type and that he might get jealous and challenge me to a duel."

Elena nodded.

"Do you think he's the type that could murder a man in cold blood?"

"Oh, darling, they all are. That's what the SOE is all about."

"Someone took a shot at me last night. In Ezbekiah Gardens. He missed me, but another man, an Egyptian, was killed, Elena."

"Oh my God, you don't think it was Lazlo?"

"It looks that way. The only people running around Cairo carrying pistols with silencers work for SOE, or the German Abwehr." I shrugged. It wasn't anything like the ball I had pitched Harry Hopkins, but I still liked a German spy ring for the murders of Ted and Debbie Schmidt. I would have to speak to Colonel Powell about Wlazyslaw Pulnarowicz. "It might be that after the party, the colonel drove back home, changed out of his uniform, borrowed someone's car, and then came back to see if I was still here. Then he followed me back to my hotel, where he tried to give my brain some air-conditioning."

This time Elena took a proper hit on her cigarette. "I'm so sorry," she said.

"Don't be. You're Desdemona in this play. Not Othello."

"All the same, it was me who put you in harm's way, Willy. It was me who made him jealous." She shook her head. "God damn the man. It's not like there was even anything to feel jealous about. We were just two old friends, catching up."

"Maybe that was true last night," I said and then kissed her on the lips. "But not now."

She smiled and kissed me back. "No, you're right. Now he would have every reason to feel jealous."

"He's not hiding upstairs, is he?"

"No. Would you like to check?"

"I think I should, don't you?"

Elena stood up and, taking me by the hand, led me out of the drawing room toward the stairs.

"Of course you know what this means, don't you?" I said. "It means you're going to have to show me your bedroom wallpaper."

"I hope you like it."

"I'm sure I will."

She led me into a hallway as big as a railway station, up the huge yellow marble stairs, into her bedroom, and closed the doors behind us. I glanced around. I didn't see her wallpaper. I didn't see the rug beneath my feet. I didn't even see her bed. All I saw was Elena and the white silk gown slipping off her shoulders and the reflection of my own hands cupping her bare behind in a full-length cheval mirror.

I LAY STILL next to the refuge afforded by Elena's naked body. I thought of Heinrich Zahler and Helmut von Dorff lying in the cold ground of Beketovka. I thought of the insane Polish colonel who wanted to kill me, and the ruthless Nazi agent on the ship, and the imprisoned German major who was working to decode some signals that might reveal me to have been a Russian spy. I thought of poor Ted Schmidt's body, or what remained of it, somewhere in the mid-Atlantic. I thought of Diana lying on the floor of her Chevy Chase house and her nameless lover's bare backside framed between her knees. I thought of Mrs. Schmidt lying in the cold drawer of a Metro Police morgue. I thought of the president. I thought of Harry Hopkins and Winston Churchill and Josef Stalin. I even thought of Wild Bill Donovan and Colonel Powell. But mostly I thought of Elena. The shadows moved across the bedside cabinet and I thought of death. I thought of my own death, and assured myself that it seemed a long way off when I was with Elena.

For a while I slept and dreamed of Elena. When I did wake, she was in the bathroom, singing quietly. I sat up, switched on the bedside light, lit a cigarette, and looked around for something to read. On a large chest of drawers were several leather-bound photograph albums, and thinking that these might contain some pictures of our old times together in Berlin, I opened one and started turning the pages. Mostly the album was full of pictures of Elena in various Cairo nightclubs with her late husband, Freddy, and, once or twice, with King Farouk himself. But it was a page of photographs taken in the roof garden at the Auberge des Pyramides (Elena captioned all of her pictures in a neat, penciled hand) that, for the second time that day, left me feeling as if a camel had kicked me in the stomach.

In the photographs, Elena was seated beside a handsome man in a cream linen suit. He had his arm around her and she looked to be on the most intimate terms with him. What was surprising was that this was a man currently occupying a cell at Grey Pillars, less than half a mile away. The man in the photograph was Major Max Reichleitner.

I told myself these pictures could hardly have been taken before the war. Hadn't Coogan told me that the Auberge des Pyramides had opened just a few months before? Hearing Elena coming out of the bathroom, I quickly put aside the album and retrieved my hardly smoked cigarette from its ashtray.

"Light me one, will you, darling?" she said. She was wearing nothing but a gold watch.

"Here, you can have this one," I said, moving to her side.

I watched her closely as she took a puff, then put it out. Unpinning her blond hair, which was long enough to come past her waist, she began to brush it absently. Thinking that I was looking at her with desire, she smiled and said, "Do you want to have me again? Is that it?"

She climbed onto the bed and held her arms open expectantly. Taking a deep breath, I knelt over her but I could not help but consider the possibility that she herself was working for the Germans. Given the intimacy in the photograph of her with Reichleitner, was it at all possible that he would have come to Cairo and not tried to see her? Elena simply had to be his contact. After all, she wouldn't know that Reichleitner had been captured by the Allies.

I put myself inside her, drawing a long, shuddering gasp from her.

Only now did the speed with which she had gone to bed with me again seem at all suspicious. I began to thrust hard, almost as if I were trying to punish her for the duplicity I now strongly suspected. Elena came with equal force, and for a moment I abandoned myself to pleasure. Then she snuggled into my side, and my doubts returned. Was it possible that she was more than just a contact?

But if she was a German spy, when had she been recruited? Casting my mind back to Berlin in the summer of 1938, I tried to recall the Elena Pontiatowska with whom I'd been intimate.

Elena had hated the Bolsheviks, that much was easy to remember. I recalled one particular conversation we had had when news of Stalin's Ukrainian terror began to reach the West. Elena, whose father had fought in the Russo-Polish war of 1920, had insisted that the whole edifice of Soviet communism was based on mass murder, but Stalin was no worse than Lenin in that respect.

"My father always said that Lenin ordered the extermination of the entire Don Cossack people—a million men, women, and children," she had told me. "It's not that I like the Nazis. I don't, as it happens. It's just that I fear the Russians more. I know that however stupid and cruel the Nazis can be, the Russians are far worse. If Hitler wants the Sudetenland, it's because he thinks he needs it as a bulwark against another Russian invasion. Perhaps the Czechs have forgotten what Trotsky did to them, in 1918, when he tried to turn their army into slave-labor battalions. Mark my words, Willy, they wouldn't hesitate to do the same thing again. The Nazis are a bad lot, but the Bolsheviks are evil. That's why Hitler got elected in the first place. Because people were terrified that the Reds might gain control in Germany. So you won't convince me that there is anything good to be said about communism. Perhaps it sounds good in principle, as an ideal. But my family has seen it in practice, and it's nothing short of bestial."

Disliking the Russians was one thing; spying for the Nazis was another. There was only one thing for it. In order to be sure, one way or the other, I was going to have to search Elena's house. If there were photographs of Major Reichleitner in an album, then there might easily be other evidence that would prove one way or the other if Elena were working for the Abwehr.

Elena roused herself, gave me a brief kiss, and returned to the bathroom.

I picked up the photo album. I wanted to see what she would say when she found me looking at it. At the pictures of her with Reichleitner. It would be instructive to see exactly how she tried to explain them. But when she emerged from the bathroom, she didn't bat an eye.

"I'm sorry," I said. "I couldn't resist having a peek. I suppose I thought there might be one or two pictures of you and me, back in Berlin."

"They're in another album," she said coolly, her only concern seeming to be that we dress and find some dinner. "I'll show you later. It's time you got ready. I thought we could go to the club. But you'll need to change. We can stop at your hotel on the way."

"Who's the man in the white suit?" I asked, putting aside the album and going into the bathroom.

"Don't tell me you're jealous," she said, pulling on her underwear.

"Of course I'm jealous. You're the best thing that's happened to me since this war started. And now I see I have yet another rival."

"Take my word for it, he's no threat to you."

"I don't know. You and he seem pretty close in those pictures. Good-looking fellow, too."

"Max? Yes, I suppose so." Elena shrugged and, sitting down on the edge of the bed, began to roll on a pair of stockings. "For a while we were, you know. Close, like you say. But it didn't last long. He was a Polish officer from Sikorski's staff. From Posen. A rare bird."

"Oh? How do you mean?"

"A German-speaking Pole who fought for the Polish army. That's how rare."

"And where is he now?"

"I'm not sure. I haven't seen him in several months. Since the summer, I think. Max did a lot of work for SOE. In Yugoslavia. At least that's what he told me."

I nodded, thinking that these were good answers—they had the merit of being possibly true.

Elena finished fastening her stocking to its garter and, opening her closet, stared at an armory of devastating gowns. She pulled one out and put it on. Then she looked at her watch again. "Hurry up," she said.

XXI

WEDNESDAY, NOVEMBER 24, 1943,
IRAN

IN ITS SOUTHERN PART, the streets of Teheran were narrow and tortuous; in the northern part, there were broad avenues. Misbah Ebtehaj, the wrestler who was acting as North Team's guide and translator, said that much of the character of the city had been destroyed by the previous shah. But North Team's commander, Captain Oster, thought that Reza Shah's modernization could hardly have altered the fact that it was not a good location for a city. The nearest river was forty kilometers away, which meant that potable water was always in short supply. Two of Oster's men were already sick from drinking the local water.

It was cold, too, much colder than they had expected, which Oster felt Berlin ought to have known about, given that Shimran, the northern part of Teheran, was built on the slopes of a mountain more than 20,000 meters high. But apart from a lack of warm clothing, everything had gone as planned.

North Team had parachuted into the remote foothills of the Alborz Mountains, northeast of Qazvin, where they had been met on the ground by Kashgai tribesmen, the backbone of the local resistance movement to the joint British and Soviet rule of Iran. The team had spent the first night in the countryside, hiding in a castle fortress that had once been the mountain hideaway of the Hashishiyun, an ancient Ismaili sect that was better known in the West as the Assassins. It seemed appropriate, Oster thought, more so when he considered that the business of the Kashgai, most of whom smoked hashish at all times of the day, was morphine. The Kashgai had seemed genuinely delighted with the weapons, the gold, and the golden pistols that North Team had brought with them from the Ukraine. Oster thought they were a fearsome, shifty lot, and on that first night, in the ruins of the fortress, he had half expected to wake up and find his throat being cut by one of these murderous-looking and intoxicated tribesmen. He had slept fitfully, with his hand holding a Mauser pistol underneath the knapsack he used as a pillow. It was hard to believe that these men, dressed like Ali Baba's forty thieves, could have found any common cause with Nazi Germany.

Ebtehaj, huge and bearded, with the shoulders of a bear and smelling strongly of liniment, and forever feeding a string of prayer beads through his rope-thick fingers, told Oster how it was that the Kashgai were helping him and his troops. It was the day after their arrival, and after a two-hour hike through the hills the team had rendezvoused with the two trucks that would take them on the next stage of their journey, a drive of more than a hundred kilometers southwest into Teheran.

"It's not that we're for Germany," he explained, "so much as that we're against the British and the Russians. Germany has no history of interference in Persia. But for these two it is a game about who will control our oil. The British have been here since the last war. But they came in greater force in 1941, to protect Russia's ass. They deposed the shah, sent him into exile, and made his son, Crown Prince Reza Pahlavi, their puppet. The German embassy was closed. All pro-German Persians were arrested and imprisoned without trial in Sultanabad, including the prime minister. But the real leader of the opposition, Habibullah Nobakht, managed to get away somehow, and now he makes war on truck convoys.

"You see, Captain, Persia is a most independent country. Yes, it is true, the country has been invaded many times. But the invader always came, looted, and then left. It was worth no one's while to stay here. What would they stay for? Persia is a desert country. But that was before oil, of course, and before Russia realized she had a back door through which she might be supplied by the Americans. Which is how you find us now.

"The British and the Russians tell us that they will not interfere in Persia after the war, but they rule their respective zones like independent provinces in their empires. The Russians make us their cesspit, sending us all their Polish prisoners and their Jews. Never have so many people come to Persia. Maybe a quarter of a million people. And these Poles, they bring all sorts of diseases. All sorts of problems. Why send them here? If Poland is Russia's ally then why not keep them in Russia? They are Slavs, not Persians. But no one listens." The wrestler laughed. "All right, so we can fix that, yes? We will kill Stalin, Churchill, and Roosevelt, and maybe they will leave us alone. Then we will kill all the Poles. Only then will Persia be good for Persians."

The trucks had brought North Team to Teheran's bazaar, a city within a city, a labyrinth of streets and alleys. Each street specialized in selling a particular commodity, and the wrestler took them to the carpet street, where he had arranged for them to stay in a disused rug factory. Still full of rugs, it proved quite comfortable. Food was brought to them. Their first hot meal in Iran consisted of bread and a soupy stew called *dizi*, and tea was served from a samovar that made Oster's Ukrainians feel entirely at home. This was just as well, for Ebtehaj told Oster that, in his opinion, it had been a mistake for Berlin to send Ukrainians on this mission. His Kashgai brothers were half inclined to think of them as Russians, and it took Oster some time to convince the wrestler that Ukrainians were not only different from Russians but that they also had more reason to hate the Russians than anyone.

On Wednesday morning the wrestler took Oster to the main entrance to the bazaar, where they were to meet one of the German agents in Teheran. Oster wore a dark suit and a cap. Since most of the men in the city wore European-style trousers, short coats, and Pahlavi hats, he didn't look out of place. Oster knew very little about his contact, Lothar Schoellhorn, other than that he had once run a boxing academy in Berlin and, for a while before his posting to Persia, had acted as an assassin for the Abwehr. Oster had half expected to meet a thug, but instead he found himself with a man of considerable learning and culture who held strong views on his adopted city. From the bazaar gate, the three men walked north, up Ferdosi Street in the direction of the British embassy.

"It's a disappointing place, Teheran," said Schoellhorn. "From an architectural point of view, at least. The modern part is rather French, and, as a result, somewhat pretentious. Like a poor man's version of the Champs-Elysées. Even the Mejlis—that's the Iranian Parliament—is not all that distinguished. Only the bazaar retains something of the old, absolutely Oriental Teheran. Everything else has been modernized into mediocrity, I'm afraid. There's the odd mosque, of course. But that's about all.

"In winter it's much too cold, and in summer it's much too hot, and for this reason, the British and the Americans each maintain two embassies. Right now the British are in their winter embassy, which you shall see presently. It's a rather ramshackle building that was constructed, poorly, by the Indian Public Works Department many years ago. Trusting Persians as little as they do, the British still maintain a small escort of Indian infantry for the ambassador's protection. Here, and at the summer embassy in Gulheh." Schoellhorn smiled. "It wouldn't do to attack the wrong embassy."

Oster glanced around, nervous that someone might overhear.

"Oh, there's nothing to worry about, my friend. It's true, the city is crawling with NKVD agents, but frankly a blind man could see them coming. None of them speak Farsi, and even in their zone of occupation to the north of the city, they employ no Persian police or gendarmerie. Which makes them less than effective. Elsewhere, law and order are the province of the British and the Americans. We shall have to be a little careful of the British, I think. But the Americans are wholly ignorant of the Persians and only manage to keep order by virtue of the fact that they are not yet as hated as the Russians or the British. The fellow in charge of the American police, a general named Schwarzkopf, used to narrate a popular cops-and-robbers program on radio—can you believe it? This same Schwarzkopf was the *Dummkopf* who led the investigation into the Lindbergh kidnapping case, and you will perhaps recall what a mess was made there—and how a German was framed for the child's murder."

Schoellhorn slowed a little as they came in sight of a large barrier covered in barbed wire that prevented further progress. Behind the barrier were two armored cars and several Indian troops wearing British uniforms.

"Beyond the barrier and those trees are the British and the Russian embassies," said Schoellhorn. "They are separated by a narrow side street, but in the wall of the British legation is a narrow wicker gate where a sentry is usually posted at night and which presents your best point of entry. A map of the British compound will be provided, but on the other side of the wall you will find lots of trees and bushes which will provide ample opportunity for cover. There's a long balustraded verandah on the eastern part of the legation compound, and very likely the Big Three will be immediately behind the French windows. To the west are stables and outhouses accommodating not horses but troops guarding the legation. As I said, they're Indians mostly. Or, to be more precise, Sikhs. They're courageous enough, no question. But I gather they're none too fond of bombardment, or so a friend of mine in the British Public Relations Bureau here in Teheran would have me believe. There was a bomb blast in the city a few months ago and the Sikhs legged it, I'm told. The minute our bombers drop their ordnance, they'll probably make a run for it."

"What about the Russian legation?" asked Oster.

"Crawling with Popovs. One in every tree. Even the waiters are NKVD. Floodlights, dogs, machine-gun nests. The building has just been subject to an extensive renovation. A new air-raid bunker, it seems." Schoellhorn lit a cigarette. "No, it's just as well your target is the British legation. From the look of things, I doubt Churchill even considers the possibility that he might be assassinated. Still, there's one thing about the British legation that makes it the safest place in Teheran."

"Oh? And what's that?"

"The water. The British pipe in water from a pure source in the hills to the north. They even sell it to the Russians. It even crossed my mind that you should make this part of your plan. You see, every morning a Russian and an American water cart turn up for their water. But then again, you'd hardly want to be inside the legation walls if and when the Luftwaffe start to bomb the place."

"Good point," grinned Oster. "Besides, if we do manage to kill the Big Three, it won't be water I'm drinking, but champagne. Eh, Ebtehaj?"

The wrestler gave an obsequious little bow. "Regrettably, alcohol is not permitted to Muslims," he said.

Oster smiled politely and stared beyond the wrestler's sturdy shoulder at the purple screen of snow-capped mountains that lay behind the city. It would not be easy getting out of Teheran after an assassination, he reflected, and suddenly Oster felt a very long way from home.

They returned to the bazaar, where, among the mosques, the crowds of people and the shops, Ebtehaj seemed to relax a little. The variety of things for sale astonished Oster: copper, book-bindings, flags, haberdashery, saddles, tin, knives, woodwork, and carpets. Once or twice he stopped to have a look at something, reasoning that not to look at all might invite suspicion. There was even a moment to enjoy a coffee at the Café Ferdosi, so that by the time they returned to the rug factory, Oster was feeling slightly more well-disposed toward Persia and the Persians. This feeling did not last long. As soon as the three men entered the factory, one of the Kashgai tribesmen walked quickly up to Ebtehaj and said something that left the wrestler looking very worried.

"What's wrong?" Oster asked Schoellhorn.

"It seems that we have caught a spy," said the German.

In the back of the factory, seated on the floor and tied to an old loom by bunches of carpet thread, was a frightened-looking man wearing Western-style clothes.

"Who is he?" asked Oster.

Untersturmführers Schnabel and Shkvarzev turned away from the prisoner to answer.

"Says he's a Pole, sir," said Schnabel. "And that he came here looking for a carpet. There's plenty of cash in his pocket to buy one. But he also had this." Schnabel showed Oster a semiautomatic pistol.

"It's a Tokarev TT," said Shkvarzev, removing a cigarette from the corner of his unshaven mouth. "Russian-made. But here's the thing." He took the pistol from Schnabel, dropped the magazine out of the Tokarev's grip, and thumbed one of the bullets onto his palm for Oster's close inspection. "It's Mauser ammunition. German-made, and flat-nosed, too. Filed down, so that it makes a bigger hole on impact. To make identification of the victim harder. It's standard SMERSH procedure."

"SMERSH?" frowned Schoellhorn. "What's that?"

"It's a Russian acronym," explained Shkvarzev. "It means 'death to spies.' SMERSH is the counterintelligence wing of the NKVD and Stalin's personal assassination squad."

Oster sighed and looked at Schoellhorn and Mehdizadeh. "We'll need to find somewhere else to stay. Can you organize it?"

"That won't be easy," said Mehdizadeh. "It took a while just to find this place. But I'll see what I can do," he said, leaving.

"What shall we do with him?" Schnabel asked, pointing to the prisoner.

"There's no time to interrogate him properly," Oster said. "We'll just have to kill him and leave him here."

"On the contrary." Shkvarzev was grinning. "There's plenty of time to interrogate him. Properly, improperly, it's all the same in the end. In five minutes I can have this fellow confess to the murder of Trotsky, if that's what you want."

Oster disliked torture, but he knew that there was no other way to be sure about what the Russians were already aware of. "All right," he told Shkvarzev. "Do it. Just don't make a meal of it."

The carpets that had been crafted in the factory were made of wool, by hand. The finished product was usually laid out on the floor, and any bumps or small imperfections flattened out with a heavy iron filled with coals from the fire. As soon as the SMERSH agent saw that the Ukrainians intended to use the hot iron on his bare feet, he started to offer information. For a moment, Shkvarzev's men seemed a little disappointed that they were not going to have the opportunity of inflicting pain on a hated enemy.

"Yes, yes, all right, I'll tell you everything," blathered the man. "I was snooping around the bazaar, hoping to find out something. Everyone in Teheran knows that this is where the resistance is centered, so I figured it might be a good place to look for you."

"What do you mean, 'look for us'?" demanded Oster.

"You're the German parachute team. One of your Kashgai tribesmen came to the SMERSH building on Syroos Street and told us that two teams of SS had landed somewhere outside the city. For the Big Three Conference. He sold us the information. We've already picked up one team, near the radar installation at the airport. And it's only a matter of time before you are arrested, too."

"Get on the radio right away," Oster told Schnabel. "See if you can raise von Holten-Pflug, if it's not already too late. And better keep it short, just in case they're trying to get a radio fix on us."

"Who's your boss?" asked Shkvarzev.

"Colonel Andrei Mikhalovits. At least he *was*—now there's a new fellow in charge. A Jew from Kiev. Brigadier General Mikhail Moisseevich Melamed."

"I know him," grunted Shkvarzev. "He's a state security commissar, third class, and the most hated NKVD officer in the Red Army."

"That's him," declared the prisoner. "Of course, who knows who'll be in charge by the end of the week. Beria's deputy, General Merkulov, is arriving tomorrow. And then his secretary, Stepan Mamulov. Beria himself will be coming here, too, for all I know."

"How many NKVD are in Teheran right now?" asked Shkvarzev.

"At least a couple hundred. And we've had about three thousand extra Red Army troops since the end of October. Commanded by Krulev."

"Any other officers you know of?"

"Arkadiev, the Soviet commissar of state security. And General Avramov, from the Near Eastern Area Office. They came here to round up the remaining pro-German suspects. About three hundred Poles. Most of them first arrested in Poland." To which he added, matter-of-factly, "They were shot. In the Russian barracks to the north of the city, in Meshed."

"What was the name of the Kashgai tribesman who told you about the German parachute team landing in Iran?" asked Oster, speaking Russian.

"I don't know." The prisoner yelped as one of the Ukrainians pressed the hot iron against the sole of his left foot momentarily. "Yes, all right, I do. His name is Mehdizah."

Schoellhorn swore loudly. "Mehdizah is another wrestler!" he said. "He was supposed to be looking after South Team."

"What about *our* wrestler?" asked Oster. "Herr Ebtehaj. Maybe he's in this, too. Maybe he tipped off our friend from SMERSH here. Maybe he's going to come back here with the Red Army."

"No." Schoellhorn shook his head. "He could have betrayed us many times already. So why didn't he?"

"If I may say so," Oster said carefully, "all of this is a very long way from the picture you were painting earlier today. How a blind man can spot an NKVD agent."

"Are you suggesting *I'm* a traitor, too?" said Schoellhorn.

"I don't know what I'm suggesting. Christ, what a mess." He removed his broom-handle Mauser from the holster inside his jacket and began to screw a silencer onto the end of the barrel. "I just wish that bastard Schellenberg was here to see this. It would be the *last* thing he would see, I can promise you that."

Oster stood in front of the prisoner, the now silenced pistol still pointed at the floor and parallel with his trouser leg.

"I told you everything I know," the Pole said, swallowing.

Oster smiled sadly and then shot the man three times in the head and face.

Shkvarzev nodded his approval. He had been wondering what the German captain was made of, how much stomach he had for killing, and now he knew. It was one thing to shoot a man in a fire-fight, with a rifle or a machine gun; but it was quite another to kill him in cold blood, as he looked you in the eye. This German was all right, he could see that now, and as Oster made the Mauser safe and unscrewed the silencer, Shkvarzev lit a cigarette and handed it to him.

"Thanks," Oster said and, placing the cigarette between his lips, drew on it deeply as he holstered his pistol again. "Did you get through to South Team?" he asked Schnabel.

"No, sir. I don't seem to be able to raise them at all. But I did receive a message from Berlin. We're scrubbed."

"What?" Oster's face collapsed into fury. "Ask for confirmation."

"I already did."

Shkvarzev sighed. "So that's that, then," he said. "We're scrubbed."

"Like hell we are," said Oster. "I didn't come all this way to do fuck-all. If I'm going to die in a Soviet labor camp, it'll be for a damn good reason." He took a long drag on the cigarette and then flicked it at the dead man's head. "How do the rest of you feel about that?"

Shkvarzev hardly had to glance at his men. "The same way as you. There's nothing we wouldn't do for a chance to kill Stalin. Nothing."

"But without those Junkers bombers," said Schoellhorn. "And the South Team. What can you do?"

"Perhaps none of that matters," murmured Oster.

"How do you mean?" asked Schoellhorn.

"Maybe I like your plan better."

"My plan?"

"We're too many and not enough," said Oster. "That's the trouble with Schellenberg's plan. Too many not to be noticed before next Tuesday. And not enough to deal with three thousand fucking Russians. But a couple of men with a water cart could do the job. You can put anything in a water cart. Machine guns. A bomb." Oster looked at Shkvarzev. "What would we need to make a decent-sized bomb, Shkvarzev?"

"Now you're talking." The Ukrainian lit a cigarette for himself and thought out loud. "Some sort of nitrogen fertilizer, rich in nitric acid," he said. "A nitrating agent to make a glycerine compound with the nitric acid—sugar, sawdust, lard, indigo, cork are all commonly obtained nitrating agents. A few grenades, some mercury, and some ethyl alcohol to make a reliable detonator. And an alarm clock and some batteries, on the assumption you don't want to be around when the thing goes off."

"Could you make such a bomb?"

Shkvarzev spat on the floor and then smiled. "Child's play."

"Then that's settled. As soon as we get to another safe house I want you to start building a bloody big bomb."

XXII
WEDNESDAY, NOVEMBER 24, 1943,
CAIRO

SLIPPING OUT of Elena's bed in the early light of an Egyptian dawn, I went onto the balcony. Beyond the extensive chaos of Garden City rooftops, it was possible to see across the Nile as far as the river island of Zamalek and the Gezira Sporting Club, where Elena and I had dined just a few hours before.

The Gezira was something straight out of *The Four Feathers,* a club so stiff it hurt, and it left me puzzled why Elena should have wanted to go there. It was like seeing the whole of the British empire preserved in aspic jelly. Everyone was in uniform or evening dress, or a combination of both. A little quintet played dreary British popular music and red-faced men and pink-looking women shuffled their way across the dance floor. The only people with dark skins were the men holding silver trays or towels over their arms. Every time Elena introduced me to someone I caught a faint smell of snobbery.

There was only one person I was happy to see. The trouble was, Colonel Powell assumed I was eager to resume our philosophical discussion, and it took me quite a while to divert him onto a subject that now interested me more.

"Do you know a Polish colonel by the name of Wlazyslaw Pulnarowicz?" I asked.

Powell looked surprised. "Why do you ask?"

"I met him last night," I said. "At a dinner party. I think I may have got on the wrong side of him. Since then, I've been informed that he is not a man to cross."

"That was also my impression," said Powell. "A most ruthless character. Might I inquire if your disagreement with Wlazyslaw Pulnarowicz was to do with philosophy?"

Thinking I had better keep off the subject of philosophy altogether, as far as Powell was concerned, I shook my head. "Actually it was about the merits—or lack of merits—of the Soviet Union. The colonel takes a very dim view of the Russians. And of Stalin in particular. I think Pulnarowicz perceives Stalin as a kind of modern Herodotus, if you like. As the 'father of modern lies,' I think he said."

Powell smiled thinly.

"If you are concerned that the colonel is ever likely to seek you out, I can put your mind at rest, in a manner of speaking. Regrettably, Colonel Wlazyslaw Pulnarowicz was killed late this afternoon. The plane on which he was traveling was shot down somewhere in the northern Mediterranean. He was on a secret mission, you understand. As a result, I'm afraid I am duty bound to tell you no more than that."

I let out a breath that was a mixture of relief and surprise. And for a moment or two, I was hardly aware that Powell had already changed the subject and was disputing my description of Herodotus.

"Herodotus only makes the mistakes that are common to all historians," he said. "Which are that he was not there and often relies on sources that are themselves unreliable. After this war is over, don't you think it will be interesting to read the many lies that will be told of who did what and when and why, and of the things that were done, and the things that were not? Although God cannot alter the past, historians can and do provide a useful function in this respect. Which persuades Him, perhaps, to tolerate their existence."

"Yes, I suppose so," I said vaguely.

Powell seemed to detect my relief that Pulnarowicz was dead, and he changed the subject back again. "Wlazyslaw Pulnarowicz was a good soldier," he said. "But he was not a good man. It is the nature of war to find ourselves with some pretty strange bedfellows."

Standing on the balcony of Elena's bedroom, I finished my cigarette and reflected that Enoch Powell was more right than he had known. My own current bedfellow was very possibly a German spy. I had to find out if my suspicions were justified. She remained soundly asleep, so I left the balcony and slipped quietly out of the bedroom. I wasn't sure what I was looking for, but I felt I would recognize it if I saw it.

On the sweeping marble staircase, I laid my hand on the wrought-iron balustrade and peered over into the hallway. Apart from the sound of a ticking grandfather clock and a stray dog barking somewhere in the street outside, the house was as quiet as a mausoleum.

At the end of a long corridor, I entered a door and found a set of stairs leading to a laundry room, a wine cellar stocked with some very choice vintages, and several storerooms that were filled mostly with old paintings. There were one or two pictures I recognized from Elena's house in Berlin and various pieces of dusty-looking Biedermeier furniture.

I tiptoed back up to the second floor, where I checked that Elena was still sleeping before opening the doors to some of the other rooms. One set of double doors revealed a whole stone staircase and, at the top of this, another door that led into what looked like an apartment complete with drawing room, kitchen, bedroom, bathroom, and library. There was even a sort of tower with bars on the windows. Just the place to lock up a mad prince or two.

I was about to call off the search and return to the bedroom when my eye caught sight of a book on one of the shelves. It was my own book, *On Being Empirical,* and, much to my surprise, I found that it had been substantially annotated. I could not understand the annotations, which were in Polish, but I did recognize Elena's handwriting. And yet she had given me the impression that my book had been beyond her understanding. This hardly counted as evidence of anything except perhaps that she was a lot cleverer than I had always supposed.

But then I noticed a small curving mark on the carpet that ran from the corner of the bookcase toward the wall beside it—almost as if the bookcase itself was regularly shifted. Taking hold of the side of the case, I tugged at it gently, only to find it was also a door.

As I advanced into the darkness behind the bookcase, I noticed a smell. It was the same smell I had detected in the drawing room the previous afternoon. American cigarettes, Old Spice, and brilliantine. I reached out for a light switch and saw a room about ten feet square. The room was equipped with a chair and a table on which a lamp and a German radio stood. I recognized the radio immediately, for it had been one of the first things they had shown us on the OSS induction training course at Catoctin Mountain. One of the eight German agents arrested on Long Island in July 1942 had been equipped with just such a radio. It was standard Abwehr issue, an SE100/11 with the controls all printed in English to try and disguise it. The disguise might have fooled a civilian but not someone who was in the trade. Back in the States, just possessing a sender/receiver was enough to get you the electric chair.

On the table in front of the radio was a little Walther PPK automatic. It seemed to make clear that Elena meant business. If it really was her gun. The masculine scent in the room suggested she had another confederate besides Major Reichleitner. I picked up the pistol. Turning it upside down, I ejected the magazine from the plastic grip. The gun was loaded, not that I had expected otherwise. I shoved the magazine back into the handle and laid it down on the table.

I tiptoed back to the top of the stone stairs for a moment to check that my dirty little mission was still a secret. And it was about then that I had the sudden sensation I was being watched. I remained standing there for several minutes before concluding I had imagined it, and returned to the secret radio room.

I sat on the chair, reached underneath the table, and drew a metallic wastepaper bin toward me. It was full of paper. I placed it between my naked thighs and began to examine the contents. It showed a great want of vigilance not to have set alight the cellophane sheets intended to help burn any plaintext messages sent or received. Abwehr agents, even the ones from Long Island, were usually not so careless. Perhaps the secret room itself had lulled Elena into a false sense of security about normal spycraft. Or perhaps the lack of a window.

I fished a message out of the bin, spread the paper flat on the table, glanced over it, and then folded it up so that I could read it later. I was about to return the wastepaper bin to its place underneath the table when something else caught my eye.

It was an empty package of Kools. Kools were a mentholated American brand of cigarettes that neither I nor Elena smoked. Smoking Kools was like smoking a stick of chewing gum. Even more interesting was what I found crushed up inside the empty packet. It was a matchbook with only one match left. It was from the Hamilton Hotel in Washington. The Hamilton Hotel overlooked Franklin Park, where Thornton Cole's body had been found. Finding this matchbook in the same room as an SE100 radio was all the evidence I needed to know that the man who had killed Cole, and very likely Ted Schmidt, too, had occupied the very chair I was sitting in.

All I had to do now was tell Reilly, and then he could arrange with the British to have the place staked out until the German agent showed up again. I snatched up the evidence—the plaintext message, the empty package of Kools, the Hamilton Hotel matchbook—and went out of the radio room. I knew I could hardly catch the spy without condemning Elena as well.

I turned out the light, closed the bookcase door, and returned to the bedroom. Seeing her stir under the single sheet, I pretended to fetch a pack of cigarettes from my coat pocket.

"What are you doing?" she asked, sitting up.

"I'm just going to the bathroom," I said, lighting a cigarette. "Go back to sleep."

I closed the bathroom door, sat down on the toilet, and unfolded the plaintext message headed OPERATION WURF. In German, *wurf* was the verb "to throw," but, figuratively speaking, it also meant "success," "a hit," "a stroke of luck," and even, "a decisive action." The message, addressed to someone called Brutus, was short, and everything about it supported the idea of some kind of decisive action. I read the message several times before folding it carefully and sliding it inside my own cigarette packet, alongside the matchbook from the Hamilton Hotel. Then I stood up, flushed the toilet, and went back to bed.

There wasn't much chance of my sleeping again—not now that I had read the plaintext message from the Abwehr. And as dawn broke, I was still repeating the message in my head. *Brutus to proceed with the assassination of Wotan. Good luck.*

It was a while since I had seen an opera by Wagner, but I remembered that Wotan was one of the gods in *Das Rheingold*. This seemed to suggest that Brutus, whoever he was, planned to kill just one of the Big Three. But surely not Roosevelt or Churchill. Neither of them appeared to match up to Wotan. No, there was only one of the Big Three who seemed to fit the bill, and that was Joseph Stalin.

Elena awoke for a few minutes and kissed me fondly before going back to sleep. I really did think she cared for me. I knew I cared for her. And I knew I wasn't prepared to send her over, no matter who or what she was. I tried to sleep a little in the hope that when I awoke I would know the right thing to do. But the sleep never came. And after a while I could think of no other way forward than the one I had first thought of. I slipped out of bed and, before leaving her bedroom, took the photograph of Elena and Major Reichleitner from her album, to make sure that I would be believed.

REICHLEITNER was still eating breakfast when Lance Corporal Armfield brought me to his cell. The major greeted me coolly. At first I was inclined to ascribe this display of indifference to the fact that his breakfast was not yet over. But as I lit a cigarette and waited for him to look me in the eye, I realized that something had happened. And that was when, looking around the cell, I saw Donovan's Bride transcripts piled neatly on the table, the task of rendering them into plaintext now complete.

"Everything is clear to me now," said Reichleitner. He was wearing a superior smile I found annoying, after all that I had done for him.

"Why haven't you tried to tell someone?"

"Don't think I won't. But, no, I wanted to speak to you first. To tell you what I require for my silence."

"And what might that be?" I smiled, half enjoying his little show.

"Your help to escape."

This time I laughed. "I think you're being a little premature, Major. After all, I need to see what you think you know and how you think that you know it. Cards on the table. Then perhaps we can make a deal."

"All right. If you want to play it that way." Reichleitner shrugged and fetched the papers off the table. "The Russians call this 'open packing,'" he said. "Even though it's deciphered, the use of certain code words still makes it hard for the layman to understand. How to read what ought to be plain, but is not. You will note the date of this particular message, please. October eighth. The message concerns a meeting that took place in London.

I nodded, more or less certain now I knew the meeting to which he was referring.

"LEO reports in his last LUGGAGE that he had BREAKFAST in GLADSTONE with a 26 who we now know was formerly a NOVATOR for SPARTA in TROY during the year 1937. Codenamed CROESUS. VERSAILLES suggests watching brief minimum, since CROESUS now works for ORVILLE and STAMP in a special capacity, and might provide future KNAPSACK. At any subsequent BREAKFAST you should stress the desperation of the situation in SPARTA and, if all else fails, you should tell him that we may have to weigh the question of his 43."

Reichleitner smiled. "LEO is the name of an agent," he said. "And BREAKFAST is a meeting, of course. GLADSTONE is London. A number 26 is a potential recruit for the NKVD. A NOVATOR is an existing NKVD agent. SPARTA means Soviet Russia, and TROY refers to Nazi Germany. CROESUS is you, I suspect, since you work for both ORVILLE—that's Donovan, I imagine—and

STAMP—that's Roosevelt, I know. KNAPSACK is information that might develop into something more important. Number 43 means last will and testament."

"Well, that part about the last will and testament ought to tell you something, Major."

"Not as much as the fact that you were once a NOVATOR for SPARTA."

"'Once' being the critical word. For example, I imagine you're no longer the enthusiastic Nazi you were back in 1933. Well, in 1938 I was a lecturer at the University of Berlin and occasionally came into contact with Dr. Goebbels. I decided that the best way I had of opposing Nazism was to pass on any information that came my way to the Russians. Only all that ended when I left Germany to return to the United States.

"Then, a few weeks ago, when I was in London researching a report for the president on the Katyn Forest massacre, I ran into someone I'd known back in Vienna. An Englishman who had been a fellow Communist and who now works for British intelligence. And, it would seem, from what you've just told me, Russian intelligence, too. We talked about old times and that was it. Or so I thought, until General Donovan mentioned these intercepts and codebooks. Naturally I wanted to know if I should expect the NKVD to try to reestablish contact. I suspect that the only reason they haven't is because I've been away from Washington since November twelfth. I doubt that they've had time.

"All the same, I can't deny that all of this would be embarrassing for me if Donovan and the president got to know about it. Embarrassing and perhaps even compromising. I would probably have to resign from the service. But I don't think I'd go to the electric chair for something I did before the United States was at war with Germany. I don't think I'd even go to prison for it. So, no, I'm not going to help you to escape. I'll take my chances."

I smiled nonchalantly. I actually felt better now that I knew what the Bride material contained.

"But, then, so will you."

Reichleitner frowned. "What do you mean?"

"Only this. That if you do decide to tell Deakin and Donovan what you know, it might be worth bearing in mind that I won't be the only person who's arrested for spying. There's you for one. Don't forget, Major Deakin's still got your name on chit for a firing squad. And for another, there's this little lady. Cairo's answer to Mata Hari."

I handed Reichleitner the photograph from Elena's album. "This was taken just a few months ago. At the opening of the Auberge des Pyramides. Quite apart from the many questions it begs about what you were doing here at that time, it also begs just as many about Elena Pontiatowska. You see, Major Reichleitner, I know all about the radio in the little room behind the bookcase. And that, on its own, would be enough to book her the firing squad after yours."

"What do you intend to do?" Reichleitner asked grimly.

"If it was just you and her and the odd bit of information about what the SOE is up to in Yugoslavia, then I think I might be inclined merely to warn Elena that I was on to her. That she should cease operations and get the hell out of Cairo. You see, we're good friends. Maybe good friends like you and she were good friends. That I don't know.

"What I do know is that it's more serious than just a bit of spying. A lot more serious. You see, I believe she's involved in a plot to assassinate Stalin in Teheran."

I showed Reichleitner the plaintext message I had taken from the bin in Elena's radio room and tossed the half-baked part of my theory in his lap.

"What was the idea with the Beketovka File, anyway? To use it as some sort of *post factum* justification for killing Stalin? Yes, that might play quite well with the world's press. Stalin was a tyrant, a monster, a mass murderer. He deserved to die because God knows how many others have been murdered on his orders. And here's the proof. This is what Germany has always been fighting against. This kind of Bolshevik barbarism. And this is why Britain and

America have been fighting the wrong enemy." I nodded. "It makes a lot of sense when you think of it like this."

"To you, maybe," said Reichleitner. "But not to me, I'm afraid. It wasn't like that at all. I don't know anything about a plot to kill Stalin."

"No? Then what about that photograph? At the very least it proves you've been here in Cairo before. As a spy."

"It's true, I've been here before. But not as a spy."

"I get it. You were on vacation." I grinned and threw my cigarette onto the floor of Reichleitner's cell. "See the Pyramids and then back to Berlin with some dirty postcards and a couple of cheap souvenirs."

Reichleitner said nothing. He was looking green around the mouth. But I was through being patient. I grabbed him by the vest and banged him hard against the cell wall.

"Come on, Max, you idiot," I yelled. "It's not just your ass that's facing a firing squad. It's Elena's, too. Or are you too dumb to realize that?"

"All right. I'll tell you what I know."

I let him go and stood back. He sat down heavily and lit a cigarette. "From the top," I said. "When you're ready."

"I've been operating in this theater for a while. Ankara and Cairo, mainly. But I'm not a spy. I'm a courier. I've been involved in some secret peace negotiations between Himmler, von Papen, and the Americans. In particular, a man named George Earle who is yet another of your president's special representatives."

"Earle? What's he got to do with this?"

"Listen, I don't deny that the Beketovka File was intended to undermine U.S.–Soviet relations. And, by the way, it's completely genuine. But there was never any talk of an assassination. At least nothing of which I have been made aware."

"How much did Elena know of your activities?"

"Almost nothing. Only that there was an important document I was required to go back and fetch from Germany. And which then had to find its way into the president's hands by the shortest route possible."

"I suppose that was where I came in handy," I said grimly.

Reichleitner shook his head, hardly understanding what I was talking about. "She's just the station master, that's all. She helps whichever German gets off the train, so to speak. Not asking questions. Just facilitating one mission and then another."

"This week a peace envoy, next week an assassin, is that it?"

"You say you're an expert on German intelligence? Then you'll know that the Abwehr and the SD don't tend to share much in the way of information or operational plans. And neither of them is much disposed to keep the Foreign Ministry or the Gestapo informed of what they're up to."

"But surely Himmler knows what's happening?"

"Not necessarily. Himmler and Admiral Canaris don't get on any better than Canaris and Schellenberg. Or Schellenberg and von Ribbentrop."

"And you. Where do you fit into all this?"

"I'm SS. Before the war I was with the Criminal Police. And, like I say, I'm just a courier between Himmler and von Papen, and your Commander Earle. I met Earle here in Cairo when I was last here. You could probably ask him to confirm my story. I'm certainly not an assassin." Reichleitner handed back the plaintext message from the Abwehr. "But it's possible I could help you catch him. This Brutus. If he really exists."

"Why would you do that?"

"To help Elena, of course. If there is an attempt made to kill Stalin, then it might go badly for her. I've no wish to see any harm come to her." He paused. "I might be able to persuade her to cooperate in bringing in Brutus. Or I could simply persuade her to tell you who this man is. How would that be?"

"All of that in spite of the fact you told me you'd like to see Stalin dead."

"I'd much prefer that Elena stayed alive." Reichleitner glanced wistfully at the photograph of himself and Elena that lay on the table. "I don't see that she has got much choice but to cooperate, do you? And what have you got to lose?"

"Nothing, probably. All the same, I'd like to think about it. Over breakfast." I glanced at my watch. "I'm going back to my hotel. Have a bath and something to eat while I'm considering your proposal. Then I'll come back here and tell you what I've decided to do."

By now it was clear to me that the major was fond of Elena— probably as fond of her as I was myself.

"What shall I do with these transcripts?" he asked.

"Don't say I told you to. But burn them. And the codebooks."

On the cab ride back to the hotel, I asked myself if I could risk telling Reilly and Hopkins what I had discovered. What was the life of a woman I was fond of, a woman who was, after all, a German spy, alongside the fate of the only man capable of driving Russia on to the Pyrrhic victory over Germany that seemed inevitable? I should probably just have walked around the corner from Grey Pillars to the American legation and placed the whole matter in the hands of the Secret Service. But then, I couldn't rule out the possibility that one of the Treasury agents was Brutus, the potential assassin. I needed time to think, and with the conference in Teheran still several days away, the small matter of a few hours seemed neither here nor there.

Climbing out of the cab in front of Shepheard's, I scratched my hand on a metal hinge. Having wrapped my handkerchief around the wound to stop it bleeding, I cleaned the cut with some iodine when I was back in my room. In Cairo, it didn't do to neglect these things. Then I shaved and drew a bath. I was just about to step into the tepid water when there was a loud knock at the door. Cursing, I wrapped a bath towel around my middle and opened the door to find myself faced by four men, two of them tall, thin Egyptians wearing the white uniform of the local police. The two Europeans with them were breathing hard, as if they'd used the stairs. One of them addressed me politely, but behind his wire-frame glasses, he had a nasty look in his eye.

"Are you Professor Willard Mayer?"

"Yes."

The man held up a warrant card. "Detective Inspector Luger, sir. And this is Sergeant Cash." The inspector did not bother to identify the two Egyptians. In their white uniforms they looked like a couple of pipecleaners. "May we come in, sir?"

"All of you?" But the two detectives had already brushed me aside and entered my room. Cash didn't look at me at all. He was looking around the room.

"Nice room," he said. "Very nice. I've never actually been in a room at Shepheard's. Officers only, you see."

"Standards have to be maintained, you know," I said, disliking him for the way he had of making me feel like I was a criminal. "Otherwise where would the empire be?"

He winced a little and fixed me with his stoniest look. Perhaps it worked on Egyptians, but it didn't work on me. But then he smiled. His smile was terrifying. It was full of teeth. Bad teeth. I turned to Luger in disgust.

"Look, what's going on? I was just about to take a bath."

"Did you spend the night in this room, sir?" he asked.

"No, I just came here to take a bath."

"Just answer the question, please, Professor."

"All right. I spent the night at a friend's house."

"Would you mind telling me the name of your friend, sir?"

"If you really think it's necessary. The house belongs to the Princess Elena Pontiatowska. I can't remember the street number. But it's on Harass Street, in Garden City." Even as I spoke, I saw Sergeant Cash pick up my bloodstained handkerchief and catch Luger's eye. "Look, what is all this? I'm with the American delegation." I looked at Cash. "That's spelled D-I-P-L-O-M-A-T-I-C."

"We'll try not to take up too much of your valuable time, sir," said Luger. "When did you leave the princess's house. Approximately?"

"Early this morning. At about seven."

"And did you come straight here?"

"No, as a matter of fact I dropped into British Army GHQ at Grey Pillars. On official business. My boss, General Donovan, will vouch for me, if required. As indeed will Mike Reilly, who is head of the president's Secret Service detail."

"Yes, sir," said Luger.

Cash replaced my handkerchief carefully on the table. A little too carefully for my liking. Almost as if he contemplated picking it up again and placing it in an envelope marked "Evidence." That was bad enough, but now he collected my trousers off the back of the chair where I had thrown them, and was inspecting the pocket. There was a bloodstain on the edge of the pocket lining.

"Look, I'm not saying another goddamn thing until you've told me what's going on."

"In that case, sir, you leave me no alternative," sighed Luger. "Willard Mayer, I'm arresting you on suspicion of having committed murder. Do you understand?"

"Who's been murdered, for Christ's sake?"

"Get dressed, sir," said Cash. "But not these trousers, eh?"

"I cut myself. Climbing out of a cab about half an hour ago."

"I'm afraid that's for the laboratory to decide now, sir."

"Look, this is a mistake. I haven't murdered anyone."

Luger had found my shoulder holster and the Colt automatic it contained. Holding the holster, he lifted the pistol to his nostrils and sniffed it experimentally.

"It's not been fired for months," I said, putting on some clothes. "I wish you'd tell me what this is all about. Has something happened to Elena?"

Neither of the two detectives spoke as they escorted me to a large black car parked outside the hotel. We drove south, to the Citadel, a centuries-old bastion that, with its needle-like minarets, was just about the most dramatic feature on Cairo's skyline. Circling the Citadel, we entered it from the back, at a higher level, close to the center of the ancient complex, and then drove through the gate tunnel and into a courtyard in front of the police station.

I got out of the car and, still closely escorted, entered the building. There, in a large room with a wear-polished stone floor, a fine view over the city, and, on the wall, a portrait of King George, my interrogation began.

It very quickly became apparent that Elena had been murdered.

"Were you involved in a sexual relationship with Elena Pontiatowska?"

"Yes," I said.

"How did you meet?"

"We were friends, from before the war. In Berlin."

"I see."

"Look, Inspector, she was still alive when I left the house this morning. But there's something you should know. Something important."

Luger looked up from the notes he had been making while I spoke. "And what might that be?"

"I need to see that she really is dead before I tell you."

"All right," sighed Luger. "Let's go and take a look at her."

The two detectives had the car brought back, and we drove to the house in Harass Street. It was now guarded by several Egyptian policemen and already subject to the close scrutiny of various scientific experts.

In the hall, Luger led the way up to the first floor. Cash brought up the rear. We went into Elena's bedroom.

She lay beside a high French window, wearing a silk gown. She had been shot through the heart at fairly close range, for the wound was surrounded with black powder. I didn't need to put a mirror in front of her mouth to know that she was dead.

"It looks as if she knew her attacker," I observed. "Given the close proximity of her assailant. But it wasn't me."

On the floor beside her body lay a Walther PPK, and I realized with horror that it was very likely the same automatic I had handled in the radio room. It would have my fingerprints on it. But for the moment I said nothing.

"You've had your look," Luger said.

"Just give me a minute, please. This was a good friend of mine."

But I was playing for time. There was something small on the floor, near Elena's hand, and I wondered if I might see what it was before I was obliged to leave the crime scene. "This has all been a dreadful shock to me, Inspector. I need a cigarette." I took out my cigarettes. "Do you mind?"

"Go ahead."

I pretended to fumble with the pack and dropped a couple onto the floor. Placing another in my mouth I bent quickly down and retrieved only one of the two cigarettes from the carpet. At the same time I picked up the object close to Elena's outstretched hand and slipped it into the pack.

"Here, here, you're contaminating my crime scene," objected Luger. "You've left one of your cigarettes on the floor." And, bending down, he picked it up.

"Sorry." I took the cigarette from Luger's fingers and then lit the one in my mouth.

"Now, then, Professor. What were you going to tell me that's so important?"

"That Elena Pontiatowska was a German spy."

Luger tried to repress a smile. "This case really does have everything," he said. "Yes, it's been quite a while since we had such a sensational murder here in Cairo. You have to go back to 1927, I'd say—the murder of Solomon Cicurel, the owner of the department store—to have such a fascinating dramatis personae, so to speak. There's you, Professor, a famous philosopher, and a Polish princess who used to be married to one of the richest men in Egypt. A man who I might add, was also shot. And now you say that this woman was a German spy."

"You can forget that business about 'now I say,'" I told him. "I don't recall saying anything about her before now."

"Is that why you killed her?" asked Cash. "Because she was a German spy?"

"I didn't kill her. But I can prove she was a spy." For a moment I thought of showing Luger the plaintext message that was still in my coat pocket and then decided it would be better to put that straight into the hands of Hopkins and Reilly. "There's a German agent radio in a secret room upstairs. I could show you where it is."

Luger nodded, and we left Cash in the bedroom and went back along the landing to the double doors that opened onto the stone stairs, and then up to the little apartment. I showed the detective how the bookcase was really a door and then led the way into the secret room.

But the German sender/receiver was gone.

"It was there on that table. And next to it was the gun that's on the floor in Elena's bedroom. The Walther. I'm afraid you might find my prints on that, Inspector. I handled it when I came in here and found the radio this morning. Just to see if it was loaded."

"I see," said Luger. "Is there anything else you want to tell me, sir?"

"Only that I didn't kill her."

Luger sighed. "Try and look at it from my point of view," he said, almost gently. "There was blood on your trousers when we arrested you. By your own admission your fingerprints are on the probable murder weapon. You were sleeping with the victim. And, to cap it all, when you came here, with some cock-and-bull story about spies, you even tried to interfere with evidence. Yes, I'll thank you to hand that button over. The one you picked off the floor when you dropped your cigarettes in the bedroom back there."

I took out the button, scrutinized it momentarily, and then handed it over to the inspector. "It's not one of mine. Sorry."

"Did you think it might be?" asked Luger.

"As a matter of fact, no. But I don't suppose that matters."

"We're not fools, sir," said Luger, pocketing the button.

"Then you'll already have noticed that none of my coat jackets is missing a button."

"I have noticed that. So I'm still trying to fathom why you picked it up."

I shrugged. "I guess I was hoping to meet a man who's missing a coat button."

"Of course it might have been there a while," admitted Luger. "Still, it is evidence. Not as good as a gun with fingerprints on it, however. Your fingerprints, you say?"

"As well as the murderer's."

"It's a pity that radio wasn't here," said Luger. "That might have made things very different."

"I imagine that the same person who killed the Princess must have removed it. And for the same reason. To conceal the fact she was a German agent. Something must have spooked him." I sighed as I realized what might have happened. "I think that must have been me. You see, I searched the house last night when everyone was asleep. At least that's what I thought at the time. Someone must have seen me and decided to cover their tracks. The fact is, Inspector, I believe I've stumbled on a plot to kill the Big Three."

I handed over the plaintext message. There was no sense in hanging on to it now. I was inches away from being charged with murder.

"I believe this message was received by someone, very likely the murderer, using that missing radio."

Luger glanced at the message. "It's in German," he said.

"Of course it is. It was sent from Berlin. 'Mordanschlag.' That's the German word for 'assassinate.'"

"Is it?"

"German intelligence is my speciality. I'm with the OSS. That's the American intelligence service. I'm the president's liaison officer with the agency. It's imperative that I speak to the head of the president's Secret Service detail as soon as possible. His name is Mike Reilly."

Cash appeared in the doorway. "No German radio, sir?" he asked.

"No German radio. And don't let anyone touch that gun in the bedroom. The professor here has confessed his fingerprints are on it."

"Actually, no. I said you *might* find them."

Inspector Luger leaned forward. "Shall I tell you what I think happened, Professor Mayer?"

I groaned inside. It was easy to see where his elementary thought processes were going with this.

"My friend is dead, Inspector. And what you think about that is of little interest to me right now."

"I think that sometime during the night, when you were in bed with Princess Pontiatowska, you had an argument. A lover's quarrel. So sometime this morning, you shot her."

"As complicated as that, eh?" I shook my head. "You must read a lot of novels."

"We leave the complications to you. This was very simple. All this stuff about a German radio is complete nonsense, isn't it? Just like the story about there being a plot to kill the Big Three."

Luger advanced slowly on me, followed closely by Sergeant Cash, until I was close enough to smell the tobacco and the coffee on his breath.

"It's bad enough that you should murder a woman in cold blood," said Luger. "But what really pisses me off is that you should take us for a pair of fucking idiots." Luger was shouting now. "German spies? Plots to kill the Big Three? Next thing you'll be telling us that Hitler is hiding in the fucking cellar."

"Well, I didn't see him when I was down there this morning."

"Why don't you tell us the truth?" Cash said quietly.

"I don't like Yanks," said Luger.

"For the first time since you opened your big trap you've said something that makes sense. This is personal."

"You were late for this war, just like you were late for the last one. And when you do finally bother to show up, you all think you can treat us like poor relations. Tell us what to do, like you owned this bloody war."

"Since we're paying for it, I think that gives us a say."

"Tell us what really happened," murmured Cash.

"You've told us a pack of bloody lies, that's what," bellowed Luger, taking hold of my coat lapels. "You're full of shit, mate. Like the rest of your bloody countrymen."

Cash grabbed hold of Luger's arm and tried to pull him off me. "Leave it, guv," he said. "It's not worth it."

"I'm going to have this bastard," and Luger tightened his grip on my lapels. "That, or the truth, so help me."

"You boys have got quite an act here," I said, grabbing hold of Luger's wrists and wrenching them off my coat. "It's a real shame to waste it on someone who's seen it performed before. By better actors, too."

"The truth," yelled Luger, punching me hard in the ribs.

I lashed back, catching Luger with a glancing punch on his jaw. Cash stepped in, just managing to hold us apart. Glancing sourly at Cash, Luger said, "Get him out of my sight."

They drove me back to the Citadel and locked me in a hot stinking cell. I sat down on the solitary wooden bunk and stared into the solitary slops bucket. The bucket was empty but it seemed to be where my life was headed.

Toward the end of the day, I heard the muezzin calling the faithful to prayer. His powerful, sonorous voice drifted through the still air of the Citadel. The sound was soothing, something felt as much as heard.

A minute after the muezzin had finished, the cell door opened and I was ordered out. A uniformed policeman marched me upstairs to a large room where Donovan, Reilly, and Agent Rauff were seated around a table. In front of them was the plaintext message I had given to Inspector Luger. I didn't mention it. I was through volunteering information.

"It seems that the British want to charge you with the murder of your lady friend," said Donovan.

I poured myself a glass of water from the decanter on the table.

"How about it? Did you kill her?"

"Nope. Someone else killed her. Someone who wanted to conceal that she was a German spy." I nodded at the table. "I found that message in the radio room."

"Would this be the radio room without a radio?" Rauff asked.

"Yes. I guess the person who took it away was worried that someone like you was going to shoot it."

"This German spy you claim killed her," said Rauff.

"Yes. You know, German spies are not at all unusual in the middle of a war with Germany."

"Perhaps it just seems that way," he said, "because you manage to make it sound like there's a plague of them."

"Well, we *are* in Egypt. If there's going to be a plague of spies anywhere, it would have to be here. Along with lice and flies and boils and Secret Service agents."

The artery on Rauff's sweating neck started to throb. It was hot in the room and he had taken off his jacket so that it was impossible to see if he was missing a coat button.

Donovan picked up the plaintext message on the table. He regarded it as I suppose he would have regarded a disputed bill from his local butcher.

"And you say that this is evidence of a plot to kill the Big Three, in Teheran," he said.

"Not the Big Three. Just Stalin." I took the paper from Donovan's thick fingers and translated from the German. "I think Stalin is Wotan," I explained. "From the opera by Richard Wagner? Only I figured that the British police might be more inclined to pay attention if I told them it was all three Allied leaders, instead of just Marshal Stalin. It's funny, but most of the people I speak to don't care very much for Uncle Joe. You included, as I recall."

Donovan smiled calmly. His blue eyes never left mine.

"It's a great pity they didn't find that German radio," he said. "A radio would have corroborated your story nicely."

"I imagine the man who killed my friend was of the same opinion, sir."

"Yes, let's talk about her for a moment. How exactly is it that you come to be friendly with a woman you say was a German agent?"

"She was beautiful. She was clever. She was rich. I guess I'm just the gullible kind."

"How long had you known her?"

"We went way back. I knew her in Berlin, before the war."

"Were you sleeping with her?"

"That's my business."

"Quite the swordsman, aren't you, Willard?" said Rauff. "For a professor."

"Why, Agent Rauff, you sound jealous."

"I think it's a fair question," said Donovan.

"It didn't sound like a question at all. Look, gentlemen, I'm not married, so I don't see that who I sleep with is anyone's business except me and the lady's gynecologist." I smiled at Rauff. "That's a pussy doctor to you, Agent Rauff."

"The British are saying that she was a Polish princess," Reilly said.

"That's right. She was."

"Is it true that when you and she were living in Berlin you were both friends of Josef Goebbels?"

"Who told you that?"

"One of her Polish friends. A Captain Skomorowski. Is it true?"

I nodded. It made sense that Elena would have told him. What better way of persuading someone that you could never be a spy than by being hopelessly, charmingly indiscreet?

"I was never a friend of Goebbels. Only an acquaintance." I nodded at Rauff. "Like me and your colleague." I took another sip of water. "Besides, this was in 1938. The United States still had an ambassador in Berlin. Hugh Wilson. We used to see each other at Goebbels's parties. I think I may even have left Germany before he did."

"Did you mention this information when you joined the service?" asked Donovan.

"I think I told Allen Dulles."

"Since he's in Switzerland, it's going to be hard to corroborate that," said Donovan.

"Yes. But why would you want to? My short acquaintance with Goebbels hardly makes me unusual in the OSS. In the early days of

COI, we had lots of krauts working for us. Still do. Everyone on Campus knows about FDR's Doctor S project. Then there's Putzi Hanfstaengl, Hitler's former foreign press chief. Didn't you bring him under the COI wing, General? Of course, that was before the FBI decided he ought to remain under house arrest in Bush Hill, monitoring German news broadcasts. And let's not forget Commander George Earle's several meetings with von Papen in Ankara. No, General, I hardly think my having met Goebbels is going to trouble anyone."

"I'll be the judge of that," said Donovan.

"Of course. But on Saturday the president is flying to Teheran to meet Stalin. Don't you think that instead of quizzing me about whether I might have been a friend of the German propaganda minister you would do better to find out who it is among the American delegation that's planning to assassinate Marshal Stalin?"

"That's exactly what we were doing," Rauff said, holding up the plaintext. "After all, this message was found on you."

"I gave it to Inspector Luger."

"He'd have found it when he searched you anyway. And let's not forget that you were the one using the German radio back in Tunis."

"I wondered what you were doing here, Rauff. I take it your clever theory is that ever since leaving Hampton Roads I've been crying wolf because I'm a wolf myself, is that it? Well, you're certainly consistent, I'll say that for you. Your stupidity looks chronic."

I retrieved the Hamilton Hotel matchbook from my empty cigarette packet. I had hidden it inside the lining of my jacket.

"Whoever killed Princess Elena also killed Thornton Cole, back in Washington. I found this matchbook in the wastepaper basket beside that plaintext message from the Abwehr."

"This is underneath the nonexistent radio, right?" said Rauff.

"It's a little complicated, Agent Rauff, so I'll speak slowly and in short words even you can understand. Cole was murdered because he stumbled onto a German spy ring. The Schmidts were murdered to help maintain the fiction that Cole had been cruising for homosexual sex—something that a State Department already nervous about losing presidential confidence in the wake of the Sumner Welles scandal was more than happy to see swept under the rug.

"The same man who killed the Schmidts—let's call him Brutus—also killed his contact here in Cairo and is trying to frame me for it. My guess is that he hopes to clear the way for an attempt on Stalin's life in Teheran."

I thumped the table hard with the flat of my hand, which made Donovan jump. I upped the tone. "Look, you've got to listen to me. Someone, an American, is going to try to kill Stalin."

Mike Reilly stirred in his chair. "Oh, there's no doubt that there's an assassination plot," he said coolly. "In fact, the Russians know all about it. But there's no American involved, Professor. That's a fantasy. There *was* a plot to kill the Big Three. You were right about that. Two teams of German parachutists were dropped into the countryside outside Teheran on Monday. Most of them have already been arrested. And the rest are being picked up as we speak."

I sat back on my chair, flabbergasted. "A parachute team?"

"Yes. They were SS. The same outfit that rescued Mussolini from the Hotel Campo Imperatore in Italy."

"Skorzeny," I said dumbly.

"As yet it's unclear if he's involved or not," said Reilly.

"Our last intelligence was that he's in Paris," said Donovan. "Of course that could be a feint."

"As many as a hundred men were dropped into Iran," continued Reilly. "They were supposed to knock out local radar so that a team of long-range bombers based in the Crimea could attack the British embassy on Churchill's birthday. When the bombers had done their worst, the two teams were supposed to coordinate a commando attack to kill any survivors. There's your Operation Wurf, Professor. A renegade SS mission."

"Renegade? What the hell do you mean by that?"

"It seems that the operation did not have official sanction."

"But how do we know that?"

"We know it because it was the German government that betrayed their existence to the Soviets," said Donovan.

I stood up from the table and put my hands on my head. Reilly's mock-turtle story was beginning to make me feel like Alice in Wonderland. None of this made any sense.

"And why the hell would they do that?" I asked.

Donovan shrugged. "As I told you last Sunday, Professor Mayer. The last thing the Germans want right now is to kill President Roosevelt. For several weeks now our man in Ankara has been conducting secret talks with the German ambassador. I imagine that the Germans want nothing that might risk compromising these peace feelers. You should have paid more attention."

"None of this explains Thornton Cole, the Schmidts, Brutus—"

"I'd say you've got quite enough to worry about right now," said Donovan. "With the British, I mean. If I were you, Professor, I'd get myself a lawyer. You're going to need one."

XXIII
FRIDAY, NOVEMBER 26, 1943,
TEHERAN

THE ENTIRE OPERATION in Teheran was directed by Beria, the head of the Soviet Security Agency (the NKVD), and General Avramov, of the new Eastern Office. Beria had arrived from Baku that same day, with Stalin. Aboard the same SI-47 aircraft had been General Arkadiev, and it had given the general some considerable pleasure to witness the Soviet leader demonstrate his intense fear of flying by delivering a spectacular dressing-down on the person of Beria himself. Stalin had been drunk, of course. It was the only way he had been able to find enough courage to get on the plane; and, filled with fear and vodka, Stalin had let loose a torrent of abuse upon his fellow Georgian when the plane had encountered some air turbulence over the Caspian Sea.

"If I die on this plane, the last order I give will be to throw you out the door, snake eyes. Do you hear? We spend all that time on a train to Baku in order to avoid having to fly, only to end up on a fucking airplane. Doesn't make sense."

Beria had turned as red as a beetroot. Arkadiev had avoided Beria's eye. It did not do to show pleasure in the NKVD chairman's discomfiture.

"Do you hear what I'm saying, snake eyes?"

"Yes, Comrade Stalin," said Beria. "Perhaps Comrade Stalin has forgotten that we went over the travel itinerary back in Moscow. It was always agreed that the last leg of the journey would be made by plane."

"I don't remember agreeing to that," snarled Stalin. "Makes no sense. Churchill and Roosevelt both had warships to carry them across the sea. Why couldn't I have a warship? The Caspian Sea is no bigger than the Black Sea. Is the Russian navy short of warships? Is the Caspian Sea more dangerous than the Atlantic Ocean? I don't think so, Beria."

"Both Roosevelt and Churchill are making the journey from Cairo to Teheran by air," insisted Beria.

"Only because they have to. There's no other fucking way for them to get there, snake eyes."

Now, several hours after the flight, in a large room on the first floor of the NKVD headquarters on Syroos Street in the eastern part of the city, Arkadiev saw that Beria was in a foul mood himself, doubtless still smarting from Stalin's comments. He and his secretary, Stepan Mamulov, were reviewing the arrangements for Stalin's security with General Merkulov, Beria's deputy. Joining them were: General Krulev, who commanded the 3,000 men of Stalin's personal guard, stationed in Teheran since the end of October; General Melamed, the head of the local NKVD; and Melamed's deputy, Colonel Andrei Mikhalovits Vertinski. Beria's ill temper had not been improved by the discovery that at least a dozen SS paratroopers were still at liberty. Of the two teams of men, one had been picked up near the holy city of Qom within hours of their landing; another forty men had been surrounded at a house in Kakh Street but had chosen to shoot it out. There were no survivors. But several were still unaccounted for.

"Although commanded by German officers and German NCOs, they're Ukrainians, most of them," Melamed told Beria. "From General Vlasov's army that was lost on the Volkhov front in 1942."

"Traitors," hissed Beria. "That's what they are."

"Traitors, yes, of course," agreed Melamed. "But not easy to crack. We've been French wrestling with the bastards all night and they've hardly told us a thing." Until Beria's arrival in Teheran, Melamed had been the most feared NKVD officer in Iran, and

"French wrestling" was what he and his thugs jokingly called the process of breaking a man with beatings and torture. "These men are pretty tough, I can tell you."

"Need I remind you that Comrade Stalin is now in the city?" demanded Beria. "That each hour these traitors and Fascists remain at liberty represents a potential threat to his life?" Beria leveled a white, pudgy finger at the center of Melamed's poorly shaven face. "You're a Ukrainian yourself, aren't you, Melamed?"

"Yes, Comrade. From Kiev."

"Yes, I thought so." Beria sat back in his chair and folded his arms, smiling unpleasantly. "You know, if none of these bastards talks, it might be surmised that you've been lenient with them because of where they are from."

"I can assure you, Comrade Beria, that the reverse is true," said Melamed. "The truth is, that as a Ukrainian I am ashamed of these traitors. No one is keener to see them talk or punished, I promise you."

"And I can promise you this, Melamed," sneered Beria. "If one of these fuckers who are still at large gets to within a hundred feet of our embassy, I'll have you shot. That goes for you, too, Vertinski. And you, Krulev, you ugly bastard. Christ only knows what you've been doing in the last four weeks you've been here. I'm furious about this. Furious. That we should have allowed the great Stalin to come to a city where there are terrorists planning to kill him. If it was up to me he wouldn't be here at all; but Comrade Stalin is made of sterner stuff. He refused to stay in Russia. So I tell you this. We must find these men and we must find them quickly." Beria took off his pince-nez. He was forty-four and probably the most intellectually gifted of all Stalin's henchmen, but he was no party wallflower. Even by the depraved standards of the NKVD, he was notorious for his brutality.

"Where are these bastards, anyway?" he asked. "The ones you've been questioning."

"We've got about ten of them downstairs, Comrade Beria," explained Melamed. "The rest of the bunch are in the Red Army barracks to the north of the city, in Meshed."

"The Germans are to be kept alive, do you hear?" said Beria. "But I want the highest measure of punishment for the Ukrainians at Meshed. To be carried out this day, Krulev. Is that understood?"

"Without questioning them?" asked Krulev. "Suppose the ones we've got downstairs don't talk? What then? We might wish that we'd kept the prisoners at Meshed alive for a bit longer."

"Do as I say and shoot them today. You may rest assured, the ones downstairs will talk." Beria stood up. "I never met a man yet who wouldn't talk, when questioned properly. I'll take charge of it myself."

Beria, Mamulov, Melamed, and Vertinski went down into the basement of the house at Syroos Street, where there was nothing that might have led a prisoner to believe that this was Teheran and not the Lubyanka in Moscow. The walls and floors were concrete, and the corridors and cells were brightly lit to prevent any prisoner from enjoying the temporary escape of sleep. The smell was uniquely Soviet, too: a mixture of cheap cigarettes, sweat, animal fats, urine, and human fear.

Beria was a squarely made man, but light on his feet; with his glasses, polished shoes, neatly cut Western suit, and silk tie, he gave off the can-do air of a successful businessman who was nevertheless quite prepared to pitch in on the shop floor alongside his employees. He tossed his jacket at Arkadiev, removed his tie, and rolled up his sleeves as he bustled his way through the door of the NKVD's torture chamber. "So where the fuck is everyone?" he yelled. "No wonder the bastards aren't talking. They've got no one to talk to. Vertinski. What the hell is going on here?"

"I expect the men are tired," said Vertinski. "They've been working on these men for a whole day."

"Tired?" screamed Beria. "I wonder how tired they'll feel after six months in Solovki. I want one of the prisoners in here, now. The strongest. So you'll see how you should do these things." He shook his head wearily. "It's always the same," he told Mamulov. "You want a job done properly, you've got to do it yourself."

Beria asked one of the NKVD officers to hand over his gun. The man obeyed without hesitation, and Beria checked that the revolver, a Nagant seven-shot pistol, was loaded. Although old, the pistol was favored by some of the NKVD because it could be fitted with a Bramit silencer, and thus it was immediately clear to Beria that the officer had been an executioner.

"Have you questioned any of the prisoners?" he asked the man.

"Yes, sir."

"And?"

"They're very stubborn, sir."

"What's your name?" Beria asked him.

"Captain Alexander Koltsov," said the officer, clicking the heels of his boots as he came smartly to attention in front of the comrade chairman.

"I knew a Kolstov once," said Beria absently, neglecting to add that the man he remembered had been a journalist whom Beria had tortured to death at Sukhanov Prison. The Sukhanovka was Beria's personal prison in Moscow, where those he had singled out for an extra measure of cruelty, or women he had decided to rape before handing them over to be shot, were sent.

The guards returned, dragging a naked man in shackles, and stood him roughly in front of the NKVD chief. Beria looked closely at the prisoner, who stared back at him with undisguised hatred. "But there's hardly a mark on this man," he objected. "Who questioned him?"

"I did, Comrade Beria," said Koltsov.

"What did you hit him with? A feather duster?"

"I can assure you, sir, I used the utmost severity."

Beria touched a couple of bruises on the prisoner's face and arms and laughed. "The utmost severity? Koltsov, you wouldn't know the utmost severity if it fucked you up the ass. You're an executioner, not an interrogator." Looking straight into the prisoner's eyes, Beria continued: "Big difference. You see, it takes a certain kind of person to beat a man with a club for thirty minutes. I can see you know what I'm talking about. I can see it in your eyes.

Killing a man, putting a gun to his head and pulling a trigger, is nothing. Well, maybe the first time it feels like something. But when you've killed as many as a hundred, a thousand, then you know how easy it is. Like something you do in an abattoir. That's just killing, it means nothing, and any fool can do it."

Even as he spoke, Beria turned quickly, pointed the revolver, and shot Captain Kolstov in the head. Before the captain had hit the floor, Beria had returned his cold, merciless stare to his Ukrainian prisoner.

"See what I mean? Nothing. It means nothing. Nothing at all." Beria handed the pistol to Vertinski, who took it in his shaking hand. Then, nodding down toward the dead captain, Beria told the prisoner, "Look at him. Look at him," and he took hold of the Ukrainian's hair, pulling his head down. "Imagine it. He was one of mine. Not a traitor like you." Beria snorted, then turned and spat onto the dead man's head. "No, he was just incompetent."

Beria let go of the man's hair and, taking a step back, turned his sleeves up another few inches and selected a rubber rod that was hanging from a shiny new nail in the wall. "All I have for you, my friend, is a promise. That before I'm finished, you will envy this"— Beria kicked the dead man's face, negligently—"this piece of shit." Beria glanced meaningfully at Vertinski and Melamed. "This clown, Koltsov, who was too soft for his own good. Because there's only one way to deal with an animal like a Ukrainian peasant. You beat him. And then you beat him again.

"You." Beria snapped his fingers at one of the other NKVD officers in the torture chamber. "Put that chair up on the table." Then he clicked his fingers at the two men holding the Ukrainian. "You two. Sit him up in that chair and tie his feet to the legs. The rest of you pay attention. This is how we amuse the spies and traitors in our midst. This is what we do. We tickle their feet." And seeing that the prisoner was now securely bound to the chair, Beria brought the rod down hard on top of the man's toes. Raising his voice over the Ukrainian's howl, Beria said, "We tickle their toes until they beg for mercy." Beria struck the prisoner's feet again, and this time he screamed aloud. "Like that! And that! And that! And that!"

Lavrenti Pavlovich Beria took off his pince-nez, placed it safely in his trouser pocket, and then licked his lips. He wasn't a fit man despite the frequent games of volleyball he played with his bodyguards, but he was strong enough, and he inflicted the beating with an economy of effort that spoke of years of practice, and some considerable enjoyment. "Energetic" was how people usually described Beria, and for the officers witnessing this beating it would have been difficult to disagree. Mamulov, Beria's secretary, had always thought vegetarians were weak and listless and held human life in awe, until he worked for Beria. Beating a man on his bare feet for a full thirty minutes was something awful to behold. A lesson from the deepest pit in hell that was not lost on any NKVD in that room.

At last Beria threw aside the rubber rod and, taking hold of the towel that Mamulov had thoughtfully fetched for him, wiped his face and neck. "Thank you," he said, quietly. "By God, I needed that, after the journey.

"On the floor with him," he ordered the two men holding the now unconscious prisoner, still bound to the chair. "Idiots," he snarled, as they tried to lift the chair down. Beria sprang onto the table like a cat. "Not like that. Like this." He placed his foot on the chair and pushed it off the table so that the prisoner fell heavily onto the floor. "It's not a fucking ambulance service. You," Beria pointed at Melamed. "Get a bucket of water and some vodka."

Beria threw the bucket of water onto the Ukrainian's head and then tossed it aside as the man, whose feet were the size and color of two pieces of raw beef, started to revive. "Pick him up," said Beria.

The guards straightened the chair, and Beria, taking the vodka from Vertinski, pushed the neck of the bottle into the prisoner's mouth and tipped it up, so that the man could drink. "Watch and learn," he told his men. "You want a man to tell you something, don't beat him about the head and mouth so that he can't talk. Beat him on the feet. On his ass. On his back, or on his balls. But never interfere with his means of speech. Now, then, who sent you on this mission, my friend?"

"Schellenberg," whispered the prisoner. "General Walter Schellenberg, of the SD. There are two teams. A North Team and a South Team. The South Team is commanded by . . ."

Beria patted the man on the cheek. "See what I mean? This bastard's not only talking but we'll have a hard job to shut him up now. He'd tell me Charlie Chaplin sent him on this mission if that's what I wanted to hear." Beria wiped the neck of the bottle and took a long swig of vodka himself. "Well, don't just stand there," he yelled at Melamed. "He's ready to split like a pomegranate. Get a pencil and paper and take down every stinking word that comes out of his mouth."

Still holding the vodka bottle, Beria collected his jacket and went back upstairs, followed closely by Mamulov. He handed his secretary the bottle. "Where are Sarkisov and Nadaraia?" These were the two NKVD colonels who acted as his unofficial pimps and procurers.

"They're at the summer embassy, Comrade Beria."

With Stalin occupying the winter embassy in the center of Teheran, it had been decided that Beria would have the run of the summer embassy in Zargandeh, about five miles outside the capital.

"They've got women?"

"Quite a variety. A couple of Poles, several Persians, and some Arabs."

"Very Rimsky-Korsakov," Beria said, and laughed. "Let's hope there's enough time, and that our guests don't arrive too early. I've never fucked an Arab bitch before. Are they clean?"

"Yes, Comrade Beria. Comrade Baroyan has examined them all thoroughly."

Dr. Baroyan was the director of the Soviet hospital in Teheran.

He also worked for the NKVD, and in that capacity he sometimes murdered troublesome patients with neglect, unnecessary surgery, or overdoses of drugs.

"Good, because I've only just recovered from that syphilis. I wouldn't want to go through that again. It was that actress, you know. What's her name?"

"Tatiana."

"Yes. Her. Which camp did we send her to? I've forgotten."

"Kolyma."

The camps at Kolyma, a three-month journey from Moscow, were the most wretched places in the whole Soviet Gulag system.

"Then she's probably dead by now," said Beria. "The bitch. Good."

Beria went into Melamed's office, ignoring the pretty secretary who was the local security commissar's gatekeeper, and threw himself down on the sofa. He farted loudly and then ordered Mamulov to "tell the girl" to bring him some tea. "And some wine," he yelled after Mamulov's retreating figure. "Georgian wine, too. I don't want any of the local piss."

He closed his eyes and slept for almost half an hour. When he opened them again, he saw Melamed standing nervously over him. "What the fuck do *you* want?" he growled.

"I have a transcript of Kosior's statement, Comrade Beria."

"Who the hell is Kosior?"

"The Ukrainian prisoner you interrogated downstairs."

"Oh, him. Well?"

Melamed handed him a typed sheet of paper. "Would you like to read it?"

"Fuck, no. Just tell me what you're doing about it."

"Well, naturally, Comrade Beria, I wanted to confer with you first, before doing anything."

Beria groaned loudly. "I thought I made it abundantly clear that it is imperative we catch the remaining terrorists as quickly as possible. You should have woken me."

Melamed glanced uncomfortably at the box of silk teddy bears that now occupied a corner of his office—presents for the young women with whom Beria was planning to spend his evening. "The comrade chairman must be tired after his long journey from Moscow," he said. "I didn't want to disturb him."

"When an assassin presents himself in front of Comrade Stalin," said Beria, snatching the transcript out of Melamed's hands, "I'll remember your thoughtfulness." Fixing the pince-nez on the bridge of his broad nose, Beria glanced over the typescript. "Very well. Here are my orders. I want the bazaar surrounded with troops. No one is to be allowed in or out until a house-to-house search has been carried out."

"Yes, Comrade Chairman."

Beria read on a way. "Wrestlers?" he said.

"They have high status in the local community," explained Melamed. "Many of them used to be bodyguards."

"Have you ever heard of this fellow, Misbah Ebtehaj?"

"He's quite famous, I believe."

"Arrest him. Go to wherever it is that wrestlers go—"

"The Zurkhane?"

"Go there. And arrest them all. Also this address in Abassi Street. Arrest everyone there, too."

Melamed moved smartly toward the door.

"Melamed!"

"Yes, Comrade Beria?"

"While you're at it, put up some signs offering a reward for information leading to the capture of the German terrorists. Twenty thousand dollars, in gold. That ought to be enough to persuade anyone who's hiding them to give them up."

"But where shall I find such a sum?"

"Leave that to me," said Beria, still glancing over the transcript. "This Kosior. He doesn't say exactly how many were in his team. Don't you think it might be useful to know that? So we can be sure how many we are still looking for. Is it ten? Is it a dozen? Is it thirteen? I want to know."

"I'm afraid he fainted, Comrade Beria, before we could establish a precise number."

"Then bring him around again and ask him. And if he doesn't tell you, beat him. Or beat one of the others until you know absolutely everything. How many Ukrainians? How many Germans?" Beria threw the transcript at Melamed's feet. "And you'd better bring the Americans and the British in on this. The time is past when we could have kept this to ourselves. Only don't, for Christ's sake, mention that most of these terrorists are from the Ukraine. They're SS. Have you got that? SS. And that makes them Germans. Got that?"

"Yes, Comrade Chairman."

"Now get out of here and do your job before I have you shot."

Melamed passed the arrest orders to Vertinski and then telephoned the British legation, asking to speak to Colonel Spencer, in command of British security in Teheran. It was the second conversation the two had had about the German parachutists. In the first, Melamed had assured Spencer that the plot had been nipped in the bud and that all the SS troopers were dead or safely in custody. Now he told Spencer that several were still at liberty. Spencer immediately offered 170 British detectives and MPs to help with the search, and Melamed agreed, suggesting that the British concentrate their searches on Abassi Street. Next Melamed called Schwarzkopf's office and spoke with Colonel L. Steven Timmermann, who promised to assist in any way possible and dispatched a team of American MPs to help search the bazaar. With the whole of Teheran, from Gale Morghe Airfield in the south to Kulhek in the north, being searched by Allied troops, Melamed then turned to the reward notices, and when these had been posted, he began fielding phone calls from some of the search teams. And only gradually did he fall to thinking about why it was that the Germans had betrayed their own assassination team to Beria himself, and about the many unusual preparations that were still taking place within the grounds of the winter embassy under the supervision of Beria's own son, Sergo.

Stalin was not staying in the main building of the recently redecorated embassy but in one of the several smaller cottages and villas that were on the grounds of what had once been the sumptuous estate of a rich Persian businessman. Until the Big Three Conference, many of these villas and cottages had been empty, and for the last two weeks, Zoya Zarubina, the stepdaughter of NKVD general Leonid Eitingen, had been scouring the local shops for carpets and furniture. New bathrooms had been installed and, unusually perhaps, in one of the villas, a portrait of Lenin had been replaced with one of Beethoven. No less peculiar, in Melamed's view, had been the decision to refurbish a large underground bunker and to drain and paint a series of secret tunnels that connected the main building with several of the villas; after all, Teheran was protected by as many as a dozen squadrons of Russian and British fighter aircraft, and any air attack of the kind countenanced by the SS general who had sent in the teams of German parachutists would have been suicide. Melamed thought there was less likelihood of Stalin needing to seek the refuge of a bomb shelter while he was in Teheran than there was of Beria requiring the pastoral care of a Russian Orthodox priest.

By late afternoon, several more of the SS parachutists had been arrested. By Melamed's final account, this left three men, two of them German, still unaccounted for. As night fell, Melamed was informed about the arrival (under cover of darkness) of some early guests at Gale Morghe Airfield that very same evening, but was given no information as to who they were. These guests had been received by Beria, personally, and then, amid great secrecy, had been taken not to the British or to the American embassy but to the grounds of the Russian embassy itself. All of which prompted Melamed to wonder just who it was in the Kremlin that could have been accorded the same level of importance and security as Comrade Stalin himself. Molotov? Stalin's daughter, Svetlana? His son, Vasily? Stalin's mistress, perhaps?

But perhaps the strangest of all Melamed's discoveries that day came just before midnight, when, mindful of Beria's threats to have him shot, he took a walk around the winter embassy grounds and found, to his astonishment, that one of the NKVD officers patrolling near the gates, with a Degtyarev submachine gun cradled in his arm, was Lavrenti Beria himself.

XXIV
Saturday, November 27, 1943,
Cairo

I spent three uncomfortable nights in a cell beneath the police station in Cairo's Citadel. No lack of precedents for a philosopher spending time in prison: Zeno, Socrates, Roger Bacon, Hugo Grotius, and Dick Tracy's brother, Destutt. None of them had been accused of murder, of course. Not even Aristotle, of whom Bacon had remarked, jokingly, that, like an Eastern despot, he had strangled his rivals in order to reign peaceably.

Philosophers' jokes are always a real belly laugh.

Missing the chance to see the city of Teheran gave me little cause for regret. Everything I had heard about the place—the water, the pro-Nazi Iranians, the haughty colonialism inflicted on the country by the British and the Russians—made me glad I wouldn't be going there. All I wanted now was to clear myself of the murder charge and return to Washington. Once there, I was going to quit the OSS, sell the house in Kalorama Heights, and return to Harvard or Princeton. Whichever would have me. I would write another book. Truth looked like a subject that might be interesting. Provided I could decide exactly what truth was. I thought I might even write another letter to Diana, something much more difficult than writing a book about Truth.

Early on the morning of the fourth day of my holiday in the Citadel I awoke to find Mike Reilly in my prison cell. Even in his tropical cream suit, he was hardly anyone's idea of the Lord's angel.

"Did the maid let you in?" I shook my head, groggy with sleep. "What time is it?"

"Time to get up," Reilly said quietly and handed me a cup of coffee. "Here. Drink this."

"It smells a lot like coffee. How do you make it?"

"With a little brandy. There's more in the car outside. Brandy, I mean. It's just the thing to settle the stomach ahead of a long flight."

"Where are we going?"

"Teheran, of course."

"Teheran, huh? I hear it's a dump."

"It is. That's why we want you along."

"What about the British?"

"They're coming, too."

"I meant the police."

"Harry Hopkins has spent the last thirty-six hours pulling strings for you," said Reilly. "It seems both he and the president regard your presence in Teheran as absolutely essential." He shook his head and lit a cigarette. "Don't ask me why. I have no idea."

"My things at the hotel—"

"Are in the car outside. You can wash, shave, and change your clothes in a room upstairs."

"And the murder charges?"

"Dropped." Reilly handed me my wristwatch. "Here. I even wound it for you."

I glanced at the time. It was five-thirty in the morning. "What time is our flight?"

"Six-thirty."

"Then there's still time to drop into Grey Pillars."

Reilly was shaking his head.

"C'mon, Reilly, we've got to cross the Nile to get to the airport, so Garden City is on our way. More or less." I glanced up again at the barred window. Outside, the early-morning sky looked very different from its usual bright shade of orange. "Besides, haven't you noticed the fog? I'll be very surprised if we take off on time."

"My orders are to get you to the airport, Professor Mayer. At all costs."

"Good. That makes things easy for us both, then. Unless we go to Grey Pillars first, I'm not going to Teheran."

Grey Pillars was only two miles west of the Citadel, and the journey, by official car, took but a few minutes. The British GHQ was always open for business and, showered and shaved and wearing the clean clothes Reilly had brought from Shepheard's Hotel, I had little difficulty in gaining access again to the cells in the basement. I found Corporal Armfield just coming off duty.

"I'm here to see Major Reichleitner," I told the bemused corporal.

"But he's gone, sir. Transferred to a POW transport last night. On Major Deakin's orders. He turned up here with your General Donovan, sir, wanting to know about some codebooks, sir. Major Reichleitner told your General Donovan that he'd burned them all, at which point the general got rather upset with him, sir. After that, he and Deakin had a bit of a chat like, and it was decided to put Reichleitner on a POW ship leaving Alexandria this morning."

"Where's the ship going, Corporal?"

"Belfast, sir."

"Belfast? Did he leave a message for me?"

"No, sir. On account of how the general told him you'd been arrested on suspicion of being a German spy. Major Reichleitner seemed to think that was quite funny, sir. Very funny indeed. Fair roared with laughter."

"I bet he did. What else did Donovan tell him? Did he tell him that I was accused of murder? About that woman who was shot?"

"No, sir. I was standing in the doorway all the time they were in there and I heard every word."

So Reichleitner didn't know that his girlfriend was dead. Perhaps that was just as well. A man facing a stretch in a POW camp in Northern Ireland needed something to look forward to.

"Have you heard? My arrest was a mistake. Just in case you were wondering, Corporal."

"I *was* sort of wondering that, sir," grinned Armfield.

"It's been nice knowing you, Corporal. I'm pleased to see that not all the English are bastards."

"Oh, they are, sir. I'm Welsh."

Reilly was waiting impatiently in the back of the car, and even before I had closed the door, we were speeding west across the English Bridge and dashing between the limousines of the British pashas, the ice carts, the gold-and-tinsel hearses, the handcarts, the donkeys, and the gharries. "Are we flying via Basra?" I asked Reilly.

"There's typhus in Basra. And, for all I know, Nazi paratroopers, too. Besides, it's a hell of a train journey from Basra to Teheran. Even in the shah's personal train." He offered me a cigarette and then lit us both. "No, we're flying direct to Teheran. That's if we ever get through this goddamned Cairo traffic."

"I like the Cairo traffic," I said. "It's honest."

Reilly handed me his hip flask. "Looks like you were right," he said, nodding out of the window at the fog.

"I'm always right," I told Reilly. "That's why I became a philosopher."

"I just figured out why they want you along, Professor," he said. "You're easier to carry than a set of encyclopedias."

I took a swig of his brandy. And then another.

"Better make it last. That's breakfast until we get to Teheran."

I was starting to like him again, thinking maybe there was more under his Panama hat than a thick head of black-Irish hair.

There were several planes on the runway at Cairo Airport, and Reilly directed me toward the president's own C-54. I climbed aboard and sat down alongside Harry Hopkins. It was as if nothing had happened. I shook hands with Hopkins. I shook hands hands with Roosevelt. I even exchanged a few jokes with John Weitz.

"Nice of you to join us, Professor," said Hopkins.

"I'm very glad to be here, sir. I understand from Reilly that but for you I wouldn't be here at all."

"Don't mention it."

"I'll try not to, sir."

Hopkins nodded happily. "It's all behind us now. All forgotten. Besides, we couldn't afford to leave you behind, Willard. We're going to have need of your linguistic skills."

"But surely the only foreign language that's going to be spoken at the Big Three is Russian."

Hopkins shook his head. "The shah went to school in Switzerland. And I think you are aware of his father's hatred of the British. Hence, His Majesty speaks only French and German. Because of the delicacy of the political situation in Iran, it was decided to keep any meetings between Reza Shah and the Big Three a secret. For the sake of the shah himself. He's only twenty-four years old and not yet secure on the throne. Until thirty-six hours ago, we weren't exactly sure he would risk meeting us at all. That's why you haven't been kept informed of what was happening. We didn't know ourselves. After the war, oil is going to be the key to world power. There's an ocean of the stuff underneath Iran. It's why the president agreed to come here in the first place."

I was already forming the strong impression that, but for my German-language skills, I would still be in a prison cell in Cairo facing a murder charge. Yet even now there was something about Hopkins's story that didn't quite add up.

"Then, with all due respect, wouldn't it have been better to have brought someone along who speaks Farsi?" When Hopkins looked at me blankly, I added, "That's the Persian name for the modern Persian language, sir."

"Easier said than done. Even Dreyfus, our ambassador in Teheran, doesn't speak the local lingo. Hungarian and a little French, but no Farsi. Our State Department isn't up to snuff in terms of linguists, I'm afraid. Nor anything else, for that matter."

I glanced around. John Weitz, the State Department's Russian-language specialist and Bohlen's substitute, was sitting right behind me, and, having clearly heard Hopkins's remark, he raised his eyebrows at me with a show of diplomatic patience. A few moments later he got out of his seat to walk back to the plane's tiny lavatory. Meanwhile, the president, Elliott Roosevelt, Mike Reilly, Averell Harriman, Agent Pawlikowski, and the Joint Chiefs were each of them staring out of the windows as the plane flew over the Suez Canal near Ismailia.

"Since we're speaking frankly, sir," I said, taking advantage of Weitz's absence, "it's still my belief that we have a German spy traveling in our delegation. A man who has now killed twice. Possibly more. I firmly believe that one of our party intends to assassinate Joseph Stalin."

Hopkins listened patiently and then nodded. "Professor, I just know you're wrong. And you'll have to take my word for why that is, I'm afraid. I can't tell you why. Not yet. But I happen to know that what you say is just impossible. When we're on the ground, we can talk about this again. Until then, it might be a good idea if you were just to can this theory of yours. Got that?"

We flew over Jerusalem and Baghdad, crossing the Tigris, up and along the Basra-Teheran railroad, and then from Ramadan to Teheran, always at only five or six thousand feet off the ground so that the lame constitutions of Roosevelt and Hopkins would not be taxed too much by the journey. All the same, I guessed it was quite a job for the pilot, having to negotiate several mountain passes instead of just flying the big C-54 over them.

It was three o'clock in the afternoon when finally we caught sight of the Russian army airfield at Gale Morghe. Dozens of American B-25s repainted with the red star of the Soviet Union sat on the airfield.

"Jesus Christ, that's a terrifying sight," joked Roosevelt. "Our own planes in Russian livery. I guess that's what it will look like if the Commies ever conquer the States, eh, Mike?"

"Painting them is one thing," said Reilly. "Flying them's another. The last time I was in this lousy country I learned that to fly with a Russian pilot and live is to lose all fear of death."

"Mike, I thought you knew," laughed Roosevelt. "My security exists in inverse proportion to your own insecurity."

The presidential plane began to make its turn for a landing, banking over a checkerboard of rice fields and banks of puddle mud.

A military escort commanded by General Connolly conveyed Roosevelt and his immediate party to the American legation in the north of the city. I went with the Joint Chiefs, Harriman, Bohlen, and some of the Secret Service to our quarters at Camp Amirabad.

Amirabad was a U.S. Army facility that was still in the process of being built, and it already had a brick barracks, a hospital, a movie theater, some shops, offices, warehouses, and recreational facilities. It looked like any army base in New Mexico or Arizona, and seemed to indicate that the American presence in Teheran was hardly temporary.

As soon as the Joint Chiefs, Bohlen, and I had changed our clothes, we were driven through the streets of Teheran in a convoy of jeeps, cars, and motorcycles to the American legation, where, on the verandah, Secret Service agents Qualter and Rauff were already on guard. I nodded to the agents, and much to my surprise they nodded back.

"Have you got a cigarette?" I asked Qualter. "I seem to have left mine somewhere."

"Prison, by any chance?" said Qualter, and, smiling wryly, he took out a packet of Kools and tapped one out for me. "Do you mind mentholated?"

"Nope," I said, quietly noting the brand. "You don't actually think I killed that woman, do you?"

I didn't really care what he thought, but I wanted to keep him talking. I was more interested in the discovery that he was smoking Kools.

Qualter lit my cigarette and shrugged. "Not my place to think anything that doesn't affect the safety of the boss. Hell, I dunno, Professor. You sure don't look like a murderer, I'll say that much for you. But, then, you don't look like a secret agent, either."

"I'll take that as a compliment." I glanced down the front of Qualter's single-breasted jacket, counting the buttons. There were three, just as there were supposed to be. "Anyway, thanks for the cigarette."

"That's okay." Qualter grinned. "They ain't mine."

"Oh? Whose are they?"

But Qualter had already turned away to open the door for the

Joint Chiefs. I followed them inside, walking up a wooden ramp that had been built by army carpenters to facilitate Roosevelt's entry and exit. It seemed the ramp had also presented the American delegation with a problem. Settled in the drawing room, the president was asking for a drink and Ambassador Dreyfus had to explain that the ramp had been built on top of the only entrance to the legation's wine cellar. He had been obliged to borrow eight bottles of scotch from the British ambassador, Sir Reader Bullard. Reilly heard Dreyfus out politely, then steered the ambassador to the door.

"Jesus," remarked Roosevelt when Dreyfus had gone. "Forget the scotch, what about the gin? And the vermouth? Mike? How am I going to mix a goddamned martini without any gin and vermouth?"

Reilly nodded at Pawlikowski, who left the room, presumably in search of some gin and vermouth.

"Take a seat, gentlemen," said Hopkins.

I sat down beside Chip Bohlen, facing the president, Hopkins, Admirals King and Leahy, and Ambassador Harriman. I hadn't seen much of Harriman up close. He was tall, with a prominent jaw and the kind of smile lines that put you in mind of a clown without makeup. He had dark hair, with big furry eyebrows that anchored a forehead as high as Grand Central Station. His father had been a robber baron, one of the big railway magnates, and I supposed he was even richer than my mother. He looked a little how I was feeling, which was nervous.

Seeing that Roosevelt was still talking to Harriman and King, I leaned toward Bohlen and said: "Since most of the interpreting is going to be done by you, it had better be you that reminds the president of any system you want to get going."

"System?" Bohlen frowned and shook his head. "Hell, there's not even a stenographer. And as far as I can see, no one seems to have prepared any position papers on questions that might be discussed. Certainly none that I've seen. Doesn't that strike you as a little bit strange?"

"Come to think of it, yes. But that's FDR. He likes to improvise. Keep things informal."

"Is that really feasible when you're discussing the fate of the postwar world? This ought to be about as formal as it can be, don't you think?"

"Nothing can surprise me anymore, Chip. Not on this trip."

"What's in the briefcase?" Hopkins asked me, pointing to the case at my side. "A bomb?"

I smiled thinly, opened the briefcase, took out the Beketovka File, and handed it over. I was still explaining the contents when Roosevelt cleared his throat loudly and interrupted.

"All right, gentlemen," he said quietly. "Let's get down to business. I'll have to ask Professor Mayer and Mr. Bohlen to suspend their curiosity for a while longer. A lot of this might not make any sense to you right now, so you'll have to be patient. All will be explained to you both eventually. I've asked you here now for a damn good reason. But I'll come to that presently. Mike—have all the delegations arrived safely?"

"Yesterday."

"How's Churchill, Harry?"

"Sulking."

"Well, I can't say that I blame him. I'll call him myself. See if I can't persuade him to go along with this. As a matter of fact, I think we're going to have some problems with General Marshall and General Arnold, for the same reason."

Hopkins shrugged.

"All the same, it's a pity." Roosevelt lit a cigarette, smoking it without his holder, which seemed to bespeak a greater nervousness. Adjusting his position in his wheelchair, he looked at Reilly. "Mike? What's our cover story to justify moving to the Russian embassy?"

"That it's quite a hike between here and the Soviet embassy. Which would mean you driving through unguarded streets when there are still some German paratroopers at large. Between three and six still unaccounted for, according to the Ivans. Equally, there might be some kind of demonstration against the British, or against the Russians, in which case we might get caught up in it."

"Actually, that's quite true," admitted Roosevelt. "Did you see the welcome we had on the way from the airport? I felt like Hitler driving into Paris."

"And there's no doubt," continued Reilly, "that the Russian and British embassies are, by comparison with ours, almost impregnable. Did you know that this embassy has been robbed several times in the last month? Anyway, the Brits and the Ivans are right next door to each other, so if something did go wrong while we were there, we'd have plenty of troops to protect you, Mr. President. Anyway, the bottom line is this: that I don't think anyone would argue if we claimed it was your safety that prompted us to move you into the Russian embassy."

For a moment I wondered if my ears had deceived me. That Reilly had said something about moving the president of the United States into the "safety" of the Russian embassy. But then Roosevelt nodded.

"You say that, Mike," he said. "But it'll cause some comment, don't think it won't. Whatever the reason we put out. Everyone in the press corps will say that all of my conversations will be taped by the Russians using secret microphones. Unless we have some kind of line on that, I'll be accused of being naïve. Or worse. Not on the ball. Lame. Sick."

"Then how about we say this?" offered Hopkins. "That in an effort to seem like we came to Teheran with no preconceived strategies cooked up by us and the British . . ." Hopkins paused for a moment and then added, "That in the spirit of openness and cooperation, we stayed at the Russian embassy in full knowledge that all our conversations would probably be monitored by the Soviets. But that we had nothing to hide from our Soviet allies. And that therefore it really didn't matter a damn if they recorded our conversations. What do you think, Mr. President?"

"Sounds good, Harry. I like it. Of course, once we're in the Russian compound we can close everything down and no one in the press will know a goddamned thing about what's going on. Eh, Mike? No one's better at keeping a lid on things than the Soviets."

"That's why we came to Teheran," said Reilly. "To keep a lid on things. But before any of this, how about if we say that we asked Stalin over for a drink and he turned us down? That he refused to come over here. That way we can make it look like he's the one who is more worried about his personal security than you are. And that this is what prompted us to make the move to their embassy in the first place."

"Good," said Roosevelt. "I like that, too."

"And after all, Mr. President," said King, "let's not forget that it's you who has come halfway around the world to be here. Not Stalin. It isn't you who's afraid of flying."

"True, Ernie, true," admitted Roosevelt.

"So when do we pull off this charade?" asked Harriman.

"Tonight," said Roosevelt. "That way we can get things under way first thing in the morning. If the other side is agreeable."

"They are," said Reilly. "But Mr. Harriman raises a useful point when he mentions a charade. I mean, it might be best if we arranged some kind of decoy that saw you leaving the legation here and going to the Russian compound. Like before, with Agent Holmes pretending to be you."

"You mean like a dummy cavalcade? Yes, that's good. And meanwhile we go there in an unmarked van, through a side door, maybe. The servants' entrance."

"Are Soviet embassies *allowed* to have a servants' entrance?" Hopkins laughed. "It sounds kind of anti-Communist."

"I for one am not sure I like the idea of the president of the United States sneaking in and out of buildings like a common thief," said Admiral King. "It sounds, well, sir, lacking in dignity."

"Believe me, Ernie," Roosevelt said, "there's not much dignity when you're a man in a wheelchair. Besides, whatever happens I'm going to be having a better time than Hull."

Harry Hopkins laughed again. "I'd love to see him now, the bastard. Thay, are thoth bombth I heard jutht now?"

Roosevelt guffawed. "You're a cruel son of a bitch, Harry. I guess that's why I like you. And you're right. I'd love to see Cordell's face right now."

"What about records?" asked Hopkins. "Stenographers?"

Roosevelt shook his head. "No, we'll just exchange the position papers that we have each prepared. Otherwise there's to be no formal record. Professor Mayer and Mr. Bohlen—if you don't mind I'm going to start using your first names. Willard? Chip? You will make what notes you need to help with your translations, but I don't want a written record of what's said here. At least not in the beginning. And all notes are to be destroyed afterwards. Chip? Willard? Have you got that?"

Bohlen and I, both of us now thoroughly bewildered, nodded our compliance. I had started to think that there was something else we hadn't yet been told. Something we might not like. Averell Harriman was looking even more uncomfortable.

"Sir," said Harriman now. "The absence of records could be dangerous. It's one thing not to have a record when it's you speaking to Mr. Churchill. You and he are on the same wavelength, at least most of the time. But the Soviets can be quite literal-minded about things. You say something, they will expect to hold you to the letter."

"I'm sorry, Averell, but my mind is made up. That's the way it's got to be for now." He looked at Reilly. "Mike, pour us some of Sir Whatshisname's scotch, will you? I'm sure we could all use a drink."

Roosevelt surveyed his drink thoughtfully. "I wish Churchill could reconcile himself to this." He sipped some of the British ambassador's whiskey. "Averell? Did he say what he's doing tonight?"

"He said he planned to make it an early night and read a novel by Charles Dickens, Mr. President."

"We need to work on Churchill again," Roosevelt said.

"He'll come around, Mr. President."

Roosevelt nodded and, catching my frown, smiled wryly. "Willard. Chip. I guess you boys are wondering what in hell this is all about?"

"It had crossed my mind, sir."

Bohlen just nodded.

"All will become very clear to you both tomorrow morning," said Roosevelt. "Until then, I must ask for your indulgence. If ever there was a time in which the president of the United States needed the full confidence and support of the people around him, that time is now, gentlemen. Great risks are involved, but great rewards are to be had."

"Whatever it takes, Mr. President," said Bohlen.

"We're a team, now," added Roosevelt. "I just wanted to make sure you boys understood that."

"You have our total support, sir," I added.

"All right, gentlemen, that'll do for now."

We'd been dismissed. I finished my scotch hurriedly and followed Reilly into the hallway, where he handed me an official-looking document.

"'The Espionage Act, 1917,'" I said, reading the cover. "What's this, Mike? A little light bedtime reading?"

"I'd like you both to familiarize yourselves with the contents of this document before tomorrow morning," he said. "It relates to the disclosure of non-security-related government information."

I said nothing. The Democrat in me wanted to remind the Secret Service agent that the United States had no official secrets act for the simple reason that the First Amendment of the Constitution guaranteed free speech. But, feeling I had perhaps caused enough trouble already, I decided to let it alone.

"What the hell *is* this, Mike?" Bohlen asked.

"Look," said Reilly, "the president is pretty worked up about secrecy on this mission. You can understand that, can't you? That's why he wanted you along to this meeting. So you could see that for yourself. And so that you might realize that you are an important part of this team."

I shrugged. "Sure," I said.

Bohlen nodded.

"The administration has taken legal advice, and all we're asking is that you both sign a document saying you're aware of the need for secrecy, that's all."

"What do you mean, legal advice?" asked Bohlen.

"Three Supreme Court judges have ruled, in private, that the Espionage Act doesn't just cover spying. It also covers leaks of government information to someone other than an enemy, such as a newspaper or magazine."

"You're trying to gag us?" said Bohlen. "I don't believe it."

"No, not gag. Not at all. This is merely to make you aware of the possible consequences of speaking about what might go on while we're here in Teheran. All we're asking is that you sign an affidavit after you've read this thing, just to indicate that you appreciate the full meaning of the act."

"What about *our* legal advice, Mike?" I asked.

"I think this is illegal," Bohlen objected, smiling nervously.

"I'm not a lawyer. Not anymore. I couldn't tell you what is and what's not illegal here. All I know is that the boss wants everyone who's involved in our effort here to sign this. Otherwise . . ."

"Otherwise what, Mike?" Bohlen asked, coloring visibly around his prominent ears.

Reilly thought for a moment. "Stalin's translator," he said, then snapped his fingers at Bohlen. "What's his name?"

"There are two. Pavlov and Berezhkov."

"And what do you think would happen to them if they said anything out of line?"

Bohlen and Willard remained silent.

"They'd be shot," said Reilly, answering his own question. "I don't think they're in any doubt about that."

"What's your point, Mike?" Bohlen asked.

"Only that it would be a shame if they ended up having to do all of the translations because the president couldn't find anyone he trusted, that's all."

"Of course the president can trust us, Mike," I said. "We're just a little surprised that you want us to sign a piece of paper to that effect."

"I know I can trust *you*, Professor," Reilly said, with extra meaning. "We have to go back to Cairo after Teheran, and I'm sure you wouldn't want to have to speak to the British police again about that unfortunate incident in Garden City."

It was my turn to feel the color enter my ears. There were no two ways about it. I was being blackmailed into toeing the line.

"Professor, why don't you have a word with Chip," Reilly said smoothly, "and point out the expediency of what's being proposed?"

Reilly walked away to have a word with Pawlikowski, leaving an exasperated-looking Bohlen alone with me.

"We just got tackled by our own offensive linemen," I said.

Bohlen nodded. "What the hell is going on here?" he asked.

"I have no idea," I said. "But whatever it is, I could sure use another glass of Sir Lancelot's scotch."

XXV
Sunday, November 28, 1943,
Teheran

0700 HOURS

AFTER LEAVING the carpet factory in the bazaar, Ebtehaj had taken North Team to a house in Abassi Street, where Oster, having refined his new plan still further, left all but five of his men there with orders to wait until dark and then try to make their way out of the city and across the border into Turkey. Oster had decided that what was now required was a small commando team of no more than half a dozen men, and after a few emotional good-byes, he, Schoellhorn, Unterturmführers Schnabel and Shkvarzev, and three other Ukrainians were driven to a pistachio farm northeast of the city.

At the celebrated court of Queen Belghais of Sheba, pistachios were a delicacy for royalty and the privileged elite. Luckily for Captain Oster and his men, Iranian pistachios were no longer the preserve of the wealthy, but popular throughout the country. Jomat Abdoli was one of the largest wholesalers of pistachios in Iran, and farmers from all over the major pistachio-producing provinces sold their crops to him. He roasted and stored them at a facility in Eshtejariyeh, to the northeast of the city. Jomat hated the British. When Ebtehaj, the wrestler, had come to him asking that he hide some Germans, Jomat said he was only too willing to help.

Ebtehaj, Schoellhorn, Oster, Schnabel, and the three others had been sleeping in the main storehouse and had just finished a traditional Iranian breakfast of tea, boiled eggs, salted cheese, yogurt, and unleavened bread when news reached them that a truck carrying Russian troops had been sighted at the foot of the hill leading up to Jomat's warehouse. Shkvarzev reached for his Russian-made PPSh41 submachine gun. Neither Jomat nor any of the six men at the pistachio warehouse were aware that everyone back at the house in Abassi Street had now been shot resisting arrest. Oster had no idea that they had been discovered. Had he known, he might have assumed that it was their turn next and acquiesced with the Ukrainian officers' desire to shoot it out.

"No," he told Shkvarzev, "we wouldn't stand a chance." Then he said to Jomat, "Can we hide somewhere?"

Jomat was already picking up a pile of empty sacks. "Follow me," he said and led them through the main storehouse and the roasting shed into an empty brick silo. "Lie on the floor, and cover yourselves with the sacks," he told them. As soon as they had done so, he tugged a metal chute over the silo and then pulled open a feeder drawer so that the silo was filled with half a ton of smooth, purple, recently harvested pistachios.

Oster had never given pistachios much thought. There was a cocktail bar at the Hotel Adlon that served them in little brass bowls, and once or twice he had eaten some; he thought he would certainly make a point of eating them more often if pistachios ended up saving his life. Besides, Jomat insisted they were a perfect after-dinner aphrodisiac. "Your Bible's King Solomon was a great lover," Jomat had told him, "only because Queen Belghais, she gave him plenty of *peste*." *Peste* was the Farsi word for pistachios.

Dust filled Oster's nose and mouth, and he tried to ignore the impulse to cough. What would he have given now for a glass of water? Not the local water that ran alongside the streets in gaping, unprotected gutters called *qanats* but the pure water that ran off the glacier in his home town in the Austrian Alps. It was typical of the British that they should pipe down the only reliably pure supply of water in Teheran, and then sell it by the gallon to their friends. A nation of shopkeepers, indeed. There were plenty of water carts in and around Teheran, but none of the other embassies trusted these. Which was just as well, he thought. The British sense of hygiene and commerce was going to be their downfall.

Nearly all of Teheran's horse-drawn water carts had been made by an Australian company, J. Furphy of Shepperton, Victoria, and had arrived in Mesopotamia with Australian troops during the First World War, before being sold on to Iranians when the Australians had left the country. The Iranian drivers of these water carts were notorious sources of unreliable information and gossip, with the result that the word "furphy" had become a local synonym for unfounded rumor. On Oster's orders, Ebtehaj had purchased a Furphy from the owner of the Café Ferdosi, and a Caspian pony from a local horse trader. The Furphy had then been taken to the pistachio warehouse in Eshtejariyeh, where Shkvarzev and Schnabel set about converting it into a mobile bomb.

The tank part of the water cart was made of two cast-iron ends, thirty-four inches in diameter, and a sheet steel body rolled to form a cylinder about forty-five inches long. Filled with 180 gallons of water, the Furphy weighed just over a ton and, carefully balanced over the axle to distribute the weight, was a fair load for a good horse. The frame of the cart was made of wood and fitted with two thirty-inch wheels. Water was poured out of the tank from a tap in the rear, and poured in through a large lidded filler hole on top. It was a simple enough job to use this filler hole to pack the empty Furphy with nitrate fertilizer and sugar, thereby making a bomb that was about half the size of the largest bomb in general use by the Luftwaffe on the eastern front—the two-and-a-half-ton "Max." Oster had seen one of these dropped from a Heinkel, and it had destroyed a four-story building in Kharkov, killing everyone inside, so he calculated that a well-placed bomb weighing more than a ton was easily capable of bringing down one small villa housing the British embassy.

Oster froze as he heard the muffled sound of Russian voices. At the same time, he saw, in close-up, Shkvarzev's hand tightening on his submachine gun. The German could hardly blame him for not wanting to be taken alive. A particularly harsh fate was said to await all of Vlasov's Zeppelin volunteers: something special devised by Beria himself, at Stalin's express order. Oster didn't much care if Churchill and Roosevelt survived the explosion, but the prospect of killing Stalin was something else again. There wasn't a German on the eastern front who wouldn't have risked his life for a chance to kill Stalin. Lots of Oster's friends and even one or two relatives had been in Stalingrad and were now dead—or worse, in Soviet POW camps. Stalin's assassination was something any German officer would be proud of.

The plan was almost too straightforward. Every morning two Iranians set off with a water cart from the U.S. embassy and traveled some two miles across the city to the British embassy to fill a Furphy with pure water. With some of the British gold sovereigns Oster had brought from Vinnica, it was a simple matter to buy off the two Iranians. On Tuesday morning, Oster and Shkvarzev, disguised as locals, would drive two Furphys onto the grounds of the embassy. If they were asked about having two, Oster would tell the British that more water was required because of the visit of President Roosevelt's delegation. According to the two water carriers bribed by Ebtehaj, the British water supply appeared underneath the roof of the embassy building in an ornamental dome with honeycomb tracery and a poll of water tiled in blue—what the French called a *rond-point*. The *rond-point* appeared on the other side of the embassy's kitchen wall. The harness of the Furphy carrying the bomb would be disabled, necessitating its temporary abandonment. The bomb would then be armed using a cheap Westclox "Big Ben" alarm clock—which to Oster seemed only appropriate—an Eveready B103 radio battery, an electrical blasting cap, and three pounds of plastic explosive. Oster and Shkvarzev would then leave the embassy with one Furphy filled with water and, having left the second Furphy behind, the two men would use both cart horses and ride fifteen miles to Kan, where Ebtehaj would be waiting with a truckload of roasted pistachios. They would then make the 400-mile journey to the Turkish border. By the time the bomb went off, Oster hoped to be in a neutral country.

Oster thought that if the plan did have a fault, it was that it seemed too simple. He spoke some Persian, and a little English, and since neither he nor Shkvarzev had washed or shaved since their arrival in Iran, he didn't doubt that in the right clothes they could easily pass for locals. At least as far as the British were concerned. If all went to plan, they would arm the bomb at around nine A.M. and, twelve hours later, just as Churchill's birthday guests were sitting down to dinner, it would go off. And while Oster did not think this would win the war, it would be enough to force an armistice. That had to be worth any amount of risk.

Oster finally heard Jomat shout that the Russians had left and, breathing a sigh of relief, he and the others began to struggle out from under the pistachios. He did not think that they would be so lucky again. With forty-eight hours still to go before he and Shkvarzev could put their plan into action, it was going to be all they could do to keep their nerve and sit it out.

0800 HOURS

THE AMIRABAD U.S. Army base was close to the Gale Morghe Airport, yet despite the noise of American C-54s arriving throughout the night, carrying matériel for the Russian war effort, I slept extremely well. This was easy. I had a proper bed, instead of a wooden pallet next to an open slops bucket. And the door of my room had a key I was allowed to keep. Like most army camps, the accommodations and facilities at Amirabad were basic. That was just fine with me, too. After three nights as the guest of the Cairo police, the camp felt like the Plaza. I saw a couple of army football teams practicing their plays on a field of mud. But there was little time to see if they were any good. Not that I cared very much either way. I wouldn't have known a good football team from the choir at the Mount Zion United Methodist Church. After a hurried breakfast of coffee and scrambled eggs, a jeep took Bohlen and me not to the American legation, as before, but to the Russian embassy.

Beyond its heavily guarded exterior walls, the main part of the embassy was a square building of light-brown stone set in a small park. On its front was a handsome portico with white Doric columns and, behind these, six arched French windows. In the distance I saw fountains, a small lake, and several other villas, one of them now occupied by Stalin and Molotov, his foreign commissar, and all of them closely guarded by yet more Russian troops armed with submachine guns.

The president was already in official residence in the main building, having been smuggled into the embassy in the early hours of the morning. But as far as most people other than the Joint Chiefs and the Secret Service knew, he was still at the American legation. Bohlen and I found Roosevelt seated alongside Hopkins, who was perched on the edge of a two-seater leather sofa in a small drawing room at the back of the residence.

On the floor was a new Persian rug with a peacock motif that matched the light blue curtains; behind the president's shoulder was an ornate table lamp and, to the side, a huge oil-fired radiator. Clearly the Russians had tried to make Roosevelt comfortable, but the general effect was as if the interior decorator had been Joseph Stalin himself.

Reilly came into the room, closing the door behind him.

"Marshall and Arnold?" asked Roosevelt.

"No, sir," said Reilly.

"Churchill?"

Reilly shook his head.

"Fuck," said Roosevelt. "Fuck! . . . So who are we waiting for?"

"Admiral Leahy, sir."

Roosevelt caught sight of Bohlen and me and motioned us to sit.

I saw that Hopkins had Reichleitner's Beketovka File on his lap. He patted the file. "Explosive stuff," he said to me as Roosevelt began to curse Generals Marshall and Arnold yet again. "But I'm sure you'll understand why we can't act on any of this."

I nodded. In truth I had seen this coming.

"Not right now. For the same reason we couldn't do anything about the Katyn Forest massacre."

And then he handed the file back to me.

The door opened again and Leahy came into the room, followed closely by Agent Pawlikowski, who took up a position of vigilance between me and the door. To my left, I had a pretty good view of the president. And to my right, I had an equally good view of Pawlikowski, which was how I came to notice that one of his jacket's three buttons was different from the other two.

I looked away so as not to arouse suspicion. When I looked back again, I knew there could be no doubt about it. The button was plain black, whereas the other two looked like tortoiseshell. The original button was missing. But was it the same as the one I had seen on the floor in Elena's bedroom? It was hard to be sure.

"Thanks for coming, Bill," Roosevelt said to Leahy. "Well, it looks like this is it."

"Yes, sir, it does," said Leahy.

"Any last reservations?"

"No, sir," said Leahy. "What about Winston?"

Roosevelt shook his head bitterly.

"Stubborn old bastard," said Leahy.

"Fuck him," shrugged Hopkins. "We don't need him for this. In fact, it's probably best he's not here. Besides, in the long run, he'll come around. You'll see. He has no choice but to do what we do. Any other position would be untenable."

"I sure hope you're right," said Roosevelt.

There was a moment or two of silence, during which time I sought another look at Pawlikowski. It was much cooler in Teheran than in Cairo, but I couldn't help but notice that the Secret Service agent was sweating heavily. He mopped his brow with a handkerchief several times, and as he raised his arm I caught sight of the .45-caliber automatic in the shoulder holster beneath his jacket. Then he caught me looking at him.

"I couldn't bum a cigarette off you, could I?" I asked him. "I left mine back at Amirabad."

Pawlikowksi said nothing, just dipped his hand into his coat pocket and took out a pack of Kools. He knocked one out for me and then lit it.

"Thanks." I was now quite certain Pawlikowski was my man. And who better than a Polish-American to assassinate Stalin? But even as I pictured Pawlikowski in the radio room at Elena's house, I heard Roosevelt speaking to me.

"With Churchill and two of my Joint Chiefs sulking in their tents, I can't afford any more losses in this negotiating team. Not now. And especially not you boys. You are my ears and my voice. Without you, this would be over before it even got started. So whatever happens, I want both of you to make a personal promise that you won't duck out on me. I want your word that you'll see this through, no matter how repugnant you might find your duties as translators. Especially you, Willard, since the major part of what happens today is going to fall on your shoulders. And I must also apologize for keeping you both in the dark. But here's the thing. If we get this morning right, I believe the world will thank us. But if we screw up, it'll be the dirtiest secret in the history of this conflict. Perhaps of all time."

"I won't desert you, Mr. President," I said, still wondering what the hell this was all about. "You have my word on it."

"Mine, too, sir," said Bohlen.

Roosevelt nodded and then spun his chair into action. "All right. Let's do this."

Pawlikowski leaped to open the door for his boss, but instead of turning toward the main door of the residence, Roosevelt propelled himself toward the end of the corridor, where Mike Reilly was already grappling with a heavy steel door. I followed the president's small party through it and down a long slope. It felt as if we were going into a bomb shelter.

Pawlikowski caught up with me and we walked down the corridor. I thought to tell him that I was on to him, if only as a deterrent, but he suddenly accelerated forward to open another door that led into yet another corridor, this one level and almost fifty yards long. It was well lit and seemed recently constructed.

We reached a third door, this one guarded by two uniformed NKVD who, seeing the president, came to attention smartly, the heels of their jackboots clicking loudly. Then one of them turned and knocked three times. The door swung open slowly, and Pawlikowski and Reilly led our small party into the vast round room that lay beyond.

There were no windows inside that room, which was as big as a tennis court and lit by an enormous brass light that hung over a Camelot-sized round table with a green baize cover.

Around the table were two rings of chairs: the inner ring, fifteen ornate mahogany chairs upholstered in a Persian-patterned silk; the outer ring, twelve smaller chairs, on each of which lay a notepad and a pencil. The room itself was guarded by ten NKVD men positioned at regular intervals around the tapestry-covered walls, stoic and unmoving, like so many suits of armor. Roosevelt's Secret Service agents took up positions between the NKVD guards along the same circular wall.

Sixty seconds later, I hardly noticed any of this. Sixty seconds later I hardly noticed Stalin, or Molotov, or Beria, or Voroshilov, his Red Army field marshal. Sixty seconds later, even Pawlikowski was forgotten. Sixty seconds later, as I stared openmouthed at the man coming through a door on the opposite side of the chamber, and then at the others who accompanied him, I wouldn't have noticed if Betty Grable had climbed onto my lap and stripped down to her ankle-strap platforms.

In any other circumstances I might have assumed it was a joke. Except that the man was now advancing on Roosevelt with an outstretched hand, wearing a smile on his face as if he were actually pleased to see the president of a country on which he had personally declared war.

The man was Adolf Hitler.

"JESUS CHRIST," I muttered.

"Get a grip on yourself," Roosevelt murmured and then shook the outstretched hand in front of him. Acting almost automatically, I started to translate Hitler's first words to the president. It was all now quite clear: how it was that Harry Hopkins and Donovan could have been so adamant that the Germans were not planning to assassinate the Big Three at Teheran, for example; and why Churchill, and very likely Marshall and Arnold, too, were "sulking in their tents."

Not the very least of what I now understood quite clearly was why Roosevelt had asked me along in the first place, for of course he needed a fluent speaker of German who had also demonstrated himself to be what the president had called "a Realpolitiker," someone who was prepared to keep his mouth shut for the sake of some supposed greater good. That "greater good" was now all too apparent to me: Roosevelt and Stalin intended talking peace with the Führer.

"The British prime minister is not here," said Hitler, whose speaking voice was much softer than the one I knew from German radio broadcasts. "Am I to assume that he will not be joining us?"

"I'm afraid not," said Roosevelt. "At least not for the present."

"A great pity," said Hitler. "I should like to have met him."

"There may yet be an opportunity for that, Herr Hitler," said Roosevelt. "Let us hope so, anyway."

Hitler glanced around as his own translator appeared behind his shoulder to interpret the president's words. It was my chance to take another quick look around the room, just in time to see Molotov shaking hands with von Ribbentrop, Stalin speaking to Harry Hopkins through Bohlen, and the various plainclothes SS men grouped around Himmler, who was smiling broadly as if delighted that things were off to a reasonably amicable start.

"Your Mr. Cordell Hull has asked me to assure you that he is quite well," said Hitler. "And that he is being well looked after. Also the Russian commissar of foreign trade, Mr. Mikoyan."

I made the translation, and seeing me frown while I spoke, Roosevelt thought to provide me with a short explanation of what the Führer had just said: "Cordell Hull is in Berlin," he told me. "As a hostage for the Führer's safe return home."

Everything seemed to be falling into place now—even the reason the secretary of state had not been invited to the Big Three.

Hitler walked over to Stalin, who was a little shorter than Hitler and resembled a small, tubby bear. All the pictures I had seen of Stalin had created the illusion of a much taller man, and I guessed that these must have been taken from a lower level. When Stalin lit a cigarette, I also noticed his left arm was lame and slightly deformed, like the kaiser's.

"Will you be all right, Willard?" Roosevelt said, and I guessed he was referring to my Jewishness more than anything else.

"Yes, Mr. President, I'm fine."

Seeing his opportunity, Himmler moved smartly forward and, still smiling broadly, dipped his head, and then, relaxing somewhat, offered the president his hand. He was wearing a suit, with a silk shirt and tie and a pair of handsome gold cuff links that flashed like alarm signals under the room's bright lights.

"I believe you are the principal architect of these negotiations," said Roosevelt.

"I have only tried to make all parties see the sense of what is to be attempted here this morning." The Reichsführer-SS spoke pompously and with one eye always on Hitler. "And I sincerely believe that this war can be ended before Christmas."

"Let's hope so," said Roosevelt. "Let's hope so."

The representatives of Russia, the United States, and Nazi Germany and their advisers seated themselves around the big green table. As host, it fell to Stalin to initiate the proceedings. With Bohlen translating, I was able to catch my breath and reflect on what was happening. That the Russians had managed to keep Hitler's arrival in Teheran a secret was almost as amazing as the fact that Hitler should have ever come at all. And already I had decided that if the talks did, for some reason, fail, Roosevelt's reputation was probably safe, for surely no one would believe that such a thing could ever have taken place.

Of the two dictators seated at the table, Stalin seemed the less attractive, and not because I could understand no Russian. He had a cold, crafty, almost corpselike face, and when the yellowish eyes flickered on me and he smiled to reveal his teeth, broken and stained with nicotine, it was all too easy to imagine him as a modern Ivan the Terrible, sending men, women, and children off to their deaths without mussing a hair. At the same time, his mind seemed sharper than Hitler's, and he spoke well and without notes:

"We are sitting around this table for the first time with but one object in mind," he said. "The ending of this war. It is my sincere belief that we shall do everything at this conference to make due use, within the framework of our cooperation, of the power and authority that our peoples have vested in us."

Stalin nodded at Roosevelt, who removed his pince-nez and, using it to emphasize his opening remarks, began to speak: "I should like to welcome Herr Hitler into this circle," said the president. "In past meetings between Britain and the United States, it has been our habit to publish nothing, but to speak our minds very freely. And I do urge each one of us all to speak as freely as he wishes on the basis of the good faith that has already been demonstrated by our presence in this room. Nevertheless, if any one of us does not want to talk about any particular subject, we do not have to do so." Roosevelt leaned back in his wheelchair and waited for von Ribbentrop, who spoke excellent English, to finish the translation.

Hitler nodded and folded his arms across his chest. For a moment he was silent and only Stalin, filling his pipe from torn-up Russian Belomor cigarettes, seemed oblivious to the effect the Führer's pause was having on the room. When Hitler started to speak, I realized, with some amusement, that the Führer had been trying to finish the PEZ mint he was sucking before saying anything.

"Thank you, Marshal Stalin and Mr. President. I should like to have offered my thanks to Mr. Churchill, too; however, since it is my belief that the three countries in this room represent the greatest concentration of worldly power that has ever been seen in the history of mankind, I also believe that we three alone have the potential to shorten the war, and that peace lies in our collective hands. Providence favors men who know how to use the opportunities fate has given them. This is such an opportunity, and to those who might criticize us for taking it, I would say that the notions of what is proper in war and peace have little to do with political reality. Morality has no place at the negotiating table, and the only truths we need recognize are the truths of pragmatism and expediency."

Roosevelt beamed like a benevolent uncle and nodded happily as Hitler continued to speak.

"And now, let me come to the subject that commands all our attention: the second front. I shall not say that I do not believe in the possibility of a second front, for that would jeopardize the whole basis of my coming here. Instead, I shall merely say that German military precision and thoroughness already ensure that we are certainly prepared for such an eventuality. The fact remains that to attempt a landing on the coast of Europe would give any sane military strategist some considerable pause for thought. The reasons that forestalled my own invasion of England in 1940 are now the same reasons that haunt your generals. The difficulty of this landing cannot be overstated, and a bloodbath seems inevitable. My own generals estimate that at least half a million men will die— German and Allied combined. In 1940 I did not think England was worth the lives of so many German soldiers, and today I wonder if you will think that a beachhead in Holland, Belgium, or France is worth the lives of as many British and American soldiers. Doubtless Marshal Stalin, whose losses have been nothing short of heroic, is thinking the same thing."

Hitler shrugged. "Oh, I won't say that we can win the war. After the defeats at El Alamein in October '42 and, more decisively, the defeat of the German Sixth Army at Stalingrad, I know that victory is now beyond our capability. We cannot win this war. There, I say it openly—as you, Mr. President, have urged us all to be open. I will say it again. Germany cannot win this war. But, equally, Germany can still make it painfully difficult for you to win it yourselves."

Roosevelt lit the cigarette in his holder and, removing the pince-nez once again, leaned forward to make a point. "I appreciate your candor, Herr Hitler. So let me be quite candid, too. The important strategic objective for the Allies is not a northern European land-ing, but rather to draw more German divisions away from the So-viet front. To this end, there are other operations available to us. A drive up through Italy, a thrust from the northeastern Adriatic, an operation in the Aegean Sea, even operations from Turkey. Any of these would oblige you to withdraw some of your forces from the eastern front. And yet, having said all that, there are many people in Britain and America who might think that the sacrifice of a quar-ter of a million men is a price worth paying for a free and demo-cratic Europe."

Hitler swept the forelock off his brow and shook his head slowly. "We all know that the Italian campaign is of value only in opening the Mediterranean to Allied shipping and is of no great importance as far as the defeat of Germany is concerned. Marshal Stalin will tell you as much himself when I am no longer in the room. At the risk of sounding pedantic, Mr. President, I must remind you of some Eu-ropean history with which Marshal Stalin is already doubtless famil-iar. In 1799, Marshal Suvorov discovered that the Alps presented an insuperable barrier to an invasion of Germany from Italy. And Turkey? Yes, that might open the way to an Allied invasion of the Balkans, but that is a *very* long way from the heart of Germany. No, gentlemen, no, Germany's weakest spot is France, which, let's face it, you and the British have had all year to invade. What is more, I do not see that you could even contemplate a French invasion until the summer of 1944, by which time it is my calculation that as many as a million more Red Army soldiers will be dead. Out of respect to Marshal Stalin, I do not say this lightly. The losses inherent in any European invasion are negligible to what he has lost already. And what he will lose. A million Red Army soldiers killed is four times as many losses as the quarter of a million British and American casualties that you and Mr. Churchill are hesitating about. Only after France has been secured will it make military sense to send more forces to Italy. In this way you will then be able to secure southern France and, after these two Allied armies have linked up, make your big push into Germany." Hitler was speaking quickly, dismissively, as if considering Allied options off the top of his head. "But not Turkey. It would be a mistake for you to disperse your forces by sending two or three divisions to Turkey. Besides, Turkey is still a neutral country, and it is my understanding that she continues to reject Mr. Churchill's attempts to persuade her to come into this war. Like Iran, perhaps, the Turks have a low opinion of British fair play after what happened at Versailles."

Stalin had spent the last few minutes doodling wolf heads on a pad with a thick red pencil. He stopped now and, removing the pipe from his mouth, began to speak. "The Red Army," he said quietly, hardly looking at either Hitler or Roosevelt, "has enjoyed a number of successes this year. But these have had more to do with simple numerical superiority. There are three hundred thirty Russian divisions opposing two hundred sixty Axis divisions. When all that remains of the German forces on the eastern front has been wiped out, there will still be seventy Russian divisions left. But this is the arithmetic of the madhouse. I would hope it does not ever come down to that. Besides, the Germans have achieved some unexpected victories. Nothing is certain save that, like the Germans, we, too, believe that the British and the Americans will be at their most effective by striking at the enemy in France, and nowhere else. From our point of view, the Führer's assessment of the task facing the British and the Americans is entirely accurate. But surely the Führer has not come all this way to Teheran—and I must take the opportunity now to applaud his very great personal courage in doing so—merely to state that he intends to remain in those countries that he has invaded. Assuming that he is as anxious to put an end to this war as we are, what are his proposals regarding Germany's occupied territories? Specifically, what are his proposals regarding those parts of Russia and the Ukraine that remain under his control? And then, also Hungary, Romania, the Balkans, Greece, Poland, Czechoslovakia, the Netherlands, Belgium, France, and Italy? I should like to hear what he proposes as the basis for a peace that Germany might regard as honorable."

Hitler nodded and took a deep breath. "My proposal is this, Marshal Stalin. A withdrawal of German troops to pre-1939 borders in the West, and the East. This would leave Russia as the dominant power in Eastern Europe. With a negotiated withdrawal—note, I do not use the word 'surrender'—the war in Europe would be over by Christmas, perhaps even earlier, thereby permitting America and its allies to concentrate on the defeat of Japan, which I imagine America still sees as its own strategic priority. Under these circumstances, Mr. President, you can hardly fail to win next year's election. For not only will you have saved two hundred and fifty thousand British and American men from certain death on Europe's beachheads, but you will also have delivered the Jews of Hungary, Italy, Norway, Denmark, and France from their liquidation."

Roosevelt looked beyond speech for a moment.

Hitler smiled thinly. "It was my understanding that we should talk frankly," he said. "Of course, Mr. President, if you do not wish to talk about this particular subject, you do not have to do so. But it is my impression that the fate of three million European Jews would have enormous importance among a very vocal section of your own electorate."

"Is it your intention to use Europe's Jews as hostages?" Roosevelt spoke curtly, and for the first time, in German.

"Mr. President," said Hitler. "My back is against the wall. The German people are facing nothing less than total destruction. You have offered us only unconditional surrender, at least in public. I am merely suggesting the existence of a factor that perhaps you had not considered."

"As the Führer will recall," Roosevelt said stiffly, "the use of the phrase 'unconditional surrender' was always intended to be only a means of bringing him to the negotiating table."

"I am here," said Hitler. "I am negotiating. And one of the chips on this card table, besides the fate of two hundred and fifty thousand Allied soldiers, is the fate of European Jewry. Marshal Stalin has some very similar chips to play himself, such as the fate of Europe's Cossacks and those White Russians who preferred to fight for Germany rather than the Soviet Union."

"We have always been in favor of a negotiated surrender," said Stalin, "and believed that the president's notion of an unconditional surrender would serve only to unite the German people. But quite frankly, I don't give a damn about the fate of Europe's Jews."

"Well, I sure as hell do," insisted Roosevelt. "And by the way, I have a few conditions of my own. I might agree to Germany's withdrawal to her pre-1939 borders if there was also a return to the pre-1933 German constitution. That means free and fair elections and the Führer's retirement from German politics."

"I might concede this," said Hitler, "if I had the right to nominate my successor as the leader of my party."

"I don't see how that would work," objected Roosevelt.

Now Stalin was shaking his head. "Speaking for myself, I care even less about German elections than I do about Europe's Jews. Frankly, I have no faith that the German people are capable of reform, and I really don't see that an election would be enough to curb their militarism. As far as I can see, the only condition I would insist on would be the payment by Germany of war reparations to Russia. This would have a twofold effect. First, it would go a long way toward preventing the German Reich from ever making war again. And, second, it would only restore that which Germany's aggressive war against Russia has destroyed." Stalin waved his hand dismissively in the direction of Roosevelt. "Everything else is of little account to us, including the matter of the Führer's retirement. Indeed, we should probably prefer to have one strong man in charge of the country rather than see it collapse into the anarchy that would surely follow on his retirement. At the very least, we should prefer him in semiretirement only, at the Berchtesgaden perhaps, with Reich Marshal Göring taking over the day-to-day running of the country."

Roosevelt smiled uncomfortably. "I don't see that I could ever sell that kind of deal to the American people," he said.

"With all due respect to the president," Stalin said, "Russia has had greater experience of making deals with Germany than the United States. There is no reason to suppose that a deal cannot be reached now. Still, I recognize your difficulties in this regard. Might I suggest that your best policy might be to present the American people with the fact that there existed a fait accompli between Germany and the Soviet Union and that there was very little you could do about said fait accompli except to recognize that fact and deal with it."

I could already see the direction these negotiations were headed in, and how Stalin was determined to have a peace, albeit at the right price. And I remembered something that John Weitz had said to me back on the *Iowa:* that Stalin's greatest fear was not the Germans, but that the Russian army might mutiny, as it had done back in 1917.

"I have two conditions," said Hitler, holding up his hand almost imperiously. "My first is that the British should return the German deputy führer, Rudolf Hess."

"I am opposed to the return of Hess," said Stalin. "The British have held Hess in reserve in order that they might make a separate deal with Germany. But what is more offensive to us is that Hess went to the British to solicit their help as an ally in an attack on Russia. This we cannot forgive. We say that Hess must stay in prison."

"Haven't the Russians tried to make a separate peace with Germany themselves?" Roosevelt asked. "Has Marshal Stalin forgotten the negotiations in Stockholm between the Soviet ambassador, Madame de Kollontay, and Germany's foreign minister, Joachim von Ribbentrop? I don't see how you can criticize the British for doing what you yourselves have done."

"I did not criticize the British," said Stalin. "Only Rudolf Hess. My objection was only to his repatriation. But since we are on the subject of negotiations for a separate peace, it did not escape the attention of our intelligence services that your own personal representative, Commander George Earle, and von Papen, the German ambassador in Turkey, also held a series of peace talks."

There was long silence. Then Hitler, smiling now, a little gleefully it seemed to me, as if he had enjoyed this display of tension between Stalin and Roosevelt, spoke up: "My second condition," he said, "is that Germany cannot afford to pay any war indemnities. All property removed from occupied territories will be returned, of course. But it only seems to us fair that each should bear his own costs. For Germany to pay war reparations to Russia would then open the way to other claims by Britain, France, Poland, and the rest. Where would it stop? And what would Russia say to paying war reparations to Poland? And what about Italy? Would they pay Abyssinia at the same time as they tried to make a claim on Germany? No, gentlemen, we must wipe the slate clean, or there can be no real peace. Need I remind you that it was the bill presented to Germany by the League of Nations, and more especially the French, after the Great War of 1914 to 1918, that left Germany with no alternative but to go to war again?"

"Speaking for myself," Roosevelt said, deliberately echoing Stalin's turn of phrase, "I care less about war reparations than I do about the return of Rudolf Hess. Neither of these matters is an issue for us."

"That is because you have lost so little," said Stalin, somewhat irritated. "I don't see how we could ever meet our lend-lease payments without receiving German war reparations."

"I think the Führer has made a good point, Marshal Stalin," said Roosevelt. "If he pays you reparations, then what war reparations will you pay the Poles?"

Hitler, trying to contain his pleasure, now seemed intent on playing the peacemaker between Roosevelt and Stalin. "But is it possible," he said, "to reach any kind of negotiated deal at all without the British? Am I to conclude by their absence that they will agree to nothing? Will Germany negotiate a peace with Russia and America only to find herself still at war with Britain?"

"Don't worry about Britain," Roosevelt said. "It's the United

States and the USSR that will decide things from here on. America certainly didn't come into this war to restore the British Empire. Or the French. The United States is footing the bill in this war, and that gives us the right to pull rank. If we want peace, there will be no more war waged by the Western allies, I can assure the Führer of that much at least."

At this, Stalin smiled broadly. I began to be concerned that the president had bitten off more than he could chew. It was bad enough for Roosevelt to try to deal with Stalin on his own, but to deal with Hitler as well was like trying to fend off a pair of hungry wolves, each attacking from a different side. For Roosevelt to have admitted to Stalin that Britain was almost irrelevant to the decision-making that lay ahead—that Russia and America would dominate the postwar world—was surely more than Stalin could ever have hoped for.

1030 HOURS

HIMMLER WAS congratulating himself, not just at having pulled off these secret talks but also at the way his Führer was handling things. Hitler actually seemed to be enjoying the conference. His grasp of affairs had suddenly improved and he had even stopped indulging in his two common mannerisms: the compulsive picking at the skin on the back of his neck and the biting of the cuticles around his thumbs and forefingers. Himmler wasn't sure, but he thought it was even possible that Hitler had dispensed with his usual morning injection of cocaine. This was like seeing the old Hitler, the Hitler who had made the French and the British dance to his tune in 1938. What would have been hard to believe but was now quite obvious was just how divided the Allies were: Churchill's refusal to negotiate, or even meet, with Hitler was understandable, but it seemed extraordinary to Himmler that Roosevelt and Stalin should not have agreed on a common position before sitting down with the Führer. This was more than he could reasonably have expected when, secretly, they had left Prussia and traveled to Teheran, leaving a stenographer named Heinrich Berger to impersonate Hitler at the Wolfschanze and Martin Bormann in effective control of the Greater German Reich.

The Russians had, he admitted, behaved with great hospitality. Von Ribbentrop said that Molotov and Stalin seemed no less friendly than when he had visited Russia in August 1939, in pursuit of the nonaggression pact. And their control of security and secrecy had been predictably excellent. No one was better at keeping secrets and manipulating public perceptions than the Russians. Secrecy was, of course, the reason that Stalin had insisted on having the Big Three in Teheran. The peace talks could not have been arranged anywhere else, except perhaps in Russia itself. Just look what had happened to the secrecy of the Allied talks in Cairo, Himmler reflected. Even so, it had been Himmler's idea to use General Schellenberg's Operation Long Jump as a way of demonstrating German good faith to the Russians. Giving up those men to the NKVD had been regrettable, but it was made easier by the late discovery that most of Schellenberg's team were not German at all but Ukrainian volunteers. Himmler cared nothing for these men, and as a result he had been able to denounce them to the NKVD without scruple. As for the handful of renegade German officers and NCOs, they would be on Schellenberg's conscience, not his.

Of course, the warmth of the Russian reception had a lot to do with the secret payment of ten million dollars in gold from Swiss bank accounts held by Germany into those of the Soviet Union. How right the Führer had been about Russia: it was the very acme of the capitalist state headed by a man who would do anything, make any sacrifice, and take any bribe to pay for the realization of his *idée fixe*. And, despite what Hitler had said in front of Roosevelt, he was already reconciled to paying Stalin a fifty-million-dollar "bonus" if a peace could be negotiated at Teheran, for this was a drop in the ocean compared to the gold Germany had on reserve in its secret Swiss bank accounts.

"In the final analysis," Hitler had told Himmler in their preparatory talks at the Wolfschanze, "Stalin is nothing more than some plutocratic tycoon looking for his next payday. For that reason alone, you know where you are with the Russians. They're realistic."

Realistic? Yes, thought Himmler, you knew where you were with the Popovs. They would do anything for money. Even so, there was no way he was going to let Göring take over the country, as Stalin had suggested as the best alternative to the Führer remaining as head of state. Himmler hated Göring almost as much as he hated Bormann, and he hadn't put his neck on the line persuading Hitler to come to the Big Three in person just to see the country handed over to that fat bastard.

In some respects, the British were just like the Popovs, he reflected. Quite predictable. Churchill most of all. Very likely the British prime minister was worried that once a peace with Germany was signed, the generous terms offered to Great Britain by Hess in 1940—a peace without any conditions whatsoever—would be made public and there would be an uproar in the British newspapers. Could the Führer have been more generous? No wonder Churchill refused to come to the negotiating table. Surely, as soon as the war was over, Churchill would be kicked out of office.

No one could accuse the Americans of not being realistic, but, unlike the Russians, they could not be influenced by money. Still, as the Führer had always argued, they could be influenced by their own paranoia. "They fear Bolshevism more than they fear us," he had told Himmler back at the Wolfschanze. "And the greatest success of the Red Army has not been defeating the German army, but in the way it has intimidated the Americans. We must take advantage of that fact. If they cannot be bribed in these negotiations, then they must be blackmailed. They are, of course, aware of the secret weapons we have been developing at Peenemünde, or why else would they have used the whole of Bomber Command to target the area back in August? It will require great subtlety, Himmler, for without telling the Americans exactly what we have, we must imply that if Germany were forced to negotiate a separate peace with the Russians, we would feel obliged to share our new weapons with them, in lieu of war reparations. Naturally, the Americans will fear this because even now it is clear that they are more concerned about the shape of postwar Europe than they are about defeating Germany.

"The vengeance-weapon film that the people at Fieseler made in May—the Americans should see a copy. And just in case they still don't believe it, let's plan to fire one such weapon at England on November twenty-eighth, the day of the conference. Not from the new site, of course, but from Peenemünde. That should help them to decide if we're serious or not. But don't fire it at London. No, choose an American air base. The one at Shipham, near Norwich, perhaps. That's a large one. A V1 rocket might have quite a chastening effect there, Himmler."

Although a V1 had been placed on a launching ramp at Peenemünde earlier that same day, it had not, in fact, been fired. In the final analysis, it had not been seen as necessary. Now, possessed of film footage of a successful V1 test flight and a list of German scientists, American military intelligence had persuaded Roosevelt that it was imperative for the German rocket secrets to be in American, not in Russian, hands after the war. Consequently, the president had already been persuaded in secret not to insist on large German war reparations, and also to abandon his demand for free and fair elections.

Since the Americans and the Russians both thought they had already made a secret deal to their own advantage, Himmler did not see how, short of a disaster—one of the rages that were inbuilt features of Hitler's character, perhaps, or Churchill prevailing on Roosevelt at last to break off the talks with Hitler—these negotiations could fail. If a peace was agreed at Teheran, Himmler felt his own achievements in this diplomatic triumph would make his name more illustrious in German history than Bismarck's.

1100 HOURS

I SIPPED the last of my water and tried to ignore a need to visit the lavatory.

The arguments had turned to France, a topic Hitler refused to consider with any seriousness. At the very least the French had no right to the return of their empire, he argued. And why should Roosevelt and Stalin be disposed to treat France as anything other than their enemy, since the current government was Nazi in all but name and actively helping Germany?

"France is hardly an occupied country," said Hitler. "There are less than fifty thousand German soldiers in the whole country. That's not an occupying army so much as an auxiliary police force helping to carry out the will of the Vichy French government. The thing that strikes me above all about the French is that because they have been so anxious to sit on every chair at the same time, they have not succeeded in sitting firmly on any one of them. They pretend to be your ally and yet they conspire with us. They fight for free speech and yet France is the most anti-Semitic country in Europe. She refuses to renounce her colonies and expects Russia and America, two countries that have thrown off the yoke of imperialism, to restore them to her. And in exchange for what? A few bottles of good wine, some cheese, and perhaps a smile from a pretty girl?"

Stalin grinned. "I tend to agree with Herr Hitler," he said. "I can see no good reason why France should be allowed to play any role in formal peace negotiations with Germany. I was very much in agreement with what the Führer said earlier. To my mind, there wouldn't have been another war at all if France hadn't insisted on trying to punish Germany for the last one. Besides, the entire French ruling class is rotten to the core."

I wished that Stalin would say more, for it was my opportunity to rest for a moment. Roosevelt was easy to work for, breaking up his statements into short lengths, which demonstrated some concern for his two translators. But Hitler was always much too carried away by his own eloquence to pay much attention to von Ribbentrop, who had struggled to find the words to convey Hitler's thoughts into English, so much so that I had felt obliged to step in and help; and, after a while, the exhausted-looking von Ribbentrop had given up altogether, leaving me to translate all of the conversation between Hitler and Roosevelt.

Roosevelt had smoked steadily throughout the negotiations and, suddenly afflicted with a fit of coughing, now reached for the carafe of water that stood on the table in front of him. But he succeeded only in knocking it over. Both Bohlen and I had now run out of water, and seeing the president's predicament, Hitler poured a glass from his own untouched carafe. Standing up quickly, he brought it around the table to the still-coughing Roosevelt. Stalin, slower on his feet than Hitler, started to do the same.

The president took the glass of water from Hitler, but as he put it to his lips, Agent Pawlikowski sprang forward and knocked it from his hand. Some of the water spilled over me, but most ended up on the president's shirtfront.

For a moment, everyone thought that the Secret Service agent had gone mad. Then von Ribbentrop expressed the thought that was now in the minds of every man in the room. Picking up Hitler's water carafe, he sniffed it suspiciously and then said, in his Canadian-accented English, "Is there something wrong with this water?" He looked around the room, first at Stalin, then at Molotov, and then at Stalin's two bodyguards, Vlasik and Poskrebyshev, who both grinned nervously. One of them said something in Russian that was immediately translated by Pavlov, the Soviet interpreter, and Bohlen.

"The water is good. It comes fresh from the British embassy. First thing this morning."

Meanwhile Roosevelt had turned in his wheelchair and was regarding Pawlikowski with something like horror. "What the hell do you think you're doing, John?"

"John," Reilly said calmly. "I think you should leave the room immediately."

Pawlikowski was trembling like a leaf, and, seated immediately in front of him, I could see that his shirt, soaked in sweat, was almost as wet as the president's. The Secret Service man sighed and smiled almost apologetically at Roosevelt. The very next second he drew his weapon and aimed it at Hitler.

"No," I yelled and, jumping to my feet, I forced Pawlikowski's arm and gun up in the air so that the shot, when it came, hit only the ceiling.

Wrestling Pawlikowski onto the table, I caught sight of Stalin's bodyguard pulling the Russian leader onto the floor, and then others diving for cover as Pawlikowski fired again. A third shot followed close on the second, and then Pawlikowski's body went limp and slid onto the floor. I pushed myself up off the table and saw Mike Reilly standing over the agent's body, a smoking revolver extended in front of him. And seeing that his colleague was not dead, Reilly kicked the automatic from the wounded agent's hand.

"Get an ambulance, someone," he yelled. The next second, seeing that both Hitler's and Stalin's bodyguards had their own weapons drawn and were now covering him in case he, too, felt impelled to take a shot at one of the two dictators, Reilly holstered his gun carefully. "Take it easy," he told them. "It's all over." Coolly, Reilly picked up Pawlikowski's automatic, made it safe, ejected the magazine, and then laid these items on the conference table.

Gradually, the room came to order. Högl, the detective superintendent guarding Hitler, was the first bodyguard to put away his gun. Then Vlasik, Stalin's bodyguard, did the same. Pawlikowski, bleeding heavily from a wound in his back, was swiftly carried out of the room by Agents Qualter and Rauff.

I sat down on my chair and stared at the blood on my shirt sleeve. It was another few seconds before I realized that someone was standing immediately in front of me. I lifted my gaze, up from the polished black shoes and over the dark trousers, the plain brown military tunic and the white shirt and tie, to meet Hitler's watery blue eyes. Instinctively, I stood up.

"Young man," said Hitler, "I owe you my life." And before I could say anything, he was shaking my hand and smiling broadly. "But for your prompt action, that man would surely have shot me." As he spoke, the Führer rose slightly on his toes, like a man for whom life suddenly had a new zest. "Yes, indeed. You saved my life. And judging from his behavior with the water glass, I think he had already failed to poison me, eh, Mr. President?"

Roosevelt nodded. "My deepest apologies to you, Herr Hitler," he said, speaking German again. "It would appear you are right. That man meant to kill you, all right. For which I am deeply ashamed."

Stalin was already adding his own apologies as host.

"Don't mention it, gentlemen," Hitler said, still holding me by the hand. "What is your name?" he asked me.

"Mayer, sir. Willard Mayer."

Even as Hitler held my hand, I felt an understanding of what the Führer and I were: two men for whom the entire spectrum of moral values had no real meaning, who had no real need of the humanities and the immaterial world. Here was the obvious extension of everything that I, as a logical positivist, believed in. Here was a man without values. And I suddenly perceived the bankruptcy of all my own intellectual endeavors. The meaninglessness of all the meanings I had striven to find. This was the truth of Hitler and all rigid materialism: it had absolutely nothing to do with being human.

"Thank you," said Hitler, squeezing my hand in his own. "Thank you."

"That's all right, sir," I said, smiling thinly.

At last the Führer let go. It was Hopkins's cue to suggest that this might be an appropriate opportunity to call a temporary halt to the proceedings. "I suggest that during our recess," he said, "we examine those documents we have prepared supporting our respective negotiating positions. Willard?" He nodded at a file that lay on the table. "Would you hand that to the Führer, please?"

I nodded numbly, and handed the file over to Hitler.

The three delegations now moved toward three of the room's four doors. It was only now that I saw how the room had been constructed so that four delegations might enter the room from four separate entrances and, presumably, four separate dachas inside the Russian embassy compound.

"Wait a minute," said Hopkins, as the American delegation

neared the door that led back the same way they had come. "I've still got the American position papers. What was it that you gave the Führer, Willard?"

"I don't know. I think it must have been that Beketovka File," I said.

"Then no harm done," said Hopkins. "I expect Hitler's seen it before. Still, it's a lucky thing you didn't give it to the Russians. Now that would have been embarrassing."

1215 HOURS

HIMMLER WAS AMAZED that the peace talks still appeared to be on track. After the attempt on the Führer's life, he had assumed Hitler would insist on returning to Germany immediately. And indeed, he could hardly have blamed him. But you never could tell how the Führer would react to an attempt on his life. In a way, of course, he had lived with the idea of assassination all his political life. As early as 1921, someone—Himmler had never found out who it was— had fired shots at Hitler in Munich during a rally at the Hof-bräuhaus. Since then, there had been at least thirty other attempts, not including the trumped-up plots that the Gestapo dealt in. During a twelve-month period in 1933 and 1934 alone, there had been ten attempts on Hitler's life. By any standard, the Führer was a man possessed of the most astonishing luck. Usually, once the shock and anger had disappeared, Hitler managed to see an escape from death as nothing short of miraculous. It was a sign of divine inter-vention, and after thirty or more attempts, Himmler was half-inclined to agree.

Surviving an attempt on his life was the only time Hitler ever talked about God with any real conviction or enthusiasm, and it al-ways affected both his oratory and his self-belief. It was a vicious cir-cle, too: the more attempts to assassinate him Hitler survived, the stronger became his certainty that God had marked him out to make Germany great. And having convinced himself that this was the case, he more easily persuaded others to think the same way.

In the middle of a difficult war, there was, understandably, less hysterical adoration of the Führer than once there had been. Himmler still remembered the feeling of shock and awe he had experienced at the 1934 Nuremberg rally, when Hitler had driven through the town in an open-top Mercedes. The faces of those thousands of women who had screamed Hitler's name and reached out to try and touch him, as if he were the risen Christ incarnate— no other comparison served as well. Himmler had seen houses with shrines to the Führer. He had met schoolgirls who painted swastikas on their fingernails. There were even small towns and villages in Germany where the sick were encouraged to touch Hitler's portrait in search of a cure. All of which only served to bolster Hitler's sense that he was God's elect. Still, it took an assassination attempt to give Hitler a lift—but usually only after a couple of days had elapsed and the guilty caught and punished, with maximum cruelty. On this particular occasion, however, Hitler returned to the villa on the grounds of the Russian embassy with his face shining and his eyes flashing, reassuring Himmler and the others in the German delegation that there was no need to be concerned about the future of the talks.

"God and Providence have made it impossible for anything to happen to me," he told Himmler and von Ribbentrop, "until my historic mission is completed."

The Führer retired to his bedroom "to rest and read these Allied position papers." Himmler felt sufficiently reassured by Hitler's show of optimism to order a bottle of champagne for himself and von Ribbentrop.

"Remarkable, is it not?" said Himmler, toasting the German foreign minister. "Who but the Führer could come through such an ordeal? To sit there for two hours and not drink any of that water. And then, having survived an attempt to poison him, to be saved from shooting by a Jew, of all people." Himmler laughed out loud.

"Are you sure?" asked von Ribbentrop. "The translator is Jewish?"

"You may take it from me, Joachim. There's not much I don't know about Jews, and I can tell you that Mayer is an undeniably

Jewish name. Besides, there is his rather obvious physiognomy. The dark hair and high cheekbones. The man is Jewish, all right. I haven't dared to tell the Führer."

"Perhaps he already knows."

"I rather think the actual assassin is a Pole, however. Or at least of Polish descent."

Von Ribbentrop shrugged. "Perhaps *he's* a Jew, too."

"Yes, perhaps. John Pawlikowksi." Himmler thought for a moment. "Is Molotov a Jew?"

"No," said von Ribbentrop. "Merely married to one."

Himmler laughed. "I bet that's awkward for him. Stalin is openly anti-Semitic. I had no idea. Do you know, I heard him tell the Führer that the Jews were 'middlemen, profiteers, and parasites.'"

"Yes, he and the Führer got on rather well, I thought. They see eye-to-eye on a great many things. For example, like the Führer, Stalin hates people with mixed loyalties. It's why he thinks that Roosevelt is weak. Because of the powerful Jewish lobby in America." Von Ribbentrop sipped some of his champagne with satisfaction. "And something else. He has the same low opinion of his generals that Hitler has."

"That's hardly surprising when you see the general he brought with him. Did you smell that man Vorishilov's breath? My God, he must have had beer for breakfast. How did he ever come to be a field marshal?"

"I think he was the only one who wasn't executed during Stalin's last purge. He was much too mediocre to shoot. Thus his current elevated position in the Red Army. Incidentally, on the subject of shooting, I don't know whether you noticed, but last night at the dinner with Stalin, every one of those Russian waiters was carrying a gun."

"NKVD probably. Beria told me there are a few thousand of them in and around the embassy. Schellenberg's team never stood a chance. It just makes me all the more glad I told Beria about them."

"Have they all been captured?"

"Beria says they have. But I'm not so sure. Still, even if they haven't all been caught, I don't give much for their chances. Not in this country. It's a filthy place. Not at all what I imagined. From what I've observed so far, the tap water is hardly less lethal than the stuff that was in the Führer's carafe."

"I rather think President Roosevelt sipped some of that water," said von Ribbentrop. "Before it was knocked from his hand."

"He seems all right." Himmler shrugged. "I sent Brandt to enquire after his health—in plain clothes, of course. But it seems that Roosevelt has gone shopping."

"Shopping?"

"Yes, the Russians have set up a shop on the grounds of the embassy. They say it's for the convenience of all the delegates, so that we don't have to leave the estate—but, oh, my, the prices! Brandt says they're astronomical."

"But what is there to buy?" laughed von Ribbentrop.

"Oh, it's well stocked with everything that might appeal to an American tourist. Water pipes, carpets, wooden bowls, Persian daggers, silver. Brandt says there is even a box of silk teddy bears."

"Perhaps Roosevelt is picking out a teddy bear for Churchill's birthday." Von Ribbentrop laughed. "Or, perhaps, some sour grapes. The son is here, too, you know. Randolph. It seems that he's an even bigger drunk than his father."

"I hear Roosevelt's son, Elliott, is just as bad. Apparently he and Randolph stayed up late last night getting drunk. There is no greater curse than the curse of a great man for a father."

"Can you imagine what Hitler's son would have been like?" von Ribbentrop asked. "I mean, if he had ever had a son. To live up to such a man as the Führer. Impossible."

Himmler smiled quietly to himself: there were perhaps only three people in the world who knew that Hitler had indeed fathered a son, by a Jewish woman in Vienna in 1913. In *Mein Kampf*, Hitler had claimed to have left the old Austro-Hungarian capital for "political reasons"; he had even written a version that had him leaving Vienna to escape conscription into the Austro-Hungarian army, preferring to enlist in a German regiment, the Tenth Bavarian Reserve Infantry Regiment, instead. But only Hitler, Himmler, and Julius Streicher knew the truth—that Hitler had an affair with a Jewish prostitute, Hannah Mendel, who had borne him a son. Mendel and her son had disappeared from Vienna sometime in 1928 and not even Hitler knew their final fate. Only Himmler knew that Mendel had abandoned her son in 1915; that she had died of syphilis in 1919; that her son, Wolfgang, had been brought up in the Catholic orphanage in Linz; that Wolfgang Mendel had changed his name to Paul Jetzinger and become a waiter at Sacher's Hotel in Vienna until the outbreak of war, when he had enlisted in the Third Motorized Infantry Division; and that Corporal Paul Jetzinger had been killed or captured at Stalingrad. Which Himmler had thought was probably for the best. Great men like Hitler shouldn't have sons, he thought; especially sons who were half-Jewish.

Himmler and von Ribbentrop were in an excellent mood when the drawing room door was suddenly flung open and Hitler stormed in. His face was wreathed in fury as he marched up to Himmler, brandishing a file in front of the Reichsführer's face.

"Did you know about this?" he yelled.

Himmler stood and clicked his heels together as he came to attention. "Know about what, my Führer?"

"It's an SD file entitled 'Beketovka.'"

"Beketovka?" stammered Himmler, and, wondering how on earth Hitler could have come into possession of the file, he colored noticeably.

"I can see you recognize the name," Hitler barked. "Why was I not shown this before? Why did I have to receive this from the Americans?"

"I don't understand. The Americans gave you this file?"

"Yes. Yes, yes, yes. But that hardly matters beside the fact that I have never been shown the contents of this file."

Himmler winced, suddenly understanding exactly what must have happened. The Beketovka File. He had forgotten all about it. The file had reached Roosevelt's hands, as he had ordered it should, and mistakenly, the Americans had simply handed it back to Hitler. As Himmler searched for an explanation, Hitler struck him on the shoulder with the file and then threw it on the floor.

"Do you really think I would have come here, ready to withdraw my forces from Russia, if I had known about this?" he said.

Himmler stayed silent. Knowing Hitler as well as he did, it seemed to him that the question hardly needed to be answered. This was the end of Teheran, he could see that. Plainly, Hitler's rage, the worst Himmler had witnessed, made it impossible that the Führer could continue to sit at the same negotiating table as the people he would hold responsible for the atrocities detailed in the Beketovka File.

"Thousands and thousands of our brave musketeers and lieutenants have been murdered by these Russian pigs, in circumstances that beggar belief, and yet you would have had me sit down and talk peace with them. How could I look my soldiers in the eye if I made a deal with these animals?"

"My Führer, it was for those soldiers who still remain alive that I thought it best to pursue these talks," Himmler said. "Those German prisoners still in Russian camps may yet be released."

"What kind of a man are you, Himmler? Two hundred thousand German prisoners have been systematically starved, frozen, or beaten to death by these subhuman Slavs and you can still contemplate cozying up to them." Hitler shook his head. "Well, that's a matter for your own conscience. Assuming you have one. But I for one will not make a peace with the cold-blooded murderers of German soldiers. Do you hear me? I will not shake hands that are dripping with German blood. You're an unprincipled swine, Himmler. Do you know that? You are a man without values."

Still beside himself with fury, Hitler marched around the room, biting the cuticle around his thumbnail and calling down vengeance upon the heads of the Russians.

"But what will we tell them?" Himmler asked weakly. He knew that the question hardly needed to be asked since he was quite certain that the room concealed hidden microphones: a large part of his negotiating strategy had been based on the assumption that the Russians would listen to their supposedly private conversations; another sign of good faith, as Himmler had described it to Hitler. But in his anger, the Führer seemed to have forgotten this.

"Tell Stalin that because of the attempt on my life you no longer believe that my safety can be guaranteed and that we are forced, reluctantly, to withdraw from these negotiations. Tell them what you like. But we're leaving. Now."

1245 HOURS

As soon as Sergo Beria read the transcript of Hitler's conversation with Himmler and von Ribbentrop, he hurried over to the NKVD villa to tell his father what had happened. Sergo loved his father and was probably the only man in Russia, including Stalin, who wasn't afraid of the state security boss. Despite Lavrenti Beria's incessant womanizing, Sergo recognized that Beria had always been a good father who wanted nothing more than to keep his son out of politics, encouraging him to be a scientist. But Stalin favored his security commissar's nineteen-year-old son, and hoped that the handsome Sergo might one day marry his own daughter, Svetlana, with whom Sergo had gone to school. To this end Stalin had promoted Sergo to the rank of captain in the NKVD, invited him to the conference in Teheran, and personally charged Sergo with briefing him every morning on what the other two leaders were saying "privately" in their respective villas.

Lavrenti Beria was nervous about the apparent high regard in which his son was held by Stalin, for he knew how capricious the old man was and feared the idea of Sergo marrying Svetlana. Stalin might have encouraged a romance between these two young people, but Beria knew that in a year's time, the boss might think very differently about it, even to the extent, perhaps, of accusing the security commissar of trying to worm his way into Stalin's family. There was no telling what a paranoid personality like Stalin was capable of.

Arriving at the NKVD villa, Sergo found his father already speaking to Himmler. Their meeting lasted only a few minutes, after which Himmler exited through a secret passage in the basement, leaving father and son alone. Beria stared glumly at his son.

"I can see you already know what has happened," the older man observed.

"Yes, but the reason I think he gave you—that Himmler no longer believes the Führer's safety can be guaranteed—that's a load of crap." Sergo showed his father the transcript of what Hitler had said to Himmler and von Ribbentrop. Lavrenti Beria read the half-dozen pages without comment. Eventually the younger man blurted out the question he had been dying to ask since first hearing of Beketovka. "Who or what is Beketovka?" he asked his father.

"It's a prisoner-of-war camp near Stalingrad," Beria explained. "For German prisoners. I don't have to tell you that Stalin thinks even less about them than he does about the welfare of his own soldiers. I haven't seen this camp myself, but I imagine conditions there are harsh. Extremely harsh. If this Beketovka File that Hitler talks about documents the camp in any detail, then it would be hardly surprising if he were upset about it. Very likely the Germans gave the file to the Americans in an attempt to support the contention that they are no more morally reprehensible than we are. Most likely Himmler has been concealing this file from Hitler. He must have been well aware of the effect it would have on him, and on these peace talks. The only question, therefore, is if the Americans were aware of that when they gave it to him. For one would then have to conclude that they meant for these negotiations to fail."

Sergo Beria shrugged. "There must be some Americans who continue to share Churchill's point of view: that we should not be negotiating with these Fascists."

Lavrenti Beria picked up the phone. "Get me Molotov," he told the embassy switchboard. And then to Sergo: "I didn't see what happened in the conference room myself. Perhaps our foreign minister can tell us which one of the Americans gave the file to Hitler."

Molotov came on the line and, at some length, Beria explained what had happened, after which there arose the delicate question of who was going to tell Stalin that Hitler was leaving.

"This is a security matter, surely," Molotov argued. "It's your responsibility, Beria."

"On the contrary," said Beria. "Without question this is a foreign affairs matter."

"Under normal circumstances I might agree with you," Molotov said. "But as I recall, it was Himmler, your opposite number, who put out these peace feelers in the first place. And you who dealt with them. Moreover, all matters pertaining to the Führer's presence here in Teheran have, as I understand it, been arranged by you, Comrade Commissar."

"That's true. However, the initial contacts were made by Himmler via Madame de Kollontay, in Stockholm. It's my understanding that these conversations were cleared by Stalin himself, through you, Comrade Secretary."

"And it was agreed that all matters relating to the handling of the German legation would be administered jointly by the NKVD and the SS. As I see it, Hitler is going home because of a security breakdown of one sort or another. Either because an American tried to kill him or because another American gave him an intelligence file right under our noses."

For once, Beria had to concede that Molotov was right. "Do you happen to recall which American it was that gave him the file?" he asked Molotov.

"It was the man who saved Hitler's life. The interpreter."

"Why would he save Hitler's life and then fuck up the peace negotiations?"

"I suspect it was just a mistake. The fellow was confused after what had just happened. I think if I had just saved Hitler's life, I might feel a little perplexed myself. To put it mildly. Anyway, Hopkins told this fellow Mayer to hand over the American position papers and he handed him something else. As simple as that. It must have been this file you describe, because Hopkins was almost at the door when he realized he still had the position papers that were meant for Hitler. Probably he was a bit rattled himself. That's what happened. The Americans fucked up, that's all. They probably thought it hardly mattered that this fellow had just given Hitler the Beketovka File, since they could hardly have imagined that Hitler had never seen an important file prepared by his own SD."

"Jesus Christ," groaned Beria. "The boss is going to go nuts."

"Blame it all on the Yank," advised Molotov. "That's my advice. Let him take the heat. There's not much point in saving Hitler's life if you then manage to fuck up the peace talks."

"But how? It was a mistake. That's all. You said so yourself, Molotov."

"Look, you know what the boss is like, Beria. And he saw it just as I did. Maybe he'll decide that it was an accident. But just remember it's our treatment of German POWs that's sending Hitler away. In other words, the Americans will find out that this is the reason Hitler's run home. Now that puts the ball in our court, and the boss won't like that at all. Better give him something he can throw at the Yanks, just in case he's feeling bloody-minded."

"Such as?"

"All right. But this is just a thought. And you owe me, Lavrenti Pavlovich. Got that? A favor."

"Fine, fine, whatever. What's this thing the boss can level at the Yanks?"

"Just this. The interpreter. He's a Jew."

"And?"

"And maybe he's a pal of Cordell Hull, the American hostage in Berlin. He might want the talks to fail without Hitler getting assassinated, and his friend Hull's life being forfeit as a result. Something like that."

"But you heard Hitler. He's threatening to massacre the rest of Europe's Jews. Why would a Jew want these talks to fail?"

"Maybe for the same reason Churchill does. Because the total defeat of Germany will require an American army in Europe. Churchill wants that army in Europe as a bulwark against us, Beria.

Churchill knows that if Hitler is left in control there will be another European war, which Stalin will win. Meaning the whole of Europe, including Great Britain, will come under Soviet control. It could be that this Jewish interpreter hates communism more than he hates the Nazis. Like a lot of other Americans."

"That's not bad, you know," admitted Beria. "That's not bad at all. You've got a devious fucking mind, Molotov. I respect that."

"It's why I've stayed alive so long. One more thing: Hopkins was telling me that this Jew is also quite a famous philosopher. Did his doctorate in Germany. Very likely he's a kraut-lover. Maybe you can make something out of that as well."

Beria laughed. "Vyacheslav Mikhailovich, you would have made a fucking good policeman, do you know that?"

"If you fuck this up, Lavrenti Pavlovich, there might just turn out to be a job vacancy."

1430 HOURS

IT WAS A BEAUTIFUL, mild, sunny Sunday afternoon. Birds were singing in the many cherry trees that grew on the grounds of the Russian embassy compound, and somewhere something delicious was being prepared. But among the president's immediate entourage, spirits were low and no one felt like eating the late lunch that was scheduled. Hitler's abrupt departure from the peace talks—he was already aboard his Condor, flying back to the Crimea, and then home—had hit Roosevelt hard.

"Things were going so well," he said, shaking his head. "We were going to make a peace. Not a perfect peace, but a peace nonetheless. Hitler was ready to withdraw his forces from nearly all the occupied territories. You heard him, Professor. You understood what he said better than any man in this room. He did say that, didn't he?"

My despair was no less profound than Roosevelt's, although for very different reasons. "Yes, sir. I think he was ready to do it."

"We had peace in our hands and we screwed up."

"No one could have foreseen what happened this morning," Hopkins said. "That nutcase pulling a gun on Hitler like that. Jesus Christ. What the hell made him do it, Mike? And the water. That was poisoned, right?"

"Yes, sir, it was," said Reilly. "The Russians gave the rest of the water in that carafe to a dog, which has since died."

"Goddamn Russians," said Roosevelt. "What did they want to go and do a thing like that for? The poor dog. What kind of fucking people would do that sort of thing?"

"It's too early to say what the poison was, however," continued Reilly. "This country is rather short on proper laboratory facilities."

"Why the hell did he do it, Mike?" asked Roosevelt. "Has he said anything?"

After the shooting, Agent Pawlikowski had been taken to the American military hospital at Camp Amirabad.

"They're still operating, sir. But it doesn't look too good. The bullet went through his liver." Reilly swallowed uncomfortably. "On behalf of the United States Treasury and the Secret Service, I'd like to offer you an apology, Mr. President."

"Oh, forget it, Mike. Not your fault."

"And to you, Professor Mayer. You've been right about this all along. Ever since the *Iowa* you've been saying that there was an assassin among us."

"I was only half right. I thought it was Stalin he was after. And half right is as bad as wholly wrong in my book."

"I think we all owe Professor Mayer our thanks," said Hopkins. "But for him, Cordell Hull would be facing a firing squad round about now."

"Yes," said Roosevelt, pressing his hand to his own stomach. "Thank you, Willard."

"You don't look too good sir," Reilly told the President. "Shall I fetch Admiral McIntire?"

"No, Mike, I'm all right. If I look sick it's because I'm thinking of all those American boys who are going to lose their lives on the beaches of Normandy next year. To say nothing of Europe's Jews."

Roosevelt shifted uneasily in his wheelchair. "Do you think he meant it, Harry? Do you really think he means to kill three million Jews?"

Hopkins said nothing.

"Professor?" asked Roosevelt. "Did he mean it?"

"It's a thought that's been troubling me a lot, sir. Not least because I'm the man who saved Hitler's life. I'd hate to spend the rest of my days regretting what happened here this morning. But I've a terrible feeling that I might." I took a cigarette from Chip Bohlen. "As a matter of fact, I'd sincerely prefer it if no one ever mentioned it to me or anyone else again. I'm going to try to forget all about it, if you don't mind."

"We're all of us walking away from here with some dirty secrets," Roosevelt said. "Me most of all. Can you imagine what people will say about Franklin D. Roosevelt if they ever find out what I've done? I'll tell you what they'll say. They'll say it was bad enough he tried to make a peace with a bastard like Hitler, but it was even worse that he fucked it up. Jesus Christ. History is going to piss all over me."

"No one is going to say anything of the kind, Mr. President," Bohlen said. "Because none of us is ever going to talk about what happened here. I think we should all agree, on our honor, never to talk about what I for one regard as a brave attempt that almost came off."

There was a murmur of assent from the others in the room.

"Thank you," said Roosevelt. "Thank you all, gentlemen." Roosevelt screwed a cigarette into his holder and took a light from my Dunhill. "But I must confess I still don't quite understand why he's gone. Hitler seemed okay about what happened, didn't he? Grateful, to you, he said. He shook your hand, Professor."

"Maybe he just lost his nerve," said Reilly. "Back in his room, Hitler sat down, thought about it some more, and realized just what a narrow escape he'd had. Happens that way sometimes, when someone escapes being shot."

"I guess so," said Roosevelt. "But I really thought I could get Hitler. You know? Win him over."

"Now you have to make sure you get Stalin," Harry Hopkins said. "We always knew there was a big risk that these secret peace talks might not work out. Hell, that's why they were secret, right? So now we go back to plan B. The Big Three. The way this conference in Teheran started out in the first place. We have to make sure that we make Stalin appreciate just what's entailed in a second front across the English Channel, and get him behind our United Nations idea."

Hopkins was still trying to restore the president's belief in himself and in his capacity to charm Stalin when, accompanied by Vlasik, Pavlov, and several Georgian NKVD bodyguards, the great man himself appeared in the doorway of the president's drawing room.

"Jesus Christ, it's Uncle Joe. He's here," muttered Hopkins.

Leaving the bodyguards in the corridor, Stalin edged his way clumsily into the room, his presence most clearly marked by the strong smell of Belomor cigarettes that clung to his marshal's mustard-colored summer tunic like damp on a wet dog. Pavlov and Vlasik followed as if on an invisible leash. Chip Bohlen was quickly on his feet, bowing curtly to the Soviet leader and acknowledging something Stalin had said with an obsequious *"Da vy, da vy."*

Roosevelt maneuvered his wheelchair to face Stalin and held out his hand. "Hello, Marshal Stalin," he said. "I'm very sorry about what has happened. Very sorry. After all your brave and courageous efforts to secure a peace, that it should come to this is a great shame." Stalin shook Roosevelt's hand in silence while Bohlen translated. "And I am deeply ashamed that it should have been one of my own people who tried to kill Hitler."

Stalin let go of the president's hand and then shook his head. "But that is not what made him angry," he said gruffly, taking the Beketovka File from Pavlov, his translator, and placing it gingerly on the president's lap. "This is what made him abandon the talks."

"What is it?" asked Roosevelt.

"It's a dossier prepared by German intelligence for your eyes, Mr. President," said Stalin. "It purports to provide details of atrocities committed by Red Army soldiers against German prisoners of war. It was given to the Führer by one of your people this morning.

The dossier is a forgery, of course, and we believe that it was prepared by die-hard Fascists in Germany with the intention of driving a wedge between the United States and the Soviet Union. Of course Hitler knew nothing about its provenance. Why should he? A commander in chief cannot see every piece of disinformation that emanates from his own counterintelligence department. When he saw the dossier, however, he assumed, incorrectly, that the lies and calumnies it contained regarding the atrocious treatment of German POWs were true, and he reacted as any commander in chief would, by calling off the talks with those he believed carried out these atrocities."

"You're saying that this dossier was prepared for my deception?" said Roosevelt. "And handed over to Hitler by one of my people?"

Stalin lit a cigarette, coolly. "That is correct."

"But I don't recall ever seeing such a file," said Roosevelt. "Have I, Harry?"

"I saw it, Mr. President," said Hopkins. "I decided that it was inappropriate for you to see it in the present circumstances. Certainly until we'd had a chance to evaluate it properly."

"Then I still don't understand," said Roosevelt. "Who gave this dossier to Hitler?"

"Your Jewish doctor of philosophy."

I felt a chill as Stalin stared balefully at me with his yellow, almost Oriental, eyes.

"Jesus Christ, Professor. Is this true? Did you give this dossier to Hitler?"

I hesitated to call Stalin a liar to his face, but it was clear what the Soviet leader was trying to do. Stalin could hardly explain why Hitler had left without bringing up the Beketovka File. And that risked the possibility that Roosevelt might lay responsibility for the Führer's departure on the Soviets themselves.

I had to hand it to him: insisting that the file was a forgery was the best way of avoiding any potential embarrassment. And throwing the blame on me put the ball squarely back in the American court.

Believing Roosevelt would never forgive me if I challenged Stalin's assertion that the file was a forgery, I decided to appeal to the president's sense of fair play.

"I did give it to him, Mr. President. When I was struggling with Agent Pawlikowski on the conference table, the files got mixed up. When Mr. Hopkins told me to hand our position papers to Hitler, I mistakenly handed over the Beketovka File instead."

"That's right, Mr. President," Hopkins said. "It was an accident. And partly my fault. I was holding on to the position papers when I told Willard to hand them over. I didn't realize I was holding them. I guess I was kind of shocked myself. Under the circumstances, it could have happened to anyone."

"Perhaps," said Stalin.

"I don't think we should forget that but for Professor Mayer's presence of mind," added Hopkins, "the Führer would probably be dead, and our hostages in Berlin, Mr. Hull, and Mr. Mikoyan, would certainly have been executed by now."

Stalin shrugged. "Speaking for myself, I think I should prefer to have seen Hitler dead on the floor of that conference room than to have him walk out of these peace talks. I cannot speak for Mr. Hull, but I know that Mr. Mikoyan would gladly have gone to the wall if it had meant us being rid of a monster like Hitler." Stalin sniffed unpleasantly and wiped his mustache with the back of a liver-spotted hand. Waving dismissively in my direction, he said, "It seems to me that, thanks to your translator, we now find ourselves with the worst of all possible outcomes."

"With all due respect, Mr. President," I said, "I think that Marshal Stalin is, perhaps, being a little unfair."

I was still smarting from Stalin's description of me as "the Jewish doctor." I was already cursed with the knowledge that I had saved the life of perhaps the most evil man in history, and I was damned if I could see why I should have to shoulder the responsibility for the failure of the peace talks as well.

"All right, Professor, all right," said Roosevelt, gesturing with the flat of his hand that I should try to keep calm.

"Are we to worry about what these parrots, our interpreters, think is fair and what is unfair?" snorted Stalin. "Perhaps your man is one of these American capitalists who wants to see his country's armies in Europe if only because he imagines that the Soviet Union wishes to make an empire for itself. Such as the British have made in India. I'm told that his mother is one of the richest women in America. Perhaps he hates Communists more than he hates Nazis. Perhaps that is why he gave the forgery to Hitler."

I wished that I could have mentioned my previous membership in the Austrian Communist Party. But Roosevelt was already trying to change the subject.

"I think that India is certainly ripe for a revolution, Marshal Stalin," he said. "Don't you? From the bottom up."

Recognizing that perhaps he had gone too far in his denunciation of me, Stalin shrugged. "I'm not sure about that," he said. "India's caste system makes things more complicated. I doubt a revolution along the lines of the straightforward Bolshevik model is a realistic proposition." Stalin smiled thinly. "But I can see that you're tired, Mr. President. I only came to tell you that, if you are agreeable, we will reconvene at four o'clock in the main conference hall, with Mr. Churchill. So I'll leave you now, to rest a while and to gather your strength for what we must discuss. A second front in Europe."

And with that, Stalin was gone, leaving each of us in open-mouthed amazement. It was Roosevelt who spoke first.

"Professor Mayer? I don't think Uncle Joe likes you very much."

"No, sir. I don't think he does. And I'm counting myself lucky that I'm an American and not a Russian. Otherwise I guess I'd be facing a firing squad."

Roosevelt nodded wearily. "Under the circumstances," he said, "it might be best if you went back to Camp Amirabad. After all, it's not as if we'll be needing your interpreting services anymore. Not now that the Führer has gone. And there's no sense aggravating Stalin any further by your presence here in the Russian compound."

"I'm sure you're right, sir." I walked toward the door of the draw-ing room. There, with my fingers on the door handle, I stopped and, looking back at the president, added: "Just for the record, Mr. President, as someone who knows about German intelligence, it's my considered opinion that the Beketovka File is one hundred percent genuine and accurate. You can take that from a man who was a member of the Austrian Communist Party when he was a lot younger and less wise than he is now. And there's nothing Stalin can say that will change that."

Standing in the door of the Russian embassy, I took a deep, un-steady breath of the warm afternoon air. I closed my eyes and re-flected on the extraordinary events of the day and my unwitting role in the history of Hitler's peace. It was a story that would prob-ably never be told because it was a history of lies and dissembling and hypocrisy, and it revealed the greatest truth of history: that truth itself is an illusion. I was a part of that big lie now. I always would be.

I opened my eyes to find myself facing a tubby-looking man wearing the uniform of a British RAF Commodore and smoking a seven-inch Romeo y Julieta.

"Sir," said the tubby little commodore, "you appear to be in my way."

"Mr. Churchill, I appear to be in everyone's way. My own most of all."

Churchill removed the cigar from his mouth and nodded. "I know that feeling. It is the antithesis of being alive, is it not?"

"I feel myself unraveling, sir. There's a dog that's got hold of the end of my yarn and pretty soon there's going to be nothing of me left."

"But I know that dog," he said. Churchill took a step toward me, his eyes wide with excitement. "I have given that dog a name. I call it the black dog, and it must be driven off as if it were the real thing." The prime minister glanced at his watch and then pointed toward the grounds with his walking stick. "Stroll with me for a mo-ment, in these Persian gardens. We may not have five miles meandering with a mazy motion, as Mr. Coleridge has it, but I think it will do very well."

"I'd be honored, sir."

"I feel I should know you. I know we have met somewhere before now. But beyond the fact you are an American and perhaps something in the diplomatic services, or else you would be wearing a uniform, I cannot for the life of me remember who you are."

"Willard Mayer, sir. I'm the president's German translator. At least I was. And we said hello in the corridor of the Mena House Hotel last Tuesday."

"Then you are the unfortunate young man who saved the life of the German dictator," said Churchill. Even in the open air, there was a loud echoing timbre to his voice, as well as a slight speech impediment, more noticeable in person than on radio. It made me think the prime minister must once have had a small problem with his palate. "And whose subsequent actions have caused the collapse of the parley with Hitler and his dreadful gang."

"Yes, sir."

"Mr. Mayer, I venture to think that you believe the failure of these peace talks is something to be lamented, as doubtless Mr. Stalin does, and your own president, to be sure. I have an enormous admiration and affection for Mr. Roosevelt, indeed for all Americans. You must know I am half American myself. But I tell you frankly, sir, that this policy was ill conceived. Hitler is a leviathan of wickedness, a bloodthirsty guttersnipe unparalleled in the history of tyranny and evil, and we have not fought for four long years only now, when victory is in our sights, to turn around and make a peace with these foul fanatics. So do not hold yourself to blame for this morning's fiasco. No civilized government could ever have countenanced having diplomatic relations with this Nazi power, a power that spurns Christian ethics, cheers its onward course by a barbarous paganism, vaunts the spirit of aggression and conquest, derives strength and perverted pleasure from persecution, and uses with pitiless brutality the threat of massacre against the innocents. That power could not ever be the trusted friend of democracy, and to have made a peace with Hitler would have been morally indecent and constitutionally disastrous. In a matter of a few years, perhaps a few months, your country and mine would have come to regret that we did not scotch this snake when we had the chance. I tell you, Willard Mayer, do not hold yourself to blame. The only shame is that such a repugnant course of action was ever contemplated at all, and akin to the man who stroked a rabid dog and said how gentle it seemed to be, until it bit him, whereof he fell sick and died. We do not want Hitler's peace any more than we wanted Hitler's war, for only a fool comes down from a tree to look into the eyes of a wounded tiger."

Churchill took a seat beside a cherry tree and I sat down beside him.

"This is only the beginning of the reckoning," he said. "The first taste of the world's judgment on Nazi Germany, and many stern days lie ahead of us. The best of our young men will be killed, almost certainly. That is not your fault, nor is it your president's fault. Rather, it is the fault of that bloodthirsty Austrian butcher who led us down the dark stairs and into the abyss of a European war. No more should you regret saving Herr Hitler's life, for it would have dishonored us all to have invited him here and seen him murdered in our midst, like some ancient Roman tyrant, for that would have been to have made ourselves look as vile and detestable as he who has murdered his way across Europe and Russia. The destiny of mankind should never be decided by the trajectory of an assassin's bullet.

"And now I must leave you," and Churchill stood up, with some difficulty. "If the black dog returns to growl at your heels, I offer you these three pieces of advice. One, strip off your shirt and place yourself in some direct sunlight, which I have found has a most restorative and uplifting effect. The second is to take up painting. It is a pastime that will take you out of yourself when that seems like an unpleasant place to be. And my third piece of advice is to go to a party and drink a little too much champagne, which is no less efficacious than the sun in lifting the gloom. Wine is, after all, the greatest gift that the sun has made to us. Fortunately for you, I myself am giving a party to celebrate my birthday on Tuesday, and I should be delighted if you would come."

"Thank you, sir, but I'm not sure that Marshal Stalin would welcome my being there."

"Since it is not Marshal Stalin's birthday—assuming that there was ever such an occasion for celebration—that need not concern you at all, Mr. Mayer. I shall expect you at the British embassy at eight o'clock on Tuesday evening. Black tie. No dog."

I found my ears were still ringing with Churchill's words long after the prime minister had gone and I was on my way back to Camp Amirabad in an army jeep, certain that I had just met the one man in the world who embodied truth and who would demonstrate the courage of truthfulness.

2100 HOURS

AT NIGHT there is no sun. There is only darkness. In Iran, the darkness comes quickly and with its own peculiar demons. I lay awake on my bed in a Quonset hut, smoking cigarettes and quietly getting drunk. Just after ten o'clock, there was a knock on my door. I opened it to find a tall, round-shouldered man, who had the loose-limbed look and large feet of a basketball player. He was wearing a white coat on top of his army fatigues and eyed the drink and the cigarette in my hand with a combination of military and medical disapproval.

"Professor Mayer?"

"If that's what's written on the tag on my toe." I turned away from the open door and sat down on my bed. "Come on in. Pour yourself a drink."

"No, thanks, sir. I'm on duty."

"Nice to know someone is on duty."

"Sir, I'm Lieutenant John Kaplan," he said, advancing only a short way into my room. "I'm the assistant chief medical officer in the army field hospital here at Camp Amirabad."

"It's okay, Lieutenant Kaplan. I'm only a little tight. No need for the stomach pump just yet."

"It's Mr. Pawlikowski, sir. The Secret Service guy. He's asking for you."

"For me?" I laughed and sipped my drink. "Asking, as in wants to talk or to tell me I'm a son of a bitch? Well, I'm feeling a little fragile right now."

"I don't think he's angry."

"No? I would be if someone stopped me from—" I smiled and started again, with the official version. "If someone had put a hole in my liver. How is he, anyway?"

"Stable."

"Will he make it?"

"It's too early to say. In themselves, most liver injuries are simple. Sepsis is the main postoperative problem. And rebleeding. And bile leaks." Kaplan shrugged. "But he's in good hands. I was a hepatologist at Cedars Sinai before the war. With anyone else but me I'd say his chances might not be so good."

"Good to meet a man who still has faith in what he does." I nodded. "I wish I could say the same."

"Will you come?"

I stood up and collected my coat off the back of my door. As I put it on, I saw that there was still some blood on the sleeve. It was Pawlikowski's blood, but I almost wished it had been mine.

I followed Kaplan out of the Quonset. He switched on a GI anglehead flashlight and led the way along some duckboards.

"What happened, anyway?" he asked. "Information is a little confused. Someone said that he tried to shoot the president."

"No. That's not true. I was there. I saw it happen. Nobody tried to shoot FDR."

"So what happened?"

"It was an accident, that's all. Around the president, I think that some of these Secret Service boys get a little trigger happy, that's all."

The lies had started.

John Pawlikowski was pale and asleep when I found him. There was a plasma drip in his arm and a couple of cannulae in his lower torso. He looked like a chemical plant.

Kaplan took Pawlikowski's arm and squeezed it gently.

"Don't wake him," I said. "Let him sleep for now. I'll sit with him awhile."

The doctor pulled up a chair and I sat down.

"Besides, being in here gives me an excuse to leave that bottle alone. I take it alcohol is forbidden in here."

"Strictly forbidden," said Kaplan, smiling.

"Good."

Kaplan went away to check on one of his other patients, and, clasping my hands, I leaned my elbows on Pawlikowski's bed. Anyone who didn't know me might have thought I was praying for him. And in a way I was. I was praying John Pawlikowski would wake up and tell me who he had been working for. So far I seemed to be the only member of the American delegation who wondered what kind of German spy it was that attempted to kill Adolf Hitler? I already had a few ideas on that one. But I was tired. It had been a long and stressful day followed by an alcohol-fueled evening and, after ten or fifteen minutes, I fell asleep.

I awoke with a start and the beginnings of a hangover, to hear the sound of a U.S. Military Police siren. Some kind of an emergency was on its way. Moments later, several cars drew up noisily outside the field hospital. Then the doors flew open and Roosevelt was wheeled inside on a hospital gurney, accompanied by Mike Reilly, Agents Rauff and Qualter, his physician, Admiral McIntire, and his valet, Arthur Prettyman. They were followed by several U.S. Army medical personnel, who quickly lifted Roosevelt onto a bed and began to examine him.

My head was clearer now. I went over to see what was happening.

The president did not look at all well; his shirt was wet through with perspiration, his face was deathly pale, and from time to time he was wracked with stomach cramps. One of the doctors attending him removed Roosevelt's pince-nez and handed it to Reilly. The doctor was Kaplan. He straightened up for a moment and surveyed the melee of people around Franklin Roosevelt with obvious disapproval. "Will all those who are not medical personnel please step back? Let's give the president some air."

Reilly backed into me. He looked around.

"What the hell happened?" I asked.

He shook his head and shrugged. "The boss was hosting a dinner for Stalin and Churchill. Steak and baked potatoes cooked by the Filipino mess boys he brought on the trip. One minute he's fine, talking about having access to the Baltic Sea or something, and the next he's looking like shit. If he hadn't already been sitting down in his chair, he'd have fainted for sure. Anyway, we wheeled him out of there and then McIntire decided we should bring him here. Just in case—"

Roosevelt twisted down on the bed again, holding his stomach painfully.

"Just in case he was poisoned," continued Reilly.

"I guess anything's possible after this morning."

"The boss mixed the cocktails himself," objected Reilly. "Martinis. The way he always does. You know, too much gin, too much ice. That's all he drank. Churchill had one or two and he's fine. But Stalin didn't really touch his at all. He said it was too cold on the stomach."

"Very sensible of him. They are."

"It made me think—I don't know what."

"Either he just didn't like them, or Stalin's now afraid of being poisoned himself," I said. "And consequently reluctant to drink anything that someone he doesn't know has prepared."

Reilly nodded.

"On the other hand . . ." I hesitated to say anything more.

"Let's hear it, Professor."

"I'm not an expert on these things. But it seems likely that the president's being in that wheelchair gives him a very slow metabolism. Mike, it could be he drank more of that poison this morning than we figured on. This could be a delayed reaction." I glanced at my watch. "It might just have taken ten hours for the poison to take its effect on him. What does McIntire say?"

"I don't think that's even occurred to him. McIntire thinks it's indigestion. Or some kind of seizure. I mean the man is under so much pressure right now. After you-know-who skedaddled, I've never seen the boss so depressed. But then he picked himself right up again for this afternoon's Big Three. Like nothing happened, you know?" He shook his head. "You should tell someone what you just told me. One of the doctors."

"Not me, Mike. When I cry wolf, people have a nasty habit of saying, 'What big teeth you have.' Besides, that kind of information would only be useful if we knew what kind of poison was involved here." I shrugged. "There's only one man who can tell us and he's unconscious." I jerked my head behind me at Pawlikowski, lying on his hospital bed.

"Well, he's awake *now*," said Reilly. The agent glanced back at Roosevelt as one of the U.S. Army doctors finished fitting an intravenous line into the president's arm to help rehydrate him. "Come on," he said, and headed toward Pawlikowski's bed. "There's nothing we can do here. Let's see what we can find out."

Pawlikowski was staring up at the fan on the ceiling so that for a moment I almost thought he might be dead. But then his eyes flickered as he let out a long sigh and they closed again. Reilly leaned over his pillow. "John? It's me, Mike. Can you hear me, John?"

Pawlikowski opened his eyes and smiled sleepily. "Mike?"

"How are you doing, pal?"

"Not so good. Some dumb bastard shot me."

"I'm sorry about that."

"That's okay. I guess you were aiming for my leg, huh? You always were a lousy shot."

"Why'd you do it, John?"

"It seemed like a pretty good idea at the time, I guess."

"Want to tell us all about it?" Reilly paused. "I brought Professor Mayer along."

"Good. I wanted to tell him something."

"John, before you do—"

"What about Hitler?" asked Pawlikowski. "What happened to him?"

"He went home, John."

Pawlikowski closed his eyes for a moment. "Mike? Give me a cigarette, will you?"

"Sure, John, anything you say." Reilly lit a cigarette and then placed it carefully between Pawlikowski's lips. "John. I need to know something right now. You poisoned Hitler's water, right?"

Pawlikowski smiled. "You noticed that, huh?"

"What kind of poison was it?"

"Strychnine. You should have let me kill him, Mike."

But Reilly was already heading toward Admiral McIntire and Dr. Kaplan. Pawlikowski closed his eyes for a moment. I removed the cigarette from his mouth.

"Professor? Give me a drink of water, will you?"

I poured him a glass of water and helped him to drink it. When he had swallowed enough he shook his head and then looked at me strangely. But I was getting used to this. And Pawlikowski wasn't in the same league as Stalin when it came to giving me a look.

"How does it feel?"

"How does what feel?" I asked. But I knew very well what he meant. Reilly came back and went around the other side of Pawlikowski's bed. I put the cigarette back in his mouth.

"How does it feel to be the man who saved Hitler's life?"

"I'll be honest, I've done good deeds that I felt better about."

"I'll bet."

"Is that all you wanted to say?"

"No."

"What did you want to say to Professor Mayer?" asked Reilly.

"Only that he was right all along, Mike. And to apologize to him. For killing his girlfriend."

"You killed that woman in Cairo? The princess?"

"Had to. She could have given me away. You understand, don't you, Professor? I was there that afternoon when you came calling unexpectedly. I was up in the radio room when you arrived. Receiving a message from Berlin. When you showed up I had to wait until you and Elena were in bed before I could sneak out the back door. Which is why I forgot to burn the signal from Berlin. I remembered later. And came back in the small hours, to burn it. I figured you would be in bed with her again, and otherwise engaged. She was a great-looking broad. Nothing between us, though. Not that I would have minded, of course. But it was strictly professional. Anyway, I had just come in when I saw you up in the radio room. I stayed downstairs while you went back in her bedroom. And after you'd left the house, I went back in there and saw that you'd taken the signal."

"But why didn't you just kill me? Why kill her?"

Pawlikowski smiled thinly. The shadows under his eyes looked like the ash on the end of his cigarette and his lips were blue, as if the priest had been there slightly before me, with the communion wine.

"After all that heat you'd made about a German spy? No way. Killing one member of the president's delegation was risky enough. But two? Besides, she would never have stood for it. She was fond of you, Professor. Very fond. So, I killed her, hid the radio, and made it look like you had done it. I'm sorry about that, Professor. Really I am. But I had no choice. Killing Hitler was more important than anything."

"Yes, I see. But who put you up to this? Can you tell us who you were working for?"

"The Abwehr. Admiral Canaris. And some people in the Wehrmacht who don't want the Allies to make a peace with Germany that leaves Hitler in power. They figured it might be easier killing him here than in Germany. That he wouldn't be expecting it here. You see, back in Germany it gets more difficult each time they try."

"But why you?"

"I'm a Polish-German Jew from Danzig, that's why." Pawlikowski took another drag off the cigarette. "That's all the reason I needed."

"Who recruited you, and where?"

Pawlikowski smiled. "I can't tell you that."

"But Thornton Cole was on to you, right? That's why he was killed."

"He wasn't on to me. But he was on to my contact in Washington. That's why he was killed. But I didn't do it. Someone else did that."

"But you did kill Ted Schmidt, aboard the USS *Iowa*, right?"

"He came to me with information that would have persuaded the police to take a closer look at Cole's murder. It was a split-second thing. I guessed that if the Metro cops managed to find out who really did kill him, then they might find my contact. And that might put them on to me. That it might stop me from killing Hitler. So I hit him and threw the body overboard."

"And on the *Iowa*, it was you who radioed your German friends back in the States, for the same reason."

Pawlikowski nodded. "I love the boss," he whispered. "I love him like he was my own dad. But he should never have tried to make peace with Hitler. You can't make deals with someone like that. I'm sorry I killed those people. I didn't like doing it. But I'd do it again, tomorrow, if it gave me another chance to kill Hitler." He grabbed Reilly's hand. "I'm sorry I let you down, Mike. And the boss, too. Tell him that for me, will you? But I did what I thought was right."

"We all did, John. You, me, the professor here, and the president. We all did what we thought was right."

"I guess so," said Pawlikowski and fell asleep once again.

Reilly took his cigarette and stubbed it out. Straightening up, he glanced over his shoulder at the president, who was already looking a little more comfortable. We went to his bed. Dr. Kaplan said that poisoned or not, he was now quite stable and was going to be okay.

"It's been a helluva long day," groaned Reilly, pressing a fist into the small of his back. "So, Professor? What do you think?"

"I think that, all things considered, I wish I'd never left Princeton."

XXVI

TUESDAY, NOVEMBER 30, 1943, TEHERAN

WHAT WERE THE CONSOLATIONS of philosophy? None. And, for most of Monday and Tuesday, Stalin's words echoed in my mind: "For myself, I think I should prefer to have seen Hitler dead on the floor of that conference room than to have him walk out of these peace talks. I cannot speak for Mr. Hull, but I know that Mr. Mikoyan would gladly have gone to the wall if it had meant us being rid of a monster like Hitler."

I'd never had much time for the pessimism of Schopenhauer, but finding one of his books in the library at Camp Amirabad, I read him again; and what Schopenhauer had said, that no honest man at the end of his life would want to relive his own life, seemed to ring in my ears like a funeral bell.

By Tuesday, Roosevelt had made a complete recovery, and the gala dinner at the British legation to celebrate Churchill's sixty-ninth birthday now loomed. I debated not going but decided that consideration of Prime Minister Churchill's feelings outweighed those of Marshal Stalin. What had still not dawned on me was how much of a leper I had become among my own people in Teheran. But immediately on my arrival at the British embassy, Harry Hopkins put me properly in the picture.

"Jesus, Mayer," he hissed. "What the hell are you doing here?"

Churchill, overhearing this, advanced on him, growling like a bulldog defending a favorite ham bone.

"He's here because I asked him, Harry. Professor Mayer is well aware that I should have regarded it as a personal insult if he had not come here tonight. Isn't that so, Professor?"

"Yes, Prime Minister."

"Excuse me, gentlemen." The prime minister's son Randolph, sober for once, took his father by the elbow. "May I speak to you for a minute, Papa?"

The prime minister turned away from my defense and stared at his son, kindly. "Yes, Randolph, what is it?"

Hopkins looked at me as if the stumps of my limbs were about to turn gangrenous. "All right," he sighed. "But for Christ's sake try to stay out of Stalin's way. Things are difficult enough as it is." Then he walked abruptly away and went over to speak to his own son, who was one of the guests.

Which was Churchill's cue to come back and talk to me. Together we chatted and drank several glasses of champagne.

"My daughter did not think to tell me that there would be party games," Churchill said, with patient good humor, as he watched Reilly and his Secret Service team search one half of the British legation, while the NKVD searched the other. "The trouble with a treasure hunt is that the searching is always more pleasurable than the finding. It is, I fear, self-evidently true of so much in life. And an axiom that even now, in my seventieth year, gives me much pause for thought. Indeed, I often ask myself the question: Will the final victory feel as good as the last battle?"

A few minutes later, Roosevelt arrived, pushed up a ramp that led onto the terrace by his son Elliott and wearing a shawl against the cooler air of the evening. Outside the front doors of the British embassy, and in the presence of an honor guard, Churchill greeted Roosevelt, who handed over his birthday present—a Persian bowl purchased from the hard-currency shop in the grounds of the Russian embassy.

"May we be together for many years," Roosevelt told the beaming Churchill, and then allowed himself to be wheeled into the dining room. But seeing me, he looked the other way and began to speak to Averell Harriman.

"Speaking as one who has been shunned many times," Churchill said, "I have always persuaded myself that it is better to be shunned than to be ignored."

Taking me by the arm, he led me back out onto the front terrace, where the Sikh guard of honor now awaited only Stalin's arrival. A large black limousine had appeared in the driveway of the legation and was now rolling up to the entrance, which was the cue for Churchill's Sikhs to present arms.

Seeing Stalin, Molotov, and Voroshilov step out of their limousine, I turned to go back indoors, but found my elbow held tight by the prime minister. "No, no," growled Churchill. "Stalin may have his way with Eastern Europe, but this is my fucking party."

Stalin, wearing his mustard-colored military jacket and a matching cape with a scarlet lining, came to the top of the legation steps. Seeing me next to Churchill, he paused, whereupon a British servant slipped between two of Stalin's bodyguards and tried to relieve the Soviet leader of his cape, prompting one of the guards to draw his pistol and jab it in the poor man's stomach.

"Oh, Christ," muttered Churchill, "that's all we need." And, in an effort to defuse the situation, he took a step forward and thrust his hand toward Stalin. "Good evening, Marshal Stalin," said Churchill. "And welcome to my birthday party. I believe this man was merely trying to relieve you of your cape."

To my horror, Stalin ignored the prime minister, neither speaking to him nor shaking his hand and slowly walked past him into the dining room.

"Well, that's got him rattled." And Churchill laughed.

"Is that why I'm here, sir?"

"I told you before, young man. You're here because I asked you to be here."

But I was no longer sure that the British prime minister did not have some ulterior motive in asking me to his party. Perhaps rattling Stalin had been a motive in itself.

At a safe distance I followed Churchill into the dining room. It looked like the interior of a small Cairo nightclub: heavy, red velvet curtains hung off large brass rails, while the walls were covered with a mosaic of small pieces of mirrored glass. The general effect was not one of imperial grandeur so much as a tawdry glamour.

A waiter dressed in red and blue, with ill-fitting white gloves, approached Stalin, bowed his head curtly, and offered up a tray of drinks that the Soviet leader seemed to regard with suspicion.

The table was set with crystal and silver and in pride of place stood a large birthday cake with sixty-nine candles. Checking the place cards, I discovered that I had been seated rather closer to Stalin than either one of us might have considered comfortable. After the incident on the terrace I had a bad feeling about Churchill's birthday party, which was hardly made better by the discovery that only six places would separate me from Stalin. I wondered if it was possible that Stalin had snubbed Churchill because the prime minister had invited me. And had Roosevelt really snubbed me, too? If the president had turned against me, I could see the evening ending only in disaster. I picked up my place card and went out onto the back terrace to smoke a cigarette and contemplate my next move.

It was quiet in the back garden of the legation with only the sound of water trickling into a large square fish pond, and the hiss of burning storm lanterns—a precaution against a possible power cut. I walked down the steps into the garden and then along the edge of the pond, my eyes fixed on the perfect white moon that lay motionless upon the surface of the water. With only the British speaking to me, there seemed to be little point in going back into the dining room.

I walked past the kitchens to a quiet domed area covered with wisteria and honeysuckle and sat down to finish my cigarette. Gradually, as my eyes became accustomed to the dark, I made out a large water cart and, on the wall, a heavy brass water tap. I closed my eyes wearily, trying to cast my mind back to a happier time—alone in my room at Princeton with just a book, the tolling of the bell in the Nassau Hall tower, and the ticking of an Eardley Norton bracket clock on the antebellum mantelpiece.

I opened my eyes again, for suddenly it seemed I could indeed hear the ticking of that lovely old Georgian clock, a graduation present from my mother. And, fetching a storm lantern from the terrace, I brought the light back to the little ornamental dome and glanced around in search of the sound's origin. I discovered the ticking coming from inside the Furphy water cart. My ear pressed against the cart's cool metal cylinder, the clock sounded quite infernal, as if, like the devil's clock, it was about to strike and the battlefield where heaven had stood, blown to hell again.

There was a bomb inside the cart. And from the size of the water cylinder, it was a big one. As much as a ton, perhaps. I glanced at my watch and saw that it was only a few minutes before nine o'clock.

I picked up the wooden shafts of the water cart and, taking hold of the leather harness, began to pull. At first the cart hardly seemed to shift, but at last, after an effort that left me red in the face and dripping with sweat, it moved and, slowly, began to roll out of the little *rond-point* dome.

I told myself that I made an absurd-looking hero, in my tuxedo and evening slippers. But all I had to do was keep the cart moving. Just long enough to get it away from the main building. I reached the gravel driveway, my shoes slipping slightly on the small stones and, stopping for a moment, I threw off my jacket before once again picking up the yoke and dragging the thing down to the main gate.

Two of the Sikh sentries came toward me, bayonets fixed, but quite relaxed and looking puzzled.

"What are you doing, Sahib?" asked one of them.

"Give me a hand," I said. "There's a time bomb inside this thing."

They stared at me blankly.

"Don't you understand? It's a bomb."

And then wisely, one of them ran off toward the main building.

I reached the gate, having achieved quite a reasonable forward motion, at which point the Sikh who had spoken to me threw down his rifle and began to help me push the cart.

At last we cleared the gates of the British embassy compound and headed down the wide empty boulevard toward the main part of the city. The Sikh stopped pushing now and ran away. Which suited me fine. I almost preferred that I should do it myself. How much better that I should be remembered not as the man who had saved Hitler's life, nor even as the man who had scuppered the peace talks, but as the hero of the hour—the man who had saved the Big Three from being blown to pieces.

There seemed nothing particularly heroic about what I was doing. I was tired and, in a way, I almost looked forward to the end of it all. So, pushing the water cart with its lethal payload, I went to find a kind of peace. The kind of peace that passeth all understanding. Final peace. Hitler's peace.

XXVII
FRIDAY, DECEMBER 10, 1943,
BERLIN

WITH NONE OF THE surviving members of the Operation Long Jump team—supposing that there were any—having yet made it as far as the German embassy in Ankara, there was much that Walter Schellenberg still didn't know about what had happened in Teheran. But from sources at the Soviet embassy in Iran, and inside the British SIS in London, he had been able to put together a rough picture of the events that followed the hurried departure of the Führer from the Iranian capital. Alone in his office on Berkaerstrasse, Schellenberg reread the top-secret account he had typed himself for Himmler, and then drove to the Ministry of the Interior.

It was a meeting he was hardly looking forward to since it was now well known to the Reichsführer-SS that the young SD chief had disobeyed a direct order regarding the use of Zeppelin volunteers. Himmler would have been well within his rights to have ordered Schellenberg's immediate execution. At the same time, however, Schellenberg had already concluded that if Himmler intended to have him arrested he would probably have done it by now. The worst Schellenberg thought he could probably expect was a severe dressing down, and perhaps some sort of demotion.

Despite the recent bombing, the Ku-damm still managed to look comparatively normal, with people getting ready for Christmas as if they hadn't a care in the world. To look at them, carrying Christmas trees and gazing in shop windows, a war might be happening somewhere other than in Berlin on a Thursday morning in mid-December. Schellenberg parked his car on Unter den Linden, where a cold wind was worrying the Nazi flag on the facade of the Ministry of the Interior, saluted to the two guards on duty outside the front door, and went inside.

He found Himmler in a businesslike mood and, to his surprise, the Reichsführer showed no immediate inclination to issue his subordinate with any kind of reprimand. Instead he eyed the report on Schellenberg's lap and with an uncharacteristic casualness invited the SD general to summarize what it contained.

"Most of the Friedenthal Section were killed or captured, of course," said Schellenberg. "Very likely they were betrayed to the Soviets by one of the Kashgai tribesmen, for money."

"Very likely," agreed Himmler, who saw no reason to tell Schellenberg that it was he himself who had betrayed the Operation Long Jump team to the NKVD.

"It was always the main risk in Operation Long Jump—the reliability of those tribesmen," Schellenberg continued. "But we think that those who did evade capture, at least in the short term, were probably responsible for some sort of bomb that was placed on the grounds of the British embassy in Teheran. Our sources indicate that there was a large explosion about a hundred yards away from the embassy at just after twenty-one hundred hours on Tuesday, November thirtieth. Churchill was hosting his birthday party at the time, and it seems that earlier that same day, the bomb, of considerable size, had been concealed in a water cart and positioned close to the banqueting room. But the bomb was discovered, very likely by the same man who was killed moving it to a place of safety. An American, named Willard Mayer."

"You don't say," said Himmler, who sounded genuinely surprised to hear this.

"Willard Mayer was a member of the American OSS, and was Roosevelt's German translator during the conference. He was also a philosopher of some note and before the war had studied in Vienna. And in Berlin, I believe. I looked at one of his books. It's really quite profound."

"Willard Mayer was also the Jew who saved the Führer's life," said Himmler.

"Then he seems to have been quite a hero, doesn't he?" Schellenberg observed. "Saving the Führer and then the Big Three. A little more than one expects from your average philosopher."

"Do you really think that bomb would have killed them?"

"By all accounts, the explosion was immense. The American's body was never found."

"Of course, with him gone there's one less witness to what really happened," said Himmler. "In that respect at least, they're fortunate. Almost as fortunate as you, Schellenberg."

Schellenberg acknowledged the rebuke with a curt nod of the head. He waited a moment.

"Well, go on," urged Himmler. "Go on."

"Yes, Herr Reichsführer. I was merely going to add that as far as the Americans are concerned, the process of rewriting the record has already begun. To read the British and American newspapers after the conference was over, it's hard to believe the Führer could ever have been there. Remarkable, really. It's as if none of this ever happened."

"Not quite," said Himmler.

Schellenberg braced himself. This was it. Himmler was going to demote him after all.

"That Jew-lover, Roosevelt, must now take the consequences for his refusal to agree to the Führer's terms."

Schellenberg smiled with a mixture of relief and amusement. It seemed as though he would be remaining in his position. And it looked as if it wasn't just the Allies who were busy rewriting history. The first time Himmler had told him of the Führer's secret trip to Teheran he had added that Hitler's departure had been precipitated by the discovery that he could not deal with an enemy as cruel and perfidious as Stalin after all.

"What consequences are those, Herr Reichsführer?"

"The war against the Allies may be impossible to win, Schellenberg," said Himmler. "I think we both know that's true. But there is still the war against the Jews. The Führer has ordered that the final solution of the Jewish problem is to be given the utmost priority in the coming year. New deportations have already begun in Hungary and Scandinavia, and special camps have been given instructions to increase their turnover."

Himmler stood up and, clasping his hands behind his back, walked to the window and looked out.

"The work will be difficult, of course. Unpleasant, even. Personally speaking, I myself find this order especially abhorrent. As you know, I have always struggled to find a just peace for Hitler and for Germany." He glanced back at Schellenberg and shrugged. "But it was not to be. We did our very best. And now . . ." He walked carefully back to his desk and, sitting down, picked up his fountain pen with its infamous green ink. "Now we must do our very worst."

Schellenberg breathed a sigh of relief. He was safe after all.

"Yes, Herr Reichsführer."

Appendix:
Excerpts from the Works
of Willard Mayer

"To be content is to have arrived at the furthest limits of human reason and experience; and there is more satisfaction to be had in the acceptance of what cannot logically be said than in all the moral philosophy ever studied by men. Reason is as inert as a noble gas and functions empirically, by its relation to real existence and matters of fact. And what cannot be tested empirically and is incapable of being proved true or false can never be an object of our reason. To be empirical is to be guided by experience, not by sophists, charlatans, priests, and demagogues."

from *On Being Empirical*

"All the objects of which we are aware are either impressions we take from the data of sensation, or ideas, which may only be gathered from an impression if that idea is to be logical. In looking to find the meaning of things, we must be empirical concerning matters of fact, or analytical concerning the relation of ideas. But matters of fact are what they are and need reveal no logical relation to each other: that facts are facts is always logically true regardless of rational inspection. Since, however, ideas may also exist as ideas regardless of rational inspection, it will be understood how it is only here, at the level of mere understanding, that there can exist the possibility of philosophy and establishing scientifically what may or may not logically be said. By the same token, since the opposite of any fact can exist as an idea, however illogical, it will be seen as a paradox how any philosophical demonstration of a fact becomes impossible."

from *On Being Empirical*

"A man need only be convinced of two principles of philosophy in order to find himself liberated from all vulgar creeds, no matter how charismatic these might seem to be: first, that considered in itself, there is nothing in an object that enables us to say anything beyond that object; and, second, that nothing enables us to say anything about an object beyond those observations of which we have direct experience. I say again, let any man take the time to be persuaded of these two philosophical principles, and live his life accordingly, which we might describe as being empirical, and it will be perceived how all the bonds of common ignorance will be broken. In this way does modern philosophy shine the sublime light of science in even the darkest places in Man's psyche."

from *On Being Empirical*

"We read a great deal about organized book burnings by Nazi stormtroopers. But in fact it was the Christians who first organized book burnings as a means of promoting their faith [see Acts of the Apostles 19:19–20]. One of my students at the University asked me today if I thought it could ever be right to burn a book, quoting Heine's 'Almansor' in support of his argument that it could not. I told him that any volume of philosophy should be consigned to the flames if it contains any experimental or abstract reasoning regarding matters of fact, human existence, and mathematics, for such a book can contain nothing but lies and specious reasoning. His eyes widened fearfully as he whispered to me he assumed I was referring to Hitler's *Mein Kampf* and that I should be careful what I said. I didn't have the heart to tell him that actually I had been referring to the Holy Bible."

from *Vienna Diary: 1936*

Author's Note

THIS BOOK IS A WORK OF FICTION that is based on a real event in history: the Big Three Conference at Teheran of 1943. The photographs of Stalin, Churchill, and Roosevelt—"the Big Three"—at Teheran, and later at the Yalta Conference of February 1945, are near icons of the Second World War. Roosevelt died before the VE Conference at Potsdam in July 1945. But most of the substantive issues had been decided in Teheran.

Some names, characters, businesses, organizations, places, events, and incidents are the product of the author's own imagination, but others are not. Many of the more obscure events described in the book really did take place, and I thought it might amuse the reader if I listed a few here.

These are, in no particular order:

- Sumner Welles, the assistant secretary of state, resigned from the administration in September 1943, following the disclosure of "an act of grave moral turpitude with a Negro railway conductor."

- A torpedo was fired at the USS *Iowa* by the USS *Willie D. Porter* during Roosevelt's journey to North Africa. He and the Joint Chiefs of Staff narrowly escaped death at the hands of their own naval escort destroyer.

- In 1943, secret peace negotiations between the Germans and the Russians, and the Germans and the Americans, were being actively discussed. The former German chancellor and ambassador to Turkey, Franz von Papen, really did meet with Commander George Earle in Ankara, on October 4, 1943. According to von Papen's memoirs, Earle claimed "to have been entrusted by President Roosevelt with the task of discussing with me personally the possibility of an early peace" and showed von Papen a document "that might serve as the basis for peace with Germany." Von Papen says that Earle even encouraged him to come to Cairo, for an interview with the president, but that he could not have gone "until I had written proof from President Roosevelt that he would undertake to negotiate on the basis of the terms we had discussed." So, the talks between von Papen came to nothing. "I can only assume that the President considered it too risky to be more specific." Similarly, while Himmler was in Posen, his masseur, Felix Kersten, really was in Stockholm, making contact with President Roosevelt's special representative, Abram S. Hewitt. Hewitt also met with General Walter Schellenberg in Sweden. Himmler had also, previously, deputed his lawyer, Carl Langbehn, to attempt peace feelers in Switzerland. The Russians were no less willing to negotiate with the Germans, and, after Stalingrad, their ambassador in Stockholm, Madame de Kollontay, met with von Ribbentrop's representatives on a number of occasions.

- Operation Long Jump was a real plan. More than one hundred German paratroopers were parachuted into Iran in order to kill the Big Three. All were killed or captured.
- Camp 108, at Beketovka, was a real camp for German POWs. The figures given in the book for German deaths in Russian POW camps are well documented.
- The murder of four thousand Polish officers in the Katyn Forest was finally admitted by Russian president Boris Yeltsin in 1992. But hundreds of thousands of Poles deported to labor camps in the Soviet Gulag system were never seen again.

MUCH OF WHAT took place at the Big Three Conference is still shrouded in secrecy. But the following strange facts are uncontested:

- Two American generals—General George C. Marshall and General H. H. Arnold—absented themselves, without leave, from the Teheran conference and went on a tour of the woods around the city. Why?
- As soon as Roosevelt landed in Teheran, Stalin claimed his NKVD had uncovered a plot to kill the Big Three. He suggested that Roosevelt—though not Churchill—should move into the safety of the impregnable Russian compound. Roosevelt seems to have believed in the plot; and, contrary to all advice, he agreed to move, thus laying the American delegation open to eavesdropping. Was there any truth to the plot? Wasn't Roosevelt too canny not to have known that all his conversations in the Russian compound would be bugged? If he did know, what was he up to? Could there have been another reason he agreed to stay at the Russian compound?
- At Teheran, Churchill was irritated and upset with Roosevelt on a number of occasions; never again were the two men friends. Why?
- At Teheran, Roosevelt collapsed with severe stomach pains. Was he poisoned? Some think he was.
- Before, during, and after the Teheran conference, von Papen, the German ambassador in Ankara (Turkey), was kept informed of what was happening by a spy who worked as a valet for the British ambassador in Ankara, Sir Hughe Knatchbull-Hugessen.
- At Teheran, Churchill spent much of the Big Three Conference marginalized by the other two principals, and on his own. Why?
- At Teheran, Stalin suggested, seriously, that the best way of making sure that Germany never again posed a threat to the security of the world was to destroy its militarism at the root: to this end he proposed the execution of 100,000 German officers and NCOs. Reluctantly, he accepted that 50,000 executions might be enough. Churchill protested vehemently.

Roosevelt said he thought 49,000 ought to be enough! This was most uncharacteristic of Roosevelt. Why did he say this? And why did he sell out Poland and Finland to Stalin? Did Stalin have some temporary hold over Roosevelt?

- The Katyn Forest massacre, for which the Russians were responsible, was not mentioned by Roosevelt to Stalin at Teheran.
- General Marshall was widely expected to command the Allied landings in June 1944. But Roosevelt handed the command to Eisenhower instead. No explanation was given for this choice, which caused widespread surprise at the time. Was the reason, perhaps, something to do with Marshall's unexplained absence for part of the conference at Teheran?
- In 1944, more Jews died in "special camps" than in any other single year.